This Family of Women

RICHARD PECK

A DELL BOOK

Published by
Dell Publishing Co., Inc.
1 Dag Hammarskjold Plaza
New York, New York 10017

Dell ® TM 681510, Dell Publishing Co., Inc.

ISBN: 0-440-18790-7

Reprinted by arrangement with Delacorte Press
Printed in the United States of America
First Dell printing—July 1984

for Isabelle Daniels Griffis

PROLOGUE

Faster than a man could ride, the news swept out of the West, blowing like the eddies that turn the autumn leaves. It gusted into a prevailing wind, sending the word before it, the Western word, Gold.

The word came down the wilderness rivers—the American, the Sacramento—to the village by the bay, a settlement no more than a Mexican fort and a Spanish mission with a new American flag planted in a sandy plaza. It was the village of Yerba Buena, newly named San Francisco.

The word billowed from there swifter than ships under sail. It rang in the Rockies and in the fever jungles of the Isthmus and at Chagres. It confounded distance and tilted a continent.

As in a war, the young men went first, inflamed and singing "Oh, Susannah." The fathers followed, quieter men who'd moved before and could tailor their hopes. Then whole families went, moving at an oxen pace and measuring the miles in months. Babies made under starlight were born under canvas, and graves beside the track marked their meandering way. They rode against the sunset, bathed in the long slant of sundown light, more gold than most of them would ever see.

Frank Wheatley heard the word singing in the wind and took it as a sign. He'd come out of Kentucky with a wife growing gaunt. They'd buried two infant sons in Indiana, the last one on the bluff above the Wabash River at Vincennes. They moved on, north and west, on the lookout for flatter land to farm.

But there were fences in Illinois. The frontier lay farther off, receding before them. People lived too close there to suit Frank Wheatley, and too far off to suit his wife. He traded cattle to satisfy his need to be moving on, but he farmed when he was between excuses for change. Much of the time, his herd was no more than a foursome of milch cows, women's work.

In Piatt County they seemed to settle. She laid out a garden and knelt along the rows, somewhere between weeding and prayer. Another child would heal her, but it wouldn't come. In the long evenings when they sat at the lampless table, the ghosts of their sons played in the raw yard and cried their taunts from the grave.

There were neighbors. In a distant walnut grove another chimney rose, a thing that closed Frank Wheatley in but gave his wife her only hope. Then one day and the day after that there was no smoke from the far chimney. Frank Wheatley and his wife walked across the fields to inquire. They stood in their neighbors' yard waiting for welcome. But a new ax was left in a log, and from the shed the cattle hollered for milking.

They pushed open the strangers' door and found another man and wife like themselves dead in the bed of diphtheria. There were twin daughters, too, in the crib. One was dead, but the other shook her small fist at them. They buried the three and took the fourth home, and Frank Wheatley's wife rallied. The ghosts of her sons played farther off now, in the timber by the Sangamon River, better behaved.

They raised the foundling as their own, but told her the truth in case she might have need to know. They named her Eleanora and called her Lena. They schooled her and spoiled her all they could, and when she was twelve or so they moved on again to Beardstown, where Frank Wheatley farmed hard in his abstracted way.

That was where they heard word of Gold and California. Around the stove at the store in Beardstown a letter was passed from hand to hand. The local boys gone West to seek their fortunes had sent back a letter worn slick with reading:

The work is tedious and heavy as we are blasting a smart amount of rock. . . . This particular place was partly worked last summer but we are taking about five dollars a day out of it in spite of mules stolen and trunks broke into. . . . The mines is full of blacklegs.

Their farmer fathers shook their heads in skepticism and pride. The five-dollar figure was widely debated. Frank Wheatley rode home so lost in thought that the horse stood stamping at the shed door before he knew where he was. Riches meant nothing to him, but he felt age in his joints and time in his tread. He wondered if there was another move in him. Finally he had to know.

BOOK 1

Faster Than a Man Could Ride

ONE

I thought I must be fourteen the winter we readied ourselves to go West. The black walnuts lay drying on a blanket till the first snow. We sugared fruit and traded off what we wouldn't need for flour and meal by the barrel. We cured ham and brined bacon and heaped the storm cellar with apples. We'd need better than a year's supply and a canvas-topped wagon.

Oh, it was cold in the black mornings when we went about our work by moonlight. Our hands stuck to the hardware of the doors, and snow blocked the storm cellar. We like to have froze where we were, and I wondered if we would. All I knew of the world was these flat fields and the timber by the river. But Frank Wheatley was a moving man, and the urge West was on him.

We were poor, I suppose, and didn't know it. We had all we wanted to eat. The barrels of apples and the hams hanging in the shed against our journey looked like riches to me. I didn't think ahead to the privations. We laid out most of our coin for canvas. My ma and I sewed it with needles big as thorns to make a new top for the old wagon. At night we burned the last of the oil to see our stitches, warming our hands with our work.

They were a quiet people, almost silent. My pa couldn't put his vision into words, and my ma dared not dream. On the white canvas she sewed over, I saw the first beads of her blood. She'd commenced to cough blood and black bile that winter, only a fleck at first and never more than she could

hide from Frank Wheatley. We couldn't turn back when we
hadn't begun.

They called me Lena Wheatley, but I wasn't theirs. I was a
foundling, though they never made me feel it. They let me
stay home from school to help them prepare, and so I found
freedom first.

I was moving past childhood with nobody to show me the
way. I didn't know that my ma had been young. No daughter
does. My breasts began to strain against my wool dress. I
wrapped a shawl tighter around and fixed it with a pin to
enclose my figure and show it to myself. On my way to
milking, I practiced a woman's small, sure steps and left off
skipping. I was always fixing to weep over nothing, and my
dreams confused me.

At Eastertime we crossed the rising river at Beardstown in
our old wagon under new canvas. Three yoke of oxen drew
it, followed by a herd of milch cows, the supply oxen, and a
saddle horse. We were a saving people, and it was for this
journey. We went in a kind of pride, leaving no doubts or
debts. I sat on the tailgate looking back, watching my world
unwind.

We'd left in the dark, but the sun rose behind us, breaking
through the trees. It seemed to set our house and fences afire.
I imagined the blinding light was real flames and supposed it
was fitting.

We ferried across the big river, the Mississippi, there being
no way to avoid the cost, and met others like ourselves at
Muscatine. Here in a campground wagons for fifty people
waited to make up a train. We'd be a hundred at Independence.
I'd never seen such a sight, all the wagons standing every
which way from one another, and the cooking fires bright in
the night.

It was a holiday, but I'd never had one. There was no
housekeeping to be done as we'd known it, and that suited
me. I'd always liked milking and mucking better than indoor
work. There were children aplenty and more to come from
the look of things. Some were too young to know they were
strangers, and played tag among the water kegs. Others were

more my age, but I hung back, not knowing how to begin
with them.

My ma sewed in a circle while we waited to form a train.
I'd thought her silent when there'd been no other womenfolk,
but now I heard her laughter for the first time. I listened to
her swap yarns with the other women free of their cabins set
far back in the fields. She carried a bandanna of my pa's
thrust into her waist, a red bandanna to dab at her lips and
hide the color of blood.

It seemed we needed a leader, and an Iowan named Powers
was chosen. He'd fought the Mexicans so they called him
Captain Powers. Behind his lead wagon we traveled a month
down into Missouri. We came at last to Independence, and
people said this marked the end of our easy going. The
government stepped in and lectured us how to move in paral-
lel lines in the way that was safest.

There were nearly thirty wagons for the hundred souls and
cattle enough for a dairy, nobody wanting to be beholden.
Muscatine was nothing to this, and I wondered at the varieties
of humankind. One lady had brought a black walnut dresser
with a marble top heavy as lead and a looking glass attached
that shone out of the back of her wagon like a beacon. My pa
and the other men called the looking glass an ''ox-killer'' and
prophesied that it would end up abandoned at the side of the
road. But the women and we girls found excuses to pass by
the wagon for a look at ourselves. I looked along with the
rest, hoping to find roses in my cheeks from the open air and
a woman's face for my hard work and years. But in the
ripples of the mirror I was a child still, thin in the face and
hopeful round the eyes.

As the leaders, the Powers family held themselves a little
high, but the rest were sociable enough. While we waited at
Independence, our wagon was pulled up alongside the Ransom family's. Mrs. Ransom had a pillow-soft bosom and a
way of pursing her lips in sympathy at any story.

She was one my ma could tell her grief to, and Mrs.
Ransom listened with arms folded across her soft front. I

listened too and heard my ma speak of the two boys she'd
buried back before my time.

"They was alike as two peas in a pod," my ma said,
putting back her head and looking up at the sky to keep her
brimming eyes from spilling over. "And into everything?
You never seen the like for mischief. I come on them one
time, and one was putting the other in the flour barrel. Oh, I
whupped them," she said, blinking away her tears.

"Of course you did," Mrs. Ransom said. "A person
would."

"But there was no harm in them," my ma said in a
faraway voice. "Until they took sick, they was like kittens
for getting into things. I think of them yet."

"It's only natural," Mrs. Ransom said, pursing her lips.
My ma had a friend now, and I saw how that helped.

Mrs. Ransom was raising all four of hers. Sarah Ann
Ransom was sixteen already. Beatrice was a year or so
behind me, and there were two younger boys, still coltish:
Lorenzo and Matthew.

My pa and Mr. James Ransom split kindling and repacked
their loads while they waited to move. Our families grew
close, though I was inclined to hang back. Sarah Ann who
was older moved across the rough ground like it was a
polished floor. Her hair was raven-dark, swept up into a
womanly knot, and her complexion was marble-perfect. I
thought she was too beautiful to live, as the saying went.

Beatrice who was childish yet was about as bad as a boy
for devilment, with a spark in her eye for warning. I was all
ears around these two to hear how sisters were with one
another. I believe in her heart Beatrice looked up to Sarah
Ann as I did, but she wouldn't let on. She was a regular little
mimic too, as good as a tentshow, people said.

Sarah Ann moved with the grace I longed for, but Beatrice
liked an audience too. Once while I was watching Sarah Ann
move in her lovely way back from a woodpile, her arms
burdened with stove lengths, there come Beatrice behind her
where Sarah Ann couldn't see. Beatrice come on like a
parade, bearing a twig or two cradled in her dimpled arm and

swanning along in imitation of her sister, flirting her skirts in
an outrageous way and making terrible prim faces.

You hated to laugh and couldn't help it, and I suppose
Sarah Ann knew she was being mocked. "I will jerk a knot
in your tail," she'd say to Beatrice when the sister went too
far. "Your sass will cost you dear." But she spoke in a voice
of such natural music, she made any threat sound a reward. I
saw how sisters set their limits and sometimes abided by
them.

Though she could buzz around your head like a cloud of
gnats, Beatrice became my particular friend. Being younger,
she was easier, and I kept Sarah Ann back for an idol.
Having them all near, even the pesky boys, was like school
without the lessons. The weather was fine, and we ate good. I
could think of nothing more to want.

We moved out from Independence one early morning when
nothing stirred but us. We were five weeks crossing the
Kansas country. It was hot enough, people said, to pop the
corn in the fields, and hotter at nights. We couldn't sleep
under canvas. We sat out on the tailgates, feet dangling,
pouring sweat. Because of snakes, nobody slept on the ground
except boastful boys like Lorenzo and Matthew, and even
they circled their bedrolls with ropes to make sure.

The drying heat made the track hard and fast. Our wheels
turned in a rhythm, and the creeks were nothing to ford. It
wasn't hard going yet in spite of the punishing sun. Young
men rode ahead to stretch their horses. Riding high between
my ma and pa, I listened to the crackling echo of the shotguns,
and saw birds fall. The hunters shared out their bounty, and
we sat around the fires at night, eating quail and partridge and
picking the bits of shot off our tongues.

Every two or three days we halted, by a stream if there was
one. The wagons were drawn into a circle to corral the
livestock, and then we climbed down and staggered on solid
ground. Children toted water and the women baked and
washed. The men rode out to find antelope or buffalo. If the
stream showed promise, they fished it.

Some of the women thought it wasn't ladylike to fish, but

my ma wasn't one of them. In the wagon she'd brought her
poles and line and hooks she'd bent herself. She had her own
way with bait, made of bread soaked in two or three sub-
stances she was a little secretive about. In an old straw hat of
my pa's in place of her sunbonnet she'd go off and sit on the
riverbank in this unknown country, resting herself away from
the wagon. I wondered at her thoughts, but she never told
them.

Within the big ring of wagons, people told stories across
the fire and played games. A boy from Wisconsin with a
sizable Adam's apple and no chest to speak of could play the
violin. He played "Money Musk" over and over until the
young folks got up two by two and danced.

Sarah Ann Ransom drew more than her share of the young
men, and now she moved over rough ground like it was a
ballroom floor. I watched her with all my eyes, for I'd never
seen her like. Though I hadn't heard much poetry, I saw it in
the way she moved. She could subdue the clumsiest partners.
Her feet slipped smoothly, nimbly from beneath their stomp-
ing boots. Sarah Ann had a way of reaching back to gather up
her skirts as she turned in the dance. A cameo brooch fixed
the shawl across her heart. I hadn't known an older girl to
envy and admire, and I studied her like a picture.

Then though I swear I don't know how it happened, I was
in a partner's arms myself, a castoff of Sarah Ann's maybe. I
was too flustered to know or notice. He was traveling with a
party from Ohio, the Brimfields, but he wasn't one of them,
not kin. His name was Evan Freeman, and the way he talked
with his jaw set was foreign to me. He was from Massachu-
setts and had walked a fair piece of the way from his home at
Great Barrington to Independence.

His shoulders were yoke-broad, and in the firelight his hair
shone yellow-white. I wasn't one to mind sitting back to
watch the others dance, and I wondered now how I liked
being in a man's arms. Was my face hot from the dancing
and my heart racing with the violin, or was it something else?
As we tried to match the music, I turned my head aside,

wondering if I could hear his heart beat if I laid my cheek against his thick chest. I had such foolish thoughts as these.

Did he dance with me only because he wouldn't wait in a line for Sarah Ann? Or for a miracle, did he like me for myself? Was he nothing but a drifter? The questions buzzed my head like mosquitoes, and though I might be fifteen soon, I felt far short of answers.

I was a natural worrier, and so my mind leaped ahead. What would I do if Evan Freeman asked me to walk? Others did, and they were noticed. Couples drifted away from the fire and strolled in the shadows. Sarah Ann Ransom would do that with a favored few, but she never went outside the corral with any of them. Other girls would, and they were remarked on.

Beatrice Ransom, who was still thirteen and saw no use in dignity, found ways to plague me. "Evan Freeman is your affinity," she'd say over and over, making sly eyes. I learned to toss my head and rise above Beatrice if I could rise above nothing else.

Without her, I might have stretched myself more to fit Sarah Ann's shadow, though that would have been a losing game. I couldn't imagine being that grown and sure. The sprouting figure I'd been so vain of all the winter was nothing now to Sarah Ann's ripeness.

On the day the Arkansas River hung like a mirage ahead of us, a shout went up. We were many days now from the last scattering of houses. The stars seemed brighter at night, more unforgiving. I reckon we all dreamed of turning back, though I never heard it spoken of. The Army had told the men when to be wary of the Apache. For nights now the unmarried men had slipped out to stand guard. They went quietly to keep the women calm, but I'd watched Evan Freeman go, catching up a long-barreled gun in his hand.

When we made camp on the bank of the Arkansas, a band of Apache was camped on the far side farther down. The party Captain Powers sent out returned to say the Apache were burdened with a hundred head of mules that looked stolen. The men told one another that the savages wouldn't attack, but they went about their chores with their rifles slung on their shoulders. We built up our cooking fires to double size to make a showing.

Beatrice and I stood up on the wagon seat to catch a glimpse of Apache firelight. Even she was awed, and her plump little hand crept into mine. When we'd jumped down again, Beatrice whirled around at me and rolled her eyes. She hadn't a whit of her sister's beauty, but her round face was expressive to a fault. She jerked a thumb over her shoulder and said, "Buckets."

We'd forgotten to fill them for the morning water, and it was our chore. Now, except for the firelight of two camps, it was pitch dark. I was ready to confess and take my medicine, but that wasn't Beatrice's way. Her brows knitted as she bent her thoughts to slipping out to fill the buckets and getting back unnoticed.

"We better never—"

"Just hush a minute," she said, "and let me think."

"There's a guard posted between every two wagons," I murmured, but she saw that and took it for a challenge.

She took my arm, and we commenced to stroll. To display our innocence, she hummed a little tune, though she was tone-deaf. We sidled past the Ransoms' wagons, and somehow a bucket was hanging from her arm. We reversed to the music of her humming, and now there was a bucket swinging from my elbow. We swapped sides in a kind of dance, and now we were strolling past my pa's wagon, attracting a pair of buckets from the hooks there. On we strolled toward the river side of the ring, keeping nearer the wagons than the firelight.

Then quick as thought, Beatrice jerked me under a wagon. We wallowed in the dirt while I did my level best not to think of snakes. Beatrice hunkered along ahead of me, and I followed her twitching backside. She'd replaced her humming with soft grunts now. We fetched up on the far side in high weeds.

Creeping on like hedgehogs, we dared never rise up for fear of being shot dead by our own people. The buckets dragging along in the crooks of my arms rattled and thumped like thunder. I felt as hollow inside as they were, but ahead of me I heard the soft whinny of Beatrice's laugh. She'd keep just enough fun in the thing to save us from fear outright, but I worried that I'd lose track of her.

I was following the slithering sound of her knees in the weeds, but there was every kind of creature slithering in this forbidding country. My throat began to close at the thought, but then I was seeing a little better in the dark, enough to keep the shifting shape of her rear in my sights.

Then she yipped once like a startled puppy, and the earth seemed to swallow her whole. Her heels flew up and her skirts went every direction. Then she was gone. I froze where I was. I couldn't go back without her. There was nothing to do but plant one hand carefully in front of the other and inch along forward, wiser than she'd been. But I followed in her wake. The slick weeds overhanging the riverbank betrayed me too and just as quick. They spilled me into space.

I went head over heels down the bank, and a bucket fetched me a sharp clip across the forehead. I fell in a heap on Beatrice where she was just rising up ankle-deep in a sandbar.

The wagons were back yonder above us, white and high as chalk cliffs in the moonlight. Downriver, not nearly far enough, the orange fires of the Apache camp threw dreadful shadows. We clung together and thought we heard the awful rhythm of tribal drums, but it was only our hearts.

Hiking our skirts, we sank our buckets in the river and were deafened by the splashing when we drew them out. The sandbar sucked at our feet, and Beatrice slopped half her water out. But we made it back up the bank somehow, in the high weeds again, inching along. The buckets bent us double, and I for one had my heart in my throat.

"How in blue blazes are we to get back in without them noticing?" Beatrice whispered. She'd waited till then to wonder. But not five yards ahead, the grass parted. We froze and heard breathing that wasn't ours.

Apache—I was sure of it, but my tongue was thick in my

mouth and my feet had turned to stone. Then in the glare of the moonlight I saw them. Their shirts were off, and they were heading for a forbidden swim. It was Lorenzo Ransom and behind him Matthew, Beatrice's troublesome brothers, making for the river.

I could have wept with relief, but there wasn't time. Without a thought, I fetched up a war cry as like an Apache's as I could make it. It split the air, and even the moon seemed to quiver. The high grass whipped and thrashed as the Ransom boys fell in a struggling heap.

"Jesus save me!" whimpered the younger one, seemingly on his knees. But Lorenzo was already halfway back to the wagons, screaming, "Apache! Apache! Load and fire!"

In the tumult that followed, Beatrice and I slipped back into the circle of wagons, almost strolling. We hung our buckets unnoticed on the hooks and dried our skirttails at the fire, never once chancing a glance at one another.

TWO

Beyond the Arkansas the wind blew hot day and night. Tumbleweeds worried the stock and tangled the wheels. It was the same road it had been, no better and no worse, but it crossed desolate land now, and every stand of scrub grass might harbor a crouching Apache. We moved with our minds cocked.

My pa walked much of the time with an old bird rifle in his hand. I rode up on the board. The oxen needed no driving and took no commands, but still I had to be in charge of something. In the wagon bed behind, my ma lay on a pallet, and I knew she felt every stone in the road. The towel she held against her mouth was red to the hem with blood.

I rode ramrod straight and made bargains with God. But we were well past Him now. Everywhere I looked was proof. Somewhere in the vacant, baking country I swapped God-fearing for superstition and thought as long as the oxen labored and the wheels turned, as long as I kept my back straight as a die, my ma would live.

I slept beside her in the wagon at night while my pa dozed on the tailgate to give us room. One morning I woke when the sun was just up, throwing its first beam and turning the arching canvas into a crimson tunnel. I woke in the pool of my ma's blood.

At first I couldn't see it for the color of the sunrise, but my fingers were glued with it, and my petticoat was stiff. I sat up and made my spine go straight and firm before I'd look down at her. I knew though that no living thing would be there. If she was alive, the Ransoms in the next wagon could have heard the awful shriek of her breathing. I looked down at my ma.

Her jaw had fallen, and her eyes looked past the arch of the roof. Her mouth was set in a silent scream, and her teeth were blackened by blood.

I took her up and held her against me. Suddenly she weighed nothing. I held the husk of her to me, and her arms hung down in an awkward way. She hadn't been an awkward woman, and I hadn't known it till now. There'd been a grace about her that perhaps I couldn't have, for I wasn't truly her child.

That was the thought that broke me. She hadn't been mine, and I'd lost her just the same. I didn't think to cry or cry out. They'd put her in a pit, and I was there already, and how black it was. I wouldn't close her eyes either, though they were empty and staring and nothing like her. I waited with my arms cramped around her, not measuring the time till my pa would wake and find us, my eyes and hers staring and empty.

I watched him stir and felt with him the night's dampness in his joints. He ran his work-twisted hand over his beard and reached for his old hat. I didn't speak to signal him. He'd look our way in his own good time, and find my ma and me tangled in our arms.

When he did, his eyes stared like ours for a moment. His hand come out toward Ma. This was the last moment we were three.

"She's gone, Lena," he said, thinking maybe I wouldn't believe it. He crawled on his hands and knees the little distance between us. Oh, it was quiet then. The people stirring around us behind their canvas spoke from far off.

Her head rocked against my shoulder, and I thought of hunters bringing home their quarry, how the heads of the dead dangle and loll.

"Did you know, Pa?"

He nodded. "She knowed too, Lena." He looked around the wagon for a way to tell me. "She knowed she was making a longer journey than we was.'' He put his hand out then in a way I'll never forget and closed her eyes.

There was no timber for her coffin. There hadn't been trees for weeks. Nor any flowers, for wherever we were, it was deep into the fall of the year.

Each family donated a wagon floorboard, and a party of men knocked them together into a long box. Another party broke the hard ground for a grave. No preacher was among us, but Captain Powers read at random from the Bible, and we sang ''Balm in Gilead.'' The women wore their bonnets, though I left mine off. The men stood uncovered in the raw day.

The hundred grouped at her grave, and I stood across the open pit from my pa, trying to memorize it. I hadn't known till now we were laying her in ground we'd never see again, or be able to put a name to. I'd never known where my ma was born, and now I wouldn't know where she died. I thought of the geese that pass over us every spring and fall, never home.

They asked me if I wanted a little cross left over her. They could hammer two sticks together, but I shook my head. They couldn't know I'd come past religion and its comforts. I thought they were fools for not knowing they'd come past it too. We'd all crossed a border, and even the hopeful knew there was no turning back.

Mrs. Ransom stepped up behind me and clasped me close. She didn't fuss me with words. She only held me so tight against her that I felt in the small of my back the child she was carrying. I hadn't noticed before that there was another baby on the way. With Sarah Ann grown, I must have thought Mrs. Ransom was too old for that. It took my mind away for a moment as it was perhaps meant to do.

But when all the others turned away, I couldn't leave the grave. I stayed on there, feeling the wind, even when my pa turned like a blind man and walked away between Captain Powers and James Ransom. It took Evan Freeman to move me. He was beside me, and I thought—crazily—he was about to ask me to dance. But he led me away instead, and my hand was lost in his great fist.

We made camp there, circling the grave, so that Frank Wheatley's wife wouldn't spend her first night alone in the ground. But the fear of the Apache was on us now, and we moved out at dawn. I'd slept the night with the Ransoms, and my pa was up earlier than the rest, scrubbing out our wagon bed with tumbleweed and salt.

I don't remember now how many days or weeks there were between the grave and Las Vegas. My pa walked and I rode. Wordless as animals, we watched our hands work. When there were stops to rest, he slathered the axles with lard and sewed canvas. In the mornings I milked and lashed the full pail to the crossbeam of the wagon where it would churn to butter by night.

In the evenings the others shared their campfires with us. We sat with the Powerses and the Ransoms and the two families both named Thompson and the Brimfields and Evan Freeman and the Strikers and the Hostetlers and people we hardly knew. We sat in grief and ate to live. My pa couldn't mourn in company, and I was healing as the young heal, faster than I meant to. But I knew now I had to be cautious in the future. I couldn't let another death bring me this low. I must learn to hold something of myself back, from everyone.

I pulled my mouth into a straight line that showed suffering, and endurance. Maybe I was a woman now, though I hadn't counted on the bleakness.

We sighted Las Vegas in the New Mexico Territory on a winter-cold day. The weather baffled us. We'd looked for heat this far south in desert country, but from here on we'd suffer for firewood.

Las Vegas was only a rude square where the road from Independence ran out. Spanish was spoken, and the fancy-saddled horses looked better than the people. All the mean houses turned their backs to the road.

The dangers of the old road on west were well known, but Captain Cook, the government surveyor, had blazed a new one through to Sucorro, though no emigrant party had been over it.

The opinions diverged like the roads. In the end the greater number formed up behind Captain Powers to follow the known way, preferring hazards they'd heard of. With him went the Rileys, the Hankses, the two families named Thompson, the boy with the violin, and the lady with the looking glass. In all, twenty wagons, including the Brimfields' and Evan Freeman's.

There'd been some simmering grudge between Mr. Ransom and Captain Powers. Men seemed to fall out first over livestock, and these two had traded some cattle. People said they were fixing to trade punches now, though it never come to that. It was just that Mr. Ransom liked his own way and had always had it before he'd been regimented into this wagon train. He didn't favor titles either, and when he talked to Captain Powers he left the captain part out. The end of it was that James Ransom chose the new road and less leadership. So, too, did the Hostetlers and the Strikers and six more wagonloads.

My pa cast our lot with them. When it was decided, Beatrice come to me with the news. It was well known by then, but Beatrice loved to babble and tell.

"It is a good thing you'uns is coming with us," she said, solemn as an owl for once, "for I wouldn't be parted from you, Lena. I'd have set my heels, and they couldn't have done nothing with me."

"You'd do just as your pa told you," I remarked, "or he'd take a razor strop to your behind."

She sniffed at that. "He ain't laid a finger on me," she said, ". . . here lately."

I was glad myself not to be separated from her and all the Ransoms. I wouldn't let myself make anything of losing track of Evan Freeman. It wasn't a parting, I told myself. There hadn't been enough between us for that. Yet on the morning the trains went different ways, I searched the longer line of wagons until I thought I saw him walking beside a team in his red flannel shirt. I thought I saw him scanning back over his broad shoulder for a last look at me.

The new road's hills were steeper, and we learned to tie fallen trees behind the wagons for brakes. Along the high ground the relentless wind swept the road free of sand, but we lost days at a time finding fords in the streams. Then there was the first snowfall. Snow in the desert. We made a week's camp where there was water, and out of endless emptiness, Indians appeared.

They paid a daily visit and spoke not a word. Mrs. Ransom and the other women cooked up vats of beans to give to the braves and their squaws.

A squaw no older than I was come up to me with a basket of dried petals and broken stems that was a treasure to her. She brewed it up on my fire into a kind of tea, and drank it down. Then she had me drink a cup I dared not refuse. Touching my arm to make me notice, she stroked her neck and patted her chest until I saw this was a medicine that would break up a cold or cool fever.

There was a day when the Indians didn't come, and it was said to be a bad sign. The men stood guard that night outside the shrunken ring of our wagons, but they couldn't do anything. In the night came a sound all around us like a thousand snakes or an engine letting off steam. It was the Apache's hissing way of stampeding cattle. They made off with seventeen head, including one of ours, but there was nothing to do but move on.

Beatrice often rode up on the board with me. Sarah Ann's patience would run thin with this younger sister, and then I'd fall heir to her. We settled our friendship and pledged it for life.

"We could draw blood and mingle it," Beatrice said in a considering way. "We could stab our thumbs and squeeze some out." But her voice fell away as she thought of the pain.

She was company for me now that I needed it, and she could fill up all outdoors with her chatter. She was awful pert, and her aprons were a disgrace to her mother, but her head was full of quaint thoughts, and she said whatever occurred to her.

"What do you reckon California will be like, Lena?"

I hadn't thought. Our journey seemed too long to have a destination. "I don't know. What do you want it to be?" I asked her.

She looked out over the barren landscape we were passing through. "I'd like shade trees," she said, "and a long lane up to a good two-story house. And a hammock on the porch. No chores, of course. I've had my fill of them. And a riding horse, naturally." Then to scandalize me, "And buckskin riding britches. I hope in California everybody wears buckskin britches, and there ain't a skirt in sight." As she spun out her dream, she arranged her bonnet strings over her lip and thrust it out to make them hang there like drooping mustaches.

It never dawned on her we might not make Sucorro. She saw nothing desperate in these miles and feared nothing but thunder and the sheet lightning that walked across the distant buttes. When we finally sighted the flag over Sucorro, she only bounced with glee while around us the eyes of strong men were wet.

We stopped at Sucorro long enough, almost, to forget the worst of our fears. It was more fort than town, built around a parade field. I never will forget the day we got there a soldier was being whipped at a post. I never saw such a thing in my life, and I remember the fish-whiteness of his back, striped in red, and the sound of the drumbeat to match the blows. I took an odd comfort in that sight, maybe because the savagery here was on our side.

In the mountains beyond Sucorro we were cold all the time. Beatrice's nose was like a red button, and we wore every stitch we had. The going was slower than we could have dreamed, and we got near the bottom of our supplies. On short rations, we cooked together and tried to make Santa Cruz. But we found the town raided by Apache and half burned out. From there to Tucson we knew hunger. We tried to eat hawks, and Mrs. Ransom lay sick for a day and a half from drinking a broth made from coyote meat.

In the first week of the new year we crossed the desert where the giant cactus grows tree-tall. The sun was warm in a dark blue sky, but the cold was bitter at night. All we'd foraged at Santa Cruz was pumpkins, and we ate them every way we could. When the cupboard was bare, we come to Tucson, much encouraged by the stout palisade fence we saw from a distance.

The novelty of us got us through its gates where we meant to wait out the winter. Here my pa and the other men planned to fatten their herds and do their trading and rent houses away from the everlasting wagons. We had some coin put back for this.

But when the Tucson people saw we were Yankees, they turned their backs on us. There'd been a company of soldiers called the Yankee Volunteers, and the people here blamed them for their defeat in the war.

They bent a little at sight of our ready money. They let us camp within the walls and would do a little trading with us, but their doors were closed. We lived then like outcasts, and our ten wagons cluttered the central square. We were barely tolerated, like gypsies. At night we sat around our campfires like we were still on the trail. Mr. Ransom speculated that the Mexicans would yield in time, but there was nothing about them that looked like yielding.

In time we settled in, as much fixtures of the dusty street as the hitching posts and the central well, and we slept better than we had since the Kansas country. Tucson posted guards on its walls, for every year after the harvest the Apache raided, taking the food and the young girls. During the day the gates stood open, and people went out to wash their clothes in the river and let the cattle graze. But all was locked and barred by night.

Beatrice and Sarah Ann and I took to making a promenade of the plaza with our arms linked. We were secure here among enemies who wouldn't stoop to harm us. But we were noticed. They'd never seen women so pale-skinned. Sarah Ann was a particular wonder to them, but dark eyes followed us all.

Here in this alien town I drew near my idol, Sarah Ann. What a proud thing it was to promenade with her. I wouldn't have dreamed of mimicking her like that scamp, Beatrice, but I tried to move with her measured grace. I suppose she noticed and would press my arm linked in hers and save a smile just for me.

She went out of her way to be kind. From their doors the Tucson women laid out for sale bits of frippery in the bright colors they favored. We were all three drawn to them like jackdaws, and Sarah Ann would say, "Here is a string of beads that would suit Lena."

They were tiny seeds of coral strung on silver, and she'd take up a strand to hold at my throat. I'd never thought of things suiting me or not suiting me. But she'd notice me in that way, and though I was confused, some of my shyness left me.

Casting her eyes up with the mock patience of an older sister, Sarah Ann would remark, "I wish in my soul that Beatrice would take a leaf from Lena's book. How starchy Lena keeps her collars and how nice she keeps her hair. I swan, I believe Lena wrenches it out with rainwater. What a good idea that would be for a certain grubby child that I could name."

Though she seemed to speak to neither of us, I basked in this praise while Beatrice kicked at the dust and scratched hard at her unruly hair, pretending deafness.

Once in our walk we came upon an old man lying in the dirt outside his house. His naked foot was thrust out in our way, and it was swollen worse than gout. His womenfolk buzzed around him, chattering in their strange tongue. They milled and bickered, but it was plain as day they had no cure for him.

Curious as cats, Beatrice and I drew nigh for a closer look while Sarah Ann held back. Showing off, the old man thrust his foot in our faces, though every move was a misery to him.

"Oh look, Lena," Beatrice said, "it's a mesquite thorn run way in and broke off."

The old sufferer's wife stood by with a wicked-looking knife from her kitchen, but he wouldn't have her near him. I remembered an old cure of my ma's and went back to the wagon to make up a poultice of sugar, soap, and white of egg. Since I couldn't make the old man's wife understand, I applied it myself.

It drew the thorn, and on that day my pa and I were allowed to rent the old man's house. Once one door opened, they opened all. The Ransoms tumbled down from their two tattered wagons to find a new home, and so did all the rest. Mud hovels were palaces to us, and we settled for the winter.

The Tucson people had no intention of leaving houses they'd rented out. I slept in the carved bed with the Mexican's big wife, hearing the ropes under us take her weight. My pa slept in the only other room, where the old Mexican lay muttering in his sleep before the fire.

It seemed that word of me spread in this place hard up for marvels. They come to think I could cure anything if I put my mind to it, and I didn't know enough of their language to tell them different. The dark eyes that followed Sarah Ann for her beauty followed me for my powers. Somebody was forever watching, even when I went out the gates to see to the cattle.

Like any foolish young girl, I had names for my livestock so sentimental I wouldn't have told them to my own people. My pa was a little this way himself. He had a pair of oxen he thought the world of and called them Thunder and Lightning.

One of my cows had calved, and I made a particular pet of the young one, calling her Treasure. But I could call all my cattle to me, and they'd come running to nuzzle my shoulder.

The Mexicans didn't know cattle could be controlled with kindness and wouldn't believe it now. They reckoned I spoke in the language of animals, and so I was credited with another miracle. I'd catch them back in the brush watching me and making the sign of the cross on themselves. One blazing afternoon when I came upon two Apache boys in breechcloths who'd roped Treasure and were leading her away, I forgot my fear and raised the alarm with my screams. From behind me, half of Tucson town stormed out with brickbats to drive the thieves away.

THREE

We wintered there, and from being intruders we became old settlers in Tucson. The women taught us the local way with cornmeal and bean paste and the Spanish names for ordinary things. My pa and the other men of our party met their match at horse-trading and got by on a language of hands and fingers when they were too shy to try the foreign words. My landlady made me a skirt and charged nothing. It was outlandishly made of many-colored ribbons woven together and would stand far out and twirl around my form if ever I went dancing again.

"Does it suit me?" I asked, twirling before Sarah Ann, and she said it did.

More Yankees come until the dust of the plaza never settled. Emigrants come over the new road, with new names and stories of where they'd come from and hardships. I heard of other graves along the road, to mark it as my ma's grave did.

John Raines arrived with his partners. Raines and his men had driven their thousands of sheep up from Mexico on their way to California. Tucson became a crowded place and richer than before. We might have lingered, but California was strong in our minds now, and every conversation turned that way.

We sensed the end of our journey and dreamed of blue Pacific waters just over a dry range or two more. I never heard gold spoken of, not even among the young men. We only spoke of getting there. It was time to be moving again, people said, to Fort Yuma and then California just beyond it. We thought we were agreed on the second week of April, almost a year since we'd set out.

For a leader, the men looked to James Ransom, but he would neither lead nor follow. Now he was restless of company and tired of town life and foreigners. They all spoke of how well they'd done without a leader to boss them, but now they began to divide and straggle the way men will. Some, like my pa, determined to linger till the April date, replenishing their herds. Some were all for pushing on as far as Pima Village which was not far. And some were champing at the bit for Yuma.

The Ransoms were the first to up stakes, though Mrs. Ransom was near her time. She wasn't a young woman. There was gray in her hair. Even her two last, Lorenzo and Matthew, had shot up like weeds and were halfway to manhood. The other women murmured, but nobody presumed to advise Mrs. Ransom.

"When Papa makes up his mind," Beatrice said to me, "it shuts like a trap." She didn't brag this time of how she'd set her heels and stay behind with me.

The Ransoms and the Strikers and three families more set out for the Pima Valley on the last day of March. We made a holiday, a fiesta, of their going. All the Yankees and half the Mexicans in Tucson turned out to see the little train off.

Sarah Ann stood making her good-byes, lovely as the morning. She'd trimmed a countrified sunbonnet with a bit of town lace to frame her face. At her breast she wore the cameo with the profile like her own. I was shy again and miserable to see them go. Because my eyes were blurry, I turned to hide in the wagon, but Sarah Ann called out to me. She took both my hands in hers and said, "Have you no good-bye for me, Lena?" I'd have hung my head, but I wanted one last glimpse of her. "We'll meet again, you know."

"Will we?" I said, wanting to believe.

"It would take a bigger place than California to keep old friends apart." She squeezed my hand one final time and left me with this benediction. Then she went to help her mother up into a wagon, and its wheels commenced to turn.

I followed their wagons out of the gates, eating their dust, wondering if I'd ever set eyes on them again, wondering if what Sarah Ann had said might someday come true. Long after she should have, Beatrice leaped out of the back of the wagon Lorenzo was leading and darted back to embrace me. We clung a moment before Beatrice ran back, vaulting up over the tailgate like a monkey.

I followed a while longer, waving until my arm ached. I hadn't let myself believe they were leaving until the day they went. Now I schooled myself not to weep. I only watched their swaying wagons out of sight.

When it came our time to go, I was glad, thinking we might catch up after all with the Ransoms. My pa and I went in a party made up of old companions and new. Mrs. Charlotte Gray was with us. She'd lost her husband to the redskins in the Santa Cruz mountains. In her hand to show us, she carried a scrap of her husband's shirt stained brown with his blood. It was all she had left of him, and so she wanted us to know this scrap of shirting as if it was the living man.

As leader we had John Raines, and so we moved at the slower pace of his great flock of sheep. The canvas tops of our wagons stood up like galleons on this woolly gray tide.

The sheep were lame and galled from their travels and loud in their complaints day and night. They would barely budge in the heat of the day. But in the cool of the evening they'd go surging off, acres of them, ganging into draws and pouring out again like the water they sought. There was comfort in their numbers, and the Apache couldn't stampede them. If a noise in the night stirred these creatures, they tumbled over one another to settle nearer the firelight.

We moved at this pace until we reached Pima and saw from afar an encampment of familiar wagons, the Strikers' and three others, huddled like sheep. But not the Ransoms'.

Young Mrs. Striker, chalk-white under her sunburn, walked out to meet us. My pa on foot reached her first. They stood amid the milling sheep. Watching from the wagon, I saw Mrs. Striker's gesture, and somehow I read this warning.

I jumped down and headed for the Strikers' wagon at a dead run, though my pa tried to head me off. Then I was up on the tailboard, clinging to it, and heaving myself up. Someone lay inside, wrapped in a quilt, head swathed in crusted bandages. I saw it was Lorenzo Ransom. He was half delirious now that he'd told his story to the others, and half dead of the wound where the hatchet had caught him just above the brow. He was near to consciousness, and when his eyes met mine, I tried not to read them. His lips were dry and cracked deep. He formed them to speak, to say my name, Lena, but I wouldn't let him say more. I heard his story from the others.

The Ransoms had traveled with the party as far as Pima Village where Mrs. Striker fell ill. She'd started a baby and lost it. They feared for her life. She was weak from loss of blood and grieving, for it would have been her first child.

They decided to wait there a week, but James Ransom refused, closing his jaw against them and saying that he and his would go on alone.

"He was like an ox scenting water," Mrs. Striker told my pa.

From Pima west the track was all but impassable with sand, and the Ransoms seemed to make no headway at all. They came to a bad hill near the Gila River where they couldn't get their loaded wagons up. There was nothing to do but unload and carry all their stores to the top and reload there. Sarah Ann and Beatrice and the boys carried everything. James Ransom had his hands full getting the oxen to move. Mrs. Ransom could do nothing. They'd hardly begun when they heard her cries from the wagon. She screamed all day, and just at sundown the child was born, a boy.

By then without their noticing, the wagons were surrounded. Twenty Apache braves and a chief sat in a circle. They'd moved up like the evening shadows, and waited.

James Ransom reached back in the wagon for his rifle but thought better of that. They stood there in the twilight, the

girls and Matthew and Lorenzo with their father. Inside, the
baby lay at Mrs. Ransom's breast.

At last the chief rose from the circle of his braves and
walked toward James Ransom, who put out his hand. The
first blow of the hatchet killed him. Lorenzo and a brave
reached the tailgate of his mother's wagon together, their
hands meshing. Lorenzo meant to get between his mother and
harm, but the hatchet whistled, catching him too low on his
forehead to take his scalp.

The sand flies on the raw flesh of his wound woke him at
daybreak. He'd been thrown down the hill and should have
been dead. He thought he was, but he could stand. He turned
to look back up the incline where the wagon stood mired in
sand. The oxen were gone, of course. All the livestock were.
It was the quietest morning of his life, and his eyes were
swollen nearly shut.

He climbed the hill, wearing his suit of blood, and found a
part of his father within an arm's reach of the tailgate. His
brother Matthew lay legless, so near their father that they
formed a strange shape in the sand, some tragic creature too
misshapen to live.

Inside the wagon he wouldn't see what was in the curve of
his dead mother's arm, but there was nothing there but death.
The girls, Beatrice and Sarah Ann, were gone. Wherever they
were, they'd be alive, and that was their tragedy.

Lorenzo began walking back the way they'd come. He saw
very little, but his feet stayed within the lines their wagon
wheels had cut. He walked all day, feeling no heat, and slept
between the wagon tracks that night, feeling no cold. On the
next day he looked up and saw Indians not a yard in front of
him.

He said he threw back his head until he could feel the sun
on the raw meat of his forehead direct. He offered them his
throat to cut. But they were Pima and gave him a pocketful of
mesquite beans to eat.

The party with the Strikers in the lead wagon met Lorenzo
square in their path. They put him in the wagon bed, and

Mrs. Striker dressed his wound while they turned back to
Pima. Before he lapsed into his delirium, he told them his
story, though his voice was nothing like the eleven-year-old
boy he'd been, and hardly human. Mrs. Striker and the other
women nursed him while the men went ahead on horseback
to find the bodies and bury them.

The men came back from that chore on the night we
arrived at Pima. They said there'd been no way to bury the
Ransoms, not in all that shifting sand. There were stones
though, and they'd built a high pile of them over the father
and mother, the baby and the boy.

I heard that story told until I was numb with it. After my
ma died, I'd made a pact with myself not to care too much
who was took or how. I'd swore I wouldn't let death and
parting bring me down, but now so soon my brave vow was
put to this test. I wondered what wicked god was at work on
us, and if he'd singled me out.

These Ransoms weren't kin of mine, and so I couldn't tear
my hair and fall into the arms of others. Here again I'd lost
what I had no real claim to. I felt a sourness in my throat and
wondered if it was seeping into my soul, if I had one.

Beatrice and Sarah Ann had been took by the savages. This
was only told in whispers, but it was told. I knew they
weren't dead and that they'd be better dead. I'd loved them
both like sisters, and perhaps that's why I'd been denied
them. Perhaps I wasn't meant to love anybody.

I wandered from the campfires, not knowing where I went,
and fetched up beside Mrs. Gray. She sat apart over a fire of
her own not big enough to warm her hands. In her lap was
the scrap of her husband's shirt, and she held it out to show
me as if I hadn't seen it a hundred times before. She was
crazed with her grief that wouldn't heal, and now I saw how
that was her solution.

FOUR

"We'll take Lorenzo in with us," I said to Pa. It was the first decision I'd made, the first of many.

We were moving on from Pima now, and the sand fleas infested us. They lived in my skirt and Pa's hatband and under our skins.

"We can take him," Pa said, "but we won't keep him. He's too near gone. Keep your head high, Lena, but not your hopes."

I rode up on the board with my back straight and my mouth pulled into a line. Behind me Lorenzo lay where my ma had been. He lay there greasy with fever, and the flies were busy on his face. I rode waiting for him to die and told myself it'd be a mercy, but I looked back every once in a while to see how he rested.

We moved deeper in the sand, slower now than the sheep. We breathed sand and ate it and drank it. I dreaded when we'd come to the place of the stones, but we were so slow going I still felt safe. One morning far ahead I saw something half sunk in a sand drift off the track. Closer to, I saw it was the chip basket Beatrice had used to gather kindling. I knew it for the little pattern of red reeds worked in around the rim.

I jumped down and pulled it out of the sand, then I trudged along beside the wagon for most of a morning with Beatrice's basket dangling from my arm. Then, though it was perfectly good, I pitched it off the trail as far as it would go. It turned in the air, and I looked away before it lit.

Finally I persuaded myself we'd passed the place I dreaded,

the burial place. I was riding up on the board through the endless afternoon when Lorenzo commenced to stir behind me. I looked back and saw he was sitting up in the oven of the wagon, clawing at the rags around his forehead.

"Oh, God," he moaned, "Oh, God, Oh, God."

I shushed him like a baby, but he carried on, saying the same words till he sank back. The bloodshot eyes in his broken boy's face darted all over the wagon.

I looked ahead then, and there was the rise up a sand hill and the pile of stones like a pyramid of old Egypt, looking windswept and ancient already. The wagons stopped to pay their respects. Some of us prayed for the Ransoms, I suppose, and some of us prayed for ourselves. My pa looked up at the sand hill ahead of us, gauging it, wondering if we could make it. I stood there close to the wagon where Lorenzo was, refusing to wonder or pray. Finally I couldn't take it any longer and crawled inside to hover over Lorenzo, and to hide from the stones. Long after that day it plagued me to know how he'd realized where we were and how this knowledge had torn him from his sleep.

We managed that hill and two or three worse ones. The track improved, and we found water at the Healy River and a safe haven at Fort Yuma.

The army physician at the fort, Dr. Hughes, redressed Lorenzo's wound and told us it might heal. I remembered ever after sitting up in the wagon caked with yellow dust in the street at Yuma. I sat there by the hour, watching the soldiers' wives on the boardwalk outside the store.

I marveled at skirts that had never been hiked to wade into streams for precious water. Their boots were fashioned close to their narrow feet, boots that would only do for boardwalks and parlors.

The skin of my face felt baked and turned to parchment when I saw the ladies' complexions enclosed in their deep bonnets. One woman rode in a trap behind a prancing horse and drove with one gloved hand, holding a fringed parasol between herself and the sun. Half dead from the desert, I sat there seeing this civilization and wondered what was real.

We could see California from here with our own eyes, though it looked no better than what we'd been through. We moved on almost before we had our second wind. The sands seemed to catch fire around us. Toward evening in this wasteland I'd walk ahead of the oxen, holding out handfuls of mesquite beans to keep them barely plodding.

The oxen began to fail us. Three died, leaving a fourth with no partner to yoke with, for the old ox that moved with the milch cows could hardly pull himself. That left us with Thunder and Lightning to pull the wagon. It rode lighter now that we were working through our supplies. The calf I called Treasure stumbled on behind the cows, who were dry now.

The fever in Lorenzo's forehead ebbed, and his strength began to come back. He sat up on the board for an hour at a time under a big-brimmed hat of Pa's that fit over his bandage. After his delirium he spoke less. He was remembering, I reckon, and it darkened his mind.

We were weeks crossing the California desert, leaving behind us the bursting carcasses of oxen and sheep. By following an old ox who broke free, we found Corrizo Creek. We made camp there and drank deep, though John Raines lost better than a hundred head of sheep from eating green greasewood along the banks.

In one of the days after that, Lightning fell under the yoke. Pa was in the wagon bed now, wandering in his mind from sunstroke. The other men helped me, and we unhitched Lightning to slump down beside the trail. He wasn't dead, and I wouldn't let him be shot. I only found an anger burning in me and that sourness again. Walking on beside Thunder, I wished I could yoke myself and be the beast I was becoming.

We reached Temecula that night and made a rough camp. I was too tired to sleep and told Lorenzo I'd walk back a piece to where Lightning was. I talked on with Lorenzo's empty eyes on me, pretending to him that I'd go back along the trail on my own if he wouldn't come. If Pa had been himself, he'd have forbidden it, but he was there in the wagon, half off his head, speaking Ma's name and hearing her answer.

Lorenzo watched me fill my apron with mesquite beans and draw off a pail of water to lure the ox. When I started off, he fell in beside me. He wasn't the boy he'd been, out for a midnight adventure. There was something bent over in him now. We walked the trail together, under a rising moon.

We saw Lightning's wet eyes rolling in the night before we made out the dark shape of him. I tempted him with beans and water ahead of his snout while Lorenzo twisted his tail and resorted to kicks. We worked the beast from both ends in this way until I thought it would soon be sunup. But at last Lightning rose up, too weak to argue with us. We drove him a step at a time back to Temecula under the white moon.

On the day after that our party made Old Long Warner's ranch and a warm welcome there. Pa was on his feet again, tottering, and John Warner sent him out a half of beef to fill our empty larder, and then he wouldn't take the dollar Pa offered for it. Thunder and Lightning were yoked again, but we traded off the old ox who walked behind for a fifty-pound barrel of flour.

While the sun still preyed on his mind, my pa told me and anyone who'd listen that we'd settle at the first water. He'd moved enough, and now he'd forgotten why. We made a last camp beside the San Gabriel River, which was a cooling tangle of watercress and rushes. The west bank stood high and thick with willows matted by wild grape vines.

That next morning we came to a collection of four houses built new in the old style that a group of Texas families called El Monte. It was an oasis of willow trees and bubbling springs, cool at midday. There was even an inn run by Mr. Ira Thompson where the Butterfield stage paused on its route between Los Angeles and the Mormons' town, San Bernardino.

I remembered now that I'd dreamed of towns like this when we were in the desert, and I tried not to blink for fear it would vanish. The leaves in the breeze made a green and silver sound, and there was water enough to spare for laying the dust of the road.

El Monte stood in a valley like the Garden of Eden, a land flowing, almost, with milk and honey. It was Bible-old too, which surprised us greatly after the rawness we'd come through. Here empires had already risen up and fallen back. The orchards were old and gnarled. The land long subdued under these leafy rows was heavy with pomegranates and olives and lemons, such strange things as these.

In the near distance, close in the clear day, stretched the vineyards and gardens of the old Spanish mission, San Gabriel Arcangel de los Temblores, "the Queen of Missions," as they still called it. It was like a whole country old as time, neatly walled in adobe and hedged in cactus. The lean, black long-horned cattle that the old Spanish padres had brought grazed as far as the purple foothills of San Jacinto and San Gorgonio.

I found an orange ripe in the road. I didn't hardly know how to peel the thing and stood there turning it in my hand. I'd thought I'd sent my childhood from me, but I was a wondering child one last time in this new world, with the orange opening like the sun in my hands. I found its segments and felt its sac of nectar break in my mouth. There'd been gold here in this California, as they'd said, lying in the road to be picked up by anyone.

There seemed many ways to live and flourish. The land was patchworking in groves now, but there was still grazing aplenty. Before he moved on, John Raines drove his great flock to the Cucamonga Ranch where Don Antonio Maria Lugo mingled the new stock with his thirty thousand sheep. There was even plain farming, aided by El Monte's bubbling springs. My pa found land to lease beyond the town where they talked American and farmed the way he knew: corn farming and hogs and melons for the sandy soil.

We had to raise a house, there being no improvements on the land. It was cheap to build as long as we let the locals do it their way, cheap and swift too, though the workers slept among their tools through the middle of the day.

The floor was earth and the walls were mud and stick. But the flat roof was as stout as ever I seen: first a cover of redwood planking, then a cushion of gravel, and over that hot brea, thick and sticky from the open pits beyond Los Angeles.

The central room where Pa and Lorenzo slept was kitchen and parlor, and behind the chimney they added a shed as a room for me. It wasn't what some would call a room, being only as long as the bed, but I'd never had a place to myself. And the bed was a wonder. They made it with four high willow bedposts that grazed the slanting ceiling. Then just imagine my surprise when the green willow bedposts refused to die and sent out branches and foliage. I nested in this bower like a creature among greenery, and slept at last away from the trail, though wagon wheels still turned in my mind, and I dreamed of my losses.

In this safe harbor beyond the end of our journey, I dreamed of those gone farther off than I. My ma come to me in my dreams, real as the living woman and as quickly gone again. Beatrice come to me, sassy as she'd been, with the chip basket on her arm and her eyes alight with mischief. Sarah Ann come, smooth as over ice, with the cameo at her breast. They wavered about my bed at night, waiting with me for dawn. I woke in this strange house and saw I was the woman here and must play a woman's part. I rose up every morning to look for my strengths.

The neighbors come to help Pa and Lorenzo sink a well and raise a Yankee windpump. Lorenzo would live with us as one of us. We were a little family now where two families had once been. We were quiet, for much went without saying. Lorenzo merely yoked himself together with Pa in their work, and one outdid the other in silent labor. The scar on Lorenzo's forehead was knitted now under a glaze of white. Except for what it meant, I didn't think it was hideous to look at. I didn't know how it was to live behind. I didn't know boys.

The neighbor women drew me into their circle. They gathered in their parlors to piece quilts and gave me a bag of scraps to start me out. Far back in their throats in the Texas way they talked of old times and the Home Place. Their conversation was like their quilts, faded remnants worked into wondrous new patterns.

"My daddy was like this with Stephen Austin," a woman, rocking, said. She held up two long fingers, clenched. "They was in the jail together at Mexico City in 'thirty-four when Texas pulled away!"

They were a poor audience for one another. A different woman, seeming not to hear, broke in, "To this day Sam Houston counts on my daddy in any little thing. *Senator* Houston is who I'm referring to."

They pinpointed the center of the world as Huntsville or El Paso or somewhere outside Galveston. They sewed bright new designs, speaking endlessly of their daddies and occasionally of their children, though they maintained dignified silences about their husbands.

But they thought I should have one. I saw that in their eyes and heard it in their heavy hints. They thought I was a motherless girl and needful of advice, but I was getting past that now and knew it when I was home again by my own hearth, learning the way of the oven built into the chimney.

The workers had built us a table. It was nothing but unplaned planks strapped with iron to four legs, but there was something solid and fine about it. Like everything else here, it looked old and settled. I scrubbed its top with a block of salt until it was pretty near white, and the mingled scent of salt and raw wood filled the house, my house.

I never thought to bring in a handful of the pink Castilian roses that grew all but wild, but there were fat white candles the Mexican women sold door to door. I set them along the table for light, and laid it thrice a day with the tin plates we'd brought. I set out a garden, and the fruit seemed to jump at me from the ground. We could grow fat out of my garden without a thing else in the world to eat.

One night something come over me that was strange to tell. I looked around in sudden surprise at the table and saw the weathered man who wasn't my pa in fact, and the wounded boy who wasn't my blood brother. There was no shape to the three of us, but here we were gathered as if it was meant to be, gathered here under this stout roof. I nearly gave way then and almost dared to take comfort in it.

In the candlelight I searched Lorenzo's face, bowed low over his plate. His wrists was far out of his cuffs, and I thought of the bigger shirt I'd have to cut for him. On his lip was the first faint hint of a mustache, delicate as the anise rooted among the roses. He was growing fast now to match his hands. *Be in no hurry,* I wanted to tell him, though I didn't know why.

He left the table as quick as he'd eaten and wandered out of doors as he always did. But this time I wouldn't let him go. After I cleared the table, I followed and found him.

He was down among the willows by the *zanja,* the ditch, looking down at something at his feet. Just where the ditch dipped was a snake, wrapping against itself. It was ribboned white and thrashing in the dust. Where its head had been was a rock and an ooze of black blood. Boylike still, he'd dropped the rock on it.

I wanted to pull back, but I didn't. "Was it pizen?"

He only shook his head.

"Come away from it," I said. We drifted along by the ditch, and I kept our shoulders close. I was no taller than he was now, suddenly. Soon he'd shoot past me.

I searched my mind for something to say, something to make him answer. I thought of the night Beatrice and I had gone for water in the Arkansas and scared him and Matthew out of a year's growth.

"Do you recollect the time—"

"No." He jerked up a shoulder to ward something off.

"Lorenzo, you'd do better to remember something. Nothing to amount to anything, but . . . something. It ain't natural not to speak of old times, and to remember."

He shook his head, but I was there in the corner of his eye, and there I meant to stay.

"You can cut and run if you want to, but it wouldn't be any use."

His voice broke, maybe because of his age. "Leave me be, Lena."

I wanted to grasp his arm, but I settled for words. "You'd do better to grieve, Lorenzo, and now. It'll only be harder later on."

I longed in my soul to say something about the scar on his forehead, how it was healed but hard. But I couldn't get words around that thought.

"You've got to go on, Lorenzo. The others—"

"The others ain't all dead," he said. His mouth snapped shut as final as James Ransom's.

"No," I said. "Beatrice—"

"Don't call her name," Lorenzo said. "Don't call any of their names. I don't want to hear them."

There was just enough light left to show that the corner of his eye was filling and flowing. He dropped down on his heels and worked his hands in the dark ground. I thought he was looking for another rock to drop on something, to fling at me. But then I heard the dry awful sob rising in his throat. He slipped sideways and fell across my feet. He writhed like the snake, crying in hard barks until he wept.

I had sense enough to let him cry himself weak. I let him give way till he gave out. At last he struggled up to his knees, and I chanced putting a hand on his shoulder.

"I ain't never going to get over it," Lorenzo said into the folds of my skirt.

But in that moment I think he was over the worst of it. We walked back toward the square of light from the door, side by side, back to Pa.

FIVE

We lived that way the better part of six years, until Lorenzo reached manhood, astride a creamy palomino, and our pa, Frank Wheatley, was old and liked his rocker by the fire. Until I was twenty, to the best of my calculations.

We hadn't prospered or meant to, but there were changes, "progress," as people began to call it. We had glass in the windows, and I persuaded Lorenzo and Pa to put me in a good floor for the house. Cool tiles would have suited it, I suppose, but I was set on the varnished board floors my neighbors had. I'd worked rag rugs and a little half-moon of hooked wool to lay before the hearth.

I got the porch I wanted too, and I didn't want a tin roof held up by tree trunks that rose right out of the ground. I wanted steps up and jigsaw fretwork like wooden icicles hanging down, and sky-blue paint on the ceiling. There was nothing fine about our place, but it was nice, real nice.

Oh, there was progress aplenty. The roads were graded now and stood up high above the zanjas and the fields. I could count six and then eight chimneys from my front porch. Pa thought the place was getting so crowded it wouldn't be fit for farming. We were old settlers now, a thing that happens quick in California, and we were apt to forget we'd been newcomers once and green as gourds.

We kept to ourselves, but I still sewed with the neighbor women. We still pieced our quilts and named our patterns: Wedding Ring, Texas Star, Pretty-Maids-All-in-a-Row. But there were changes here too. When they spoke of Old Times now, they were remembering when El Monte was four houses smothered in willow wood. There were so many of us now that we filled up all the corners of the parlors where we met and wondered if we hadn't better close our membership to new ones.

Now as we sewed, we passed from hand to hand the pictures of party gowns from the pattern books and laughed to scorn the old calicoes and tattered shawls we'd come West in.

"How did we manage in them times?" we asked one another, and I learned to make their comfortable clucking sound.

One lady among us was so clever with her hands that she could cut out our silhouettes from black blotter paper that were, we said, real enough to speak. Our refreshments were fancy now, pretty instead of plenty. Lettuce curled from our sandwiches, and one lady trimmed her crusts. Some of them grew beds of mint just for their tea, and while the rest sewed, one member or another would stand up and give a reading. They read poems of flowers and forgiveness and princesses waiting on castle walls. I could listen by the hour and marvel at the way the words wove.

They spoke of me behind my back, and I knew it. They saw I kept myself busy, but they thought it was time I was wed. Of course nobody spoke to me on the subject. I kept my neck stiff, and that spared me advice. I didn't want their pity either. I was a plain girl and becoming a plain woman. I knew it, but I had good sense, and good sense showed me that plainer ones than me had married early.

I read no poetry, and my seams were more stout than fine. I sewed a deal of hickory shirts for Pa and Lorenzo. To the other women I suppose I looked to be somewhere between a maiden lady and a hired girl. Instead of advice, they gave me bottles of their rosewater because they said my hands could be pretty if I'd see to them.

It was no longer a pioneering kind of place. Twice a year Lorenzo hitched up a pair to the spring wagon, and with a basket of lunch in the bed we made the trip to Los Angeles to do our trading. Pa cared nothing for town, but Lorenzo and I went.

We'd make an early start and roll over the road high above the sand hills and pink owl clover. The mornings smelled like verbena. I wore a sunbonnet I saved back for this, and Lorenzo wore his flat-crowned, wide-brimmed black hat with the thong strap under his chin to hold it. He looked rakish, like a bandito—like Joaquín Murrieta.

He'd have sooner saddled up his palomino and ridden to town on that, for he looked fine astride a horse and must have known it. On horseback he began to leave the skinny kid behind and cut the fine figure of a lanky man.

But he sat up on the board of the spring wagon with me. I rode proud beside this brother of mine and hoped some empty-headed girl wouldn't come along to steal him away and spoil things. I had hopes now of keeping us as the family we were. I had hopes, dampen them though I tried, to spare myself the disappointments that always come.

I looked forward to town and always put by my egg money for it. But it wore me out, and I was always ready to leave for home when it was time. Between every one of our visits the place grew to where you wouldn't know it.

There was no bank, but there were two hotels, the Bella Union on Main Street and the Lafayette. There was always some progress to goggle at. Once, Don Abel Stearn's Arcadia Block sprang up on Los Angeles Street facing down Aliso. It was a tremendous great structure and threw the whole road—the street into shadow. Then another time Don Juan Temple's market house reared up under a tall clock tower. Lorenzo and I marveled at how town people must always know the time of day and need a clock to tell them.

He would always make straight for the livery and the feed-and-grain, but I'd find myself in Temple's General Merchandise where I fingered the finery and saw my first brocades. I wondered where a person would wear such stuffs as these. As at Fort Yuma once long ago, I glimpsed the great world.

Another day came in my life to change me, to change everything. It was my baking day, and I had the house to myself. Over at the Cucamonga Ranch there was a cattle sale and a rodeo of sorts, and Lorenzo was bent on going. It was the sort of thing men like, and Lorenzo wanted to make a holiday of it for himself and Pa.

Our pa was failing though he wouldn't let on or see a doctor. But the men went, starting early, and Pa worried my mind the whole day. I was sure it would be too much for him. It was dark when they come back, and Pa sashayed through the door first, almost jaunty. The dome of his poor old head was frail and pale as an egg, but his cheeks were reddened by the day, and he was grinning from ear to ear. Lorenzo followed, grinning too, the pair of them like two clowns. I stood there with my hands on my hips, wondering what had got into them. Then there was another man in the doorway.

He doffed a battered old hat, and the firelight caught his tangled blond hair. He was dressed like a vaquero, and his clothes were like his face, weathered and wind-whipped. The seams in his face and a day's growth of beard kept me from knowing him. And a wedge-shaped scar cut one of his light eyebrows in two.

From the first look, something spoke inside me, and my heart turned over. But there I stood dumb as a post, forgetting my manners. But he smiled and looked me up and down, seeing me there before my own fire.

At last, Lorenzo said, "Lena, say how do you do to Evan Freeman."

Then I remembered how flushed and greasy my face was from the baking, and the state of my apron and my hair. And how men, who never think, will spring a thing like this on a person.

"My lands," I said, working my hands in my apron. I made myself stride across the room. My walk was awkward, and I knew it. I walked with the rolling gait I'd picked up from the neighbor women. "Land sakes," I said, glad now that the fire had flushed my face and hid my blushing. I put out a flour-covered hand for Evan to shake.

I'd put their supper back, and for a mercy there was plenty.

Pa was too tired to eat and repaired to his rocker. But before he sat down in it, I thought maybe Evan might have noticed the little squares I'd crocheted for the chair arms.

We had a coal oil lamp now for over the table, and I blessed myself for trimming the wick and scrubbing out the chimney. The three of us sat there long after we'd eaten, to hear Evan's stories.

In all his wanderings and work, he'd been near us a dozen times without knowing. We marveled at that even though we weren't off the place for weeks at a time. We marveled that he'd been as near as Diego Sepulveda's ranch, breaking horses all one season. He'd worked on the old Jurupa grant too, helping build Louis Rubidoux's mill. We marveled that we hadn't met again until today.

Here and there Evan had been, working his way. He'd brought the Bixby brothers' sheep down the Fremont Trail to San Bernardino. He'd gone up to the gold fields for a look at Mokelumne Hill and Hangtown. While he told us of the gold fever up there, he turned his calloused palms up on the table, to show us he'd found no riches, or maybe hadn't been looking for them. He'd met Kit Carson on the Overland Trail, and he'd been up in the Shoshone country above Fort Bridger on a night when his legs froze hard to the saddle.

He spun out his yarns till I forgot to look aside when our eyes met. I wondered how he got the scar in his eyebrow and finally asked. But he only looked quick toward Lorenzo in a way that gave me to know it was something to be understood only between men, so I figured it had to do with a woman. He'd lived rough. Lorenzo was seeing it in his hands, and I saw it in his eyes.

When I wasn't watching Evan, I was watching Lorenzo. He leaned across the table to drink these adventures, and I worried they'd give him ideas.

Later, when Lorenzo went out to see to the chores, Evan and I were left on our own, for Pa was sound asleep in his chair. I bustled away from the table and reached for the kettle on the hook in the fireplace. Evan's hand closed over mine, and I let him lift the kettle and pour it into the pan.

I couldn't think of anything but how red my hands looked in the dishwater and how a lock of loose hair was worrying my cheek. I felt impatient with myself and the world, and Evan, come marching in here like he'd never been elsewhere.

"Don't ask Lorenzo about the scar on his forehead," I said. "We don't speak of it."

Evan had pulled down the cloth and was drying the plates with his thorny hands. "You mean where the Apache caught him with the ax, trying to lift his hair?"

My hands splattered the water. In my surprise, I looked right at him. "You mean he told you?"

Evan nodded like it was natural. "While we were riding back today. He said how they killed his folks and his brother and the newborn, and made off with the girls. What was their names?"

"Beatrice," I said, whispering and looking over my shoulder to the door. "And Sarah Ann. We don't talk of them. Lorenzo's almost a man now and growed, but that's a place in him that never healed."

"Seemed like he wanted to tell me," Evan said, a little quieter to match my voice.

It plagued me, what Evan said. I lived with these two men, Lorenzo and Pa, and did for them. For days on end they wouldn't hardly string two words together. I thought that when men were off together they spoke not at all. But the minute my back was turned, Lorenzo was talking, and freely, to Evan Freeman who wasn't much more than a stranger. I had half a mind to ask him why men were that way, but I supposed there was no answer.

I made the washing up last as long as ever I could, wishing Lorenzo would come back to the house. Was he out there doing nothing, to give us time alone? Evan stuffed the cloth up on the roller for the towel where it didn't belong. Then he took up the pan of water to throw out in the yard.

"Fling it free of the porch," I called out after him. "I've got a bed of iris just under the rail, and they don't need soapy water."

He nodded like he knew, but I bit my lip for speaking so

sharp, speaking like he wasn't company at all. When he come back I was so near my wit's end I was ready to wake Pa, but Evan caught at my apron tails and loosed the tie. It was provoking, but there was nothing to do but slip the apron over my head. When I turned, he took me in his arms.

He was too quick for me. One hand slipped around my waist. The other caught up my hand in a grasp. He took a little sliding step sideways to make us dancing partners as we'd once been long ago on the trail.

"Do you recollect that boy with the violin?" Evan asked me. He spoke near my forehead, and his face grazed my hair. I wondered if I'd been waiting for this right along and hadn't known. In a story book I might have, and perhaps there was some truth in stories. He was changed from what I remembered. He was squarer and broader, somehow more certain. I didn't know if I'd been waiting, but he'd better not think so. A minute more and I might melt there against him if I didn't speak.

"All in the world that boy could play was 'Money Musk,' " I said. "I hear that tune yet in my mind."

"In my mind too," Evan said. Though it was nonsense, we moved on, circling in our dance with no music but "Money Musk" in our minds and Pa's snoring.

"What if Lorenzo comes back in?" I said, never pulling away. I'd about give up on Lorenzo ever coming back in.

"We'll just keep a-dancing," Evan said. "There's worse occupations." I wondered if he was the kind of man who has an answer for everything.

"I won't have you putting notions in his head," I said, trying to stiffen. "All your rattling around and punching cattle and living hard. That all sounds good to a young kid who don't know any better."

"I been thinking of settling down," Evan said. He turned me in the dance till the firelight was on my face.

"Hereabouts?" I asked, looking down.

"Not far. Down at the Rafaela Ranch, on the old Nieto grant. They're looking for a foreman."

"Is that a step up?"

"It's a step."

I wouldn't dance with him any longer. I was no hand at dancing anyway, and I was dizzy from trying, or something. I put my hand out on the chimney to catch my balance. Next to my hand was the silhouette the clever lady at the quilting had made of me. I'd pinned it up there because we had no other pictures.

Evan was behind me, standing closer than he had any business being. "Why, that's you," he said and reached past me to smooth the paper where it had begun to curl.

"Is it a likeness?" I turned my profile to him.

"It don't do you justice." Then it come to him that it was time to go. He found his hat, and I walked him out onto the porch. "I'm working over at Duarte right now, just temporary. I'll be back if it's all right."

I nodded. What else could I do? But I expect I thought it'd be better if he didn't come back. It'd be better to leave us as we'd been, and things as they'd been.

But at the bottom step he turned back, a little braver in the dark. "Could I have that likeness of you on the chimneypiece?"

I turned back to the house, embarrassed into flight to get it for him.

When he was gone, I took the lamp into my room and turned it up till it blazed. On the wall I had a little shard of looking glass, and I studied myself in it as I hadn't before.

Before, I'd only looked to see if the knot I wore low on my neck had caught all the strands. Now I pulled out the pin that held my hair and let it tumble. I shook it free and studied my face like it was the map of some unknown country.

I didn't wonder if I was pretty enough. That was vain, and mirrors don't tell everything. I wondered if change was coming and if I'd be equal to it. I wondered and searched the eyes of the girl in the looking glass, but she didn't know no more than me.

SIX

I wouldn't marry him all that summer. I didn't plan to marry him in the fall. Twice a week he come calling over from Duarte until his horse turned in without being told, until he was family and I was outnumbered.

He brought me gifts, and no man ever had. He brought me a bottle of Hoyt's German cologne that smelled of lavender. I counted on his coming and baked like I was trying to win him, though I scorned myself for that.

He come on the Fourth of July, and the neighbors were setting off fireworks. Lorenzo fired his shotgun into the locust trees in the yard. That time Evan brought me a set of long-toothed tortoiseshell combs with brilliants set into their backs. They were the kind the Spanish women wore in the glistening black buns high on their heads, stately and vain.

I touched the combs in their fitted box. I ought to have thanked him. He was generous, and he'd tried to please me, but the tongue in my mouth belonged to some cautious woman, cautious and not kind.

"I couldn't use them. I don't wear my hair thataway."

"Maybe you could dress it higher," he said, close to my ear. But I didn't. I kept the combs in the fitted box and never wore them until years later when I was someone else.

He walked me one August night out into the yard and kissed me as we stood beside the pink oleander tree. I felt the bristles on his chin and fought my thoughts, and changed them to these: This thing is happening to me that happens to women. I can feel myself slipping, and it would be easy to go limp in his arms and think of nothing but his nearness. It would be so easy, but wouldn't I pay for it later? I didn't fear Evan. I didn't even fear myself much. I feared love and then loss. Seemed like if ever I clung to anybody—or yearned to—they vanished and left me lonely. True, I had Pa and Lorenzo still, but I knew that couldn't last.

"I couldn't marry you," I said when he asked. "Look at my pa. He's near enough helpless. Lorenzo lets him think he's farming, but he's not. He's wore out."

Evan was wise enough not to show me the truth, though I saw it in his eyes. My pa wouldn't stand in anyone's way much longer, not even his own.

"And Lorenzo," I said. "He can't get along here without me to keep house and see to things. What's to become of him?"

"They need hands down at Rafaela," Evan said. "He'll be glad for the company and the life. A boy his age gets restless, and you've seen that yourself. We'll take Lorenzo with us."

That meant he'd already spoken to Lorenzo. Such things weren't taken for granted. That meant they'd gone behind my back the way men do. I was used to having things my own way and making decisions, though I had a job to admit that even to myself.

I knew I was in love now for the first time and the last. It was deep water to me, and I knew I could drown and die of it. I was frightened as a deer. Though I tried to keep my fear from showing, I blamed Evan for not seeing it. Why did he rumble at me in his reasonable voice when I was scared and he ought to leave me be?

"Maybe later on," I said, pulling my mouth into a straight line to show him I was practical, and calm.

"I'll be proud to have you as my wife. I've asked no other, and won't."

Then one day near November when the wind blew rain in off the ocean in sheets, I come in with the egg pail on my arm and found Pa on the floor.

Lorenzo and I got him into his bed and sat with him in turns, letting other things go. Pa continued to cling, the breath growling in his throat. I'd come awake in the chair where I tried to sleep and find his eyes on the ceiling beams and his mouth working. I'd have thought he was rallying if there'd been any strength there to call upon, and I thought he was past knowing me.

I'd loved this man who wasn't even my pa, and so I was losing him. You loved and then they left you. But he was precious to me then, more than before. Just at that time of night when I looked for him to slip away, he spoke.

"Them boys," he said, perfectly clear, and I moved nearer.

"Them boys," Pa said, worn out from the words. I thought his mind was adrift, but he turned his head and looked straight at me, seeing me. "Them boys of mine who died."

I nodded at him. He'd gone all the way back to the baby sons he'd buried all those years ago.

"Them boys of mine," he said, "couldn't have been more to me than what you are."

Then he died, never turning his head away from me.

The sound I made brought Lorenzo on the run. I howled my grief into the bedcovers and clawed at them. I screamed my throat raw at death who had robbed me again.

I mourned him a month and on that day in a black dress I married Evan Freeman. The preacher who'd buried Frank Wheatley joined us, and we set out in the spring wagon with Lorenzo following on the palomino.

The land hadn't been Pa's, and the house wasn't what people wanted nowadays. We sold off the stock, and I was glad enough to be quit of the chickens. I brought my household goods, but the bed they'd built in my room was too tall to get through the door, and too narrow for marriage.

We were wed in the morning, and so we were at the gate of Rancho Rafaela by twilight.

We come over territory that was open country still. It was raw land patterned with grazing sheep and cattle as far away as the high hump of Palos Verdes. There was nothing for miles except for the ranch house of the Yorbas and the others of Los Alamitos and Santa Gertrudis and Los Cerritos. But these looked to me more like forts than homes for people, and they were no more than dots in the distance.

These tremendous spreads were carved from the land granted to Don Manuel Nieto nearly eighty years before by Governor Don Pedro Fages, speaking for the king of Spain. But there were new owners now and new boundaries, and we'd soon hear talk of fences. There'd be talk shortly of rails to be laid and groves and high-waisted Yankee houses picketed and prim. But in that first day of my marriage, I saw no promise here.

Just at sundown we rattled across a riverbed and up a rise past a barn to the open gate of the Rafaela Ranch. I saw it was like a town gathered behind a wall with corncribs and barns and a granary standing out among the hills.

Inside the gate the courtyard came alive with waiting people. All the hands and vaqueros and dairymen were in the dry square, watching for the newlyweds. When they saw us, a shout went up and a cannonade of gunfire that left the air hazy. They threw their hats and called out comments to Evan I tried not to hear. I glanced back at Lorenzo to see a smile very like a smirk on his face. But his eyes were wide at this bustling new place, and he was ready to find his feet here.

Before us the main block of the house, two stories under a tin roof, stretched a hundred feet long. This was where the owning family, the Claypools, lived. Their windows were high and small and sunk deep in the adobe.

From the main house two low wings ran out to meet the wall and enclosed the square. At a door in the left-hand wing I saw a Chinaman standing with a boy like him at his side. They waved their aprons in greeting.

A dozen hands reached for the bridles to lead our horses on, and as the path ahead of us cleared, I saw at the door of the main house three women standing, the Claypool women grouped together, their full skirts overlapping. They stood at the back door of the main house and never waved, but only watched.

My heart fell when Evan led me into the foreman's room in the right-hand wing. It wasn't as much home as I'd left. It was only a big empty barn-space, floored in broken brick. Evan saw it through my eyes, and faltered.

A long table stood between backless benches, and another table to work from was shoved against the rough wall. At one end of the room a pair of leather chairs were pulled up to a blackened fireplace. At the other a bed was set up. It was a castoff from the main house, with a black walnut headboard rising halfway to the high ceiling. At the top the shape of a pomegranate was carved in the wood, showing seeds. There wasn't a rug or a curtain in the place.

"It's a good-sized room," he said to me, clearing his throat, "but I know it's not what you're used to, Lena."

Later I was to know that a lot of the help lived out in hovels called *jacals* made of nothing but willow brush and tule. But he was wise not to tell me and expect me to count my blessings.

"What I'm used to is lost to me now," I said, "and here I see I'll have my work cut out for me."

The hearth was too small to be any earthly use. I'd be cooking and baking in the out of doors like a squaw. The water piped into the house from the windpump didn't reach this wing, so I'd be toting water.

"I'll have wages," Evan said. "You can have things to make it better."

I nodded because this was no time to show discontent. For the month since Pa died, I'd lived in a dreary dream. Now I'd awakened to my wedding day with night coming on fast. I'd lost my father and my home, and I'd gained this vacant barn and this stranger. I saw Evan now like I'd never set eyes on him before.

I supposed I was married, so I wondered what to do about supper. With the thought, the door opened, and a sharp-eyed, black-eyed Mexican girl, a servant from the house, pushed in with a tray of supper sent over from the Chinaman's kitchen. It was his wedding gift, the only one we got.

We ate his hearty supper of mutton stew tangy with onions and fragrant with spices. We sat together at the end of the long table, and I ladled out the stew over baking-powder biscuits. There was a pot of scalding coffee and a pint of cream yellow as butter. It was a feast, and we made it last, quiet as an old married couple, until the candle guttered.

Evan went out to draw a washbowl of water. He brought it back and then stood out in the yard while I washed the dust of the road off myself. There was no place to hang up my dress, or a drawer to fold it away. Everything was awkward here, and drafty, though I was trembling anyway. I made piles of my dress and petticoats and stood my shoes against the wall. Then I slipped into a much mended nightdress. He'd laid a good fire in the hearth, but its warmth didn't reach across the room.

I lay carefully on one side of the bed and watched him silhouetted against the firelight while he washed himself in my water. His suspenders hung down, and his shirt was off. I watched the curve of his bare back as he bent to scrub his face. I thought of what I knew of men and what I didn't.

Toward the end, I'd bathed Pa like a baby and used the softest sponge I could find to soothe his old flesh that hung down like flags. I'd scrubbed Lorenzo's naked back when he sat naked as a jaybird in the horse trough. But Lorenzo was more brother to me than if we was kin. I'd turned away from his evidences of manhood because I'd have kept him a kid if I could. It come to me that I didn't know anything about a man, or what this one would want from me.

This was my wedding night, and I felt more ignorant than innocent, and not pretty enough. I'd brushed out my hair and hoped it lay untangled on the pillow. A man wanted beauty—and youth, but I'd buried my youth more than once. I lay there defenseless.

When he come to me, we lay looking up at the starlight through the breaks in the roof. He'd slipped naked under the covers, and I'd looked away. I folded my hands across my breast like a dead woman, so my arm wouldn't brush his bare side.

Evan lay there beside me, swallowing before he spoke. "There's many a pair starting out with worse prospects."

"Many," I said.

"We've got our strength."

"I only know how to work, Evan. That's all I ever done and all I know."

I felt his hand move beside me. "That's enough to know," he said, speaking low.

"Is it, Evan? You've been with . . . other women, and they knew what I don't."

He found my hand with the new wedding band on it. It was clenched at my breast, and my fingers were freezing.

"They wasn't good women," he said. "Don't think of them."

He covered me and warmed me with himself. I could all but hear my heart, and he must have felt it against his chest. His hands moved down me, and he edged my nightdress up. His hands were hard and his nails were ragged, but he'd be easy with me, and that took away some of my fear. His arms were around my naked waist now, and his mouth was wet against the hollow of my throat.

I saw then how my body would leave me and follow his. My hands were still clenched, but on his back now, and my legs loosened. I'd have forgotten myself then and gladly, but that would be fatal. There was only this moment left to speak.

"Evan, will you never leave me?"

"Never," he said, muffled against me.

But I knew he would. I knew it even then, and in a moment or two later when I cried out in pain, it wasn't for the reason that he thought.

SEVEN

Evan and I settled in beside the busy, bald square at the back of the Claypool family's Rancho Rafaela. The dust boiled continually in my dooryard though I fought day and night to keep it out of the house. There was always something happening, but it wasn't homey, of course. It was a town of men, and so it was part parade ground and part prison yard.

Opposite our wing was the Chinaman's kitchen. He and his boy cooked for the Claypools and the men from the bunkhouse. Lorenzo took his three meals a day there and would walk across the square to look in on me. He was taking on the ranch hand's ways, roughening enough to be one of them, but he wasn't quite lost to me. Against all reason, I come to think of my past life as the happy times, and Lorenzo was my link.

It was my job to cook for the dozen milkers who didn't feed at the same time as the other help. My table was full of hungry men at every odd hour. I learned to cook in quantity and the way of the big, hump-backed oven out back. I could beat up enough batter for a hundred buttermilk biscuits at a time, and my feeders learned me early how they liked a hash made of *carne seca*. They wanted fiery peppers diced into their scrambled eggs and fruit pies three meals a day, and they licked their tin plates clean. I reckon they'd have done that for any cook, but they give me credit and called me ma'am.

Beside my door was an olla well wrapped in damp croker sacks and a dipper for drinking water. Beside it I set out a washstand and a lump of lye soap as a sign to the men that I wanted clean hands at my table. They remarked on this peculiarity of mine all around the square and out in the barns.

The Chinaman across the way was my confederate. Every morsel in our mouths, save only sugar and coffee, grew on the property. I had me a key to the storeroom next door where the apples were kept, enough for sauce year-round. Everything else filtered through the Chinaman, who was butcher and greengrocer to me. He sent everything across by the boy and steered me right by sending me the right ingredients in the right quantity. But he wouldn't know me and maybe didn't speak my language. Whenever anybody come near him, he threw his apron over his head and liked to have fell down laughing, which I suppose was only nervousness.

I worked a long day, and that will cure most ills. I was in charge of things too, and that never hurts. Now and again I even found a little leisure to work a rag rug and hem curtains for my windows. I'd have settled for this, but there were changes coming. I knew what one of them was.

Evan knew, and was pleased, but I thought the secret still safe from other eyes for a little while more.

At a distance, I'd seen the Claypool women from the big house. They were Mrs. Claypool and her two maiden sisters. I knew about the Claypools from the men who fed at my table. Men are worse gossips than women, and stranger still, they believe what they tell.

I'd heard that Mr. Randolph Claypool had been a cotton planter in the state of Georgia. Back in Mexican days he'd bought Rancho Rafaela from the widow of old Don Manuel Nieto, and then after statehood he sent back to Macon, Georgia, for his wife, Narcissa Claypool. Though it wouldn't have been a part of Mr. Claypool's plan, she brought her spinster sisters, Miss Bertha and Miss Eugenia. They'd come around the tip of South America in a sailing ship. The men always said it was Claypool's tragedy that the ship hadn't sunk.

They said he'd fancied himself a rare judge of horseflesh and women at one time. But his years and his wife and blended whiskey had brought him low. He couldn't hardly sit his horse now for gout, and they said he spent his days up at the office in his house, drinking julep and talking to Jefferson Davis like he was right there in the room.

My pa had worked for no man and bowed his knee to no man, but that was the past now. In the scheme of things here the Claypools were our betters. Once when Mrs. Claypool and I had both been at our doors, she inclined her head in my direction, but we'd got no nearer than that.

I decided I wasn't quite a servant. I didn't rightly know what I was. My milkers showed respect, and I couldn't fault Evan. Marriage isn't courtship, but then only a fool expects it to be. I suppose I was content.

Then one day the child of one of the house servants brought me a note. I opened it and read:

> Mrs. Freeman,
> Be good enough to step up to the door of the house.
>   Narcissa Claypool

Jerking my apron off, I followed the child back to the house. If the note was a test to see if I was literate, I meant to pass it at once. The child vanished inside and shut the door in my face. I had to lift the iron ring and send a thunderclap echoing within.

At last the door opened, and Mrs. Claypool put out her head. She was older up close, with a wide parting in her flat hair and rice powder caked above her brow. It was the first truly hot day of spring, but she wore a net collar to hide her neck. She looked at me like I was a peddler, but then she seemed to know me.

"I have been meaning for us to meet," she said. "You are settled in, I think."

I nodded, though she hadn't quite asked me anything.

"I don't hear anything but good reports of you," Mrs. Claypool said. "You keep a clean house, they tell me, and you keep to yourself."

I wondered in my mind what choice I had but to keep to myself

"My sisters and I—that is, Miss Bertha and Miss Eugenia—have often remarked on it. We've said it isn't right for a woman to have to be always in the society of men and never to hear any conversation."

She paused, but I could think of no reply.

"You have organized your work so you have a little time in the afternoons once in a while?"

"I have."

"Then bring some of your sewing and come up to the house this afternoon. We sit out front on the veranda."

"That's good of you," I said, dreading it already.

"You're not a Southern woman?"

That meant nothing to me. I didn't hardly think of where I'd come from or what it had been called.

"You're not from the South?"

I shook my head.

"Nevertheless," said Narcissa Claypool.

I reported with my sewing in the black dress I'd been married in. I had no collar or cuffs or a brooch to relieve it, but it was unpatched and the only thing that I hadn't skimmed milk in. A servant led me through the house and out onto the porch at the far side where there was a green lawn beyond, like a secret garden.

The porch was latticed to screen the sun, and the women sat in this shade. Narcissa Claypool sat in an upholstered chair. Her sisters sat facing her in plainer chairs, too few to make a proper circle. Nearer the door was a straight chair. The maiden ladies would have to turn their heads to see me there, but I was directly within Mrs. Claypool's vision.

She looked up from her petit point. "Yes, there you are, Mrs. Freeman. I want to make you acquainted with my sisters, the Misses Calhoun."

Bertha, gaunt and long-necked as a sand hill crane, turned her beak and nodded. Eugenia rolled her peculiar, full face around and smiled at me, though her eyes danced madly. She had the look of a porcelain doll left long on a shelf.

I had no fancywork to bring, but I was pleating a shirt for

Evan, and that was the daintiest work I had on hand. Before I
had my needle threaded, the conversation I'd been sent for to
hear was flowing. Though their drawl was odd, they talked
like the women at the quiltings in El Monte had, of Home
and Old Times.

"I swan," said Miss Bertha, stabbing at her tapestry, "if
Mama was alive to see how we have to live out here in this
purgatory, she wouldn't rest easy in her grave."

Miss Eugenia put her hemming down. "But, Bertha, how
could Mama be restless in her grave if she was alive?"

"Be still, Eugenia," Mrs. Claypool said.

"When I think of them darkies we had!" Miss Bertha said.
"Why these people here don't even speak English. I don't
know how they understand each other. I don't think they do.
And lazy? Why, we wouldn't—"

"What is this *we*, Bertha?" Mrs. Claypool said into her
sewing. "It's *we* this and *we* that all the livelong day. I call
to your mind they was *Mr. Claypool's* darkies. It was *Mr.
Claypool's* house. If it wasn't for his kindness and mine that
you two been living on for thirty years, you'd both be at the
Poor House."

Mrs. Claypool's jaw went firm and she looked at me to
show me how sisters could be put in their place.

But not for long. Miss Eugenia said, "With that rube,
Lincoln, up in the White House, nobody'll have any niggers
at all to speak of."

"Be still, Eugenia. You wouldn't know Lincoln if he
walked up on the porch."

And so, I thought, this was the conversation I'd been
favored to hear. I seemed to listen to it for days before
a servant brought out a silver-laden tray. Legs dropped
down from it to make a tea table, placed before Mrs.
Claypool.

They were reverential about their tea, and I saw the sudden
grace of Mrs. Claypool's gestures. She slipped off her thimble,
and her little white hand opened the lid of the silver pot to see
how the tea was steeping. She poured out then from the

teapot and a squat creamer, mixing tea and cream and adding water from an open jug to make a proper strength. Her hands, I thought, were like small plump doves, fluttering just enough.

Mrs. Claypool passed me a cup, and I never touched china like this, thin as seashell and patterned with moss roses. Even the silly sisters' hands came out for their cups in gestures that were pretty to watch. It stirred me there for a moment when I saw how things could be.

"Move your chair nearer," Mrs. Claypool said to reward me.

When I did, Eugenia took me in with her dancing eyes. "Oh, you're in black. It gives me dismal thoughts." Eugenia was in darkest blue with a hoop in her skirt and much fringe.

"I lost my father in the fall," I said, smoothing my black skirt.

"I have told you to be still, Eugenia," said Mrs. Claypool.

"Oh, well, you will have to excuse my remark." Eugenia waggled her chins at me. "When we lost our papa, I cried for a year."

"You were not more bereaved than the rest of us," Bertha said.

"I told her to be still," Mrs. Claypool said, "but she won't."

"But, Mrs. Freeman, you have something now to occupy your thoughts," Eugenia said, burbling on. "Something to look forward to." Her strange eyes were acute all of a sudden, and I missed her meaning.

"I don't call that a suitable observation for an unmarried woman to make." Mrs. Claypool sighed.

"Me either," said Bertha.

By itself, my hand moved to cover my waist. I'd thought I wasn't showing yet, but even these witless women saw. I blushed to my roots in a way no man could make me do.

These sisters hadn't meant to mention what they were

soon calling my delicate condition. But once Eugenia had broken the ice, they chatted cheerfully of babies and birth-bed horrors they'd heard tell of. And they hoped I wouldn't suffer unduly, these childless three.

EIGHT

Evan and I spoke little aloud of the child to come, not knowing what we'd have to offer it. Besides, it didn't do to babble on and build your hopes. The child might not live. We might not raise it. But it was alive in me! Already it could kick the sewing off my lap, and I was getting bigger by the day. When I reached past the men feeding at my table, they looked away in kindly confusion.

Evan would come in at night and find me still about my work with my body swollen and my hair plastered in wet ringlets on my face. He'd look at me, and I could see the pride in his eyes, and a little guilt.

Once, to hear how it sounded he said, "I wouldn't mind a boy. We can always use extra hands here."

I looked up from whatever work was in my lap. "I'm not having a boy to live in the bunkhouse like Lorenzo," I told him, "or to be at everybody's beck and call like you. No, indeed. I want something better than that for my child."

I didn't know that till I'd said it, but I knew it then.

"Besides," I said, "it might be a girl. I've been thinking in that direction." That wasn't quite so either, but now I believed it. From that moment I believed I was carrying a girl child.

Evan gave me an uncertain look, like I might be able to decide whether it was to be boy or girl. "Well, if your mind's made up," he said, and his voice trailed away.

The new life in me took possession of my thoughts. I moved heavily through my days at my usual pace, but the pains low in my back were like fire, and my feet swelled to split my shoes. I lived in a kind of dread and exultation, like I myself was about to be born.

The nearer my child came to her birth, the more I wanted for her. I knew the folly of wanting and the hazards of hope, but I wanted things for this child I couldn't name, things bigger than my world. These thoughts, vague and sharp-edged, nagged at me while the summer deepened and I drew near my time.

A Saturday came, silent and sun-dazzled. Those not out on the land had gone to town for their Saturday night, riding like madmen and burning up all eighteen miles of bad road from here to town. Lorenzo had gone with them, never wanting to be left behind. I didn't like to think what he got up to at Los Angeles. They'd all be back Sunday morning, heavy-headed at their chores and grinning back at their adventures.

I stood in my doorway, scenting the summer, and then I heard the hoofbeats long before I saw the horse. Afterward, years afterward I remembered knowing then the rider was bringing news to turn my life.

The palomino came through the gates at a gallop. It was Lorenzo making straight for where I stood, vaulting off his horse, shaking a page of paper in the sun.

"Lena, look." It was the little newspaper they put out at Los Angeles, the *Star*. Lorenzo pointed to a notice among the advertisements. The sun blinded me, and I turned to shade the page. Lorenzo laid his hand on my shoulder, a thing he never did. The notice read:

FRIENDS OR RELATIVES SOUGHT

Anyone acquainted with Sarah Ann Ransom
is urged to communicate with Major
Lassiter, in command of Fort Yuma.

That was all it said. Lorenzo's fingers closed on my shoulder. He'd pulled off his hat, and the sun beat down on him. The scar on his forehead showed clear and white. I'd long since ceased noticing it. Now that he was a man, the scar had woven itself in the furrows of his flesh.

"Lorenzo, don't," I said. "Don't get your hopes too high. Don't want it too much."

I wanted to take the paper and tear it to pieces and scatter it. I wanted to turn back the day so it would end the way all our days did. But Lorenzo heard neither my words nor my thoughts.

"I've got to go, Lena. Today. Now."

In the end, Lorenzo set out for Fort Yuma on the following day, after the heat of it. Evan went with him. Behind their horses they tied a third in case they'd need it for another rider on the trip back.

Word of their mission swept the ranch. Even through their thick adobe walls the Claypools must have known. Only I said nothing. For reasons I knew and maybe some I didn't, I'd have kept Lorenzo back if I could.

If it was his sister, if it was the Sarah Ann we knew, what could she be by now? If the Indians were done with her, what could be left? Then after Evan and Lorenzo rode away and were only plumes of dust in the distance, did I think to ask myself that other question: "What of Beatrice?"

They were gone so long I thought they might be dead. I thought I might have my child in their absence. Sleep came hard to me in those weeks. It came late and left me early. I tossed and sweated in my bed and remembered back seven years to Sarah Ann. She come back to me real as she had been. I'd admired her and that kept her memory fresh. Though I didn't remember a word she'd ever spoken, it was her beauty that haunted me now. I saw the perfect line of her cheek and the skin white as marble within the sunbonnet. I remembered how men fell over themselves for a look at her, or from her.

Sarah Ann had taught her sister Beatrice to read and write. Beatrice hadn't been to more school than she could help, but Sarah Ann taught her. She drew letters and numbers with a stick in the dust of our encampments, for Beatrice to learn.

Sarah Ann and Beatrice, too, come back to stand around my bed, waiting for dawn with me as they'd done long ago when they were newly lost.

I woke one morning in September, sure I'd overslept. The courtyard outside was awake before me in the gray light. Horses stamped, and I heard voices.

I couldn't move quick now, but I made for the door to find Evan there, blocking the space. He took me by the shoulders, saying nothing, and when I saw he was shielding me from whatever was outside, I fought past him, wild to know.

They'd ridden through the night on this last leg, white with dust. Lorenzo was there in the square, helping someone, some figure down from the spare horse.

The light was dim, and I was still groggy and thick from sleep and surprise. I stood there blinking to see while Lorenzo took the other figure by the hand and led her nearer to me.

I stared and stared as they drew nearer, only half persuaded this wasn't another of my dreams. The figure with Lorenzo hung back like a colt at the end of a rope. She dug her heels in the dirt and tried to twist free. She moved and writhed like nothing human.

But then she was there before me, facing me. I covered my face with my hands and screamed. I screamed like nothing human myself until I'd raised the place and shutters fell back and men ran from everywhere, pulling on their shirts and catching up their guns, fearing some invasion.

NINE

I got their story from Evan and Lorenzo. In the first days back from their journey they talked more than ever I'd heard from either of them, though it wasn't easy for them. Seemed like they needed to account for every hour away, to prove they'd done right to go, and bring her back. I put together their stories in my mind, dreading every word, wishing I didn't have to know, or act on what I learned.

They crossed the desert in the worst time of year, living from their canteens from well to well. It had been a long time since Evan had been out on the trail, but its ways come back to him, and he taught Lorenzo what he remembered.

Though there was less danger of marauders, red-skinned or white, along this stretch now, Evan fell back on old habits. They'd make a quick camp to cook their supper, but Evan would kick dirt on the embers and they'd ride on a mile or two to sleep in the dark. Evan knew and Lorenzo learned it was better to sleep in the dark than by a fire that might attract anybody.

They'd stuffed blankets into their ponchos for bedrolls, but Lorenzo rested no better than I was resting back home. He lay in wait for the stars to fade and an excuse to make another early start.

The sand was so soft they couldn't trust the horses to the picket pins, and so before they slept they tied their horses to themselves, winding the lariats around their legs. Lorenzo's palomino wasn't used to such treatment as this and jerked through the nights, dragging Lorenzo from such sleep as he got.

At Fort Yuma they found a good-sized town now. Lorenzo wouldn't dismount or wash himself before he found Major Lassiter at the fort. Lorenzo had dreamed, waking and sleeping, of finding his sister there. He dreamed of Sarah Ann as I was dreaming of her. He dreamed, he told me, of finding her in a cool cotton dress up on a porch somewhere, out of the sun, waiting in a bentwood chair for him to be there.

It didn't turn out that way. When he and Evan located Major Lassiter, he made them welcome, but they saw at once he meant to caution them and keep their hopes down.

Sarah Ann wasn't there. They'd only heard the rumor of a woman who called herself that. A soldier in Lassiter's command had been out hunting on his own when a Mohave brave come up to him. He told of a white woman among the Mohave who'd bought her for blankets some while before from the Apache.

He told the soldier he'd bring the woman to some open place and show her. He'd sell her back to her own people for a certain amount of beads and a good saddle. He'd have to take her from the Mohave by stealth, so he wanted it made worth his while.

The soldier agreed to this out of curiosity, but he demanded to see the woman before they come to terms. In a second meeting, the Mohave brought him a woman, an Indian woman from the look of her. But when he asked her name, she took up a stick and wrote in the dirt: *Sarah Ann Ransom*.

Major Lassiter said it could be another Indian trick, but he was willing to find the Mohave brave again, and very soon he did.

The planning was careful in the military way. The soldier who'd dealt before with the Mohave dealt with him again. Lorenzo bought a saddle and was shown the kind of beads the Indians valued. They set out on the appointed day, a party of them, for the bend in the river where the woman would be brought.

They reached the spot when the sun was in the west, and nobody was there but the soldier waiting. It worried Evan, he said, for he'd been out in a good many lonely places, and he thought of ambush. The well-armed major and the soldier leaning on his Sharpe rifle were cold comfort.

They waited till they thought they'd been deceived. Just when the major was turning his horse, they saw them on the far riverbank. A brave and a squaw stood outlined against a rise of sand. The man led the woman into the water, gripping her upper arm. They waded across and stood finally by the horses, dripping in the sand.

Lorenzo, half off his head from waiting, stepped up nearer and called the name. "Sarah Ann?" But the woman made no sign and only hung her head in an abject way. Her hair was dark and glossy and spread in greased hanks about her shoulders.

Her face was only a little lighter than her hair. When he stood before her, he saw the slanting lines of the tattoo marks that marked her cheeks. She wore a bark dress that barely covered her. He saw nothing in her he could know. He only saw one more savage like the savages who'd killed his ma and pa and the newborn and Matthew.

Evan stood nearby, watching the brave for any sudden move and looking at the squaw. "She's not a white woman, Lorenzo," he said because somebody had to say it.

At that, she seemed to take fright and pulled away from the brave to throw herself on the ground. She tried to bury herself in the sand. She thrashed at their feet. Even in an animal it would have been pitiful, Evan said.

They were fixing to go then, but the major dismounted and walked to the woman. He reached down and lifted her up with his gloved hand. Then he gestured for them to look and turned her ear back. They saw the white flesh there, dim in the evening light.

"Break off a branch and bring it to me," he said to his trooper.

He put the stick in the woman's filthy hand and said, "There is nothing to fear. Write your name."

They said she looked back to the empty country on the far side of the river. She looked back like she thought maybe there'd be somebody there to call her back. But there was nothing there but night coming on. She turned back and wrote in the sand:

SARAH ANN RANSOM

Lorenzo read it. He moved toward her, and she shied like she expected a blow. He saw then that her eyes were blue.

"Oh, my God, are you my sister?" he said. "Did you have a brother once, a brother named Lorenzo?"

He said she looked up at him in great surprise. Her mouth hung open, and her eyes burned into his. Her mouth moved and moved again before she could form the word.

"A brother," she said.

"Yes," he said, "a brother named Lorenzo."

She waited a long time and then spoke low, but they heard her. "And Matthew too."

They paid off the brave and brought her back to Yuma on the spare horse. They brought her to the little hospital at the fort where years ago we'd taken Lorenzo to have his wound dressed. A nurse scrubbed her and fought her to take her dress, and lost.

She was dark as an Indian still, and nothing would ever erase the tattooed streaks that fanned over her face. They tied her hand and foot to the hospital bed at night, and Lorenzo paced the parade ground outside, mourning the living.

He sat by her bed all one day, searching his mind. They'd scrubbed the grease out of her hair, and it stood up around her head like black straw. She sat up uncomfortable against the soft pillows, wearing a hospital gown, but she clutched her foul bark dress in her scarred hands. She made hardly a place in the bed, and where the gown gapped Lorenzo saw how the bones stood out in her and how near to starvation she was.

He tried a dozen ways to make her talk and then watched her try to eat the food they brought her. The blue eyes in her baked face studied him. Only their look convinced Lorenzo

that she hadn't been robbed of reason. He knew she was
Sarah Ann now. He began to put together in his mind that
other girl she'd been with this disfigured, ruined woman now.
He had his doubts then, though he never quite told them to
me. He wondered then if he'd have done better to leave her
where she'd been.

I believe he even thought of leaving her there in that
hospital bed and let the Army deal with her. But of course
there was more he had to know. He needed to know bad
enough to beat it out of her, but she'd been beaten before. He
saw that.

She ate with her hands, both hands—then and long after.
She was hungry, but she held the food in her mouth like she
had a struggle to swallow such stuff.

"Shall I feed you?" Lorenzo said and reached for the fork
by her plate, but she threw up her arm to defend herself.

"Sarah Ann," he said, "when the Apache—"

"Mohave!" she cried out. She slapped at her breast and
pointed to herself. "Mohave."

He wondered why it mattered which name he used since
they were all savages, but he saw the way to her.

"And Beatrice? Is Beatrice Mohave too?"

He'd reached her now. Her head fell forward, and she
pushed her tray away. Lorenzo thought she was weeping, but
she'd lost the power to. He saw in her face though that
Beatrice was gone. He knew it was only Sarah Ann now.
Only Sarah Ann, apart from him, left of all their people.

TEN

I took Sarah Ann in, this thing that had been Sarah Ann. There was no question about it, just like there'd been no question about taking in Lorenzo long ago. The Claypool women stood at their windows and stared, and the men buzzed in the bunkhouse, but nobody thought of another plan. There was none. It was left to me to do what might be right.

"Do you know me?" I asked her time and again in those first days. "I'm Lena. I'm that girl you was with in the wagon train. I'm Lena, Lena, Lena. Look at me."

I'd get right in her face to make sure she saw me. Had they blinded her as well as struck her dumb? When they took her mind, did they take her memory with it?

"Sarah Ann, I was Lena Wheatley. I had me a calf and called it Treasure. I had me a sunbonnet, and I tried to tie the bow under my chin like you tied yours.

"Look at me, Sarah Ann. Have I changed that much?" But there I went too far when I saw how changed she was. I decided then to go farther.

"Listen to me, Sarah Ann. I had a ma like you did. We buried her on the trail, and you was there. You saw them put her in the ground. I had a pa too, and he's gone now, and it like to break my heart. I didn't lose them like you lost yours, but they're gone."

It was useless. It tore me up, and I never come near her. "Oh, God, Sarah Ann, know me!" But she said nothing, not even with her eyes.

I kept water on the boil in the old tallow vat and made her bathe and bathe again. I worked her over with lye soap and a stiff-bristle brush, but she wouldn't be white. Even her raw, sore skin defied me.

I thought I'd made progress when I got her to wear a skirt, but I only worked that by hanging up the nasty bark dress on a peg where she could see it. I told myself: *Don't be disgusted. She can't help herself. Her mind's gone.* But it never lasted. I looked up once, and though she had on the decent skirt, she was bare-breasted. I got a waist on her at last, and she seemed willing to wear a shawl over it, so anyway she was covered.

Getting the moccasins off her, those deerskin things decorated with porcupine quills, and getting proper shoes on her feet was a battle still before me. The bed was another. Evan hung a blanket across one corner of the big room we all had to live in and feed in and sleep in. He set up a camp bed behind the blanket. Sarah Ann would sit cross-legged on it, all day if I'd let her. At night though, she curled up on the floor beside it, jerking in her sleep.

My work had to go on, and the men had to be fed. They weren't easy at my table now, with the heathen there in the room, squatting behind the blanket. They talked lower and left quicker. The life I'd known and made began to collapse, like an adobe wall that melts faster than you can mend it. I took to thinking that the time before Sarah Ann come back had been the good days lost to me now.

I couldn't hardly make myself look her in the face. They'd cut gashes in it to work the dye in. I'd tried words with her, and they hadn't worked. More desperate with every day, I grabbed her hand and planted it on my own body for her to feel where the child was, riding low and within days of being born if I hadn't killed it with work and worry.

I held Sarah Ann's limp hand against this life and said, "You see? You see that this child is coming? You got to be a woman and help me." But her hand fell away. It seemed to me she was close to speech then, but not close enough.

I'd talk to Evan like she wasn't there with us and maybe

able to understand. We were never alone now, and had to face it.

"This won't do, Evan, and I'd think you could see it. We can't manage here all in one room with another coming and the men feeding and Sarah Ann everywhere I turn." She was there as I spoke, standing half hidden behind the door. "You'll have to find us a house somewheres on the place. I won't have my child here in this room. I mean it."

He found us a place outside the gates, above the dry river. It had been a house first, then a bunkhouse, and then a wool barn. There was a walled yard to one side where the sheep had once been run in to shear. It would do for a garden now, manured in advance. Evan's men fitted out the house for us and whitewashed it inside and out. They flattened syrup tins to patch the roof, and Evan and Lorenzo killed rats for two days. They brought out better than three wheelbarrow loads of dead vermin.

It was a place where they hung peppers to dry from the rafters. They hung there still in long clusters, hot and red in the cool gray shadows. There was the beginning of a kitchen at one end of the main room and a bedroom behind and a loft above. It was still mostly barn, but bearable.

I let Sarah Ann find her own place in it if she would. We set her bed up in the loft, but she slept before the fire on the stones. She slept in the skirt and shawl she wore all day, and she never took off her moccasins.

"You just as well let her wear them moccasins," Evan said one night when I was tired out. "She's set on keeping them, and it seems like they give her some comfort."

I turned on him then, I suppose I'd been waiting to. "Is that the thanks I get for trying to make a human being out of her? We just as well turn her out and chain her to the side of the house for the world to see. I do my best, Evan, and I've got her against me. Have I got to fight you too?" I was loud with him, and he slunk off like men do.

I thought my baby would be born before the week was out. Now I was frantic to find a way through to Sarah Ann before that birth. I didn't want this baby born into a house with a dumb savage like a shadow in the corner. It could mark a child to come into such a world.

But I was getting beyond the end of my ideas. I could only think of them moccasins that moved silent as snakes across the floor. I got out my other pair of shoes, the good pair I saved back. I swung them by their laces in front of her face until she had to see them.

"I want you in these shoes, Sarah Ann, and now. These is a white woman's shoes, and you're a white woman. Take them things off and put these on."

She sat hunkered by the hearth. Her hands crept down past her bare ankles to cover her moccasin toes and hold on tight to them.

"Did you hear me?" I grabbed a fistful of her hair and twisted till I knew it hurt her.

"Take them off," I said in a whisper, "and don't lash back at me. Don't even think to. If you hurt this child in my belly, I'll kill you."

I was that near crazy myself. I'd never spoke such words, but they rolled out of me with ease now. My blood sang in my ears, and I was ready with more threats.

But her grip on the moccasins loosened, a finger at a time. She slid the things off her feet, and there where it must have pained her with every step, something fell out of one of the moccasin toes and wobbled across the brick.

I saw the black and white thing where it lay, but I was too big now to bend. Sarah Ann's hand moved out to cover it. But then she took it up and opened her palm for me to see.

It was the cameo brooch that Sarah Ann—the other Sarah Ann—had always worn at her breast, when her breast was full and fine. It was the cameo with the perfect white profile so like her own had been once.

She looked up at me, the first time our eyes had really met. Then she did something more terrible than I could believe. She turned her head slowly, slowly until I saw again the wicked tattoo marks spread all the way back into her hair. She turned her blackened profile for me to see and compare with the cameo.

                             *   *   *

I stood there with her, both of us under the long red swags of drying peppers. We seemed to be there together in the cool white and red room till time meant nothing.

I felt a wetness on my leg, and now it was soaking through my skirt. The pain knotted in me and turned my womb into a cauldron. I thought of knives and heard somebody shrieking. It was me, shrieking and shrieking till I couldn't catch my breath between. She saw that my baby was coming. She helped me somehow. I hung on her and she dragged me along. Without her I wouldn't have made it as far as my bed.

The baby, a girl as I'd thought, was born just at midnight. Sarah Ann left me and went out into the yard, bringing back a sharp stone to cut the cord. But Mrs. Claypool had sent her servants down from the house, and they brought towels and rags torn in strips and a clean knife. Evan hovered there in the corner of the room.

I was wore out so they all left me, and I dozed with the baby at my breast. Later I woke and could see past the bedroom door to the end of the big room. Sarah Ann was out there squatting down before a pan on the hearth. She was peeling potatoes. Though she threw the peelings on the floor, her knife worked fast in a practiced way as she went about the first work she'd done.

I named the child Opal and thought she'd live. She wasn't hearty, and the blue vein throbbed in her temple, but she was a feeder. Her little tiny hand you could almost see through closed around my finger and clung tight. We'd both survived our ordeal, and on the third day I was reaching for my apron.

Sometimes after I'd fed the baby, I handed her over to Sarah Ann. I longed to keep the baby mine and only mine, and it went against the grain to hand her over. Still, it seemed to calm her to hold Opal. I can't explain it rightly, but it brought something more human to her face. And, too, it was my way of getting her to sit in a chair like a Christian instead of forever squatting. Sarah Ann would sit in a chair, all day if I'd let her, as long as she had the baby in the crook of her arm.

But it seemed like whatever I tried was doomed. I come back one time from cooking for the men to find Sarah Ann opening the top of her dress. I saw she meant to pretend to feed the child, or pacify it with her breast.

Her breast was whiter than her throat. I snatched the baby away, expecting Sarah Ann to sulk. She often seemed to sulk, though there was no real way of telling. Instead, she looked up at me with the ghost of a smile. She patted her own breast and made a little gesture like she was pointing to herself.

"You could talk if you wanted to," I told her, holding Opal close. "Don't think I don't know," though I wasn't sure, not absolutely.

Sarah Ann's mouth opened, and her cracked lips fought to form a word. "My," she said, "baby."

I stamped my foot on the floor. "No! Not your baby. *My* baby. Remember that."

She only shook her head and seemed to smile again, like I was too dense to know what she knew. A chill come over me then like a warning. She put up her brown, scarred hand and pointed straight at Opal. Then her finger moved down, slow, until she was pointing at my belly.

I stood there like a snake had me in thrall. Opal fussed, but I was deaf to her. I couldn't take my eyes off Sarah Ann. "That's right," I said, trying to be certain, "my baby, from my body."

I watched her finger move. It turned in the air until she trained it on herself, like the barrel of a gun. It pointed down her body and came to rest at her belly.

I couldn't breathe for looking. Her hand moved up again and slipped smoothly inside her dress and closed over her breast. She nodded at me then, wise as an old woman, wise as a witch.

I knew what she'd told me. I knew it right then. She'd made herself clearer than words, but it couldn't be true. We couldn't be that cursed. There couldn't be a child starting in Sarah Ann, a child planted there by some savage. But there was.

ELEVEN

I dreaded telling Evan, and I wouldn't tell Lorenzo. But I daren't wait till they could look at her and see for themselves. Men are slow to see, and I couldn't wait alone with this knowledge weighing me down.

She was there when I told Evan, though whether she listened or not, I don't know. He was late, and I put a bowl of cornmeal mush in front of him and then liked to go crazy waiting for him to eat it. Now that I'd brought myself to it, I couldn't wait a minute more.

"We've got more trouble than we knew," I said, standing over him.

He looked up quick. "Opal?"

"No." She was in the other room asleep, in the basket by our bed.

He looked then at Sarah Ann. She was somewheres there in the room as she always was.

"I thought she was doing better," he said, meaning the shoes and the clothes.

"I can't tell you, Evan." My voice broke, though I never let that happen around him. "I been studying to tell you for days, and now I can't." He was looking up at me, but I looked away from him. I wanted him to reach out and take my hand, but I'd only jerk mine away if he did.

"When we got her back . . . She's going to have a child."

His spoon clattered on the table. "She told you so?"

"In her way."

He looked down at his empty bowl so he wouldn't look by

chance at her, wherever she was. "That means before we got her back—"

"Yes, don't speak it aloud."

He pushed back from the table, keeping his eyes down. "Well, there's nothing to be done about it now."

"I'll tell you what I'd like to do," I said, finding a stronger voice. "I'd like to turn her out. I'd like to take her up in the hills and leave her. I'd do it too, if it wasn't for Lorenzo."

"Don't talk like that, Lena. You don't mean it."

"I don't know what I mean. I don't know what to do."

"Lorenzo will have to know," Evan said, working his hands. "I'll break it to him."

She began to show, and her skirt strained around her. When I could bear to think of it, I supposed she'd have her child at the end of the winter. She'd wear the shoes regular now, and the waist and the shawl held in place across her breast with the cameo brooch. She'd even wear an apron for her work, though she was slow to see the need of it.

All this raiment only made her more hideous in my eyes. The decent clothes warred with her savage face. We'd all tried to bleach the tattoo marks from her cheeks. Even Lorenzo and Evan bent her face to tubs of bubbling sulphur from the sheep dip, but their concoctions only blistered her flesh. She was marked for life.

She wouldn't catch her hair up in the swirling knot I remembered. The most I could get her to do was plait it into braids, and then she wanted to wear them hanging down her back. Finally, she'd coil the braids on the top of her head and fix them there, but she had to be told and told again.

The child in her seemed to give her strength, though carrying Opal had sapped me of mine. She did a day's work at my side, and she liked to garden. She'd weed by the hour, and from the door I'd see her rise up in a row, arms flailing, to chase the birds off. We pulled together in our work, but I give up trying to talk to her. I couldn't fight my disgust at what had been done to her and what she'd become. Besides, if she spoke, I feared what I'd learn.

She'd go up to help me with the cooking for the men and on the days we made cheese. But she didn't like the wall that enclosed the square behind the ranch house. She didn't even like passing through the gates though they stood ajar. She wouldn't eat with the men, not even with Evan or Lorenzo. She had her peculiarities and she stood by them. At times I wondered if we weren't peculiar to her.

Lorenzo come down from the bunkhouse of an evening, oftener than before. I thought it would be a comfort to me, though he come mainly to be with Sarah Ann. I was the one who needed the company, for Evan was often out at night now, riding with the men to hunt the coyotes that preyed on the sheep. Evan was out more than he needed to be, and I tried not to blame him for keeping clear of this house.

Lorenzo come, and we sat around the table in the evenings. Sarah Ann would sit with us if I let her hold the baby. She said nothing, of course, and he and I said little.

I called him boy still, but he was a man. His arms were thick and muscled in his sleeves. He wore a black silk shirt that shone in the lamplight and knotted a kerchief at his throat. He was handsomer than could be good for him, but not vain the way such men get.

I'd said to him, "Don't break your heart, Lorenzo. You won't get through to her. It can't be done."

Even then I may have wondered. He was no wiser than the rest of us and greener too. But there was a gentleness about him and a patience longer than his years. I'd seen him break a colt without the sting of the switch, though it took him any amount of time.

I sat with them in the pool of lamplight where Sarah Ann held my sleeping child in her shawl and Lorenzo gazed at her with his terrible patience. I was more sister to him than she was if he'd but know it. I wanted to pound the table and rise up and tell them, "This is my child. This is my brother!" But Sarah Ann possessed us all, even my thoughts.

I didn't have Lorenzo's patience. At first I thought he

didn't coax her to speak because he was as lost as I was. And
he was a man. Would he want to hear how she got this child
that was in her? Did he want to hear how them savages used
her? Would he dare listen to know how they held her down
and raped her? I knew then that I hoped she'd been raped. I
hoped she hadn't been willing.

I thought he sat there because he didn't know what to do,
but soon I saw he was gentling her like he'd gentle an animal.
I saw him waiting till the time was ripe.

One night I give up on both of them. I'd taken my dishpan
of water to fling in the yard, and I kept on walking. I
stumbled along through the tules by the riverbed. The moon
was bright enough to show me the way, and I saw how I was
more surefooted here than I was in my own house. I was out I
don't know how long before I made myself go back. The
lamplight from within threw a long yellow shape on the
packed earth outside. As I stepped nearer the doorway, I
heard Lorenzo's voice, and they didn't see me there on the
sill.

She was standing with my baby held high on her shoulder.
Lorenzo was looking up at her. Across the corner of the table
his hand was out in the air. She was showing him her
thickening waist and his hand was there almost touching the
apron that stood out from her body.

"You'll have a baby too," he said in a tone I'd never
heard from him. Sarah Ann was looking down at him, and I
couldn't read the expression on her ruined face. The lamplight flickered on the tattoo streaks. Behind this mask perhaps
she was proud. Anyway, she nodded, like she knew what
he'd said, like she was anybody.

"That baby inside you," he said. "Do you want it there?"

She jerked her head away and rocked my baby in her arms,
but all he had to do was touch her arm to make her look.

"Was he a good man, or bad?" Lorenzo said.

I stood in the doorway, and it was too late to leave them
again. I saw against the light how alike their profiles were.
Their eyes were alike too, pale blue. I'd noticed that before.
They had identical eyes.

"Good," she said. "A good man."

He'd brought these words from her, and I put up my hand to stop more from coming, but nobody saw me. To them, I wasn't there.

"Would you go back to him?" Lorenzo asked her, though I saw this cost him something to say.

"Too late."

Lorenzo ran his hand around the back of his neck. It was too late for him too, so he had to go on.

"Them . . . people killed our folks. They done this to me." He touched the scar on his forehead. "They done that to you." He put his hand up toward her cheek, but she moved as if he could reach her.

"Apache," she said, fetching up a sigh. "Not Mohave."

He waited then, casting about for the right words. "Did the Apache kill Beatrice?"

She folded my child closer to her and went stiff all over. But she was trying to speak, casting about for the words like Lorenzo was. "With the Mohave," she said, shaping each sound, "a time of . . . no food."

"A famine," Lorenzo said, and she nodded.

"Many dead," she said in a clearer voice now. I marveled at how well she could speak, if only to Lorenzo.

He put his hand up to his eyes now, and I felt his pain stinging at my eyes. I'd known all along he'd hear too much, and now he was hearing it.

But she was eager to tell him something more. Her eyes darted, and she clutched my child in one arm while she pointed to the floor. "Buried," she said. "Buried!" Something went through her, some excitement.

"Yes," he said, "I understand."

But she was shaking her head like she thought he didn't understand. "Mohave," she said, ". . . burn . . . the dead."

"Cremation," Lorenzo said.

She nodded though she wasn't sure of the word. "But . . ." Then she left off. He'd led her past her limits. Her mouth sagged open, and she put her fingers to her lips, as if to say the words wouldn't come.

But Lorenzo was saying, "The Mohave cremate their dead, but they give Beatrice a Christian's burial."

She followed his words with her eyes. Then she nodded and pointed to herself. "For me."

"They was good to you," he said, though I saw it come hard to him. "And to Beatrice. They showed respect."

Then I was frightened at her look. She was smiling now, and there was no mistake about it. But it wasn't a white woman's smile, cautious and composed. It was the smile of some primitive Indian woman. Lorenzo saw it too and drew back. He'd been so near, but she'd slipped free of him.

"Respect!" she said, ringing the word. "He was . . . a great . . . warrior . . ." She seemed to strangle on her pride. Her hand was in the air, invoking something beyond anything we knew, something we were blind to.

"Who was a great warrior?" Lorenzo said.

"My . . . husband."

He came out of his chair, and it fell back behind him. He reached out to grip her arm, but stopped himself. She hadn't flinched, and that made it worse. She had another word for him, and I saw it forming.

"Wife," she said. "No . . . widow."

They were both standing now, and Lorenzo looked about himself, for strength. "Your—the man is dead?"

She looked at him like he was the slow-witted one. "That . . . is why . . ."

"That's why you let yourself be led away from them? That's why you come back to us?"

She nodded, satisfied that he understood, but he was trying to speak sense to her now, struggling to.

"Not widow," he said, "and never wife." He took her by the shoulders in an awkward way. It was the only awkward gesture I ever saw him make. "Don't never say that. He wasn't a white man. You wasn't churched."

But she just looked at him, proof against him. Then I saw in that moment the Sarah Ann I'd known all them years ago. She was looking at Lorenzo like he was the small boy he'd been and she was the big sister who knew better.

TWELVE

I watched Lorenzo then, all I could for days and weeks. What Sarah Ann had found tongue to tell him brought him low, and he couldn't hide it. He could face up to her half-breed child, this papoose coming there'd be no place for in the world. He'd looked death in the face as a boy, and though this was worse, he could face it.

Like me, he'd lived in hope she'd been raped, though he wouldn't have spoken the word. But now he'd heard her speak of a redskin as her husband, and so he was shamed. We all were. We were plain people and didn't pretend, but we had our pride.

Though God had left me long ago, I prayed to him that Sarah Ann's child would die. I reasoned with God that it was a mercy to the child. "Spare mine, but take hers," I prayed, and then fell into a fitful sleep where I dreamed of throwing her red child down a well. Then I awoke, sickened at myself.

If I was Lorenzo, I wondered if I wouldn't be unmanned. I wondered if Evan thought so too, but men won't tell you. They'll turn to their work or, worse, they'll cut and run.

There was work aplenty, heaven knows. We were coming up to shearing time, and though Lorenzo worked with the rest of us pretty nearly around the clock, I didn't like the emptiness of his eye. I wondered too if he was looking for an easy cure when there wasn't one.

We sheared twice a year, in the spring and the fall. It was the hardest work of the year, and the best time too. Rafaela blossomed then like a city, banked in milling sheep. The

Basque herders who lived out on the range with their flocks
drove them in. And the shearers rode in from the south, their
saddles bedizened with silver. There were forty or fifty of
them, Mexicans all, flashing smiles and knives. We had the
extra cooking to do and the chuck wagons to load while the
men brewed dip and cleared out the barns where the extra
help slept. On top of this was the oat wheat to be planted to
get the benefit of the winter rains. I thought that with all this
to be done, and Sarah Ann silent again, Lorenzo would make
his peace with himself.

I'd have given whatever I had to ease his mind. It come to
me again that I was more sister to him than Sarah Ann was. If
I'd been in her place, I'd have kept my mouth shut tight
against the truth.

While these thoughts ate at me, my hands were busy with
their work. Sarah Ann and I braided the twine into cords for
tying up the fleeces into balls. We sewed sacks and cooked
and baked outdoors from long before sunup, carrying the
baby Opal with us to our work. She slept in a laundry basket
up on bricks to keep the lizards off her. I'd plant her there by
the oven for the warmth of it while we began our baking by
starlight.

On Sunday the Mexican shearers rode in, elegant and
proud as matadors. They wove their bridles of horsehair and
tooled fantastical designs on their saddle leather. They wore
big sombreros with mushroom brims, anchored to cords that
caught under their noses. There was white lace, even ruffles,
down their shirtfronts.

On Monday they'd put all this finery aside and were in the
pens, waist-deep in sheep. All the hands sheared to show they
could keep pace with these experts. Evan, too, and Lorenzo.

The new wool barn was fronted by the long narrow corrals,
each holding a hundred sheep half crazy with fear. The men
moved among them, weaving like prizefighters, then stooping
to grab a hind leg to throw the sheep down and part it from its
wool. They tossed the fleeces to others on the fences to pack
them into great balls. These were passed on to others to jam
into sacks and tamp them down.

Everyone turned out to work or watch. Even Mr. Claypool stood beside the chutes, leaning on a malacca cane and counting the critters. He kept a notched stick to record each hundredfold.

By noon there were enough of the sheared to begin the dipping. The vats of dip bubbled on brick stoves, evil as lava. Beyond them was the mouth of the long sheet-metal bath that steamed and sent up yellow clouds of sulphur. The men prodded the wild-eyed sheep through this brown, bubbling hell, and the beasts swam and sank and swam again to the shallow end.

For most of a month we put the flocks through this. The air was heavy with bleats and curses and the drifting fluff from the wool and the lint from the sacks. The sky was busy and the earth thundered. When we could sleep, we slept like the dead, deaf to the roar of naked sheep mobbed for miles around the ranch.

In the dark of the mornings the wagons rolled out under their burden of wool. They made for Wilmington where the steamer shipped them to San Francisco. Then it was over. The dust settled, and the mountains come back to us, as silent as Sunday.

Lorenzo hadn't come back to us in the evenings after that time Sarah Ann called herself wife. I might have blamed him for that, but I blamed her. Then on the night after the shearing was over, there he was in the doorway. Later, I reckoned I saw his news in his face before he brought himself to tell us. Maybe I did and maybe I didn't. But in the first moment I saw some change coming and would ward it off if I could.

It was after supper, and we were all there around the fire, too worn out to move. Evan was there, for once, sitting across the hearth from me. The baby was asleep on a pallet at our feet with Sarah Ann drawn up on the floor beside her. She'd woven a cat's cradle between her hands from fleece twine to make the baby watch. Opal was fast asleep, but Sarah Ann went on working a pattern of twine knots, weav-

ing a web and then letting it fall free through her brown
fingers. She was showing now. Her belly was big, and
Lorenzo wouldn't look there.

He stood over us until Evan urged him to drag up a bench
and sit. I began to wonder then if there wasn't some conspir-
acy between them and Evan had more warning than I did.
They talked mantalk for a time, but it was only a prelude.

They talked of a war back in the States. We in California
were a state now ourselves, but we still spoke of "back in the
States," and this war was between the states. Even here there
were divided loyalties, and men argued about them. I thought
it was wind and would blow away.

Lincoln was no sooner in the White House than the Southern states had begun to pull out, "secede" as they said. A
man named Beauregard had fired on Fort Sumter back in
April. Lincoln had ordered the blockade on Southern ports
and called for volunteers. Lorenzo spoke more of this than I'd
heard him on any subject. Evan mainly listened, but close. I
listened closer too.

"A man set on soldiering," Lorenzo said, "could ship in a
steamer from San Pedro for Panama and sail on another from
Chagres up to the port of New York." He told us of patriots
at Los Angeles who'd pay passage for men willing to sign on
with the Union forces.

Lorenzo was trying for a mustache now. It straggled on
his upper lip, and I thought it would spoil his looks.
"I'm thinking of soldiering myself," he said. "They say
the Thirty-sixth New York is a good regiment, under General
Devins."

Sarah Ann moved and may have heard. Evan would have
spoken, but he looked toward me instead, and then away.
They'd both sit mute as stones while Lorenzo talked. I saw
that. I was the only one to talk sense. I rose up, and the
mending in my lap leaped out of it.

"No, Lorenzo, I won't have it. Whatever this war is, it's
got nothing to do with us."

He looked up, trying to smile like he could pass this off as nothing. He was sitting on the low stool, and I towered over him.

"Lorenzo, I don't ask you for much, but I ask you for this. Don't walk away from us and get yourself killed to prove you're a man. It won't signify when you're dead in a ditch."

Don't walk away from *me,* I meant. He'd be dead to me the minute he was gone from here. This was my time to call in my debts. This was the time to tell him I was all the mother he had and more sister than he knew. Now I should speak of love, for it welled in me. Love for him thickened in my throat like a sob, but it was too dangerous to speak. If I spoke of love and he left just the same, then I'd have lost him twice over.

"The war's likely to end before I can get into it," he said, mumbling the words. "I'm scared it will be."

"Scared you won't be killed in it?" My lip curled. I'd show him my contempt. It was safer than love.

"I'll be back, Lena," he said.

"Oh, yes, you'll be back, like as not." I pointed at his arm. "And there'll be an empty sleeve. Or you'll come back on one leg and a crutch. Then what good will you be to yourself or to the rest of us?"

Sarah Ann listened. I felt her listening, but she was no good to me. Neither was Evan. I turned on him, nearly stumbling over the baby. She was awake and looking up at me with astonished eyes.

"Haven't you got anything to say, Evan? Don't you need this boy by you? Ain't there work enough and then some right here?"

I'd counted on him to hang his head and say nothing, but he looked up instead.

"I was his age once, Lena. It looks good then, the living hard, the smell of the gunpowder and . . . moving up at night. And the songs they sing to march by. When I was a . . . younger, I wished for a war to fight in. I liked the braiding and the boots. It don't make so much sense to me now, but it did then. You ought to try, Lena. You ought to try and see it."

So Evan betrayed me too, and in front of the others. He looked away into the fire and left me too. But I couldn't be finished. If there must be this war, here was my battle to win.

"Lorenzo, haven't we all been through aplenty without you going to court trouble? Ain't that scar on your head memory enough? And look here at your sister, at Sarah Ann." I pointed straight at her as she sometimes pointed to herself. "Boy, how much grief do you want?"

She huddled at my feet looking down, hiding behind the mask of her face. They all listened to me. My voice rang in the rafters, and the baby whimpered. But I'd lost, as I might have known I would. The sob was wide in my throat, but I wouldn't show them tears, not any of them.

"I don't know why I try," I said, sinking back in the chair. "I don't know why I try to keep us together and make a family of us. Why do I want it so much when the rest of you don't care? We aren't more than a bunch of strangers. I don't know why I try with any of you. I swear I don't." I looked for my mending, but it was gone too.

Lorenzo stood to go. I wished he'd go without a word, but I wasn't to have even that.

"Will you kiss me good-bye, Lena?"

"No. You'll have to go without that, Lorenzo. You can't have everything your way, not quite."

He was going then. When his hand was on the door, I called out after him, "Lorenzo! When you're gone, I hope in my heart you'll know why you went."

He half turned back, but his hand lifted the latch.

"You're going because you couldn't stick it to stay. You want to be gone before Sarah Ann's half-breed brat is born. That's more than you can handle, so you'll leave that blight for me. Go on then. But remember, a man would have stayed."

He went the next morning early, sooner than he'd planned. I kept to the house till he was off the place, but I watched from the window. Evan was out in the yard to see him away, along with the men turned out early from the bunkhouse to clap him on the back.

Even old Mr. Claypool tottered out and sent for Lorenzo at the last moment. He shook his hand and give him a gold coin, not knowing that Lorenzo wasn't off to join the forces of the Confederacy.

THIRTEEN

The birthing was in my bed. I thought Sarah Ann would drop the child like a beast of the field and never cry out. But she shrieked her share and her hands grappled at the headboard. She writhed like the Christian she'd been raised.

It was a girl child, another one, and I didn't know if this made things worse or not. I supposed it did. Before they could get it washed and placed on Sarah Ann's breast, I searched it, trying not to hope. It was red, but red as a newborn is, purple and angry from the womb, and bawling its head off. On the soft curve of its head was a quantity of hair too dark, but then Sarah Ann's hair had always been near black, and beautiful to look at once.

Its eyes were blue, but then a baby's always are unless the rule didn't hold for the mixed breed this one was. I left it in the room busy with the Claypools' serving women. Too many of them had come down from the house to help and to satisfy their curiosity.

"A girl," I told Evan where he sat in the big room at his supper. It was evening after a long day in a dry season. We hadn't got the lashing winter rains we'd come to count on. The drought people feared to speak of was on their lips now. I poured me a cup of coffee and sat down across from him at the table.

"What do we do now?" I asked as if he'd know. "I don't want that half-breed near my child."

He wiped his mouth with the back of his hand. There was

some white running in his straw-colored hair, paling it to no particular color. "We don't have much choice," he said.

I sighed and let him hear it. "If we're to keep it with us—"

"I thought you just said you didn't want it near Opal."

"What I want doesn't matter. What I want never does. It's what's got to be. You walk out of here every morning of your life scot-free, and I'm left with the full load. If I don't find a way to deal with things, then everything slides, and this won't slide. If we're to keep that . . . child, it'll have to be ours. It turns my stomach, but otherwise it wouldn't be fair."

He looked up, squinting at me. "Fair to who?"

"Fair to the child, of course. Who else?" But he had no answer for that. "You'll have to be father to the both of them," I told him. "Are you willing?"

He worked his jaw with his hand. "Seem like whatever I say, you'll bite my head off, but yes, I'm willing."

"And I'll have to be mother to her unless she's so ugly that I can't stand it."

"What'll Sarah Ann say about that?" Evan asked.

"Sarah Ann? She ain't said anything yet. She's worse than an animal. They're meant to be dumb. I think she's out to spite me. She could talk if she wanted to. She talked to Lorenzo all right."

I wished I hadn't said that. I wished I'd forgotten how them two, that brother and sister, had talked and left me out.

"I reckon the Apache whipped the speech out of her," Evan said. "They'll tie your tongue with a thong and lead you by it till they've pulled the words out, till they've pulled out all you are."

"I don't want to hear it," I told him. I'd seen evidence he hadn't. I'd seen the scars grooved deep on the soles of her feet. I'd seen the slick burn marks on the insides of her thighs, but it didn't do to tell.

"They could have cut out her tongue for all the use it is to her, or to me."

"A child might help her," Evan said.

"She's past that," I said, surer with every word, "and if

she raises it as her own, she'll make it more savage than it is. She can't do for it. That'll be left to me as things always are. Surely you see?''

"I see you want it that way," is all he said, and I let it pass though I didn't like the way he'd said it.

"Hard as it is to take, the child will have to be ours. There'll be no room for her in this world if people know."

"People hereabouts know already," Evan said.

"Hereabouts isn't everywhere. Are we going to stick here all the rest of our days?'' Till the moment I spoke, I'd supposed we would live here always, but he'd goaded me.

I didn't think Evan could surprise me, but then he did. He pushed his empty plate aside, and put out his hand on the table, under the lamp. He opened it, palm up, and I saw how the callouses stood up like pillows in the heel of it and along his square fingers.

"Give me your hand, Lena. Put yours in mine."

"What for?" I said, but I did as he asked, feeling a little shy with him.

We sat there a moment with my hand closed in his, but there was nobody to see. Then, looking aside, he spoke words I'd never thought to hear from him. "Oh, Lena, you was pretty once. You had the look of a doe in your eyes, and you moved that swift and neat.''

I could have wept then, and it might have been our salvation. I hadn't let him touch me since Opal was born. There'd been nights when I wanted it, though a woman should never want it, or need it. But Sarah Ann was there in the shadows of the house, very likely awake. I'd thought later, maybe. Later, he might want a son like men do. But now with this stranger child among us, I wanted no more children ever. I had more now than I wanted. Of course, I couldn't tell him, but he knew.

I must draw him away from us and back to what we must do. "A name," I said at last. "I suppose we'll have to name her."

I'd thought of a name for Sarah Ann's child. We'd call her

Effie. It was sensible and not outlandish. And plain. It wouldn't surpass the shaped, smooth sound of *Opal*.

"Effie," I said, and Evan nodded, drawing back his hand.

She was Effie Freeman then, and for two more winters after her birth we had no winter rains. People forgot the sound of water guttering from the eaves. The brea of roofs we hardly needed softened in the sun and ran black down the powdering walls. Wells dried and cyclones of grasshoppers swarmed, picking clean. Fence lines were lost in the carpet of dead cattle. They said a man could walk from Wilmington to Los Angeles on carcasses and never set foot on soil. We were deafened day and night by the bawl of hungry calves.

At last, to put the survivors out of their misery and fight the stench, the vaqueros had to drive herds of cattle and sheep, horses and mules over the Palos Verdes headlands into the sea. They said the breaking skeletons of the stock crusted on the rocks below like branching coral, white in the sun that showed us no pity.

The sun and the fences, people said, had finished the old ranch life hereabouts. Among too many others, Mr. Claypool had overstocked his grazing land. Evan had seen this coming, but it wasn't his place to say. Claypool had sown his land with sheep in the tens of thousands and cattle beyond counting, and he's reaped this arid whirlwind.

Below Rancho Rafaela there wasn't enough mud in the riverbed to mix adobe, and so the big house and the outbuildings went unpatched and began to climb down into the earth. We were fighting a losing battle here, while back in the East word would come of the war still raging there and of battlefields full of the blue and gray dead. I wouldn't let myself think of Lorenzo for days at a time, declaring him dead in advance to save my mourning later. Still, he come to me in my dreams like people will.

We heard that the war preyed on Mr. Claypool's mind. He never left the house now, and they said his desk was deep in battlefield maps. He saw the South slipping, and being from there, he began to slip too. One morning a serving girl come down to us to say Mrs. Claypool had found him stretched out across his desk and free of this world. The sound of his julep glass breaking on the floor had alerted her.

The neighbors rode in to pay their respects, and the bankers come to make their offers. It was hard times, but Evan said that's when bankers thrive. There was talk of irrigation and orange groves here, which wasn't a life we knew.

In the days after Mr. Claypool's funeral, I watched Mrs. Claypool and her two sisters driving out in a little underslung buggy behind her span of Shetland ponies. She took the track that led to the ocean, the three women all in black, making for the beach. We heard she planned to build a cottage there for the three of them to spin out their days by the Pacific. She was said to be studying a house with jigsaw porches and a single servant along a stretch of beach that was yellow with sand verbenas.

The dairy herd was drying and the bunkhouse was emptying and the earth itself was checkering and opening at our feet. The days of the place were numbered, and I followed Evan with my eyes. I watched to see how he would go.

The two babies squalled in the house day and night. Opal had been quiet, but the new one woke her now with cries, and they tried to outcry one another. I'd watched Evan endure this and then stand out in the yard, searching the stars, perhaps for an answer or a sign. I watched him make up his mind to go, and I was sour in my throat again, too sour to stay him even if I could. I knew he'd leave us behind because that's what men do. I thought of walls, and why shouldn't I? Every wall of the ranch was coming down now, though they'd stood stout for years. Thinking of Evan and me, I noticed how quick them walls were to come down.

When he was determined to go, he was ready with his reasons. "I'd as well go before they have to turn me out," he told me in a musing way like his plan was in an early stage. "Mrs. Claypool won't have much more need of me. I'll fix it so you can stay on here awhile."

He said he meant to head north where there was another rush on now and big talk of gold again and silver with it. He'd known the gold country this side of the Sierras ten years ago when it was already pretty well staked out and played out. Now they were talking of new finds in the Washoe, the Nevada country.

I'll say this of him, he didn't promise me riches. He didn't talk big, not that I'd have believed him. He said the Indians there, the Paiute, ate grasshoppers and were glad to get them, that you hadn't seen rough country if you hadn't seen the Washoe.

"Then why go?" I asked him, showing no more interest than I could help.

"Because if such talk keeps out the banks and the bush-whackers and the claim-jumpers, it sounds good to me." Though I wouldn't ask him more, he said, "I'll go on ahead, Lena. I'll send for you and Sarah Ann and the girls when I can."

I nodded at that. I'd wait, for I had no place else to be, but I wouldn't wait in hope. That makes it longer, every minute of it. On the last day I pulled my mouth into its line and held it firm as I watched him to the door.

But he turned and come back to me, taking my face in his hands. He smoothed a strand of my hair back over my ear, gentle with his thorny hands.

"You know I'll send for you, Lena."

"I know you mean to."

On the very day that Evan went, I had a letter from Lorenzo, the first word I'd had of him in better than a year. It ran only a line or two, and I could hardly make it out. He'd been taken prisoner, held at Belle Isle near Richmond, Virginia. If I was still able to weep, I'd have wept now in relief that he was out of the battle and whole enough to write.

But I reminded myself that all these thousands of miles

between us amounted to death. I told myself the boy Lorenzo, the brother I'd treasured once, was a memory to me now and nothing more. From this day on Evan must be a memory too, and no more substantial than that. I turned from these men and drew in on the family left to me in the crumbling house, this family of women.

BOOK 2

Morning on the Mountain

FOURTEEN

I was called Effie, not the sort of name one bears willingly through the length of life. But I began as Effie, the second daughter of Evan and Lena Freeman. A lie, but a necessary one.

To keep from lying with every breath, they told me very little. I was even older by a few months than they said so I'd seem to be a full year younger than that other child, Opal. So that I could be her sister and believable in the role. It was my first role, of many.

They told me I was born on a ranch in southern California, and it may have been true. I remember a house with a bricked floor and red peppers hanging in clusters from the rafters. There were spiky manzanita branches, bleached as driftwood, in the dooryard, and somewhere just out of reach, the relief of the sea. I remember a low wall edging a garden perished from drought. And two women.

I had two mothers, and none. Even before she could stand, Opal stood between me and the woman called Lena. Some unseen force more subtle than Opal stood between me and the woman called Sarah Ann.

I called the wrong woman Mother, but before I learned to let go, I yearned after them both with a kind of fierceness, perhaps because I was embraced by neither.

Opal was confident of Lena's embraces and clung to her. When I came near, Opal had a way of slapping out at me with her little starfish hand, saying, "No. Getaway."

Unwelcome there, I went in search of Sarah Ann, but she

had a way of loosing my hand when it closed around one of her leathery fingers. Sarah Ann let me near her, and her strangely blue eyes watched over me, but embraces were beyond her.

The purple lines that scored her face and made strangers stare meant nothing to me. How could she be hideous when she was the one who fed me? She'd take a morsel of stringy mutton into her mouth and chew it. Then she'd take it out and give it to me to swallow.

It was our way, but apparently it was wrong. Lena came in and there was an argument. Lena spoke as she sewed, in quick flashing jabs. Sarah Ann spoke in single separate words that rarely rose above her throat.

"That's nasty." Lena pointed at the glob of food moving from Sarah Ann's mouth to mine.

"No," Sarah Ann said. "Nothing . . . wrong."

"Throw it on the fire," Lena said, standing over us. "We are human beings, not animals," she said to Sarah Ann. "Try to remember."

Nothing more of that time comes back to me except for the important day I learned at last the purpose of the chamber pot and a way of getting to it in time. That meant Sarah Ann no longer had to pack my underdrawers with moss. I recall too our leaving: the yawning mouth of a wicker trunk that held all we owned. I remember the flurry of departing and the last looking back over parched ground.

We traveled on a steamer up the coast and rounded Fort Point into San Francisco Bay. The fog rolled off to reveal a city that climbed in a casual way up the soft green and brown hills. Sea birds wheeled above us, and the rudder chains thundered into the water.

I remember how the bowsprits of the masted ships at anchor angled in over the embarcadero. The carved figureheads of pious, voluptuous women stared down with painted eyes. In the street there were pigs ready for market and workmen finishing a great funeral arch draped in purple crepe. At the keystone was a medallion of the new martyr, Abraham Lincoln. His face was an inkblot against the white oval. It linked in my mind to the black and white cameo always fixed at Sarah Ann's breast to pin the blanket she wore for a shawl.

We were in some important place, but the journey continued to unfold before us. We were to join my father—to join Evan Freeman. I couldn't remember him, and so I wasn't sure we needed him. I sensed no urgency in Lena either, only the weary need to get wherever we were finally to be.

Then the four of us were coming down the plank from another steamer, a riverboat docked at Sacramento. From there on twenty miles of track were laid as far as Folsom. Beyond that over mountains and desert and above the aquamarine Tahoe we traveled in a top-heavy Concord coach.

The well-traveled road that crossed the valley of the Carson led up again through Gold Canyon to Virginia City. From our fellow passengers I heard of this city roaring in riches built directly upon the fabled Comstock lode where silver blended with gold.

But Virginia City wasn't Evan Freeman's kind of place. To reach him, we traveled farther east into the full desolation of a desert like the blind side of the moon. Nothing moved but horned toads, and the rivers oozed with tar. At last we were set down and climbed from the coach to reel like sailors on the dry land of some nameless camp, and Evan and Lena were reunited.

A man I'd forgotten stood there, limed with dust. His ragged hat was in his hand, and his face was stubbled. He was there to meet us, while other men weathered like him stood back, looking on. It was Evan, and he put out his arms so Lena might descend from the coach into them. From behind, I saw her just touch the brim of her bonnet and square her shoulders so she would alight with dignity.

Then she was in his arms, only for a moment because of the onlookers. Her bonnet dipped, and I saw Evan's gnarled hands holding her shoulders.

We lived many places in the years when Opal and I were children, in the desert and in the mountains and up canyons where Evan Freeman staked claims nobody else wanted. He was bearded now like the prospector he was. I remember him only as a man grayed to old age by the alkali dust, with a permanent squint set in his eyes by the sun. What he'd have done with riches we were never to know. I don't think he craved wealth. I suppose he only wanted space around him, a thing no wife can understand, let alone a child.

We lived in canvas-fronted shanties and in wickiups and in a hut once where the roof was a patchwork of calico shirts slung over pine boughs. In time I came to know in a child's way that it was Sarah Ann, not Evan, who kept us alive. Lena survived only for Opal. Sarah Ann flourished in this open air, and I began to step in the shadow of her long stride.

She set snares for jackrabbits and could skin her catch with three strokes, pulling the pelt over the heads in a final shriek of skin. She could fish an empty river and come home with a full creel. I worked to be like her, little knowing I was her child. I turned my face wisely to the wind the way she did and saw how she could conjure up food from a stone and witch water from tar. She planted gardens where they'd never been and would never be again, and she stood silent before sunsets, hearing them almost.

Finally our pinching shoes gave out or we outgrew them, and we all wore moccasins like Sarah Ann's. Then Lena made her stand. She had Evan build a single-room house for us along the Reese River. The water was good drinking, and the mines were on the surface here. There was even a little settlement in the making.

With time, the house had a floor and even glass in one of the windows and a little straggle of yard. But here the mines were only holes in the ground, and whenever Opal was out of sight, Lena wandered among the pits, sure the child had fallen in. Lena was uneasy here, and Evan grew restless. He spoke of better prospects elsewhere, and soon he left us here and went off questing.

Without him, Lena relinquished what little hold she kept on me. I was a trial to her. I'd have eaten with my hands and swiped my tin plate clean with a hunk of bannock bread like

Sarah Ann if I could have got away with it. My plump, bronzed arms were a reproach to Opal's pale matchsticks.

I was free to follow Sarah Ann outdoors, scenting the wind and scanning the distance and trying to be whatever she was. But Sarah Ann noticed what I was becoming and rounded on me.

We were on the sand bank of a river that wound ironically through the desert, and I thought we'd come to fish. But Sarah Ann took up a stick and began to scratch letters in the wet sand. Letters built into a whole alphabet, learning I didn't know she had. Lena taught Opal in the house. It was understood that Opal must be educated against the day when a miracle happened and she at least would be freed from our captivity in this sulphurous wasteland of endless nothingness.

"Opal must have her chance," Lena said over and over, reciting like prayer.

But in our sand-bank schoolhouse, Sarah Ann taught me my letters and how they joined for words written bold and big across the ground. She taught me my words and how to string them together, forming their sounds deep in her throat as if she was trying to hear them herself.

She made me take up a stick and write in the sand, copying to learn the shapes. It was so natural a method that later when I was expected to poke a steel nib into an inkwell and write in little crabbed letters across a notebook, the penholder lolled in my hand and rolled away down the desk.

Sarah Ann, who spoke only a word at a time, taught me to write and to speak with a curious kind of precision. I learned out of doors where words ring and the mountains hear. She was a strict teacher, but at least I had the echoes of my own piping voice for applause, my first applause.

Even then I may have known she was turning me back to a world where she had no place, though she could have held me to her without trying. I wasn't Opal, but I, too, was being given my chance.

Evan Freeman came back to us, older each time. He spaced his visits and came sometimes with coins and pouches of gold dust, sometimes not. Once he brought a double eagle worth twenty dollars. Lena hid it in her mattress.

I didn't know what coins were for, though Opal seemed to be born knowing. I liked better the bear's skin he brought once. It hadn't been a very elegant bear even in life. There were bald patches, and though the claws were on, the head was not. But he could do something wonderful with it, quick before we noticed. He'd drop into a crouch, wearing the skin. The Evan we knew was gone again, but here was almost a bear, lumbering around the table legs and crawling for the corners.

With earsplitting screams, Opal flew into her mother's arms and buried her face, but I danced about, shrieking, "Bear in the house, bear in the house!" while Evan lurked and grew more bearlike. Lena laughed with her hand over her mouth like a girl. Even Sarah Ann watched from the shadows, and her eyes glittered at this playacting. But once the table went crashing and a lamp with it, and so Lena cut off the claws and shaped the skin until it was bear no more, only a rug to throw over the bed.

Evan brought a snakeskin once that unfurled like an evil, silver pennant across the room, all its scales turning to prisms in the light. But Lena wouldn't have it in the house.

He tried to play with us, but I grew too loud in our roughhousing and Opal always retreated in tears. I'd sit on his knee by the hour, and he saved the other knee for Opal, but she'd only perch momentarily like a bird. And he wasn't encouraged. Once Lena said, "Evan, it will only make it worse for them when you're gone." I knew then that Evan was only a visitor here and we weren't to count on him.

Yet I did, hating to see his preparations to be off again: his boots set at the door with their toes pointed toward escape, the new pick handles he whittled of white ash to have a set of proper tools to leave with.

He'd go in the cool before dawn, but I'd wake at the sound of pans and picks jangling from the panniers of the "jenny," the mule. I'd watch from the window while he circled the

jenny, cinching the straps. Lena was there with him, a shawl
over her shoulders and the wind billowing her nightdress.

I never thought she dreaded his going. I thought she made
every day the same, but now when she thought no one saw,
there was a difference in her. Their hands seemed to meet and
part across the mule's swayed back, and Lena would look
away as if this was all the good-bye she had for him.

It was like a dance, Evan stepping back, Lena turning
away and returning. At the last, her head would burrow
against his shoulder, and her hair, loose about her, hid his
face. Neither clung. They only stood joined against the gathering horizon, and then he'd go. She watched until he was part
of the distance and the brightening day. From the window I
watched too.

But we were never quite alone, not as things were then.
Indians' faces appeared at the window, often at night, though
no ear, not even Sarah Ann's, heard their approach. People
still remembered the Paiute Wars and the battle of Pyramid
Lake. The fear of Indians seemed almost to stop Lena's heart.
Her hand clamped her throat, and her face went blank with
terror.

"Here's one time you could make yourself useful," she
spat out at Sarah Ann when black, staring eyes had appeared
at the nighttime window. But Sarah Ann could do nothing. I
never saw her frightened of anything else, and so I remember
her fear then and how she cowered in the far corner of the
room, hiding her marked face against the wall.

Lena learned to offer the Indians cans of hot coffee and
what bread we had. Through the cracks in the door I watched
them sitting in a solemn pattern on the ground, portioning out
the food. I admired the beadwork on their moccasins and the
red flannel woven into their braids. Then they'd be gone, so
silent we couldn't be sure. In the morning the stack of
firewood against the house would be added to, often up to the
roof, their payment.

Miners in the camp looked out for us as Evan's absences
lengthened. They came to plant their boots on the rag rugs of
our floored cabin and to sit in the novelty of our female

company. They'd have dandled me on their knees and remembered distant daughters, but by then I was much more than an armful. Opal fled from them, but lurked in the corner to listen.

Lena came to count on them and washed her hair and Opal's in lye soap, drying it in the long afternoon sun before the evenings when visitors came. Her aprons were burlap now, but she wore a fresh one to admit them. She knew how they liked their coffee and what a woman's hand at baking meant to them.

Though she never admitted the pleasure of it, she held a little salon in that room of backless benches. While she made the place ready, we'd catch her humming scraps of an old song called "Money Musk."

In a relay through the evening, the miners stepped out onto the porch to drink from the bottles they left in a row there, never taking liquor in Lena's presence. Opal, who already longed to be a lady, learned her manners from these courtly outcasts.

These are my memories of that time, and then a final one. Evan had gone away in the fall. It was March now, and blazing hot. There was no wind, almost no air. Scraps of cloud clung to the far peaks and never moved.

Though we wouldn't hear from him in his absences, Lena expected him back now. Then one day there were Indians in the yard, strangers to us. Sarah Ann saw them first and made a run with me to the house.

From the window I watched Lena walk out to meet them in the yard. They were on horseback, and the chief dismounted before her, where she stood with her hands clenched in her apron. The Indian held out an object, an offering wrapped in a woven blanket. The brown arms were outstretched and in the upturned palms, this gift. Lena didn't want to take it. She couldn't understand its meaning.

At last in this slow-moving drama two miners who lived near us were drawn in. I wearied of watching and turned from the window, but then the air was pierced by a keening shriek. It was Lena's voice as I'd never heard it.

Evan had been prospecting alone in the desert. There he'd got lost and injured his foot, with the pick or from stumbling on a sharp stone or from a fall. He wandered no one knew how long, maddened by thirst.

These Indians found him and took him to their camp to care for him until he died. They brought to his widow what they could of him, wrapped in a woven blanket. They'd cut the heart out of his body and dried it in the desert air, for her to bury.

FIFTEEN

Lena took us to Virginia City to give Opal her chance. For the journey she wore her old black dress split now beyond mending. From the wicker trunk she resurrected a broken bonnet and trimmed it with black ribbon. She wore a widow's weeds, but after the first shriek, she never mourned Evan Freeman. I don't think I did either though he was the only father I was ever to know.

Lena buried his heart in the straggling grove beside the river, and that night we sewed into our skirt hems the coins Lena had managed to save over the years. We sat in our meal-sack petticoats, leaning into the lamplight, sewing gold dollars and quarter eagles and the single precious double eagle into our skirts. Lena's stitches were quick and sure. Opal's were elegant until she wearied. Sarah Ann's looped like thongs, and mine were haphazard.

On the night after that we fed the benches to the fire, and though it made no sense, gave the floor a final sweeping. The morning of our going, we hefted the light burden of the wicker trunk among us, two to an end, and walked a mile to flag the stage for Reno.

We stood waiting at that roadside, chilled by change, knowing that Sarah Ann would be the first to see the Wells Fargo coach coming. I must have been ten that spring: woman-sized already but still child-shaped. Opal was hardly more than half my size, but her little wizened face, like a quick study of Lena's, was oddly aged by expectation.

Standing between us were the two women. Beneath the

tunnel of Lena's bonnet, her mouth was set against uncertainty. Sarah Ann wore an old wide-brimmed felt hat of Evan's and turned her hawk's face to the wind.

"I won't look back," Lena said, perhaps to Opal. "Every house I ever lived in fell down behind me. I won't look back at this one." And while we wondered where we'd lay our heads next, there was a swirl of yellow dust against the sunrise, the stage to take us away.

It was a long journey and the final lap after Reno was almost perpendicular. The coach lumbered up off the desert floor on the Geiger Grade through pinnacles of red cinnabar rock into air too thin almost to breathe.

We rode in the steady line of wagons bringing up timber for the mines and firewood. There were people with empty pockets going both ways, and here and there in the traffic a carriage with sidelamps of pure silver. The foaming horses dragged the stage around a last curve, and there climbing Sun Mountain was Virginia City.

There was a throb to the place audible far off, the steady roar of stamps in the mills below the town, the measured jolt of dynamite deep in the mountain, and the tinkle of mechanical music. Then we were in C Street tangled in teams and people so jaded they never looked up at newcomers. We crept past an endless row of saloons: the Crystal Bar, the Sawdust Corner, the Delta, the Black Crook, the Fashion. There was a smell to the place, a smell of beer and money.

In front of the Wells Fargo office, we clambered down out of the coach into a churn of mud and manure. Opal was lost and found again with her nose against the plate glass of a jeweler's window where bars of silver were arranged on velvet among glittering necklaces. They were diamonds, the first we'd ever seen.

Somehow Lena knew of a respectable boardinghouse up on B Street. In this seething crowd there were hands to point the way and other hands to bring the wicker trunk on behind us.

The streets running up the mountain were as steep as flumes, flanked with plank stairways. We climbed above the towering roofs of C Street, not daring to look down. While B

Street was nowhere near as fine as A Street and Howard Street at the top, there were mansions here beyond my comprehending, an Odd Fellows' Hall, even an opera house. At last we stood before a tall frame house with a high bracketed porch. Lena hiked her skirts and led us up to the door.

"Don't get your hopes up, Opal," I heard her whisper. "Keep your head high, but not your hopes."

Then she turned back to Sarah Ann and me on the step below. She looked at the man's hat crammed on Sarah Ann's head and at my wrists hanging far out of the plaid shirt I wore for a jacket over a faded cotton skirt. "And you two," Lena said, "hang back."

There was a handle to turn in the door that rang a bell, but we couldn't know that. Lena knocked and presently the door opened. A towering, hard-faced woman stood there over us. Her white hair was piled high above a brow like veined granite, and she wore the finest dress I'd ever seen. It was of corded gray silk that fell in folds behind her. At her throat was an enormous brooch of human-hair flowers beneath a glass oval.

"I'm Sophie Wilhelm," she said, looking down. "What's your business with me?"

We waited for Lena to speak. I could only stare at the back of her black bonnet, but at last she raised her chin. She kept her hand tightly clasped over Opal's.

"We are looking for lodging."

"I don't take women as a rule, not even to board. They aren't worth the trouble." Mrs. Wilhelm looked over our heads, out over the town. "Can you pay?"

"We have money," Lena said in a faltering voice. "It's sewn into our clothes."

Mrs. Wilhelm looked down at us, or through us. "That makes good sense around here. You're a widow, I see. Are these your girls?"

"Opal," Lena began, ". . . yes, these is my girls. Opal here and Effie behind. They're no trouble."

"Is that a fact." Mrs. Wilhelm's mouth twitched. "And is that there an Indian woman?" She gestured at Sarah Ann. "I'm bound to tell you I've got no time for redskins. I was a friend of Captain Storey, the finest man who ever stood up. We lost him to the Paiutes."

Lena's bonnet dipped. "She's not an Indian. She was took by the Apache, but we got her back."

Somehow I'd always known that, but I'd never heard it said that I could remember. Sarah Ann's fingers dug into my arm. I felt the bite of her broken nails.

"Are the two of you kin?" Mrs. Wilhelm asked Lena. "You don't favor one another, but then with her it's hard to tell. They marked up her face pretty bad, didn't they?"

"No," Lena said. "We're no kin, but . . ." Though her voice fell away, Mrs. Wilhelm seemed satisfied.

"I get fifty dollars a month, full board."

"It's high," Lena said.

"A head," Mrs. Wilhelm went on. "Fifty dollars for each of you. That girl at the back looks like a good feeder."

Lena turned aside. "Is there anyplace else?"

"No place decent and nothing much cheaper. I wouldn't like to see you at Crazy Kate's. I don't know where you come from, and I don't want to know, but you got to watch every step you take in Virginia City."

Opal, in front of me, fetched up a sob. She could turn them on and off, but this one was real.

Then like an answered prayer, Mrs. Wilhelm was opening the door wider and standing back. "I bet you anything I live to regret it," she was saying, "but you might as well come on in. I can't stand here with the door ajar all day. We've got such a thing here as a Washoe zephyr, and it's a wind that'll blow the pictures off your walls and your walls with them. Come on in. We'll work it out somehow or other."

She walked straight back through her house down a long hall over the first polished wood floor I ever saw. She walked like a man, but her hand drifted back to draw her skirts after her in a womanly way. On that hand was a sapphire the size of a calf's eye.

"I could do sewing for people," Lena offered to her back.

"Yes, and so can every widow of every man lost in the Yellow Jacket mine fire. And they're all down there on C Street begging outside the saloons," Mrs. Wilhelm said over her shoulder. She took up an apron from a halltree and fitted it over her magnificent dress. "Or," she added obscurely, "they're down on D Street itself."

I wondered as a child might what D Street was, and what could be worse than begging outside a saloon.

We followed her through a grand dining room to a kitchen with a cast-iron range. A girl about my age stood over it, stirring a pot of soup. She wore a rag around her forehead for a cap, and when she turned around to us, there was a vacant look in her crossed eyes.

"That's all the help I can get," Mrs. Wilhelm said, pointing at her. "You can't get help here. The Chinamen will do your laundry, but that's about the extent of it. I had a woman come in to clean and change the beds. She was a good worker too, but one time she come to work with a diamond brooch on her apron that must have cost six, seven thousand dollars. She'd bought shares in the Gould and Curry mine, you see, and it went through the roof. Finally she was fixed for life and put her feet up. You can't blame her."

Mrs. Wilhelm planted her own bejeweled hand on her hip. "That's the way things are here in Virginia City. It's been boom then bust then boom again for years—*bonanza* and *borrasca* we call it. But now that they can smell the Big Bonanza coming in, you can't get a lick of work out of people. They're all down there in C Street trading shares and going crazy. I tell you it wasn't like this in the old days. Then we pulled together."

She fell abruptly silent and seemed to study us.

"I can work," Lena said, ready to pull off her bonnet and begin.

"You'll all work," Mrs. Wilhelm said. "There's plenty of work for all."

Opal shrank at that, and Mrs. Wilhelm noticed. "You'll

have your bed and your board and a little besides. Are you dressed in your best as I see you now?''

Lena nodded quickly.

"Then you'll need decent clothes."

Opal brightened. Mrs. Wilhelm noticed that too.

"We're grateful to you," Lena said. Then, desperate enough to push her luck: "I'd like to send Opal here to school if they've got one."

Opal flinched. "Mama! You know I'm too old for any school." She bristled with outrage. "I'm near enough thirteen."

"She'll be twelve in the fall," Lena said quietly to Mrs. Wilhelm, though she never liked to contradict Opal. "And she's delicate."

The twitch reappeared at the corner of Mrs. Wilhelm's mouth.

"If your girl's too delicate to work and too old for schooling, I'd call that a problem, wouldn't you?"

"We'll take care of it," Lena said meekly while Opal simmered.

"And what about that big girl yonder?" Mrs. Wilhelm gestured at me.

"Oh, she can work," Lena said.

"And what about schooling for her?"

Lena hesitated. "I never thought . . ."

Our landlady glanced quickly at me and Sarah Ann. Then she said to Lena, "Well, they're your girls."

"Can the Indian woman cook?"

From that moment, Sarah Ann was "the Indian woman" to Mrs. Wilhelm. I thought it was hard of her since she knew better. Later I saw it was a kindness to let Sarah Ann be what she seemed.

Of course she could cook. She'd snatched us from starvation time and again, though she'd been nowhere near a fancy range with ovens and a reservoir like this one. Sarah Ann turned back her cuffs and advanced on the stove.

The cross-eyed girl at the soup pot was already jerking at the knot in her apron tails, ready to be gone. I never saw her again. From that day to the last the kitchen was Sarah Ann's, and she slept on a pallet in the warm pantry behind the range.

We stood there, all of us, watching her begin. Then the bell in the front door sounded through the house.

"There, you see?" Mrs. Wilhelm said. "I've got to be in two places at once."

We followed her back along the hallway, leaving Sarah Ann at her post. Oddly, she was the first of us to find her feet in this complicated place.

Mrs. Wilhelm opened the door to two boys who'd brought up our wicker trunk. Already it seemed a foreign object or something remembered after long forgetting. The trip had unraveled it further.

"What in the Sam Hill is that?" our landlady wondered.

"It's ours," Lena said faintly. "Our things."

"What things?"

"Oh . . . bedding . . . and our nightdresses . . . odds and ends."

"I'd as soon not have it in my house," Mrs. Wilhelm said, not altogether unkindly.

But of course this was all we had, and we opened it right there on the stoop, Opal and Lena and I, digging in it for our poor past. There were the battered dolls Sarah Ann had made for Opal and me, the little half-savage figures with the sewn faces and the gopherskin fur coats and the wigs cut from the ends of Sarah Ann's own braids.

We forgot—even Opal forgot—that we were too old for dolls. Lena felt around in the trunk for the flat box she'd always kept by her. It was a box of long-toothed Spanish combs. I'd never seen her wear them, but she found the box and held it against herself.

Once we were standing upright and clutching these things and very little more, Mrs. Wilhelm said, "I think we better burn the rest."

SIXTEEN

The house on B Street closed me in at first. In the desert
I'd been surefooted, following in Sarah Ann's way. Here I
slipped and fell with regularity on the wickedly slick board
floors that I learned to wax myself. There were lace curtains
in the parlor and gaslight even in the little attic room that
Opal and I had to share.

I was used to a plank bed with a cowhide thrown over it.
Here the beds were too soft for sleeping, and there was a
bathroom with plumbing that puzzled me. I was a long time
coming to terms with the grandeur of the place. Opal settled
right in.

Like all houses there, the place was badly built. People
lived, as they said, between fires. The homes were so flimsy
that the ceaseless wind, the Washoe zephyr, crept through
every crevice, bubbling the paper on the unplastered walls. A
flickering lick of flame would have brought the whole town
down, and in time it did.

We lived in Mrs. Wilhelm's house nearly four years, the
years when Opal and I left the mystery of childhood and
entered the confusion that follows it. Opal entered in haste, I
not hastily enough.

Though we dragged our feet considerably, we both went to
school in the old schoolhouse out South C Street. We started
out that first morning with our spellers in straps dangling
from hands that trembled.

"You're not to know me when we get to school," Opal
decreed. "I have enough of you at home." She flounced on

ahead of me, but I was in no hurry to get there, and I had enough of her at home too.

But when the schoolyard came in view, thronged with the tough big sons of miners and daughters as brawny, I began to look better to Opal. Her steps flagged until we were walking side by each. Before we got there she was hanging on my arm. We were scared of course and both too proud to show it. But I was big enough to defend myself, and once Opal got her bearings, she could stun the roughest scholar of either sex with a look.

I remember very little of our schooling except that Opal nearly died of shame and I of monotony. I'd been taught better elsewhere, and Opal naturally knew everything already.

To give her her due, she did seem to know things she'd never been taught. From the first day that she had a good pair of button boots to replace her moccasins, she simpered along in them, swaying her bottom like the best women in town, or the worst. It made me laugh, but I never laughed in her face. In a showdown, I could have whipped her one-handed, but I'd have lost later to Lena.

Mrs. Wilhelm could have turned us all into her servants, but she never quite did that. Like many of the blunt, she was more subtle than she seemed. Nobody could have called even Sarah Ann a servant though she rarely left the kitchen. It was her kitchen. This was mining country, and the value of staking a claim was understood. Sarah Ann staked hers and panned bannock bread instead of gold, and kept the range hot and busy.

She was content there in her crotchety way and grew peculiar. Out of her pay she bought a pair of silver hoops to hang in her ears, and time began to rob her of her teeth. She'd always dipped snuff when she could get it, and here she could get all she wanted. Mrs. Wilhelm, who gave way to neither man nor woman, made certain to keep on the right side of Sarah Ann.

Lena was taken on as a kind of junior partner in the running of the place and given a room of her own. She beat rugs and polished furniture like any parlor maid. She even answered the door because Opal refused to and I apparently wasn't presentable. But she also dined with the boarders at supper. So did Opal and I, after we'd carried in the food. Serving rankled Opal beyond reason, and no power on earth could make her wear an apron or put her hands in dishwater.

We kept four chambers for roomers and fed seven boarders. While they may have been miners once and Irish to boot, they were gentlemen now. Many were married men who fed—dined—with us when their wives were Down Below, which was our way of describing any place in the world that wasn't Virginia City.

A good many wives were Down Below all they could be. One of them, Louise Mackay, had made it all the way to Paris and wasn't inclined to come back. Her tall handsome husband, John W. Mackay, was often at our table. I had no idea he was one of the most famous men on earth.

He and his partner, James Fair, had located a layer of silver ore the year we came to Virginia City. Along with two partners, James Flood and William O'Brien, these men controlled the great Consolidated Virginia mine—the Con Virginia. Theirs was the Big Bonanza that Virginia City had waited for all its life, and they were the Bonanza Kings.

In a town built upon risk, Mrs. Wilhelm took no chances. She wanted the luxury of picking and choosing her boarders, and for that she needed the respect of their wives. She studied Mrs. George Hearst and Mrs. James Flood not to be like them, but to provide an alternative for their husbands and men like them.

She saw how tired these plain men were of their wives' affections. These former miners came to us in retreat from calling cards and crystal chandeliers. At Mrs. Wilhelm's they found all the sober comforts of a men's club. Nothing tinkled, and there was horsehair where there might have been brocade.

Sarah Ann completed the plan. Her campfire cookery, her platters of cured ham and fried steak, her cornbread and redeye gravy were what these men had dreamed of when they were poor. Her lattice-topped pies drew the occasional tear around our table.

We weren't servants because servants fussed these sudden millionaires. Sophie Wilhelm and Lena and Opal and I were the wives and children these men remembered before their own families had grown grand and demanding.

Mrs. Wilhelm liked a brisk crossfire of conversation at her table Opal and I were evidently to be seen and not heard, but she expected Lena to play a role, though well down the table. Shy in this high-powered place, she'd rather have eaten after the men, but Mrs. Wilhelm wouldn't hear of it.

"I wouldn't have a thing to say to them," Lena said, almost pleading. "I wouldn't know what to say."

"Shoot! They're only *men*," our landlady said. "Get you a good dress and use a little face powder. I do."

My mother—Lena, I mean—took her place and sat through these bounteous meals, anxious and bewildered. But one gentleman or another held her chair as she sat, and she grew to expect it.

Being only men, our boarders would have droned forever on the subject of mining and money, the quality of ores and the ventilating of mines, and eternally, the price of shares.

"You men make me about half tired," Mrs. Wilhelm said to the tycoons of her table. "You talk up a stock till it goes out of sight and people beg you to buy. Then you let it drop and buy it back cheap and make yourselves another million you don't need. I'd be ashamed to mention it, let alone talk it to death."

By ill chance, Mr. Dan De Quille who wrote satires for the *Territorial Enterprise* was at the table that night. He was considered a caution, and in his sly way he reminded her that on good advice she'd bought Con Virginia at a dollar a share in 1870. "And as you don't need reminding, Sophie," he said, "it's right at five thousand." His keen gaze dropped to the double strand of fine pearls on her bosom. She glanced down, vexed to see them there, and the shoptalk rumbled on.

Mr. John Mackay came as close as any to playing Mrs. Wilhelm's conversational game. He was the finest natural

gentleman Virginia City ever produced, and he managed to
draw Lena out. The wife he adored, Louise Mackay, was in
Paris, looking for a title to marry her daughter, Eva.

"You are a widowed lady, I believe?" Mr. Mackay said.

Lena couldn't look up, but she nodded.

"It takes fortitude," he said kindly.

"It does," Lena said, though I only saw her lips shape the
words.

"When I met her, my dear wife was a young widow with a
daughter," Mr. Mackay said. All his conversations turned
back upon Louise Mackay. "She was poor," he said, "but
proud."

That stirred Lena and she nearly smiled.

"I've sometimes wondered," he said, "if I didn't win the
mother because of the daughter. There's nothing my good
Louise wouldn't do for Eva."

Another woman would have rushed to reassure Mr. Mackay
that he was loved for himself, but that seemed not to occur to
Lena. She'd been sitting hunched in her new gown, but her
chin rose as high as a hostess's, and she looked across at
Opal.

"Everything a woman does is for her daughter," she said
in a voice that stilled the table. "There's nothing she wouldn't
do for her."

Her answer wasn't for Mr. Mackay. Lena never really had
anything to say to anybody but Opal, and Opal had heard. I
know because she pretended not to and looked away, far
away, stifling a little yawn.

The only man at our table who was utterly devoid of
conversation was Mr. Terrence Kinsella, who was employed
in the management of the Tiger Tail mine. He was a bachelor
with cheaper quarters than ours over an auction room down
on C Street. Because he was mute and miserly, it was thought
he'd profited by the inside word on stocks and shares.

Mr. De Quille could never let this sleeping dog lie and
would jog Terrence Kinsella's elbow, saying, "Here is the
source of all our fortunes, if we could but make this great
sphinx speak."

Terrence Kinsella would only blink his small pig eyes and say, "Me? I know nothing that isn't generally known," and this was taken as proof he knew a great deal more. Some said he was pumping his whole hoard into real estate and vacant lots at The Bay, which is what we always called San Francisco. Others said he kept it in coin under his bed.

He sat at the table with a napkin wedged under his collar button and looked deceptively wise. I despised him and thought him old. He must have been thirty. And fat. I was fat too, at least plump beyond pleasing, but Mr. Kinsella was truly and permanently fat. The watch chain across his front was stretched taut, and he had a round, slick face and a cowlick of black hair that stood up in a fan at the back.

I was as quiet as he, but only because nobody drew me out. Instead, I sat noticing how often his watery eyes were fixed on Opal across from him. I supposed he admired her elaborate way with knife and fork, and perhaps he did.

From the first night, seemingly, the cutlery flashed expertly in her hands while I kept my chin near the tablecloth and fed steadily and without style. We'd used a knife and fork before, though never both at the same meal. But like a fine athlete, Opal was always in training to be a lady. She could dab a damask dinner napkin at the corner of her sharp little V-shaped mouth and never touch flesh. Mr. Kinsella, who never missed a meal, seemed unable to tear his eyes from her.

Terrence Kinsella and Lena both watched Opal, but she wouldn't notice them or give anything back.

I was capable of cruelty too. In the kitchen while I washed the nightly dishes, Sarah Ann watched me from her distance. I'd turn away, thinking she was freakish and maybe crazy. It shames me still.

With her first wages, Lena bought the yardage and a tartan sash to make Opal a splendid outfit for school. She bought nothing for me to wear, but I didn't care. Opal babbled far into the night about fashion and clothes, killing for all time any interest I might have taken in the subject.

Lena had spent her all, and Mrs. Wilhelm noticed. One Saturday afternoon she swept me up and bore me down to C Street. She marched me into Rosener Brothers' store and chose a length of gray wool serge of a finer weave than Opal's, and a good deal more besides, including button boots.

In stages it dawned on me that all these things were meant for me. Somehow, as Mrs. Wilhelm was fingering a long swatch of taffeta tartan, I found my tongue.

"Opal says I better never wear any bright color around my waist since I'm thick."

"Opal's a jackass," Mrs. Wilhelm said, never looking up from the tartans. The mountains moved, and I thought they might swallow us whole. I'd never heard such talk.

She glided from the store like a ship under sail, I at her side. Along C Street men in every station of life nodded and touched the bills of their caps or the brims of their stovepipes. Mrs. Wilhelm had never been a stranger here.

She wore a fine sealskin cloak, raven-black, and her kid gloves buttoned above the elbow. All of her hats came from The Bay because no local milliner could be dissuaded from plumes that waved and buckles bejeweled. She dressed with the rigid sobriety that revealed as clear as day what she'd once been. But I was still a little short of understanding what that was.

I followed her up the stairs over Levi Strauss's store to the workroom of a little seamstress. She was a lame woman who did dressmaking for Mrs. Stewart and Mrs. Sharon, senators' wives both. I stood in my shift before her triple mirror in a daze while the seamstress scuttled around me, taking measurements. The pincushion at her wrist bristled.

"I'll leave room on top for later," she remarked to Mrs. Wilhelm, who nodded. Vaguely I understood this reference to a future bust. "And plenty in the hem. She looks growed to me, but she'll want skirt to the floor in time." Mrs. Wilhelm was nodding still.

These were things Opal was half dead of hankering for: skirts to the floor and a bosom. She waited in torment for breasts, smearing patent salves on her chest. And here I was being picked up and flung in the direction Opal longed for.

As we climbed Taylor Street, Mrs. Wilhelm said, "Don't think I'm taking your side. You're not my responsibility, and I know how quick a girl comes to be spoiled."

I could think of nothing to say, but she never depended on replies.

"I'm charging the goods and the dressmaking to your mother—to Lena. She can pay them off a little every month."

Dimly, I saw. Mrs. Wilhelm liked seeing justice done, and the rougher the justice, the better. Lena understood too. Ever after, I got from her if not my share, at least a sop.

On another day when I'd come home from my final fitting, Mrs. Wilhelm posed me in the parlor and called for Opal. In the mirror on the wall, I caught a glimpse of someone— myself I saw the way of the serge over my shoulder and the crisp line where the sleeve was set in. There was room at the bust, and the jacket buttoned close at my waist. The jacket hinted at a figure I might achieve. Below it I could see only a suggestion of the knife-pleated skirts. I moved a little to watch them sway.

Just as I heard Opal's step on the stairs, I chanced a glimpse at my face. I'd brushed my hair out of its braids for the occasion, and it fell down my back, black and flowing. I didn't know what I thought. But now Opal was rounding the newel post. She saw me planted there in the center of the rug under the gasolier.

Her hand clapped over her mouth, and her eyes expanded to normal size. I heard a strangled sound, but it might have been Mrs. Wilhelm. Opal's stare fell down me and ended with my new button boots. The heels were high.

She turned, faster than I knew she could travel, up the stairs, making for her mother.

SEVENTEEN

"I hate that old bitch," Opal said idly of Mrs. Wilhelm. She'd hated her every minute since that long-ago day when I returned from my fitting. Time had passed now, as Opal had prayed it would. It was an October night in 1875, and so I was thirteen and Opal was fourteen, and reaching for twenty.

"I hate this house. It's a damned jail to me."

Somewhere, probably in the schoolyard, she'd picked up the notion that a really sophisticated woman was free to use any language she liked. Her ideas of becoming a lady had altered somewhat, and she simpered less. Now, she liked to make a quarter turn and speak over her bony little shoulder, glancing just above your head.

There was hardly room to maneuver in our little room under the eaves, but Opal could pace the smallest space as if it was a piazza. She was pacing now for the effect and to break in her new dancing slippers with the French heels. She teetered past the cot where I sat, making for the window again, wearing only her petticoat and a complicated corset and the slippers.

The patent salves, or prayer, had done their work. She had a sort of bosom now and knew how to augment it. Her waist was still child-small, but that was an advantage. At fourteen, she was all the woman she was going to be, and she was prepared to build upon that. Now she was at the mirror, sweeping up her sparse, pale hair, trying to find enough of it to make a coil at the top of her head. She was going to her first party, a ball.

The new dress, ironed twice by Lena, lay across her cot. Opal had campaigned for black but settled for pink. There was a garland of silk rosebuds around the low neck, for augmentation. Currently, Opal hated Mrs. Wilhelm for smiling slightly at this grand gown and Opal's first waver atop the high-heeled slippers.

"She thinks she's so damned high and mighty," Opal said through the hairpins in her mouth. "I'll get out of here, you see if I don't. I'll get away from both of them, and you too."

I glanced at her cot and had that most sisterly of thoughts: If she'd leave, I'd have the room to myself.

"Why, I'll be sixteen in a year or so, and that's old enough to get married. I'm ready now, for that matter."

"I'm not going to get married," I said, "ever." I was in that phase.

Opal was darkening her eyebrows just a little, with lampblack. "Who'd have you?" she said. "You're a cow. The only one that'll ever marry you is a Cousin Jack."

A Cousin Jack was our local name for a Cornish miner, who ranked in Opal's hierarchy somewhere between a Chinaman and a Paiute. She made lists of wealthy men and kept an album of clippings about them.

Without effort she'd got Mr. Terrence Kinsella to partner her to the Canavans' ball, a party to be held down in a station of the New York mine. It was to be the event of the season and an absolute separating of the sheep from the goats.

"Well, what are you up here for if you're not helping me dress?"

I stood behind her at the mirror, holding her dress high while she climbed up into it. She shook out her skirts and tried to pull the little cap sleeves down off her shoulders. She liked me there as a lady's maid, but then she caught a glimpse of me in the mirror, looming over her.

I had a figure now. I hoped it was good and knew it was big. Opal's narrow pale face seemed to stare out of my cleavage into the mirror. "You really are a cow," she said, with a backward jab of her sharp little elbow. In a final flourish she took up her gloves and clattered down the attic

stairs like a neatly shod little pit pony. She paused at the top
of the flight leading down to the front hall. Lena was there
below, waiting for her, staring up into the shadows.

Opal wouldn't look down at her, but I did. Lena hadn't
changed as much as we had, but she was different now.
Except with Opal, she had a surer hand. It wasn't in her to sit
long at a table presided over by another woman. She wasn't
quite mistress of this house, but she'd made herself indispensable. She burdened herself with the running of the
place until there was less for Mrs. Wilhelm to do. Our
landlady often sat over a cup of coffee in the kitchen now,
coaxing conversation out of Sarah Ann.

Lena stood at the foot of the stairs in another gray silk
dress. At the collar was a little silver pin set with an opal.
Her dress hung against the thinness of her figure, but she
stood erect—rigid as before, a little more imposing now.

She no longer drew her hair back into its countrified knot.
She dressed it higher with the tortoiseshell combs that she'd
finally taken from their box.

As Opal descended, Lena ran her hands down the smooth
sides of her skirt. Finally, the pride and love burned so bright
in her eyes that I had to look away to keep from being
blinded.

While Opal was still on the stairs, the bell sounded in the
door, and Lena turned to open it to Terrence Kinsella. He'd
hired a closed carriage, which couldn't have been his idea,
and he wore a boiled shirt with a high collar that bit into his
chins. He hung there in the doorway, panting from the exertion and the expense.

With the merest suggestion of drama, Lena stepped aside
to reveal the stairs. Opal stood there with one hand caressing
the back of her neck. The train of her skirt ranged far above
her on the stairs.

Terrence Kinsella saw her and his stovepipe hat fell from
his hand. The trap was no sooner baited than it was sprung.

Lena lingered at the door and watched them away. Down
in the street the horses stamped, and there was a flash of

flame from the sidelamps. She closed the door and turned to the dark parlor, something lost and aimless in her step. She'd forgotten I was there on the stairs if she'd noticed. I wanted to say something to make her notice, and it couldn't be about me.

"Opal will marry Mr. Kinsella, Mama."

She started as if a stranger had spoken. Perhaps she hadn't minded being alone. "Don't talk like a fool," she said. "It's only a party. It's only tonight."

But we both knew Opal better than that. She'd build on anything and had never been denied.

"Besides, she's got plenty of time, all the time in the world."

We both knew better than that too. Opal never waited.

"I can give her what she needs," Lena said. "She can look to me for what she wants."

But the words hung heavy in the shadowed hall. She'd seen Opal's album with the articles cut out of the *Enterprise*. Opal knew by heart the descriptions of the Comstock silver tea service made by Tiffany in New York for Mrs. Hearst. And the hotel Lucky Baldwin was building on Market Street at the Bay. And the tiara Mrs. Stewart wore to the opera when she was in Paris. Opal's mind was filled to the brim with these glories, and she wouldn't wait.

"It isn't Opal I'm worried about," Lena said. "You're the one I'll have trouble getting off my hands."

I climbed the stairs then, a moment too late, and when I passed Mrs. Wilhelm's room she called me in. I knew she'd heard what had been said downstairs. She heard everything. She'd slipped her teeth into her mouth, and the water in the glass beside her bed was still swaying. She wore a nightcap and looked a little shrunken against the pillows. There was a book of household accounts beside her hand, and her spectacles were on her nose.

"Well, how did she look?" she said, meaning Opal of course.

"Her best."

"Yes, and then some if I know that little minx." She almost smiled. "Do you mind not going to the ball?"

I'd never thought of it. "Not if it meant going with Mr. Kinsella."

She snorted. "She'll marry him all right. There's bigger fish, but she's got him on the line. I hope she does. I've always wondered what he's worth, and she'll get the money out of him. You can bank on that."

"Isn't he too old?" I asked.

"That's not a man's problem. It's a woman who can be too old."

She raised her wrinkled hand, and the sapphire winked as she made an impatient gesture. I thought she was waving me away, and I turned to go. But then she said, "Don't begrudge Opal what she can get. She hasn't a lot to sell, and that kind always sells short."

I looked back blankly at her.

"You don't know what I'm talking about, do you, Effie?"

"No, ma'am."

"You ought to listen to me. I know a thing or two about girls and what they get up to and what they're worth."

I thought that was a peculiar thing to say. If she'd ever had daughters of her own, they were lost to her now. I'd come to think that *Mrs.* was a title she'd conferred upon herself. Opal was sure of it.

"You don't want to envy Opal. You're going farther than she is. She'll have to settle for what she can get. You're going to have what you want."

I only stared at her there in the bed, wondering if her mind was wandering.

She sighed impatiently. "Yes, you'll have what you want, so you must be careful what you wish for."

I must have gaped at her.

"I see you don't know what I'm talking about. I'll explain, but I never say a thing but once, so listen. Opal's been carried around on a silk cushion since she was weaned. You weren't. That'll work for you. You'll do for yourself just as I've done. If you've got sense enough."

Her eyes were sharp and bright as diamonds behind the spectacles. "It's time you got your wits together. You're nearly a woman. And you've got something Opal can't be given."

I waited to hear what it was. She smacked the bedcovers, at the end of her patience. "Why, girl, you're going to be a beauty. You're halfway there now. Haven't you seen the men turn and look at you on the street?"

I swallowed, dry in the throat. "The boys at school never—"

"I'm not talking about boys. Heaven preserve us from boys. I'm talking about men." She made an exasperated sound deep in her throat that she must have picked up from Sarah Ann.

"Oh, go to your bed," she said. "You wear me out."

EIGHTEEN

I went to my bed and lay up there staring at the low ceiling. I hadn't meant to stay awake till Opal came home. Far from it. I meant her to find me sound asleep and uninterested. But I was kept wakeful by Sophie Wilhelm's words, that I would be a beauty.

I wondered if she was only being kind, though she was always more exact than kind. Of course I'd seen men looking at me, and in a general way I knew why men looked at women and girls. They'd looked, of course. They looked at anything in skirts. It was said there were nine men to every female in Virginia City, and I could believe it. I thought they stared at me because I was big and ungainly.

On nights darker than this one I sometimes wondered if I was growing up to be a man instead of a woman. It had kept me awake and tossing many a night while Opal dreamed of grandeur.

Certainly I seemed of some other sex or species than hers. I was big, and my thickening eyebrows threatened to grow together above my nose. I had a jaw as firm as any man's and thought myself lucky not to be sprouting whiskers. In fact I had sprouted hair, down below, and this had liked to worry me to death before I learned it was normal.

But as to beauty, I couldn't know, not if I stared in a mirror till Christmas. I cast about to think of beautiful women. Famous women, beauties perhaps, came to perform just up the street. I'd never been in Piper's Opera House, but I'd seen the bills pasted up outside with the engravings of actresses.

Lotta Crabtree was a favorite there, but she looked like a little girl with an elfin face though she was a woman grown.

In some forbidden book I'd read about Lola Montez. It was said she'd had skin like a magnolia petal. My skin stayed summer-bronze the year round even where it didn't show. I knew Lena thought my coloring a disfigurement and turned back to Opal's pallor with satisfaction and relief.

My coloring made my eyes greener than they were, and bigger. I feared they might keep getting bigger, and bulge like a hanged man. When they hanged Jean Millian, the murderer of Julia Bulette, they said his eyes bulged out until they lay like crabapples on his cheeks, bleeding down his chin. Thrilled with horror, I lay in my bed with my eyes tight shut. And Lola Montez was no help to me. She'd been "perfection of a kind." I'd read the phrase.

Tossing on my cot, I seemed to remember everything that ever happened to me, none of it very encouraging. Inevitably, my mind skipped back to that day in the spring. I smelled again the sharp stench of chalk and my teacher's shirtwaist that seemed daily starched but never laundered.

I was wedged into my school desk, thinking I was dying. There was a warm stickiness between my legs and finally a spatter of blood where I could see it. If I fell on the floor in a faint as I longed to do, anyone could see it. I stared at my geography book even through recess, never daring to move for fear this wound was fatal.

At the final bell, I galloped home swerving around Opal. I'd thought I was making for Lena, but it was Sophie Wilhelm I met on the stairs. She took one look at my face and another down at my skirt. I was too frightened to speak, and like any child, unwilling to hear bad news. She took me to the bathroom and cleaned me up, soaking the spots on my skirt in cold water and introducing me to this mystery.

"Every month?" I said, feeling the world pull its drawstring tight around me. "For the rest of my life?"

"Well," she said, "not if you live as long as I have."

I was determined not to tell Opal, but of course I did that very night, upstairs in our beds.

"Oh, that," she said. "Of course." As if she'd been born with this knowledge.

"Has it happened to you?" I thought she was so little and spindly that perhaps it hadn't.

"Happened to me? Why I've had it better than a year."

"I never knew," I said. "You must not have much pain with it."

"Pain?" she said from her bed. "You don't know what pain is. I'm sick unto death every month I live."

There was never any getting around Opal, and I supposed there never would be.

I must have slept, but I was awake again. The curtains at the dormer window stirred in a sultry breeze. As the room took shape in pink light, I saw that Opal wasn't in the other cot. Still, I'd have drifted off again, but the door of the room banged back. I'd heard no one on the stairs.

Sarah Ann stood there in an old nightdress with a lumberman's jacket over it. Her braids hung long and black to her waist. In the gathering reddish light the tattoo marks on her face looked like furrows. In two strides she was beside me.

"Up," she said. "Up and out."

Then because I couldn't move fast enough to suit her, she dragged me by the arm down through the creaking house. There was wind at all the windows and the clatter of bells and the boom of dynamite I took for thunder.

We were down the porch steps and in the street. Still she wouldn't turn me loose. When it should have been dawn-cool, it was hot as summer and bright as noon. Standing above us against the mountain was a wall of fire.

The volunteer fire companies were dragging their engines up the sheer rise of Taylor Street, but the air itself was ablaze. A fiery curtain was moving down the mountain, and the wind made a chimney for it. Whole walls of frame houses were turning high in the air, bursting apart. I stood there still in Sarah Ann's grip, as if only I were to be saved.

Our house was black against the orange flame. Lena stumbled down the porch stairs. The air was full of cries now and commands and the sounds of crazed horses and the blast-furnace roar of the fire itself. Far below us the bells in the steeple of Father Manogue's church pealed steadily in the last moments before they fell.

Lena stood in the street, dressed as I had seen her earlier this night, every hair in place above her combs. She could think only of Opal, but Opal wasn't there. She ran to Sarah Ann then, for shelter I thought. Then she cried out, "My god, Sophie's still inside."

Sarah Ann let go of me and bounded up the steps. In this short burst she ran as I remembered her running for the sport of it in the desert. Her black braids lashed the air, and she vanished into the house.

There was a halo of light around it as the shingles caught, blazing along the entire rooftree. I felt the air hot in my lungs. It was time for flight. People were running past us now with nothing in their hands. But Lena wouldn't move from the spot without Opal. And I wouldn't have moved without Sarah Ann, though I couldn't think why. Lena and I would have stood there and burned to death rather than survive with only each other.

Then through the panicked crowds the closed carriage that had carried Terrence Kinsella and Opal to the ball pulled up beside us. The door fell back, and Opal in her silk finery tumbled down into Lena's arms.

At that moment Sarah Ann strode out onto the porch above us. The fire was licking at the wooden eyebrows of the windows and the glass was bursting out. Sarah Ann stood there a moment, dazzled by the light, and in her arms was Sophie Wilhelm in her nightdress.

We stood there, all of us together, our eyebrows singed and our skirts scorched. And then the roof fell through the house. Sarah Ann tried to turn Mrs. Wilhelm's face away, but she saw.

"Everything gone," she said, "and nothing to show for my life."

One side of her mouth sagged, and her head lolled back.

Sarah Ann took her weight. I thought the shock had killed her when I saw the glaze come into her eyes. But there was life in them still, and they were fixed on Lena. Something passed between Sophie Wilhelm and Lena Freeman then, something I couldn't see.

NINETEEN

The Great Fire that raged through Virginia City in that October dawn of 1875 leveled two thirds of the town. Leaving twenty thousand people homeless, it burned out a hundred saloons, every church but the Presbyterian, and to Opal's great relief and mine, the schoolhouse.

The town was down; yet there was widespread rejoicing. By a miracle the fire kept clear of the mineshafts where it might have burned forever underground, barring the way to more riches. As long as the great vein of silver could be tapped, what happened to the city on the surface couldn't matter much.

It rose again on earth that still reeked and smoldered. Out of the rubble of C Street rose the new International Hotel, six stories tall with the only elevator in the West. John Piper built the second of his opera houses on the smoking foundations of his first. Father Manogue raised the great cathedral of his St. Mary's-in-the-Mountains. And every whore on the D Street Line rebuilt her little one-room "working gallery," with the aid of her clients. All the games Virginia City played were played again and for higher stakes.

This is the town remembered now, the town that grew old and derelict and finally ghostly when the mines played out. But it was a proud place in its new brick and stone. Sophie Wilhelm raised a fine brick house there, paid for with the last of her mining shares. She spent her last penny on it and sold her sapphire ring to furnish a bedroom for herself. The stroke she suffered during the Great Fire left her helpless. Her speech was only a little slurred, but she was bedfast now. We were all the family she had, and she needed one last roof over her. Lena needed more than that.

Mrs. Wilhelm passed the reins to her, but not the whip. That was just as well, for Lena wasn't the businesswoman she would become. She'd hoped for nothing more than another boardinghouse like the one that had been. But the fire had changed the rules of that game.

Our gentlemen boarders were looking farther afield now, to spread their empires to the Atlantic states and to Europe and to make their wives welcome at courts beyond our ken. Only Terrence Kinsella lingered behind, still ripe for Opal's plucking.

Lena fought against that and dreaded a showdown. She reasoned even with me that Opal could do better. Lena wanted to keep her forever, and in her innocence and desperation, she thought a boardinghouse would buy her.

We were still in rented rooms at Gold Hill when Lena told her plan to Sophie Wilhelm, and I well remember the old lady's look of amazement. "What makes you think a boardinghouse would keep you? Even with the girls off your hands, it wouldn't bring in anything like what you'd need. I had my shares, you know."

"But what can I do?" Lena was near to hand wringing. "You know I don't want Opal off my hands. Kinsella's not half good enough for her. She's far too young to marry, and when she does—someday—I want to be able to provide for her. I know what it is to go to marriage empty-handed."

She fell silent then, and the room echoed with her need. At last, Sophie Wilhelm said from her bed, "You'll need more money than you've ever seen to buy what you want. And then you'll lose."

She said it matter-of-factly as she said everything, and it rang with an awful authority. I was lurking in the corner, and I cowered at the thought.

"I don't care what I have to do," Lena said. "But where do I begin?"

"Where I did, I suppose," Sophie Wilhelm said, wearily. "You better send Effie out of the room so we can talk."

*   *   *

Behind closed doors, plans were laid. I was witness only to their results. Mr. Kinsella was prevailed upon to wait a while for Opal, or more likely to fend off her entreaties. It was probably Mrs. Wilhelm who reasoned with him, and she arranged the loan from the Bank of Nevada in his name to buy Lena time until the new house was finished, and functioning.

We moved into it in the following summer, the Centennial Summer of 1876. I remember the scent of wet wallpaper paste and the bunched globes of the gasolier that would blaze above the pink and silver parlor. Behind its plain facade, it was dauntingly luxurious except for the kitchen that was an exact copy of Sarah Ann's domain in the former house. Mrs. Wilhelm was wise enough to make Sarah Ann at home immediately.

Opal and I were to sleep up under the roof above the two floors of bedrooms. We were to have separate rooms, which was progress indeed. Opal repaired to her room on the first day to arrange the new wardrobe that was Lena's first bribe. Mr. Kinsella was often at The Bay now, on business. But Opal in new plumage bore his absence without pining. She regarded herself as an engaged woman.

A peculiarity of the new house was that our rooms connected to the main floor only by a rear stairway down to Sarah Ann's kitchen. Lena's room below us opened to both front and back stairways so she could monitor the house. Her chamber was in a suite with Mrs. Wilhelm's. There from her carved bed Sophie Wilhelm presided until in time Lena learned the business.

It was, of course, a brothel.

How early did I know? Not at once. I knew, or thought I knew, what prostitution was. You couldn't grow up in Virginia City without knowing about the notorious D Street Line. I'd had a forbidden look or two at it. I'd seen the "soiled doves" out on the little front porches of their working galleries calling out to the men.

I'd seen their hair brazen in the sun of broad daylight and

their flesh-colored stockings when they planted slippered feet up on the porch rail. Their faces were busy with paint, and the lace hung in tatters from their gray petticoats. They drank straight from the bottle and knocked the ash from their cigars over their porch rails.

How could I have associated them with our lady boarders who arrived, singly, on the evening train from Carson, summoned from discreet distances through a network Sophie Wilhelm knew well? They arrived in traveling cloaks with hoods that framed unpainted faces. And once ensconced, they only left the house for brief afternoon strolls, in pairs like nuns.

There was Bernice who was the first to arrive and to pass inspection up in Sophie Wilhelm's room. I took Bernice for a schoolmistress. She wore spectacles that rode high on the bridge of her nose and sewed a fine seam. She sat in the parlor in the afternoons working in bright wools a motto for a sampler that would hang framed on the wall: SEE NO EVIL. Her voice rang splendidly in the echo chamber of her prominent nose and she said she came from Boston, though not directly.

There was Chloe of the cultivated singing voice who made a great stir when she arrived with her own rosewood spinet piano, and a greater stir upon leaving when Lena impounded the piano for unpaid debts.

There was Lottie who dreamed of setting herself up as a hairdresser back in St. Louis, and who practiced on everyone, gossiping nonstop in a hairdresser's way.

And there was Emelie who'd come from England in the chorus of a notorious leg show called *The Black Crook*. She said she'd been a great star of the theater, and I admired her accent that rippled through octaves, and I studied her gift for mimicry.

There were many more than these over the years. They came and went and in the interests of variety were replaced after a time. Some failed to last the night. Others lingered half a year, often leaving in tears to be quitting such a refined situation. Though I wasn't supposed to know it, a girl slit her throat one afternoon in the best front bedroom, and her body had to be left there until night when it could be taken away under cover of darkness.

Lena tried to keep the truth of where we were from Opal and from me, too, lest I turn traitor. That was the reason for the back staircase that led only to the kitchen, as if we were to live out our lives at the rear of the house, deaf to the birdsong in this great cage of women.

While I listened at keyholes, Opal turned a deaf ear at first. Naturally, she knew. She had a keen nose for corruption, but she was biding her time and amassing a trousseau for herself and evidence against her mother.

At night Lena made sure that Opal and I were in our rooms. She'd have locked us in if she dared. But by day we drifted through the house, though if Opal was gathering evidence, she had to do much reading between the lines.

Our lady boarders outdid themselves in propriety. They had reasons beyond my imaginings for decorum. If they hadn't risen well above hair pulling and brawling with broken bottles, they wouldn't have been here at all.

They were bawds, of course, and experienced ones at that. I suppose they were sunk in every kind of viciousness and despair, and the patent medicines they swilled for their "female complaints" reeked of opium and grain alcohol. But when I was near, they might easily have passed for early suffragettes had they been more badly dressed.

They made a pet of me and told me I should take more trouble with my appearance. They taught me proper posture, and when my waistline began to shrink a little, they chirped encouragement. I learned a great deal from them, all either improving or innocent, and a hundred recipes for face cream and barley water.

Those who could read were the prey of sentimental fiction. Those who couldn't recalled the same scenes from their own histories: the deathbed tableaux of family members and the partings of unrequited love. They wept easily and recovered quickly, and they all lusted after respectable futures. The romantic ones dreamed of elderly, undemanding husbands.

The sensible ones longed to be landladies of superior boardinghouses.

I admired their overnice manners and the demure but stately way they sat slightly aside on the settee. From Lottie I learned the patience to brush my hair five hundred strokes. She even tamed my mane and dressed it into a long looping style arranged over one shoulder. It was a coiffure very popular at the time, called "follow-me-lad."

Sarah Ann registered her opinion of that and much else about our life by stepping up behind me in the kitchen once and brushing out my new hairstyle with painful, stiff-bristled strokes.

My memories would be different if I'd ever seen the inmates of our house by night. But I had no more than hints of that. The mud box at our front door was big as a bathtub to accommodate any number of men's boots. And I saw clearly the fear that fell across these women when Lena walked into the room, more imperious every time. I lay in my room at night hearing the drifting tinkle of piano music while I read some saccharine novel and waited for something wonderful to happen.

On nights when I listened carefully, I heard Lena's voice calling up the front stairs, "Company, girls!" But I never saw them paraded and prodded and made to bend to their tasks. I never saw what they had to do for men who paid to keep me housed and fed and childish a little longer.

Indeed I never saw a man in that house but once. And I shouldn't have seen him. He was the last man in the world I should have met. And I fell in love with him.

TWENTY

Lena became a familiar figure in Virginia City for her sealskin cloak and the stylishly severe hats that replaced her bonnet and the black kid gloves that buttoned above the elbow. On C Street when some worthy wife drew skirts aside and tried to snub her, Lena failed to notice. When the men tipped their hats, she nodded as if she didn't know them.

I saw this for myself, for I was expected to accompany her to the Bank of Nevada with the nightly receipts in her black leather reticule. Once, when she heaped a high pile of twenty-dollar gold pieces on the marble counter, a hapless young teller said more in admiration than anything else, "Ah, Mrs. Freeman, the wages of sin!" She had him fired.

Her reticule became famous in its own right, the source of legends. It was rumored that the corpses of newborn infants were conveyed out of the house in it and that it was crammed with the knives and needles of unspeakable surgery. But Lena had no fear of these fictions told against her. She was stoutly defended against all the world but Opal.

Opal and I were safe from the town's scorn, for we knew nobody. In our isolation, Opal was free to dream of some abstract idea of social life. She described to me at length the "at-home" gowns she would receive in as a married woman. She lectured me on the etiquette of engraved calling cards and fish forks.

We were all dressed up—and dressed very well—with no place to go. Yet Opal would always have a destination as long as there were dressmakers and jewelers. She began to take me along on her endless shopping expeditions, perhaps because Lena longed so desperately to be there in my place. Opal refused to be seen in public with her mother.

We were sampling the delights of the new soda parlor on C Street one autumn afternoon. In Dolly Varden hats, we sat at a little round table and sipped root beer, feeling the bubbles in our noses and dreaming of champagne. Opal bristled with black grosgrain bows on a changeable-silk dress that would have done justice to a woman fuller of figure and years.

A young girl came up to our table and hesitated there, working her hands. I didn't know her by name but remembered her from our school days. She was a poor girl, dressed now as I'd been on my first day in Virginia City.

"Opal Freeman?"

Opal looked up at her through narrow eyes.

"You won't recollect me," the girl said, "but I need a favor. I need work . . . bad. Your mother—"

"We don't need a maid," Opal said, glancing away. But I'd seen her eyes. There was caution there along with the cruelty.

"That's not . . . what I meant." The girl was writhing now. "I could do what them women does that your mother hires."

There was a moment of frozen silence. Then Opal acted. She stood up and jerked her head for me to follow. We left the girl behind us with her hopeless eyes cast down. Shamefully, I was glad to be pulled away. Opal never spoke, all the way home.

What passed between her and Lena I never knew, but in two days' time Mr. Kinsella was summoned from The Bay. Opal's trunks stood in the front hall, packed and labeled. She wouldn't travel with Kinsella without being a married woman, not even in the chair car of the day train to San Francisco. The judge at Silver City married them. Opal had just turned fifteen.

Later we learned, indirectly, that they'd taken a house at The Bay in a neighborhood that was said to be growing fashionable.

*   *   *

I hadn't seen the passion trapped inside Lena until she lost Opal. She burned with love for her daughter now, and it ate her to her edges. The empty shell of the woman turned to me, and Lena came to count on me a little.

I'd find her at the office desk in her bedroom with the accounts book open and the pen in her hand suspended over it. Her hands were exquisitely kept now, manicured every day by Lottie, or someone like Lottie. Lena had bought herself a ring, another opal in a perfectly simple setting. She sat over her account book, staring away into space, lost in the irony of what she'd wrought, or in something more hopeless than irony.

I began to take on some of her responsibilities. She let me keep the books for the enterprise, at least one set of them, though officially I still wasn't supposed to know what sort of enterprise it was. But I could pay the wine merchant's bill and keep the laundry accounts. When we needed new stairway carpeting, I ordered it from W. & J. Sloane at The Bay. Then one day when we were waiting for spring, that world ended too.

It was a Sunday morning, cold still with ice on the windowpanes. I came down early to breakfast in Sarah Ann's kitchen. I thought her very old, rock-and-desert old, and very strange. She must have been over forty, so I supposed anyone that ancient was bound to be half senile. There was hardly a tooth in her head, and she didn't speak for days on end. Her temper was short too and not improved by the fussy appetites of female boarders. I didn't think of her much, and yet I was often in the kitchen, barely aware that she counted on my being there. She was like the stove. I warmed my hands at her without noticing.

I'd just made a plate of flapjacks vanish when Lena came in from the front of the house. She was by now the sort of woman who seems perpetually dressed, whether at midnight or dawn. Her hair was up and a watch in a gold case hung from her snowy shirtwaist. But there was disarray in her eyes. Something made Sarah Ann turn, and we both looked at Lena.

Behind her a tall man loomed in the doorway, taking in the kitchen. He seemed just to have pulled a coat on over a shirt unbuttoned down his chest. He'd come directly from a bed, and in this house.

His eyes were fixed on Sarah Ann. When I looked again at her, another woman seemed to have replaced her. It was still Sarah Ann under her crown of black braids, with the tattoo marks raked across her sunken cheeks. But it was someone else too, a young girl almost, with the ghost of some great gracefulness lingering about her.

No one spoke. Not Lena behind her hand. Not this unaccountably changed Sarah Ann whose blue eyes were wide and wet now. The man strode across the room as if it didn't exist. A second before he embraced Sarah Ann, her arms came up and her hands clutched at the air and she cried out, deep in her throat, "Lorenzo."

He took her in his arms, and her head fell against his shoulder and buried there. Only when he turned back to us did I see the scar old and glazed against the furrows of his forehead.

TWENTY-ONE

Like a chapter from the sort of novel I read in my room, it seemed that Lorenzo Ransom was Sarah Ann's brother, long lost. Surely I'd heard of him. When Sarah Ann cried out his name, I seemed to know it, but he'd gone away before I was born, leaving these women who didn't reminisce.

Manlike, he was appalled to find us in a brothel and to be discovered there himself. He'd come to Virginia City to see the town as people did in those days. I wanted to think he'd ridden up the Geiger Grade tall in the saddle of his own horse. But he'd arrived by train and spent the first night in the town's best bordello. Somehow, he and Lena had failed to meet the night before, and she'd encountered him on the stairs the following day.

I couldn't understand how they recognized each other. Perhaps his scar revealed him to her, but how could he know this madam with the proprietorial hand planted on the hip of her expensive skirt? But somehow they did. They saw through the years and the changes in one another.

Sarah Ann moved about her kitchen with a lightened step from some forgotten dance. She fed Lorenzo with a kind of passion, and I came upon them once, he silent at the table and she standing beside him. His arm was around her waist, holding her to him, and her head was cast back to keep the tears from falling.

Then, not seeing me there, he said, "Do you blame me, Sarah Ann? Do you hold it against me that I left you and went off?"

Her head shook, scattering tears. "No . . . no. You was . . . only a boy."

"That don't excuse me," he said. "That don't excuse me staying away."

But she was shaking her head yet, as if none of this mattered to her, that only this moment mattered. "I left you behind once," she said. "Remember?"

He looked up at her in wonder, and something in his face broke before his voice did. "Oh, girl, that wasn't the same."

I thought I would see him break and sob like a woman then, and so I fled.

He wouldn't live under our roof or even use the front door, but he came to us from his room at the International Hotel, ringing a change in Lena. For hours at a time she was too distracted to mourn Opal.

She'd loved him and loved him still as much as Sarah Ann did, but the air between Lena and Lorenzo was charged. I came suddenly into the kitchen upon them too. They weren't touching. They weren't even standing near, and Lena's eyes were like pale coals glowing.

"I've done my best and better than that. You've got no call to criticize and no right. Where were you when the both of them needed you? Where were you when *I* needed you? Oh, yes, Sarah Ann forgives you anything, don't tell me. You expect to be forgiven. Men think that's their right, don't they? But you listen to me. If you'd been willing to face up—"

But they saw me there, and Lena clamped shut her mouth, while I lamented the days when I'd still fitted behind doors.

Have I said it already? Lorenzo Ransom was the handsomest man I'd ever seen. Perhaps the handsomest man I was ever to see. And I loved him from the first moment. I prepared myself to love him unnoticed, but he noticed me at once. He looked from me to Sarah Ann and then to me again, just as Sophie Wilhelm had done that first day we'd appeared at her door.

He was nearer forty than thirty, and I was only sixteen, but I'd forgotten my scorn when Opal married a man twice her age. Then my heart nearly burst with pleasure when Lorenzo asked me to go out riding with him. He wanted me out of that house, of course, thinking it was an unsuitable place for a young girl growing up.

Since I was no horsewoman, I had to admit it, and he seemed surprised. He seemed to think that riding must be in my blood and that I could leap on any half-broken colt and subdue it. He hired a palomino for himself and a dreary, barrel-bellied pony for me, and Lena let me have a divided skirt. I'd have liked a buckskin skirt with fringes and a conch belt and a wide-brimmed hat with a lariat thong under my chin and gauntlet gloves. I'd have liked a costume to make me someone else, fascinating and just what Lorenzo wanted.

He said he needed me by him to show him the town, but he cared little for the place. We took the roads out, and he favored the ones where we were quickest away from the noise of the stamping mills.

My legs stuck out from the pony's sides, and my skirts drifted up time and again above my boot tops. Tugging at my hem, I nearly unhorsed myself until Lorenzo looked down from his great height and gave me a little knowing shake of his head, as if to say he'd seen his share of female limbs and two more couldn't matter.

He wore a low-crowned Spanish hat with a feathered band and a sheepskin vest that showed the set of his shoulders thick through the thin flannel of his shirt. He was elegant without trying down to his boot heels, and he seemed to me a god. I lay awake wondering how the scar on his forehead had happened and how it had managed to make him more handsome. In the frostbitten mornings I leaped from bed to ride with him early, marveling that I'd ever longed to sleep late.

I knew nothing of how to draw a man out, and so we began by riding in silence while I studied his profile. Beneath the black of his sideburns, his shaven jaw was blue-black in the shadow of his brim. There was something of Sarah Ann in him. Where she'd grown gaunt, he was hollowed and tightened by the weather.

We were reined up at that high ground out toward Gold Hill where it was said you could see to Utah. The horses stamped and steamed, and he was leaning into the neck of his with his forearms propped upon the pommel. I thought he was surveying the long view, but he was studying me.

I felt the hot flush of blood rising up my neck. I wanted him to look at me, to admire me, and more than that. But my throat was dry and I couldn't swallow.

Finally he said, "Your . . . Sarah Ann wasn't always like you see her now. Maybe you remember."

I could remember her no different. If I prized her at all, it was for her way of never changing even when everything else did.

"She was a beautiful girl," he said, "like you."

My heart lurched and the morning sang in my ears. But I didn't believe him. I wasn't like her and could think of no reason why I should be. It was Sarah Ann's strangely pale blue eyes you noticed, but mine were greenish-turquoise as if they couldn't decide if they were brown or blue.

"Mrs. Wilhelm calls her 'the Indian woman,' " I said.

"Does the old lady know no better?"

"Oh, she knows better. She knows the Indians took Sarah Ann, and we got her back."

"I got her back," Lorenzo said, looking away far off. "I wonder if I was right to do it."

Then he turned his horse, saying no more, and I was glad. I didn't want a moment wasted on Sarah Ann or on anyone else. I wanted the two of us to ride like the wind, far faster than I could ride. I wanted to hear it over and over in my mind, that Lorenzo Ransom thought me beautiful.

In time, over weeks, I heard parts of Lorenzo's story that I strung together like bright beads. He told me how he'd gone off to the war as a green kid spoiling for a fight and how he'd been captured at Gettysburg by Jeb Stuart. He made me see him standing barefoot in a field plowed by war with his rifle thrown down and his face wet with tears.

"That's when I stopped being a boy," he said. Another

kind of man would have bragged of his valor, and so I was the more in love with this one.

He made me see the prison where they put him, Belle Isle, midstream of the James River in Virginia, where six thousand men fought each other to eat the carcasses of dogs and where the cornbread was called "solid shot." He even sang a scrap of song they sang to taunt their captors: "Down with the Traitors! Up with the Stars," though it only meant shorter rations. Finally when there wasn't much left of him to save, he was in the prisoner exchange at Camp Parole in Maryland.

Lorenzo had seen the world since then—great cities that shrank the only town I knew. He'd seen New York, and when he was flush he'd stood at the bar of the Hoffman House with the swells. I savored his stories and embroidered on them in the meaningless hours between our meetings. His was the world I'd hoped men inhabited, men who lived by their wits and fists, growing leaner with the years, not thick and fat and stupid. Men as pared as bobcats who'd never stretch watch chains across straining checkered vests.

While he told me of racehorses and barrooms full of swells and dandies, I wondered about his women. I even conjured them up: sly, worldly temptresses with waists Lorenzo's hands could span and had. Dainty-footed Delilahs alighting from carriages in swirling veils that shadowed sloe eyes. Women wicked and knowing and lovely beyond my faintest hope for myself and all at his feet as I was.

At last, despairing, I had to ask. "Wasn't there some girls somewhere to steal your heart?"

"Maybe a couple," he said, and I watched the knuckles of his steady hands bunched on the reins.

"Not one girl in particular?" I asked, priming the pump.

"Oh, they were all particular," he remarked, pulling on his chin. And that was the end of that.

He told me these things and opened these doors. When I wasn't lost in listening, I'd find his eyes on me. I hoped he was falling in love with me though I couldn't think why he should. I only hoped and thought I might deserve one miracle.

Wherever he'd been, he'd always moved on. He'd hired on

with General Frank North's brother, Luther, as a hunter-supplier for the Union Pacific Railroad. They sent him to the plains country where the Republican River feeds into the Missouri. He told of the trains rolling east in a steady line crammed with buffalo hides. The plains were thick with skinned buffalo as far as the eye could see, "like a vision of hell."

"It's Pawnee country, with some Ponca and Omaha," he said. "I hadn't gone out there just for the railroad work. I'd gone because it was Indian country. Do you know why, Effie?"

I didn't, though his hand touched the scar on his forehead.

"I went out there because I hated redskins," Lorenzo said. "It didn't matter to me who they were. They were all the same to me, and I hated them all worse than a rattlesnake. Even in the war when I was heartsick of killing, every time I squeezed off a round, I made like it was an injun in my sights. Long after that, I never put my head on the pillow without dreaming about them. Finally I had to get back to where they were to get quit of them."

"And did you?" I asked for fear he'd say no more, but his mind was back in the plains, and he didn't hear.

"The Pawnee lived with the buffalo, moved with them, made a religion out of them. They're great hunters, the Pawnee. They used every ounce of the animal. They ate the hump ribs and stuffed the guts with chunks of tenderloin to boil for a soup, and they sucked the marrow out of the bones. What they didn't eat right then, they jerked for winter.

"The white man came in and mowed down the buffalo a thousand a day, taking their skins and leaving the rest to rot. And the Pawnee starved. I saw them suffer and lose the only ways they knew. That'll purge the hatred out of you."

Telling me that led him, nearer the end, to telling me of the scar on his forehead. He took me back to that time when he and Sarah Ann and Lena were all younger than I was. He told me of the wagon mired in the sand and the circle of Apache braves. I watched him wake from the hatchet blow to find himself among his dead, and Sarah Ann gone. He told me how of all his people Sarah Ann was finally returned to him.

While he told me this, he reached out and took my hand as if this was the story he wanted me most to hear and understand.

"I've done more talking to you, Effie, than to anybody else," he said, filling my cup to overflowing. I believed he had told me everything then. I was that young.

TWENTY-TWO

In remembering that time, I imagine it was always morning on the mountain. I see Lorenzo and me outlined against the rough, reaching peaks with our faces turned toward his world and our backs to mine.

For a treat, Lorenzo took me to a play at Piper's Opera House. Forgetting my disgust at Opal's primping, I ran to the seamstress with a page torn from *Godey's*. I must have a grown-up gown, and if Lorenzo thought me beautiful, I must improve on that if I could think how. I plucked at my lawless eyebrows and blanched at blemishes and picked at my food and counted heavily on the new dress.

It was to be white with rosebud-sprigged ribbons striping the skirt, and a high neck with fluted lace that stood up. My bust was in evidence enough without laying it bare. I settled for a bouquet of cloth flowers planted awkwardly in the center of the bodice. It was like every young girl's first party gown: perfection for an evening and an embarrassment ever after.

When the night came, I went first to Mrs. Wilhelm for her inspection. She was vague and wasted now, doll-like in the big rosewood bed. She clucked and chuckled and made me turn this way and that, nodding her approval. I left her and went down the back stairs to the kitchen, hearing Lorenzo's voice raised against Lena's.

"God damn it! It's like talking to a newborn babe. Haven't you told her anything?"

Knowing he meant me, I waited in the shadows for Lena's

reply, but I heard only the hiss of her whisper. I thought he was railing at her for keeping me ignorant of the business she ran. It rankled me that he thought I was too young and witless to know a brothel when I lived in it.

I wouldn't have thought Lena's business was wrong. Without a word, she'd made me believe it was a necessity, that if it was evil, I had my share of blame to bear. I'd gathered from Lena something more: that men were quicker to find fault than to provide. All the Evans and Lorenzos of life were soon gone where you couldn't follow, leaving a woman to manage as she could. I must have believed her. It left its mark on my life, but that night I dreamed Lorenzo would never leave me. Better still, he'd take me with him. He'd free me from myself and this place and take me someplace new as morning. Ready to go at once, I stepped into the kitchen.

They turned with the guilt of grown-ups to see me there. It spoiled my entrance and my hopes for the dress. I remembered Opal on the stairs, posed in her ball gown with the train arranged up the steps behind her. Sarah Ann was there in the kitchen, standing apart. She'd been listening to Lorenzo and Lena. Now she was looking at me, seeing me eager to launch upon life. But she didn't matter. Only Lorenzo mattered.

I floated down B Street on his arm. The evening glittered and the town hung like Babylon about us. Matching his stride, I felt the sweep of my skirts.

"Do you reckon people will think we're a handsome couple?" I asked him, boldly.

"You'll come to a time when what people think won't matter so much to you," he said. But that wasn't the sort of answer I wanted, and so he said, "I expect we'll pass muster."

I was destined to spend a good part of my life in theaters, but nothing prepared me for that first night at Piper's Opera where I made an awful fool of myself.

It was a magic place as theaters must be. Half hidden in the wing, a dwarfish dark-haired man pulled on a rope, and the curtain mysteriously rose, inviting us in. The play was Augustin Daly's *Under the Gaslight*, already an old favorite, but all too new to me.

Charles Wheatleigh played the hero, Snorkey, and Mrs. F. M. Bates was the heroine, Laura. The villain was a desperate character named Byke who terrified me by merely walking on the stage. Early in the first act, my palms were damp inside my gloves.

The great scene of the play took place in a warehouse along an invisible railroad track. In it the evil Byke overpowers Snorkey, a one-armed Civil War veteran, and carries him off to tie him to the tracks. The tension in Piper's mounted. A woman in the next row fainted at Byke's speech: "Now then, Mr. Snorkey, hunt me down, will you? But when you hear the roar of the wheels along the rails; when you hear the whistle shriek and feel the head of the train crashing into your brain, then you'll remember Byke!"

I was horrified. To make matters worse, Mrs. Bates as Laura was locked in the warehouse with stout doors separating her from the tracks. And there, we all knew, poor Snorkey was trussed and ready for the locomotive.

By now I was finding it hard to breathe. The bouquet throbbed on my breast, and my fingers dug deep into Lorenzo's sleeve. The sound of a train whistle came from offstage, drawing clearly nearer. Poor Laura darted about the stage, tearing her hair and trying to batter down the tremendous doors with her bare hands. Back and forth she ran past a pile of pickaxes stacked among the warehouse freight.

The train whistle grew louder, and many of the audience were out of their seats. I was standing on mine, and of course I'd forgotten that this was a play. Laura drooped against the door, beyond help or hope; the train whistle deafened. Then I disgraced myself.

"Get one of those axes, Laura!" someone shrieked. Lorenzo flinched, for it had been my voice.

But Laura seemed to hear me. Her head jerked up, and she lunged for the ax, spun around, and demolished a thick oak door with a single stroke. Snorkey was saved.

I collapsed in my chair, too relieved to feel anything for a moment. But what I'd done crept over me in a wave of mortification, and I longed to die before the house lights came up. When it was over, I tried to hurry Lorenzo out and thought of throwing my shawl over my head.

Half blind with shame though I was, I noticed through the crowds the dwarfish man I'd glimpsed pulling up the curtain. There was a foreignness about him, and the satin tie under his chin was flowing and florid. He stood leaning into the lobby with his head around the door, and he was gazing straight at me.

I turned away from those foreign black eyes boring holes in me. Of course the whole town must be staring and pointing at the fool I'd made of myself. I vowed never to set foot in a theater again.

"You think I'm nothing but a child," I said to Lorenzo. We'd walked far along B Street, he for the air, I for the dark. My face was still hot with shame in the cold night.

"You hadn't been to a play before," Lorenzo said, kindly. "It was your first time."

"And my last," I muttered darkly. "You should have known Opal," I told him, trying for irony. "She always acted three times her age. I used to laugh at her for it. I ought to have learned from her instead." We walked farther along while I simmered at myself.

"You don't want to grow up too fast," he said. "There's plenty of time to be grown up."

"And where will you be by the time I'm grown, Lorenzo?" I strangled on a sob. "You'll be far away from here, and we both know it."

"That won't make much difference," he said. "You've got a head on your shoulders and a pretty face to go with it. One of these days you'll meet—"

"Who will I meet, Lorenzo?" I said, blazing out at him. "One of those men who come to our house with twenty-dollar gold pieces in their pockets? Shall I sashay out to the parlor and take him away from one of the whores?"

He grabbed my arm and it hurt. I thought he might slap me, and I was ready for it.

"Be careful how you talk, Effie." He meant it to sound menacing, but it only sounded elderly and superior.

"You make me careless, Lorenzo. I'm at my wit's end. You've spoiled me for anybody else in the world. I love you, Lorenzo. I want you to kiss me. I want—"

He spoke quietly and kindly, but even then I knew I was lost. "It wouldn't do, Effie. There's been a bad mistake, and I've made it."

"No, I've made it," I said, ready to sob now. "I haven't known how to make you love me."

He'd turned me toward him and took my hands in his. I could only see the white front of his shirt. He bent and brushed my forehead with his lips. It wasn't the kiss I wanted. It was a kiss for a child, with something final in it, something of a farewell. Yet he moved nearer than he meant to. I wasn't just wishing; I knew something in him wanted to take me in his arms and hold me like a lover. I knew it, and I knew he wouldn't let it happen. Lorenzo who never wavered had come near the brink and stepped back again. We were near the house before he spoke.

"I think we'll have a talk with Lena and your mother."

I half heard it.

"What did you say, Lorenzo?"

"I think you heard. But you shouldn't hear it from me. You need to hear it from—"

"Tell me now, Lorenzo. I'd far better hear it from you."

Time skipped a beat before he said, "It was an evil wind that blew me here."

Something awful began to break in my mind.

"You're Sarah Ann's child, Effie. Not Lena's. Evan and Lena . . . they took you as theirs, but you're Sarah Ann's."

I missed my footing in the dark, but his grip kept me steady. All my life turned around and laid itself bare, or seemed to. I saw Opal as a baby clinging to Lena's skirts and striking out at me with her tiny, commanding hand. I saw Lena in her gray silk dress turn toward the darkness of the parlor, away from me. I wouldn't see Sarah Ann yet, but my mind whirled.

"Who was my pa?"

"Let Sarah—"

"Who was he, Lorenzo?"

"He was an Indian. She called him—he was her husband. And I am your uncle."

We'd come down the narrow path beside the house to the back door. The kitchen was empty, and the lamp over the table was turned low. With her sixth sense, Sarah Ann, my—Sarah Ann stepped out of her little pantry bedroom behind the range and saw us there. Her hair was brushed out of its braids and fell down her back. She was just pulling a flannel robe over her shoulders. She saw us and read it all in our eyes. But she stood there still as a stone.

"Will you get Lena?" Lorenzo said to her. "I'll find her if you don't want to go."

But she was past us and through the swing door to the front of the house, fleet in her bare feet. Lorenzo and I stood waiting. I hoped we'd stand there forever and nothing more would happen. But the door swung again, and the two of them came in, these two unknown women, these strangers to me.

Lena was wearing her best dress, the color of claret wine. Her face was gray, deathly in the light. She stared past me to Lorenzo, and it was all there in her look: the accusation and the resignation. She looked tired as she used to be long ago, bone-tired.

She wouldn't look at me. Instead, she said to the room, or to herself, "I did what I thought was right."

It wasn't, I wanted to scream out. Or was this only later? *You wouldn't be my mother and yet you kept me from her.*

But it was Lorenzo who spoke. "Tell her why, Lena. Tell her why you thought it was right."

She was standing almost in Sarah Ann's shadow, but we were all separate there in the room, out of reach of each other as we'd always been. Lena knotted her white hands together against the dark red of her dress.

"There's no place in this world for a half-breed girl."

"Or a girl brought up in a whorehouse." I got it said before Lorenzo's hand closed on my arm again.

"I won't be accused," Lena said. "Not by any of you." Her voice had risen, but now it fell. "I have business to attend to." She turned on her heel and struck at the door, swinging it open. She marched through it and was gone.

I didn't know how to do then what must be done. I took a faltering step toward Sarah Ann. The table was between us and we kept it there. I looked past the scars on her face to find myself in it someplace. Her mouth worked, and I took it for a sign that she was determined not to speak. But she did, clearly.

"He was strong," she said, "and beautiful."

It was my father she meant, and I saw him then, just for a moment. I saw him then and never again. It wasn't my imaginings. I caught a glimpse of my father in a vision, strong and beautiful in a man's way and outlined against an enormous sky.

BOOK 3

A City
Built
on Hills

TWENTY-THREE

I was born Constance Nichols, a San Franciscan heart and soul, at the corner of Market and Powell in the old Baldwin Hotel. I squalled into being on a January night in 1881, the daughter of Eve Waring and Anton Nichols. Theirs were names to conjure with though I learned of their fame only gradually in a child's way

We lived in a hotel, a convenient kind of life for theater people, and a safe bastion. San Francisco society in those days was ruled by former miners and their washerwomen wives who suspected that show people were not up to their sudden new standards. We were proof against the snubs of the better neighborhoods in the Baldwin, that preposterous old pile of plate glass and pride.

Every window was a bay, and the grand staircase was guarded by a female figure of hollow bronze uplifting a bouquet of electric lights. This lushly vulgar domain of birdcage elevators and potted palms was my first glimpse of the world. In a curious way it may even have set me on the course I was to follow as a life's work.

For a lullaby I had the clank of the cable in its slot below our windows on Market Street, and I soon slipped free of nannies and found my way out past the doormen and set forth to help the gripmen on the wooden turntable at our corner. While they reversed the little red and gilt cable cars for the trip back up Powell Street, I clung to their boots, giving my all, setting small heels below a froth of petticoats. I knew every gripman and doorman and waiter in the restaurant by

name. I was looking for love with the innocent promiscuity of
the newcomer to this world.

My father, Anton Nichols, was the great showman of his
century: stage manager, theater builder, impresario, creator
and destroyer of great performers. My mother stood on the
threshold of her career as the most exquisitely beautiful woman
in the world. All my life I was asked about the fabled Eve
Waring, even offered bribes to write "sketches" of her for
the newspapers of distant cities. I've written nothing.

I remember her first as a blend of scents: the frangipani
perfume from Paris and beneath it the lavender of sachets. In
the dark her face that people stood on chairs to glimpse was
invisible. I saw only the mesh of the "fascinator" that haloed
her head and shoulders as she stood above me, thinking I
slept.

Blinding at close range, her beauty was best seen on the
stage that she could fill to overflowing. But she wouldn't
permit me to see her there at her work.

In his varied career, my father had followed the shifting
vogues from minstrelsy to melodrama to musical extravaganza.
He'd trailed cowed companies of leading ladies who threatened suicide on his account and bellicose actors who challenged him to duels. He'd reached the top despite theaters
that burned and trunks perished in train wrecks, tenors—all
the disasters. But all that was in his past. My mother, Eve
Waring, was his final achievement.

I began by thinking all fathers were elderly and with time
on their hands. He'd been a dandy and still waxed the points
of his Napoleonic "imperial," snow white against the burst
veins of his face. He was remembered for doeskin trousers
and gloves of vivid purple and walking sticks of Madagascar
vine. Now his suits and linen came soberly from London, and
the cane he had to depend on was of English holly. Still, he
never went out without a white rose in his lapel. If he forgot
it, the florist off the Baldwin's lobby ran after him down
Market Street past Lotta Crabtree's fountain, waving a rosebud in a twist of fern.

In his last years, my father made something of a British gent of himself. But in the days when there'd been a vogue here for all things French, he'd cultivated a slight continental rolling in his r's. I've read that he was an English younger son, a ruined priest, an Armenian from Fresno, a Pole, a Frenchified Russian. I expect the truth is that he'd invented himself.

My father's practiced way with women never left him. The society queens of Nob Hill consulted him for their amateur theatricals. He was more gentlemanly than their husbands, and wittier, and he always went in at the front door. In the San Francisco of those days he was a highly visible figure in a city that needed its landmarks. And then there was his wife.

There may have been nearly fifty years between them. The year of his birth was long lost, and hers was a dark secret, darker as the years went by. She couldn't have been more than a girl, hardly twenty, when I was born. When I was a small child, she was in the first blush of her great and durable beauty and already of no particular age.

She'd been a struggling actress, miscast in small parts and walk-ons in the late seventies. Anton Nichols saw her brief moment in a play called *The Danites* from the story by Joaquin Miller. Marching backstage past the leading lady, he confronted my mother to tell her she had one chance for greatness on the stage. When she asked him what that chance was, he gave her his card.

I know this much because of someone else, a dwarfish young man who was already embarked on a career to surpass Anton Nichols's. He was a frequent visitor in our suite during my childhood because he assisted James A. Herne in the management of the Baldwin Theater downstairs.

He had a high pompadour of black hair and flowing cravats, and there was something about him of both a monk and a clown. His name was David Belasco, and he was beginning his rise to a theatrical empire of his own.

My mother always had an annoying habit of being perfectly frank about what could be known otherwise, and closed-mouthed about everything else. Because Belasco could have told the world, she told me how they'd met.

She'd come from the famous silver-mining town in Nevada, Virginia City. In her teens she left home, abruptly I believe. The night she waited on the platform at Reno for the through train to San Francisco, she met David Belasco.

She said she was standing on the platform in the middle of the night, weeping. That always struck me, for I'd never seen her weep. Belasco was soon at her side. He'd been working behind the scenes at Piper's Opera House in Virginia City, and he'd caught a glimpse of her there. He could hardly have missed her, though she always said she'd been an ungainly ugly duckling. She and Belasco met on the platform at Reno and rode in the train to Oakland. It was Belasco who convinced her to try her luck on the stage, and that, she always said, robbed the Palace Hotel of a first-rate waitress.

I've often wondered if David Belasco and Anton Nichols had both been in love with my mother. But that was only one of many questions I could not ask. They had professional reasons for rivalry too, but they joined forces to promote my mother's career.

Belasco staged the once-notorious Biblical play, *The Passion* by Salmi Morse. The romantic Irishman, James O'Neill, was to play the role of Christ. Belasco wanted Eve Waring for the Magdalen, and my father let her take it.

There was more Sunday School in the play than sensation. Still, it created a furor in San Francisco. It was denounced as blasphemy from every pulpit while night after night audiences wept and fell to their knees in the aisles. This went on at every performance until the play was closed by a court order.

Belasco opened it again for the Easter week of 1879, but the performers were arrested and fined for portraying Scriptural characters on a stage. The play closed in the kind of noisy scandal so gratifying to actors. Anton Nichols paid my mother's five-dollar fine. And they were married.

My father turned all his consummate casting skills upon my mother. He assessed her unique beauty and found the roles to exploit it. There'd been a vogue for fierce glamour, the tigress allure of Lola Montez and Adah Isaacs Menken. When my mother began, the style had changed in favor of pale, girlish nymphs: Lotta Crabtree and Marie Zoe, "the Cuban Sylph."

But the tide was turning again. Perhaps my mother turned it. The dawn of the monumental beauty was breaking. It was to be the bold, knowing beauty of Mrs. Patrick Campbell and Lady Randolph Churchill, the unapproachable, sculptured presence of Ethel Barrymore. These were profiles and busts that could have been carved for the cornices of public buildings, and were. These were figures from a frieze, stonily sensual and larger than life.

With her heavily browed turquoise eyes and the burnish of bronze beneath her flawless skin, she was an exotic. My father found exotic roles for her. She learned her craft by playing any number of Moorish slaves and Eurasian temptresses. She was a Latin courtesan one night and a Romany princess the next, and she was always noticed.

My father looked next for older, more worldly roles to suit her maturely magnificent figure. Her career made a great leap in a play called *The Bauble Shop*. Augustin Daly's famous company of players brought it to San Francisco, but the leading lady refused to leave New York. Father bullied Daly into giving Mother the part. She was in her twenties, and the role was that of Lady Kate Fennel, an experienced woman of forty-five. My mother learned versatility in these varied roles. From that one on, she had the reviewers at her feet.

My father opened these doors, and my mother walked through them. Of course he did more. He coached her unmercifully, drenching her in his experience. My earliest recollections are of him giving Mother her lines and walking her through the scenes.

"Don't bump, girl!" he'd thunder from behind his script. "Never bump!" He meant the furniture, and she learned to glide across the most cluttered stage with an easy inevitability. He rehearsed her before she rehearsed with any cast, and nobody ever saw the beginner in her.

She was a quick study from the first. Long after my father was gone, I've seen her take the script for a new play into her room after lunch, or perhaps out into a garden somewhere, and return by tea time, letter perfect and already declaring herself bored with the play.

Anton Nichols formed her, and she was the legacy he left to the world. He even named her. It was said he took the name *Waring* from the first directory of the American Speaking Telephone Company. As for *Eve*, Mother always said he named her that because he thought he was God.

She needed a name that would look right up in lights, for her real one was Effie Freeman.

TWENTY-FOUR

I was the ordinary child of these extraordinary parents, this old campaigner and this young goddess. I'd have to live a long lifetime to match my father's well-worn wisdom. And my mother was matchless. She stood now at center stage, and I in the wings, wondering who I was.

From the start she was never out of work, and my first lesson was to learn to take her absences for granted.

"It was just as well," she said with maddening certainty after I was grown. "I knew nothing about small children. You were far better off without me."

My father was freer, and I must linger over him a little now, for I was soon to lose him. We looked across countless years at one another. I don't know what the terms *husband, home*, and *daughter* could have meant to him, but I do know he thought all the world a stage and that he'd been hired to manage it.

He banished all the hideous hotel furniture from our suite and had the rooms done over rather like sets. The layered draperies that crisscrossed at the bay windows were replaced by gold and white curtains that looped only once and hung in a shimmering gold fringe. David Belasco came up to do the lighting, a thing he had a genius for. The lampshades were of amber and peach silk that puddled the room in soft sultry light.

A curtain seemed just to have risen upon Act One in our drawing room, though the drama consisted mainly of entrances and exits. My father was too welcome elsewhere to hold court at home. My mother wouldn't entertain theatrical people if she could help it, and society people wouldn't know her. It was as simple as that, or so it seemed to a child.

To stage-manage me, my father hired a changing cast of nurses, nannies, governesses. They seemed always to be leaving, and they were all British, or trying to be. Exercising two of his enthusiasms, Father insisted on English governesses who could speak French. As a result, my French accent is of an English spinster who's just crossed the Channel for a day at Dieppe.

My father took me for afternoon outings. Girl children going out were always outrageously overdressed and topped by great out-of-scale bonnets that flared like petals to make flowers of our faces. My face wasn't up to this, but I was beribboned and buttoned and bundled and made to carry either a muff or a nosegay, depending on the season. Bedecked, I was thrust into Father's presence while the nurse cowered in the wings.

I'd stand there, toes turned in, while he surveyed me with mounting rage. Then he'd roar past me to the nurse, "Woman! This is a child, not a trick pony. Take her off and remove three articles from her costume!"

Father had misfiring ideas of what might entertain a child. On our outings he sometimes forgot I was there. Once for lunch I entered Collins' & Wheeland's at his side, but like many good restaurants then, it was for men only and we were expelled.

We sometimes went to Woodward's Gardens, probably for the pleasure it gave Father to get there. Though his idea of transportation was a private railroad car, he made an exception of "The Ladies' Car" that ran to Woodward's. This was one of the old balloon horsecars outfitted in some hopeless vulgarian's idea of female taste. There were plush-covered divans in place of seats, and the ceiling was a mobile Sistine Chapel of frescoes. It was transport for the fair sex and their escorts, a splendid opportunity for Father to play to the audience of female passengers. I was still too young to be mortified.

The pleasure garden surrounding Robert Woodward's mansion on Mission Street was the single most famous spot in California. The house was turned into a "Museum of Miscellanies," crammed with curiosities of the two-headed chicken variety. On its grounds were balloon ascensions, winding paths for strolling lovers, and a rather tame kiddies' ride called "the revolving boats." We'd stand on the brink watching solemn children turning in skiffs on the perfectly still water. I never thought to want a ride, and Father never thought to ask me.

Then as now there was a hunger in San Francisco for instant culture. Woodward's Gardens were dotted by copies of famous sculptures, and I remember one in particular. It was a plaster copy of Hiram Powers's "Indian Girl at the Grave of Her Lover." The pose was sentimental, but the figure's beauty was profound—pristine and half primitive. We always made our way to it, and once Father murmured, "Your mother—to the life."

He was the only playmate I had, and I lived for our excursions. Near the end of our time together my birthday was coming, and I had a choice of treats. I asked to be taken inside the Mark Hopkins house.

It stood on Nob Hill among the palaces of the Nevada silver kings and the Big Four railroad money. We'd often walked past the two-million-dollar Charles Crocker residence and Leland Stanford's that covered two acres and the chocolate-colored stone mausoleum of the Floods behind its bronze fence. I puzzled Father by wanting to see inside one of these horrors.

He wrote to the caretaker, and we had our tour. We entered the oak doors of an English castle and crossed the moat into a doge's courtyard and then on to galleries from Versailles and baronial halls from Glamis. We followed a servant through the rape of Europe where paint passed for tapestry and wood for stone and plaster for everything. It was breathtaking in its way.

Finally, we issued out of the lurid stain-glassed light into the honest January sunshine. Then, unnatural child that I was,

I said smugly, "It was nothing but a big fake. It ought to be sold for scrap."

My father stared down at me with the first real curiosity in me he'd ever shown.

In the summers when my mother could get away, we were a whole family for the days we spent at Monterey. It was near the end of its long era as an old California place, still a jumble of tile roofs and thick adobe walls and courtyards behind curly iron gates. The hitching posts were still old Spanish cannons, and there were bits of whalebone embedded in the paths.

The place was fashionable now because of Charles Crocker's new Del Monte Hotel, but we always took Señora Bonafacio's house, near enough the hotel grounds to hear Ballenberg's band, but private. Mother was already finding privacy hard to come by.

I loved that house and my room in it. The candle by my bed played on the rough walls and the old doors of the Spanish cupboard. It was stark and lovely and told me old stories. Once, Mother looked up at the hand-hewn rafters and said, mysteriously, "There should be red peppers hanging there."

The Del Monte Hotel was another matter, bristling with verandas and fashionable hats. We went there to play ninepins on the lawn and to promenade on the paths. That was the only time I ever walked between my parents with a hand to hold each side.

I remember the slippery sound of Mother's surah silk dress and the parasol to match every change. We took drives along the bay and watched the artists painting the mission church at Carmel. It was the day that needed painting, to be framed and kept forever.

At night people came back from the hotel after dinner. I lay up in my room scenting the cigar smoke that wafted up with the voices and laughter. Once, my mother looked in on me. Though she said she did this every night, I was never sure. The candlelight captured all the beads below the neck of her dress. The necklines of those years were very daring, called "low-and-beholds."

Unexpectedly, she said, "You may creep halfway down the stairs and watch through the railing. But see, don't be seen." She went away, leaving the door open and the candle flame wavering. I crept down at once and stared through the railings across the smoky, low-ceilinged *sala*.

My father was telling a story to three guests, arranged at their ease and half smiling. The men were in black evening clothes, one handsome, the other hearty. A woman, deep among the pillows of the low divan, was the only rival to my mother's beauty I had ever seen. She sat to display her wasp waist. Her hand, alive with diamonds, was at the astonishing pillar of her neck. She was playing the role of a lovely woman listening to a story.

Later I learned who she was: Mrs. Edward Langtry, Lillie Langtry. The handsome man was her leading man, Maurice Barrymore. The hearty one was Freddie Gebhart, her lover.

Throughout her life my mother said that actors were fools and knaves, that actresses were vain and vicious. She made exceptions, and Lillie Langtry was very naturally one of them. Mrs. Langtry was a woman whose helpless white hands had battered down every door and forced society to accept her on her terms, or without terms. That was a living proof of a future my mother wanted for herself.

TWENTY-FIVE *

In San Francisco we were not alone. My Aunt Opal and Uncle Terrence Kinsella lived in a ridiculous house on Pacific Avenue. It was in that first block after Franklin Street in the new Western Addition, and it stands there yet after so much else is gone.

My memories of this household blend many years together because nothing ever seemed to change there, though the Kinsella twins, Jacinto and young Terrence, grew to their differing kinds of manhood in that house.

Thought she rarely took me anywhere else, my mother gathered me up and took me there for Sunday visits that seemed fearfully frequent. My father, I believe, always begged off.

I often wondered why Mother went. Never did two sisters differ more, and never were two less sympathetic. Once when I was in a sulk, I dared ask Mother why she bothered with them. In that way she had of bringing the whole world up short, she said, ''They're the nearest thing to family you've got in the world, my girl, if something should happen to me.'' And so the heavy burden of the Kinsellas was shifted onto my shoulders though I still refuse to take responsibility for them. Opal Kinsella and Mother were locked in the kind of rivalry that can only begin in the jungle of childhood, and it was a bond between them that rendered husbands and children beside the point. I don't imagine the Kinsellas had ever been in the Baldwin Hotel, not even the lobby. Aunt

Opal was thus fixed in the role of hostess and Mother as guest, each thinking she had the better part.

How carefully they girded themselves for the battle. My mother said that clothes bored her, but she chose carefully when she dressed for Aunt Opal: some supremely simple afternoon frock that spoke silently of Paquin and Paris with a hint of bustle behind, an absurd fad that suited my mother better than any other living woman.

Aunt Opal gave thought too. One of her choices will stand for many: a billowing peacock silk at-home wrapper with a frothy jabot encased in flannel trimmed in deep flounces of Valenciennes lace. She was a wan little wraith of a woman, colorless in her soul. Her dresses all seemed ready to rise and stalk out of the room without her, leaving her denuded and resentful.

Mother's mounting fame was Aunt Opal's sole claim to distinction of any sort. The neighbors on Pacific Avenue stood in their bays, baldly waiting for a glimpse of Eve Waring ascending the Kinsella steps. A beleaguered little serving girl opened the door. Behind her, Aunt Opal waited to join battle.

The Kinsella parlor was meant to bespeak high culture. Art-glass windows depicted the Waverley novels, and a bust of Dante stared from the chimneypiece. Aunt Opal had heard Oscar Wilde speak when he lectured in San Francisco, and ever after a vase of sunflowers sprayed in gilt paint stood on the hearth, darkening through the years.

Part of the furniture was Uncle Terrence Kinsella, who lived behind a newspaper in what must have been the only comfortable chair in the Western Addition. He was a well-to-do man who owned real estate all over the city, the sort of man who could make money while lying asleep in his chair. He only rose out of it, in horror, when he had to spend some. He rarely spoke and was not encouraged.

The Kinsella twins, a couple of years older than I, were far from identical. Aunt Opal named one of them Jacinto surely because she'd heard that all the oldest California families bore Spanish names. Like many of her plans, this one went awry, and he was always called Jack. He'd inherited his father's figure and lay on the carpet at his mother's feet, strikingly like a pug dog. Her hand drifted down—for many years—to fondle the spiky hair above his moon face.

His brother, young Terrence—Terry—was another matter. He was clean of limb if not of mind, the sort of boy who couldn't settle until he'd jerked my hair ribbon out of its bow. He had a dozen ways of trapping me in distant corners to pinch and grab and worse. Once when I was seven and he was nine and needful of knowledge, he lured me to his mother's sewing room upstairs.

There, with a hand strangely practiced, he managed to take all the clothes off me, save only my white cotton stockings anchored by fasteners that defeated even him. I stood there chilled with foreboding and the climate of the sewing room while he examined me from all angles. What might have happened next I don't know because the door opened upon us. It was his brother Jack who'd somehow strayed from his mother. Jack took one look at my nakedness and wrinkled his small snout in disgust.

"What did you want to do that for?" he asked Terry, witheringly. Then he vanished, but he didn't tell on us or we'd have known.

Jack was phlegmatic, but Terry was a moving target, tow-headed with a whippet's face, and he never lay at his mother's feet. She had to find other ways to ruin him. I always went to girls' schools, and the two Kinsella monsters, the weighty one and the wily, were a nightmare to me.

Aunt Opal followed the every move of society people. Their names fell like rain across her carpet from Sloane's, though they themselves never set foot on it. I believe she kept scrapbooks about them. Uncle Terrence's money derived from the silver bonanza at Virginia City. Somehow she implied that while he was from this rough place, she was not, which I was sure couldn't be right.

There were topics where she never trod. One was the childhood she'd shared with my mother. The other was Mother's career, but she was of two minds about it: whether

to accuse Mother for pursuing it or to pretend it wasn't
happening. Though she got through her long days by poring
over newspapers, she kept herself carefully ignorant of the
theatrical notices.

But here, too, she was given trouble. Sarah Bernhardt
came to San Francisco fresh from the Comédie Française
on her world tour in 1891. The public naturally demanded she
play her Marguerite Gautier in *La Dame aux camélias*. My
mother was cast in a supporting role much smaller than she
was taking by then. It was an adroit idea: San Francisco's
great beauty paying Bernhardt homage as her handmaiden.
The audiences devoured it, and Bernhardt included my mother
in a series of supper parties well publicized by DeYoung's
Chronicle and Hearst's *Examiner*.

On a subsequent Sunday Aunt Opal's silence on the subject
threatened to deafen the entire Western Addition. But it was
young Terry who betrayed her this time.

"Say, Aunt Eve," he said, "what's that French actress
Sarah Bernhardt like up close? They say she—"

"Terrence!" Aunt Opal cried out, bringing her own husband alive. "Leave the room. This is a Christian home!"

But the afternoon was spoiled.

They were all spoiled as far as I was concerned. I felt my
life leaking away in that airless parlor. I balanced a teacup
(from Shreve) on my knee, and Aunt Opal set my teeth on
edge by always calling me "Connie." But they were opportu-
nities to study my mother. She sat sphinxlike and slightly
aside, commanding the room until Aunt Opal's sharp whine
seemed to fade.

She could do with silence what Aunt Opal longed to do
with words, and there was that mystery in her quiet that the
critics always mentioned. Perhaps it wasn't a mystery at all.
She may have sat through those Sunday afternoons running
over her lines and laying her plans for the future she was
beginning to foresee.

Somehow, the clocks moved, and the afternoons always
ended. The cab came back for us at four with the welcome
sound of hooves stamping in the street.

At the door, Aunt Opal always fired final volleys across our stern. "Oh, that hat," she'd say of one of Mother's perfect cartwheels. "It's as plain as a mud fence. I wish you'd go to my milliner. She'd be such a help to you."

We returned once from an afternoon like this to find the manager of the Baldwin waiting in the lobby. Behind him were all the staff and servants, even my favorite waiter from the restaurant. They stood to meet us. Mother stepped ahead of me, drawing her skirts behind, keeping me back.

It was Father, and they were there to tell her and to catch her if she fainted. Father had rung, and when the chambermaid went in, she found him there on the floor with the rosebud in his lapel and the long life gone out of him.

On the day of his funeral the theaters in distant New York dimmed their lights. In San Francisco, they were closed.

I should think a thousand people followed us to Laurel Hill, the old Lone Mountain cemetery. They were show people mostly, muted in their motley. The Kinsellas were there too, though when Aunt Opal saw who her fellow mourners were, she kept to an open carriage down on the road and sat glittering in jet beneath a black parasol.

It was a leaden day with a wet white fog rolling in off the Bay, but that only made the flowers brighter. In England, Ellen Terry had ordered a great floral piece to be sent, and somehow it wasn't funereal. The florist had contrived to make it look like the exuberant sprays sent to opening nights. Over Anton Nichols's coffin was the blanket of burnished chrysanthemums from the Bohemian Club. Everywhere, in hands, were little fistfuls of flowers people had bought from the carts along the streets.

It was a celebration as any gathering of theater people always is. David Belasco was there, his black curls dampened by fog. And Maude Adams, half child, half woman, like a Cassandra burdened by sorrow too soon.

The wardrobe mistress had sent Mother the black dress she was wearing in Wilde's *A Woman of No Importance*. We stood on the brink of the grave, together but untouching while I felt my childhood being hollowed out from under me.

I stood beside her, half hoping that I was my father's truest mourner. I was just thirteen then and looking for simple definitions of love. I wondered if my mother had ever loved him, and how.

A clergyman read from First Corinthians, and the breeze fluttered the gilt Bible pages.

> *O death, where is thy sting?*
> *O grave, where is thy victory?*

I stood there, thirteen, between the grave and my mother, feeling my father's spirit soar into the unknown air, leaving me.

TWENTY-SIX

She summoned me to her room. Perhaps it was at the end of the day we buried my father. At any rate, it was evening in an empty world.

They had occupied separate bedrooms, as I thought all married people did, and so there was nothing of Father there. The room hung in Mother's scent. It was dimly lit except at the dressing table.

I went, thinking this was the time to balance the burden of mourning between us. That we might be two sorrowing women together promised the dignity I longed for. I went, half willing to share my grief.

She sat on a chaise in a shadowed corner with her feet, shod in heeled slippers, stretched before her. Beneath her flowing robe she was corseted. I'd never seen her without her corsets. Her hair was down, full and tangled. Her face was composed and solemn, but then it often was. She gestured for me to sit in a nest of pillows on the floor below her elbow. There wasn't room to sit nearer. There never was. We sat in a long silence, my hand on the chair arm in case she would take it.

At last in that thrilling, low voice she said, "Your father made and lost a good many fortunes in his life. He died neither rich nor poor, but we could manage on what he left."

Then, because she was after all a mother, she added, "Though there won't be anything left for luxuries.

"We could take a little house somewhere—across the Bay, in the country, somewhere. We could live that way, just the two of us, and I suppose we could manage. Women can do that on their own. Women can manage.''

I looked up at her in surprise. ''Would you leave the stage, Mother?''

''If you wanted me to.''

That failed to ring true, even from this most convincing of actresses. Surely this was a performance, with my own role already written. I looked around for a way out. At thirteen there seems always a way out if you could only find it.

''I don't think what I want matters much,'' I said foolishly.

Her eyes snapped, but she let me get away with it. ''Opal may be right,'' she said, ''though she rarely is. You may be coming to the age when an actress for a mother will embarrass you. It might bar a way you'll want open. It's very easy for a mother to embarrass a daughter without meaning to.''

''Were you embarrassed by yours?'' I asked, too pertly, but there followed only a pause.

''No,'' she said finally. ''I hardly knew my mother until it was too late. But we were talking of us, weren't we?''

We were, and for the first time. She'd banished Father already, and I had no one to place between her and me. My mind lunged forward, ahead of the sullen child I was.

''What would you do, Mother, if you didn't have to take me into account?''

Her eyebrow rose, as if I'd muffed my lines, but she was still equal to them.

''I don't welcome the idea of staying on the stage. I've never liked it and I never will. In front of an audience you court failure every night of your life. You're naked on that stage, just when you thought you wouldn't be. And you are always someone else, some stranger.

''But I'd go on with it. What else can I do? I'd work harder than before. I'd do it for the money because it's a crime to be poor. And I'd do it because I've always wanted to be . . . shall I tell you this?''

''Yes,'' I said, ''please.''

''I've always wanted to be . . . recognized for myself. It's ridiculous, I know. Women are only valued for how they look or for the work they can do. Yet I wanted to be . . .''

Loved, she meant. *Loved,* but she couldn't say it.

''. . . to be valued for who I am. I never was. I went from being overlooked to being looked at. I want there to be something else. Not here. I don't care what people think here. But somewhere, somewhere very grand and fine.'' Her voice trailed off into thoughts I couldn't follow.

''Would you marry again?'' In the romances I read marriage was always the solution.

She looked rather blank as if I'd missed the point, and I had. ''I couldn't say. You don't marry later in life for the reasons you married early. Do you understand that?''

I didn't of course, and she saw that. She drew herself up, away from us both. ''I want to provide things for you I never had. I want to give you everything a young girl deserves.''

On this cruelly conventional note, our interview ended. It was time to go; I'd been given my cue. I struggled up from the pillows, all arms and legs. How awkward I always felt in my mother's presence, and how long into life it plagued me.

I shambled to the door, round-shouldered and drooping, but this was no time for posture. My hand was on the knob before she said, ''What is it to be, Constance?''

I stared at the door, refusing to look back. ''It's not fair. Why should I have to decide?''

''Because it's your decision to make, and I will abide by it. We both will.''

My heart pounded, and whether it was from anger or fear I don't know. ''Then go on acting,'' I said loud in the room, ''and make us lots of money and . . . do what you want.'' Then I flung out of the door like any child.

I was in my own room, separate and sealed off, before I knew what had happened to me. She'd opened her heart to me only to close me out. At just the age when a girl hopes to declare her independence from her mother, mine had declared hers from me. Worse, she'd made me set her free. I threw myself across the bed and wailed for my father who had left me helpless and alone and at the mercy of my mother.

TWENTY-SEVEN

I had set my mother free, and she went. San Francisco would always be the center of my universe, but it was only a way station in hers. The theatrical syndicates forming in those years swept her off, and she was always on tour. I stayed behind, going to school at the Clarke Institute and being looked after by the Baldwin staff and one last, lingering governess.

"Don't wander about the town," my mother wrote on a postcard from the Planter's Hotel in St. Louis. "And stay out of the shops. You're sure to run into your Aunt Opal in one of them. She'll have you in an orphan asylum if she thinks I've abandoned you."

Worse yet, Aunt Opal might take me under her wing. This was unthinkable, and for many years I slunk by habit past the entrances of The Emporium and City of Paris, furtive as any thief.

Within a matter of months my mother seized her first opportunity for an English tour which established her London fame. She rushed back to San Francisco, her mouth set against the hazards of her first Shakespeare roles—and an American actress daring Shakespeare on his native ground.

She was always very good at quick changes, and I was entered as a boarding student at St. Mary's Hall in Benicia. It was a school for the daughters of solid citizens, so she must have arranged it through my father's clubmen friends. The last of my English governesses departed, wafted off on a wave of chamomile and Yardley's, and I went up the Bay to Benicia to chart the choppy seas of a girls' boarding school.

In that first English tour I believe my mother vanquished London with a look. When I saw London for myself a few years later, her Hermia and Silvia were still recalled. She sent me a photograph, the only theatrical one of her I ever had from her hand. In the photo she is Olivia in *Twelfth Night*. I set it in a frame on my bureau to confront my schoolmates. They saw it in sidelong glances and doubtless thought of their own mothers creaking in whalebone around redwood mansions and hovering too near their lives.

My education till then had been a relief map full of peaks and valleys and yawning voids, but a daughter was dispatched to St. Mary's to be finished, not educated. When I arrived, the headmistress asked me only what my religion was. The word *none* was forming in my mouth when I picked Episcopalian out of the air of the place. I wasn't my father's daughter if I couldn't devise a history for myself, and on the spot.

We students thought ourselves more worldly than our teachers, and there may have been truth in that, but it kept us from learning more at their feet. We concentrated on exchanging dubious information among ourselves and wasted long nights speculating about the Opposite Sex from our safe distance.

Like Frenchmen in the Foreign Legion, we were preoccupied with sex and in general agreement about our theories. One was that while boys were nasty, they might get better later, whereas we girls could hardly be improved upon. Another was that sex led to babies though probably not every time. Then, inevitably: all of our parents were far too old to be in the running. One girl whose father was fifty was sure of it. Considering the advanced years of my late father, I was less sure than she but managed to keep my mouth shut.

One of the girls kept a theatrical photograph of Eugene Sandow at the bottom of her handkerchief drawer. Sandow the Strongman was a vaudeville headliner of that day, famous for his physique. In the photograph he was posed as Samson holding up a stone column and naked as the day he was born except for a provocative, outsized fig leaf. Through endless evenings of fudge and fantasy we exhausted poor Sandow by passing him from hand to grubby hand.

I had nothing to offer these sessions except the long-ago day when my cousin Terry undressed me, but that was old news and embarrassing. I was more comfortable when the subject turned to improper novels, particularly the works of Ouida. I got through drear months of my life in the company of Ouida's square-jawed guardsmen who suffered at the hands of her icy heroines. From them I moved to Marie Corelli. I was never caught with my nose in one of these documents, but I was thought to be bookish and threatened with eyeglasses.

I wasn't particularly bookish, then or ever. In the long run I had too literal a mind for fiction. There was something else struggling in me, and if I hadn't been banished to Benicia it might never have surfaced.

The place is nearly in sight of San Francisco, but it was a Devil's Island to me for all the exile I felt. I couldn't be homesick for my parents who were in their ways departed; I was homesick for my city.

I fell into the habit of trying to capture it in charcoal sketches. Every free hour found me up in the little gazebo above the school, recreating my city in drawings as detailed as possible. I don't know why my homesickness for the place took this form. It was sure to be misunderstood.

The San Francisco I missed was not a beautiful place in the 1890s. It was in its awkward age as I was. The long, jerry-built rows of frame houses were knocked together without thought or style and crowned at the heights with ugly mansions. Goats grazed on its hilltops against the lines of flapping laundry. The telephone cables drooped above the gray streets. When it essayed elegance in the courtyard of the Palace Hotel or the endless excess of the Baldwin, it only made itself absurd. But I loved it.

My drawings grew more precise—never artistic, but more visionary. I began to draw a city that would live up to its peaks and vistas. I turned houses open-faced to the views and scrapped all the boxed-in, fern-tangled parlors of the Western Addition. Mine was a city of ironwork and stucco to remember the Spanish days, and long, startling distances to herald a new century coming.

Every adolescent girl tries to recreate the world in the image of her choosing. This was the form my notion took. I anchored my castles in the air among the hills of San Francisco, hidden in the pages of my art tablet.

The Domestic Sciences teacher discovered my work, coming across one of my drawings for a hillside house. She mistook this for an interest in the scientific arrangement of kitchens, a subject far nearer her heart than mine. I was set the task of designing endless kitchens and won a school prize for one of them. Domestic Sciences became my best subject though I'd hardly set foot in a kitchen and never wanted to. But as I've said, we never took our teachers very seriously.

We saved our seriousness for ourselves and one another. Our teachers were the New Women of George Bernard Shaw's philosophy. By day they preached revolutionary new roles for women and the Moral Force of womanhood on the march for outlets. By night their students dreamed of the perfect husband and marriages that would solve the future without further exertion.

As the semesters passed, our midnight discussions shifted from sex to marriage, apparently a different topic altogether. Our popular heroines were the American heiresses who'd married European titles. Virginia Bonynge's father had once been a gardener at Woodward's Gardens, and now she was a viscountess. Maud Burke was about to become Lady Bache-Cunard, and in far-off New York Consuelo Vanderbilt was being primed for the duke of Marlborough. We began to calculate our own chances at a belted earl, whatever that was.

I hung on the edges of these conversations, less sure of marriage than most, and so did another girl named Rose Conklin. At first she was too shy to know. Rose wept away her first full year at St. Mary's, sodden with homesickness.

Perhaps we became friends because neither of us could claim families with country places down the peninsula or membership in the Burlingame Country Club. I suppose the Conklins could have bought and sold the families of far more pretentious girls, but Rose was so manifestly good that she was widely overlooked. And neither of us longed to be a viscountess. She was the ideal companion—not long on scheming but perfectly willing to go along. She was pretty too, and prettier still the more you knew her.

I spent my school holidays with the Conklins, growing up among them, living for vacations and basking in their glow. They lived in a house on Filbert Street beyond Van Ness. It was bedecked with "candle-snuffer" turrets as nonsensical as the Kinsellas, but the doors stood open to the world, and something wonderful was always baking in the oven.

Mr. Conklin had made his fortune in the wholesale grocery trade and came tieless to the table—coatless, too, if it wasn't Sunday. He was mainly silent like all fathers except mine, and always wreathed in smiles. He appeared to want nothing more beyond three hearty meals a day and a good cigar.

Mrs. Conklin was a stout woman, pretty and round-faced like Rose, with wisps of hair escaping and beads of perspiration on her upper lip. She had servants but worked along with them, setting the pace. I expect she'd been a farmer's daughter once. She knew nothing of San Francisco society but urged her daughter on in a shower of encouragement. She seemed to believe that society was only a group of kind people who gave amusing parties.

Mrs. Conklin assumed me as another daughter. I'd never known a mother's embrace, but now she met us on the stoop, pulling us both to her soft bosom, dispensing kisses. The idea of an actress was beyond her. In Mrs. Conklin's world women worked outside the home only when they were driven by direst need. She pitied me and fussed over me, and I had to make it clear that my mother sent me a generous allowance from London. Otherwise, she'd have given me an allowance herself.

She was perfection of a kind, but no daughter is ever satisfied. Rose went on occasional campaigns to improve her mother. We pored over the advertisements and urged upon

Mrs. Conklin all sorts of smart and unsuitable clothes. Though she dreaded dressmakers, Livingston Brothers had recently introduced "ready-to-wear."

"But where on earth would I wear such getups?" she asked.

Then we were inspired and said, "To tea at the Palace Hotel."

She pulled a face at that, but then said, "Shall we three go together?" And so it was decided.

We went, and Mrs. Conklin had a new dress—robin's egg blue with a fichu—and nearly a fit. She balked at the hats of that season and wore an old one, but her gloves buttoned well above her elbows, and she wore a string of pearls that may have been real.

The Palace stunned her and would have stunned Rose and me, too, if we'd let it. At the Baldwin I'd have known the waiters by name, but here they were dressed as footmen, one behind each chair, making us whisper. But when the tea arrived, all was well. Mrs. Conklin poured out in this familiar ritual and might have been safely at home.

Those were the happiest times in that carefree decade of the nineties. Bicycling was the rage, nearly a religion. Rose and I could never wait to shake ourselves out of our school serges and don the new uniform: scandalously short "rainy-daisy" skirts and trilby hats, suitable for cycling. We pedaled in Golden Gate Park where speed-crazed young men called "scorchers" were lassoed off their bicycles by zealous policemen. We swept through the park with the wind burning our cheeks, feeling new freedom, though we encased figures that didn't need them in corsets and dreamed of waists like Lillian Russell's.

We stopped for refreshments in the tea garden left from the Midwinter Fair of 1894 or at the fashionable new café, The Wheelman's Rest. There we were uncomfortably near young men in loud caps and plus fours who boasted in groups about their cycling and favored us with glances. But we were true boarding-school girls. Being this near the famous Opposite Sex sent us palpitating back to our bicycles and our theories.

On one sobering Sunday night when we were returning to school on the ferry, Rose said, "I wouldn't mind if we never grew up." And I knew what she meant.

But we did, and gladly. It was suddenly the spring I was seventeen and almost four years since I'd seen my mother. She'd returned at least once to this country, but only as far as New York for a short season there with the Empire Theater Company. She'd cut this brief engagement short to return to England, and I never wondered why. It seemed exactly what she would do, and I was secretly relieved.

She wrote and I wrote, but she began to grow mythic in my mind, a heroine lovely and unreachable as any of Ouida's. I had the idea still that I was only a minor creation of my mother—a slender shadow she'd once cast before moving on. I couldn't in my heart believe I was a person in my own right or ever would be. Still, I'd learned to do without her.

Then that fragile structure came apart and collapsed. I fell in love, and my mother re-entered my life.

TWENTY-EIGHT

My mother wrote briefly but often, growing more foreign—
English perhaps. At first she stayed at Buckland's Hotel in
Brook Street and wrote on flimsy paper. Later the letter paper
grew stiff and engraved, emblazoned with the occasional
coronet. She wrote from country houses at weekend parties,
and her handwriting loosened to fill the luxurious page:

> . . . Lord Roseberry . . . and the present Prime Minis-
> ter as well . . . and Mrs. Humphrey Ward, who writes
> . . . Lady Curzon and the duchess of Manchester who
> are both American women, quite a perfect party and
> lovely weather too. . . .

From my remote outpost I saw that my mother moved now
in a world that boarding-school girls only dreamed of, and
she'd seen for herself what became of the American heiresses
who'd married titles.

Dropping these splendid names at St. Mary's would have
proved fatal. But Rose was safe and so was her mother. In
her innocence Mrs. Conklin assumed that West Dean Park
and Welbeck Abbey and Nevill Holt engraved on the statio-
nery were hotels instead of the stately homes they were.
When Mother mentioned she'd been one of four hundred
guests at Chatsworth, Mrs. Conklin pointed out that the
Palace Hotel right here in San Francisco rented out twice that
many rooms.

I was only a little wiser and must have thought this distant highroad my mother traveled now would never cross my path. Certainly she was far from my mind when first I fell in love.

It happened in a predictably improbable way. On my weekends with the Conklins I'd taken to going off on my own. Rose wasn't the kind of friend who clings, and after years of boarding school, we liked a little solitude. I went about the city with my sketchpad, liking the heights where the views were best. I liked Telegraph Hill best of all.

It rose a stone's throw from the heart of the city at the top of Chinatown. Yet it seemed countrified and miles away. Once it had been "Signal Hill" with a semaphore at the top to announce the arrival of the sailing ships. When the city built around it, only the hardy and the poor dragged the lumber up to build their shanties on squatters' land.

There was nothing at the top but frame cottages like miners' shacks with perhaps a pane of purple glass in the attic window for style. Everything was on a slant, and the houses stood buckling above sheer drops. Volunteer nasturtiums and tin cans rambled down the ravines in jungles of undergrowth.

Beyond all this casual squalor were the finest, longest views anywhere, over bay and city and through the Golden Gate to the sea. It was always summertime at the top. I had a dozen sunny corners where I could sit on the ground and prop my drawing pad to sketch and dream.

One of my favorite spots was against a board fence up where Filbert Street narrows to a high, winding path. There I created a dream city with minarets for romance and wide clear-glass windows to catch the sunset. This was my private place where I sat drawing with my back against the warm planks. Then, once, from just on the other side of the high fence I heard a baritone voice richly reciting a Wallace Irwin verse in ripest Irish brogue:

> O Telygraft Hill she sits proud as a queen
> And th' docks lie below in the glare
> And th' bay runs beyant'er all purple and green
> Wid th' ginger-bread island out there,

And th' ferry boats toot at owld Telygraft Hill,
And th' Hill it don't care if they do
While the Bradys and Caseys av Telygraft Hill
Joost sit there enj'yin' th' view.

When there was nothing more to hear, I realized I was
being watched. I looked up, with only time to cover my
sketch. A head thrust over the fence and a face looked
down—festooned with a ginger-colored mustache over a grin
broken in the middle and crooked at the corners. It was a
square and craggy young face with a mop of gingery hair to
soften it.

He propped himself on the fence. His shirtsleeves were
rolled above his elbows, and his bare arms were muscled and
paint-spattered. "Ah, the young architectural lady again, I
see."

I'd been discovered. Worse yet, I'd been watched before,
and through a fence. I staggered up, and the drawing pencils
slithered away into tall grass. My feet meant to flee, but that
would mean turning from him. I looked down my starchy
shirtwaist to consult my watch with exaggerated care. I felt
all the wrinkles in my sat-upon skirt.

I was sinking fast, and he was saying, "Step into my
parlor, as the spider says. There's a gate around front and
coffee on the boil."

"I couldn't," the boarding-school girl murmured. But I
could, and did.

And often again at every opportunity. His name was Joe
Fletcher, and he wasn't an Irishman. The brogue had only
been for the poem. He was a farm boy from Bedford, Indiana,
with the flat ring of those hills in his voice.

He'd called me the young architectural lady, but he was an
architect in fact, a graduate of the University of California,
which he put himself through. He hadn't found a firm to hire
him, so he kept body and soul together as a painter. He
painted portraits and stencils above chair rails and menu
covers and murals for saloons. He had paint under his fingernails and splotches of chrome yellow on the elbows of his

best and only jacket. He had plans in his head and the future
at his feet and he'd noticed me. He was twenty-one and thus
four years older.

Mrs. Conklin approved of my beau, who came for Sunday
dinners with his hair slicked down. Rose and I commissioned
one of his minor works. Her mother deplored Mr. Conklin's
tobacco habit, and so Joe painted a quick portrait of her
inside the lid of Mr. Conklin's cigar box. When he opened it
to reach for a Havana, there was his wife's face, staring
straight at him more in sorrow than in anger.

I was so much a part of the Conklin family that Joe took
me for a distant relative. To salve my conscience I spoke
offhandedly of an actual aunt and uncle elsewhere in the
wilds of the Western Addition. But I didn't tell him then who
my mother was. The first time I'd been able to deny her, I
had.

Joe worked in his shed on Telegraph Hill. His easel and a
drafting board deep in blueprints were there, but he lived in
rooms down below in North Beach among a jumble of spa-
ghetti parlors and churches with saints' names.

Here life was lived in the streets. Vegetables were sold at
the curb, and the laundry flapped from house to house over
our heads. Girls walked arm in arm with young men, and Joe
crooked his elbow for me to do the same. At St. Mary's,
we'd been grilled in ladylike behavior, but North Beach had
ways of its own, and Joe invited some of my primness to be
gone.

But I was prim still and maybe priggish and wouldn't go to
his rooms in North Beach, though I made very free of the
hilltop shanty that he called his studio. There was a spirit
lamp for coffee and a disreputable old sofa with the springs
coming through.

Once between weekends I left my sketchbook there, as if
by accident. I wanted him to look at my drawings and house
plans, but I hadn't the courage to ask him. He plagued me a
little by seeming not to have noticed them, but he had. At last
we settled on the lumpy sofa, and he went through them,

saying so little at first that I blurted out, "Are they any good? I care, you know. I don't want this just as a . . . pastime."

"I see that."

He was absorbed in my work as I'd hoped he'd be. Still, I had to say, "These houses in my head, Joe—they're not there because I dream of being a housewife. I've never even known that kind of life. I was born in a hotel and grew up in a school." I wanted to make myself so clear to him, or was it to myself?

"I see that too." He might have added that I wasn't as hard to understand as I thought, but he never patronized me, not once. "I see it in your work. Your houses are visions. In fact, they're not homelike enough."

He pointed at a picture I'd drawn, and I saw how stark and forbidding it was. I'd shaved off all the fakery—the gimcracks and gingerbread—but I'd left it cold. It was free of plaster cherubs and Boston ferns, but the result was empty and inhuman.

"You're getting there," he said, looking up at me. "You're halfway there, but you've got to open up your work to let people in. If a house is going to rise off the page, it has to be a place where people want to be. It's shelter, and people want a place where they belong."

It was only the truth, but I'd had no way of hearing talk like this. I expect I'd have believed it even if I hadn't been falling in love with him.

"Come on." He pulled me out of the sofa. "You've been working in a vacuum. You've been trying to reinvent the wheel. Let's go and look at some examples."

We went up Russian Hill where his great teachers at the university, Willis Polk and Bernard Maybeck, were building the first of their revolutionary houses.

"Look right there," he'd say, "really study it." It would be a doorway, free of stained glass and silly false pillars, but it was wide and welcoming too and burnished with a finish that warmed the wood and beckoned you inside. "What does the shingling on that wall remind you of?" he'd ask of simple brown shakes, softened with silver.

"The Pacific," I said, "and driftwood and the fog."

"Yes," he said. "It's a San Francisco house drawing on the colors here and the salt air. It isn't a copy of anyplace else, and yet it's already settled in because we need roots here."

We went from these newest examples to the oldest of all, Mission Dolores down on Sixteenth Street. Here a fortress-church had stood for a century before I was born, but it was as economical and workable as the newest house on Russian Hill.

"The old padres brought their Spain with them, but it's California now," Joe said, and I began to see with his eyes.

I came back from our walks with my mind burning and my hands itching for pencil and paper. "But it's ridiculous to hope for, isn't it? No woman's ever taken a degree in architecture from the university."

"No woman until now," he said. "They'd make it harder for you than for a man, but it won't be impossible unless you let it be. You can do it, Constance."

I wasn't sure. I only saw he thought so.

"You'll have a long row to hoe," he said. "Even if they give you a chance, they'll try to push you toward woman's work: designing kitchens if you're lucky."

I only smiled because I knew that much already.

"Of course, one of these days I'll have my own firm," Joe said, "and I'll be wanting a partner."

A more sensible girl would have taken that for a pipe dream. A more confident one would have found a proposal in it. Gathering my hopes, I took it literally.

I was in love, and I hadn't expected it. At school we looked down on our teachers because they were all spinsters, but there was a spinster lurking in me. I was straight-laced to cover my uncertainty and too brisk, seemingly, to mind not being pretty. I'd cultivated a certain facade to fool my schoolmates and succeeded in awing a few of them. Every young girl needs her masks, but I feared and hoped Joe Fletcher saw through mine.

The best times were when we were alone together in the long Saturday afternoons up on the hill. I sat sketching and watching Joe at his drafting table. I loved watching him work: the flex of his arms under rolled shirtsleeves and the squint of his eyes under the green eyeshade. I loved watching him breathe.

He was always broke, and it never mattered. His friends were the same, seething with ambition and making three meals from one in the little red-wine-and-pasta places off Washington Square. These penniless poets and painters lived from one year to the next for their great event, the Beaux Arts Ball.

I hoped we'd go. It sounded the ideal antidote for life at boarding school, but his friends awed me. They'd all managed to lose their inhibitions somewhere and were given to reciting their own advanced poetry at a moment's notice and displaying their paintings in the park. They'd been to the university too, even some of the girls.

"Don't lay out any money for your costume," Joe said, not looking up from his drawing board. "Nobody does." And so I knew we were going.

"And we'd better get someone for Rose," he said. "It's about time that girl began to unfurl her wings."

Rose was the best possible audience for my accounts of Joe and his friends, but I hadn't succeeded in bringing her along. She was more shy than I was and all too happy to sit up late to hear of my adventures secondhand. She was prettier than I was, but there was no drawing her out.

Somehow, though, I managed to tempt her with the Beaux Arts Ball, but she wouldn't let Joe find her an escort. We ransacked the Conklin household for our costumes. Rose said she wanted to go as a ghost with a sheet over her head and eyeholes cut out. But that was taking modesty too far.

"This is a ball, Rose," I told her, "not Halloween."

Finally, she went as an Old California señorita in Mrs. Conklin's hired girl's best going-out attire. It was a full,

layered skirt edged in flirting lace and a white blouse that
pulled—slightly—off the shoulders and a black mantilla that
she hugged and wrapped to cover her bosom.

I went as a gypsy of sorts, wrapped in the shawl from the
Conklins' piano. Rose daubed my face with brownish
greasepaint, but I was ever the least exotic of creatures. My
eyes weren't gypsy dark or my mother's indescribable turquoise.
They were an indefinite hazel, so we lined them with charcoal and hoped for the best.

I was thin, just before Anna Held made the svelte
fashionable, and I couldn't even pretend to be pretty, not with
a mother as beautiful as mine to linger in my mind and haunt
my nights. But I wanted to be beautiful now, or whatever Joe
Fletcher wanted.

While we made one another up, Rose said, "Will you
marry Joe?" She always gave me too much credit, thinking I
could attain anything I wanted.

"I don't know. I'm going to be an architect."

"A *what*?" Rose inquired.

Joe arrived as a pirate with an eyepatch and a papier-mâché
parrot stuck on his shoulder, and away he bore us with a girl
on each arm. We went first to a preball party at Arnold
Genthe's studio across from the old University Club. There
was a skylight, and the walls were hung with Genthe's extraordinary back-lit photographs. It hadn't occurred to either
Rose or me that photography was an art too. In splendid
black evening clothes among his guests' ridiculous costumes,
the handsome Arnold Genthe led Rose away.

"Let me show you some of my work, Miss Conklin," he
said, taking her tremulous hand. But she was soon back,
breathless and wide-eyed.

The ball was held in the old Mark Hopkins mansion that
I'd been in before, but it was an art school now. Its gaudy old
interiors faded before swirling dancers under bobbing Japan-
ese lanterns, and the orchestra blared "Ta Ra Ra Boom De
Ay!" Joe's friends swept up Rose for nearly every dance, but
she spun back to us like a top. What little I knew of dancing

didn't seem to apply. Here the partners locked each other around waist or neck, weaving and capering in great shows of abandon. My makeup ran in brown rivers, and I trod on Joe's toes time after time, and it was all wonderful.

At the height of this frenzy, a girl whirled past. Her blouse was drawn down to display her fine shoulders, and her partner had wrapped himself in a mantilla to make her laugh. It was Rose, and we were seeing Life. Couples vanished up the grand staircase to the shadows above, but not Joe and I. He was more brother than lover all evening, and that was right too. I was free to dream in his arms of a future I hoped we both foresaw. It seemed too simple, like all miracles.

He brought us home on the cable car, the pirate between the gypsy and the señorita. Exhilarated by the evening, Rose and I were ready to bolt inside like the schoolgirls we were for the pleasure of replaying every moment. Joe opened the front door for us and bowed Rose inside, but he held me back.

"If you can spare Constance for a moment, Rose," he said, "I'd like to make passionate love to her under the porch light." He turned up his eyepatch as if he meant business, and Rose fled.

"Now you've shocked her," I said when we were alone and both my hands were in his. "Was that the point?"

"The point was to give us a little privacy. Next time Rose has an escort of her own, or Rose doesn't go."

His arm was around my waist now. "Next time," I said. "Will there be a lot of them?"

"More than you can count." Our lips were touching now, and kissing. We hadn't kissed before. He'd made us both wait. "All our lives," Joe said.

In that month I graduated from St. Mary's Hall. The place had done its best with us, and its worst, and now it was over. On an ashy-gray May morning we wore our mortarboards and white robes to collect our diplomas. In the afternoon we changed into pastel gowns and worked velvet vine leaves into our hair to commit a Maypole dance.

The Conklins were there, beaming with pride. Mrs. Conklin mothered Rose and me impartially. Then when the punch was being poured, the headmistress drew me aside to give me a cablegram.

It was the lightning bolt that divides the perfectly blue dome of day. A message from my mother, a congratulation I thought. But no. She was sending for me, claiming me in this first moment of freedom. I'd forgotten the perfection of her timing. And I was to start almost at once.

I ran to Joe Fletcher, to his shanty on Telegraph Hill. It seems to me now that I was still wearing the Maypole dress and the vine leaves in my hair. I burst through the door, gasping from the climb, and outrage.

"My mother has sent for me."

He looked up from his drawing board.

"My mother is Eve Waring."

"Yes?" he wasn't much surprised. He seemed maddeningly mature today.

"Well, shall I go—to London?" I was beside myself or I wouldn't have asked that.

"Does she need you?"

"Of course not. She doesn't need anybody." How dense he was. "Do *you* need me?"

The perilous question hung in the air. I tried to see his eyes in the shadow of the green eyeshade. Perhaps he didn't. Perhaps my worst fear was real and no one needed me.

"I want you," he said.

"Then why—"

"Then why not go to your mother," he said, "and then come back to me."

Still, I couldn't catch my breath. "You think I'm too young, don't you? You think I'm too young to do anything but run to my mother the minute she happens to remember me."

"We're both young," Joe said, "and there's plenty of time."

Not at seventeen there isn't. I hung there in the door, out of everyone's reach. "But what if something . . . terrible happens, and I'm kept from coming back?"

"You'll come back to me," Joe said. "I love you."

I went, hoping he was right. I went, answering my mother's summons, over land and sea to London.

TWENTY-NINE

I walked down the gangplank of the old SS *Majestic* into another world. I hadn't expected my mother to meet me at the ship. I remembered enough to know that. But if not she, who? I set one foot on English soil, and the crowds parted. A young man, unquestionably English, stood before me.

His unformed face cried out for a monocle, and there were pouches like soft-boiled eggs beginning beneath his pale eyes. A high Curzon collar did nothing to strengthen his chin. He carried a walking stick caught loosely under his well-tailored arm with the full conviction that it wouldn't fall clattering away.

"Miss Nichols, I believe," he said with numbing assurance. Somehow his soft hat was off his head and in his hand in the least servile of gestures.

He was Lord Guy Carville-Paget. I would come to know that he rejoiced in a string of other Norman names too, and another title to follow upon the death of somebody or other.

I was too green to appreciate how suavely he walked us through the customs barrier and onto the boat train. We had the compartment to ourselves, which meant that a number of empty seats had been purchased. I was at sea still, hardly able to cope with his unchallenging questions. Had I had a calm crossing? Could this in fact be my first trip to England? Did I not need a rug for my knees (in this stifling compartment) to keep the drafts off?

The train screamed and banged all its doors before Lord Guy Carville had quite dealt with my hand luggage and settled himself opposite. By then the pages of an English picture book were fluttering past the windows, but he managed to gain my full attention.

"People think me an awful fool," he said, quite unabashed. "You'll hear such rot talked about me. I hope you won't believe it all. It's just that I'm young."

He was, not more than twenty. I wondered if he shaved, or ever would.

"If you'd . . . tell me a little more about yourself," I ventured. "After all, I'm letting you lead me into unknown country."

Then Guy Carville reproved himself at length for not explaining properly. He was, he said, my mother's "dogsbody," sent to collect me and see me safe to London.

"Eve—your mother—had a matinee or she would have come herself of course."

"Of course."

Guy Carville fingered his collar. "It isn't, you see, quite the thing for me to collect you, but it was by way of being an emergency, don't you see."

I didn't.

"I mean to say, a young lady, unmarried, doesn't travel with a man. She's never alone with a man anywhere, unless he's a relative, which I'm very sorry to say I'm not."

I thought back to those long unchaperoned afternoons on Telegraph Hill with Joe and saw they were out of reach.

"I see. But if we're not to be alone, why do we have this compartment to ourselves?"

Guy looked about as if surprised to find the place untenanted. "Well, you see, it wouldn't do at all if other people were here to observe. It's not what you do; it's the look of it."

"I don't know as I follow the logic of that."

Lord Guy sat back almost relieved. "Oh, my dear Miss Nichols, don't look for logic *here*."

I smiled, helpless. "I think it's very good of you to risk compromising us both to . . . collect me."

"I am one of those," he said, "who'd go to the ends of the earth for Eve Waring. Southampton is nothing."

She'd bidden me over a longer distance than that, so I supposed this was a sort of bond between me and the foolish young man. There were pauses between his explanations. Since they weren't awkward, they might be merely polite.

Or his opportunity to study me. He was capable of it without seeming to. I'd dreaded people who had gazed upon Eve Waring and then looked for her in my face. I'd better be ready to disappoint.

"You're very like Eve, you know," he said.

I blinked at him. "It's all right. Don't be kind."

"No, truly." He edged forward, nodding. "There's something there, perhaps in the determination of the jaw."

Never having thought of my jaw, I found it clenched.

"If my mother and I are at all alike, she must have changed a good deal in four years."

"Eve?" he said. "She never changes. She changes other people."

This was all I'd let myself hear as London roared deafeningly nearer.

On the bewildering platform at Waterloo Station, another figure briefly joined us in this unfolding drama. She'd made her way up from the third-class carriages.

"Please, miss," she said, bobbing without deference, "I am Hoskins." She wore a caped coat dreadfully like mine.

"Your maid," said Lord Guy well below his breath. She rode on the box with the cabby in our journey across London.

"I don't suppose," I said to Guy, "that if . . . Hoskins had ridden in the compartment with us, it would have helped the look of things."

He shook his head wisely. "No use at all. Servants can't chaperon, unless, of course, you haven't worked free of your nanny. But nannies as a rule don't travel—they're like Swiss wines."

I expect my brow beetled. "I see."

He sighed. "That last bit was meant as a joke, you see."

But it was too late to laugh. "But . . . Lord Guy, if

Hoskins can't chaperon and you dealt with my luggage, what was she there for?''

"Ah, a lady never travels without her maid.''

I sank back against the dusty plush seat and decided not to think.

My first recollection of London is of a sign against the sky, picked out in incandescent lights:

EVE WARING
in
Clyde Fitch's
The Moth and the Flame

In a surge of approval that surprised me, I noted that her sign outshone William Gillette's in *Secret Service*.

"She is everywhere you look,'' said Guy, "and her face is for sale in every tobacconist's. There are Eve Waring hats and Eve Waring cloaks, and they are everywhere except on Eve Waring. She is always that step ahead.''

I could nod knowingly at that.

My mother had taken the lease of a house and the furniture with it in Half Moon Street, that back way into Mayfair. It was a Georgian house in a row of them, blank at first look and then elegant. A century of London smoke had darkened and furred the brick to black velvet. Against it, the brasswork at gate and door gleamed from daily polishing under the direction of an austere butler austerely named Blaine. There was a beautifully traced fanlight over the door, and above it the long windows of a drawing room across the width of the house.

Guy led me up to that room, and when I turned back to him in the doorway, he had quite unfoolishly vanished.

My mother stood in the curve of a piano against the far windows. The pale London light slanted about her onto the parquet, leaving her face in shadow. She'd arranged herself there with one hand resting on polished rosewood, her cloud of black hair only a little darker than her obscured face.

I lingered in the doorway, childish again and considering

flight. She stirred and took a step forward, only one. Her
arms opened, but she drew them close again. Her head was
on one side, uncertain or pretending to be. She had never
asked for a photograph, and I'd never sent one. I might be
some other girl sent to announce Constance Nichols's un-
timely death. I wished it were so.

"Can it be Constance?" She strode to center stage, and her
silken skirts sighed, recalling Monterey. She was garbed as a
voluptuous governess. The skirt was dark, and the shirtwaist,
though silvery white taffeta, buttoned high on the neck and
lay in pressed pleats. It was a summer season of flounces and
fripperies and much layered lace, and so she had left herself
untrimmed.

She decided on a little, theatrical laugh, more girlish than
she was, to cover the moment. Because I was slow in
approaching, she put out her hands and clasped mine, but not
to gather me in. Something in the room said we were each to
take a final step to bring us together. We didn't, but she
covered that too, dropping my hands and stepping back to
look at me.

I looked at her. She was more splendid than before, and
surer now. Not older, but more . . . complete. Invincible, I
thought, until I dared look at her remarkable eyes.

"As you see," I said, "I'm quite grown."

"Oh, not quite, surely." She'd planned her smile but had
forgotten her eyes. There was something in them, and I half
read it—a pleading. I felt the tug, and the threat.

"I want you to like it here," she said in a voice like music,
"as much as I do."

But that wasn't what her eyes begged for, nothing that
easy.

"So many people want to meet you," she said. Though
they would have terrified me, I wished they were all here in
the room this minute, passing between us, releasing us from
one another. Oh, how I wished it.

"You must make a very long . . . visit. You must stay."

"Until the fall," I said. "Then I want to go back and—"

"Oh, longer than that." She urged me with her eyes, but she looked through me into a future.

"Until the winter then."

"Must I bargain with you?" she said as if she made bargains.

"A year," I said, "and then I—"

"Ah," she said, almost enfolding me, "then you'll be someone else."

THIRTY

In that golden summer of 1898 God, an Englishman, was in His heaven and my American mother reigned below.

She had aimed impossibly high and succeeded—not to have her face sold over tobacconists' counters, but to be accepted in the world's highest and mightiest society. She had come from mountains, but this was her peak to scale. I didn't like to think what more she could want for fear it involved me.

Yet it was impossible to think clearly about myself in her presence. I was meant to think of her, and I did. She had her wits about me.

This exquisite woman had turned all her disadvantages to account. She was a foreigner in this insular, self-anointed society. Her beginnings were more than obscure in a tight circle turning upon background and family. Somewhere she had learned to be a hard-bitten businesswoman though women were not supposed to know what money was. She was a woman alone too, among women whose sole achievement lay in having made the right match. She was even unforgivably beautiful.

But driven to find them, she had discovered two strengths within herself that amounted to weapons. I'd glimpsed them both before. Now I saw them put to use. Praised for her air of mystery on and off the stage, my mother could make a convincing show of disarming frankness. The English always admired blunt candor if it cost them nothing.

I well remember a dinner party given by Mr. and Mrs.

Hwfa Williams. The topic turned to Mrs. John Mackay as it often did. She was the wife of the Nevada silver king, holding forth now in her Carlton House Terrace mansion and ludicrously grand. Mrs. Mackay suffered more than her share from slanders about her past. A minor charge was that she'd once been a laundress before she snared John Mackay for his money. There were other rumors worse, but this one was repeatable between the sexes, and so it persisted at parties.

My mother spoke out against it, stilling the table. "I grew up in Virginia City where Louise Mackay lived," she said, "and if she'd taken in washing, she'd have had no need to marry money. Washerwomen commanded exorbitant wages and were liable to come to work wearing diamond brooches."

Mother's glance slid briefly to the many carats nestled in the cleavage of Lady Londonderry.

The table stirred at this word of such deliciously American barbarism. "But, my dear," someone said, "did your people actually know the Mackays?"

Mother shook her head. "They were very prominent at Virginia, and we were nobody in particular."

A bracing pall descended, quenching all fires. Mother had championed her fellow countrywoman, and as always, at her most forthright, she'd revealed nothing of herself. A minor triumph, but they added up.

There was that other quality in her too: She'd translated her essential loneliness into something that looked like insolent nonchalance.

While Mother was an actress and couldn't deny it, she seemed to pass off her spectacular career as the casual pastime of a mildly gifted amateur. If she'd burned with artistic zeal, she might at best have been invited in to perform after dinner. Worse, she might even have been paid. She'd learned a careless pose from the English, and used it against them.

The marchioness of Ripon had declared, admiringly, "Eve Waring doesn't give a damn about the stage," and such a pronouncement from such a personage made everything all right.

You could of course buy a ticket to see her on the stage

(unless you were her daughter), but that was presumably some other woman up there behind a careful mask of makeup.

Strange how little credit she allowed herself when the playwright Pinero credited her with the success of his *Sweet Lavender* and *The Benefit of the Doubt*. Years after her heyday, the memory of her roles in *Lady Windermere's Fan* and *An Ideal Husband* kept Wilde's works bright while dimming the repute of many another actress.

Even on matinee days she was at home by five o'clock, presiding behind a silver pot. In these high circles, no husband took tea with his own wife, but a horde of husbands applied to Mother at teatime. She held this court against a screen of American Beauty roses, each clump sent by an inspired admirer who thought himself original. There was rarely a chair to spare for Lord Guy.

She was no more a woman's woman than she had been, but in the matter of female friends, she made some judicious choices. On some afternoons, all men were barred, and she sat over cucumber sandwiches with her fellow American, Lady Randolph Churchill, who came down from Great Cumberland Place for a gossip.

Lady Randolph was a great beauty too, and wise. I remember glancing into the room to see them together, their richly glossed dark heads close in the exchange of some scheme or scandal. These two Amazons had both conquered London, but Lady Randolph had conquered first, and so perhaps my mother was learning more than she was sharing.

She cited Winston, Lady Randolph's elder son, to me, extolling him: "No money there," she'd say, "but such a lot of brains. And what a lot of good his mother is doing his career."

But in the unlikely event that he could be made to notice me, Winston Churchill struck me as pompous and a thought short on personal charm. At parties I'd heard him—you could hear him at a great distance—lecturing the company on the need to put down the Boers for the sake of Empire.

Though Mother performed six nights a week, she went on to dinner parties, arriving necessarily late with the air of a lazy, luxurious woman who'd dawdled over her dressing table. She dropped like a panther on glittering rooms where hope flared in the hearts of quite elderly men, and died in the eyes of their wives.

If I thought she was too intent upon herself to take me seriously in hand, I was very much mistaken. She had great plans for me and no taste for failure. I was to be made over into a young Englishwoman, with prospects. I was to be married off and married off well, and I was to be settled in England, the only place that counted. If she couldn't show her love, she was ready and willing to exercise her power.

Naively, I'd thought a grown daughter, and a plain one, would embarrass her. But I only accentuated her own ageless-ness and beauty. The process of my transformation began undemandingly enough, and I was never given the chance to rebel. She never issued commands; she simply caused events to occur.

It was at first largely a matter of clothes. Mother, who cared nothing for them, was a fashion plate now. But dress was always a uniform for her, if not armor outright. All her evening gowns were cut from the same simple pattern, leav-ing her unbejeweled arms and shoulders bare and burnished with their coppery inner glow. Bustles were passé now, and she'd eliminated trains. Her skirts were sculpted at the knee to turn in a slow swirl onto the floor in a line that faintly recalled a Beardsley drawing. Many another matron came to grief by trying to have them copied, and by wearing the copy. Everything she wore was attributed to Worth. In fact, all her dresses were run up by a nameless dressmaker who arrived at Half Moon Street in a closed cab.

She wouldn't share this anonymous miracle-worker with me. I was sent out to spend long days at dressmakers and milliners along Bond Street. It got me out from underfoot and occupied my time in the mindless way appropriate for a young lady. I was attended doggedly by Hoskins.

In novels of high life, maids were their young ladies' confidential confederates, but Hoskins was a figure from real life—Hoxton, in fact. Her single facial expression was a pursing of the lips, and her terse conversation was limited to, "I couldn't say, miss, I'm sure." Evidently I was to be severe with her, and she was showing me how.

I'd have preferred a little companionship, but the Half Moon Street staff were massed militarily under the wooden butler, Blaine, and took all their commands from him. There was a cook who never came out of the kitchens, two parlor maids who scuttled at my approach, and a woman who came in to do the heavy work and did it without taking off an uncompromising straw hat. But Hoskins was all mine, or I was all hers.

I found I couldn't fill my days with shopping. Hoskins and I would sometimes end up as far afield as the British Museum or St. Paul's. Somehow, I hadn't dared to take up my sketchpads, but at St. Paul's or Westminster Abbey I'd scribble a little architectural detail on the back of an envelope I meant to send to Joe. Keeping my hand in, I did some light sketching while Hoskins bristled behind me, refusing to settle into a pew. She may have taken the dimmest view of making drawings in a church. She may have taken a dim view of the Church of England. I was never to know. Dealing with Hoskins as a fellow human being was a losing game. Finally, I was forced to know that there's no need for communication with the better sort of servant.

Mother's hairdresser, who was as impenetrably French as Hoskins was implacably English, dealt with my hair. It was put up at last. Not only was it mouse-brown, it wasn't nearly full enough to rise in oceans of waves to the necessary high knot. The hairdresser did her grumbling best with pads and wires to provide fullness and height. I went about strangely extended as if a bomb had detonated in my vicinity.

I went about a great deal because my mother saw to it that I was invited everywhere a young girl could go. I needed tea gowns and evening gowns and enormous hats for my enormous hair. Since this was the summer that the future king of England took his first perilous drive in a motorcar, all females were provisioned with linen dusters and motoring veils, and even goggles.

In its way this narrow world of endless rules was wider than the one I'd left. In distant America a young woman "bowed" at her debut, going nowhere before this formal introduction. In England girls tumbled directly from the nursery to the ballroom floor, prized for their ignorance, which was meant to bespeak virginity.

"No one will expect you to say anything of any consequence," Mother said.

She worried that I'd become a "bluestocking" and might bore dinner partners with my intellect.

"It's my own fault," she remarked when Guy was with us to keep the tone light. "I should never have sent Constance to school—like a boy."

But she was only being English. There a carefully brought-up girl didn't go to school, where her thighs might thicken from games and her mind be twisted by suffragette spinsters who would kill her matrimonial chances.

No one inquired into my intellect when Mother sent me out upon the social waters, expecting me to float.

In those rarefied rooms that wiser people than I had fought to enter, I sat dazed by grandeur and monotony and ptarmigan pie. When the table grew heated and brilliant over the Irish Question or What to Do about the Boers, I let my eye wander over Adam fireplaces and dadoes carved by Grinling Gibbons. I stared glassily through Palladian arches to Canova's statuary in classical niches, and dreamed of houses on San Francisco hills.

I met no one my age. Mother steered me to dinner parties made up of the eminent and the noble. But they all seemed elderly to me. The eminent had lived long enough to achieve, and the noble to inherit.

Because she was late or had gone elsewhere, I often went on my own, which seems strange now. A man must see me in to dinner, but I couldn't arrive with him unless I meant to be engaged to him before we got there. Hoskins, my watchdog, delivered me to the butlers of great houses in St. James and Belgravia, and there I was at the mercy of hostesses. The kind ones gathered me in. The others merely motioned me into rooms of blank faces.

I was expected not only to survive but to come home and report. If she hadn't joined the party, Mother was at home, waiting. Guy Carville was generally there too, even at this hour when gentlemen didn't call. Mother required him as an escort when there was no one else, and this chaste role gave him long hours. A room began to feel unfurnished without him. His presence ceased to annoy me, but no daughter can fully forgive a young man for being in love with her mother.

In those midnights she began to learn a bitter truth that any more experienced mother could have warned her of. What was important to her was simply not important to me. I didn't distinguish between a younger son and an elder son. I never knew which viscount would become a duke and which wouldn't. I barely knew Sir Ernest Cassel from Cecil Rhodes, and I didn't know a Conservative hostess from a Liberal. I was hopeless and took a secret pleasure in it.

After one long day when there'd been a garden party that gave way to two teas followed by a dinner, I recalled coming home twice to change, from white to pink to lavender, but my mind was otherwise blank.

"Yes, but who *gave* the garden party?" Mother asked, heaving with impatience.

The name was on the tip of my tongue.

"Marie Corelli was there," I offered, "with a lapdog." I was suddenly aware of Guy. "A real dog, I mean, in her arms. And the poet—Le Gallienne would it be? He was there, and so was Shaw. And Harold Frederic."

"Literary," Mother said, her hand pinching her chin. "Mrs. T. P. O'Connor, was it?"

It was.

"And who took you in to dinner?" she asked, skating over teatime.

Dinner had been an ordeal. "A very muscular man who lectured me on the subject of good wickets—right through from the melon glacé to the Caroline glacé."

Guy stirred.

"Cricket player?" Mother raised a famous eyebrow at him. "Not C. B. Fry?" Guy said.

"Yes, that's who," I said.

He buried his small pink face in his hands. Apparently I'd been in the company of celebrity and hadn't properly appreciated it.

"Nobody else made a fuss over him," I said, idiotically in my own defense.

"No, Constance," Mother said bleakly, "they wouldn't."

In such moments she wasn't Lady Windermere's mother; she was mine, a far less rewarding role. And though this was a brief interlude of reality, she continued to speak to me across almost visible footlights. Her voice rang unwaveringly, but she worked her hands and paced. Her studied grace began to forsake her, and little awkwardnesses crept in when I'd driven her near her limits.

On that night or another like it, she trusted herself to say no more and retired for the night. I followed her out into the hall to unhook her as usual, but she absentmindedly let me return to Guy. He was only halfway through a brandy, and lingered on. After all, the servants were in their beds, and they were the public most easily shocked.

I dropped onto the divan across from him and fetched up a moan. "It's all so *meaningless*."

"Not to your mother," Guy said.

"Why is what she wants so much more important than anything else?"

Sensibly, he left that unanswered and studied the brandy in the balloon.

"I believe I should just tell her outright. I have a young man at home, and I'm not interested in—"

"She knows about your young man."

Of course she knew. I'd come armed with a picture of Joe and planted it on the stand beside my bed. It was a photograph taken by our friend, Arnold Genthe. Joe was posed in a soft shirt open at the neck. There was both the farm boy and the artist about him, with a glint of the visionary in his eye. It wasn't inscribed. He wasn't given to written endearments as his letters were proving. But he was my young man whether Mother deigned to notice or not. I rushed home every night to be greeted by him, and to reassure him. I wrote him detailed letters, and more frivolous ones to Rose Conklin. I clung to them both.

"Are you engaged or anything like that?" Guy never put a personal question. When I looked up, he seemed not even to have spoken. His small chin hung in space, and he stared aside.

"Not exactly. Where I come from young women aren't— sold on an auction block to perfect strangers. We take the trouble, and the time, to get acquainted first and to find— common ground. We marry for love, not advantage. Most of us."

"Barbaric," said Guy, though his tongue was in his cheek.

"I'll tell you something more barbaric," I said. "I mean to enter a university when I go home and take a degree. Me, a worthless female. Think of it!"

"Monstrous," Guy said mildly.

"I have a good mind to march up the stairs and tell her I'm leaving on the next boat. Things can only get worse."

"Ah, I shouldn't want to see you do anything like that. It would make both you and your mother unhappy. Then I should be made to be unhappy."

"Then what would you have me do?" I began to heave with impatience until I realized I was copying . . . her.

"I should think your best course is to find some suitable man here at one of these parties just as you are meant to do—good family, that sort of thing, and—"

"Fall in love with him?" I said, immensely disgusted.

Guy's pale eyebrows rose. "Seem to fall in love with him, perhaps. Rather gradually . . ."

I was brought up short by this piece of female guile. "I see," I said. "Pretend to play along. But how long can I—"

"For as long as you are here." Guy appeared so detached, so . . . innocent that again he might not have spoken at all except that he looked rather pleased with himself.

"That's clever," I said, half meaning it.

"It's damn clever," Guy said, "come to that." He straightened himself and set his brandy glass aside. "I told you that first day in the train, dear Constance, that I was thought a fool. I didn't mean an utter fool."

He was rising to go.

"But, Guy, you're the only Englishman I know," I said mischievously. "I don't suppose—"

"Me?" he said. I'd expected him to color alarmingly, but he only waved the notion away. "I wouldn't do at all. You need someone your mother will take seriously."

That was rather sad if one thought about it, but I was thinking of myself. "But how shall I choose?" I asked him. "All Englishmen are alike to me. They all dress as waiters and talk of nothing but good wickets and murdering birds. How will I know a suitable one from the other sort?"

He was on his feet now and sighing one of his sighs. "You will be given no trouble there. The suitable ones are all quite unlike me."

THIRTY-ONE

It was a summer of perfect weather, or so it was always to seem. The Thames shimmered with kingfishers above Boveney Loch, and white clouds thick as sheep grazed the deep blue heavens.

England basked in the afterglow of old Queen Victoria's Jubilee Year. Bunting in Union Jack colors lingered on lamp posts in this blazing noon of a great empire that ruled the world and saw no omens though the sunsets were blood-red.

I resisted its allure all I could, sending letters like lifelines back to Joe and to Rose. I contemplated Guy's plan too, the scheme to find myself a phantom lover to fill the time and draw my mother's fire. And then I found him.

Drawing me deeper into a plan of her own, Mother deputized me to stand in for her on official occasions. To the disappointment of the assembled crowds, I appeared in Eve Waring's place to open some charity bazaar, some sale of work, some fete to provide milk for slum children. If London theatrical people were behind the charity, Mother stood aloof and sent a check. When it was an event where a society figure was more welcome than an actress, she went. She accepted more than she could manage, and then I played the role, learning how to cut ribbons with a gloved hand.

After one of these harrowing occasions, I went on with Hoskins grim and uncomplaining at my side to the duchess of Manchester's garden party. My mother was somewhat mysteriously away for the day as she often was, but she made sure of my invitation.

The hostess was not only a duchess, she was an American: once Consuelo Iznaga of New York. Mother never lost an opportunity to point out the prospects for an American woman with the sense to act upon them.

A very smart barouche bristling with footmen met the train at Windsor. We rode in this style to the house the duchess had taken for the season. It stood in gardens sloping down to a screen of trees beside the river. When we drew up, Hoskins was led away between two footmen, like a rather distinguished prisoner, to a servants'-hall tea. I was received with less pomp.

Consuelo Manchester stood on no ceremony, looking me over and keeping comparisons with my mother to herself. She'd been bewitching and was still blond, with an arch expression on her durable face to cover all occasions.

As a hostess, she was rather vague, and I soon found myself strolling the grounds where the other guests were in tight knots. At least the gardens were lovely and the day lovelier, and I was used to looking on. I'd have been content but for my too-grand fund-raising hat which was overbearing and badly anchored.

Somehow I found myself on a knoll above the tennis lawn where a man was displaying an expert backhand in a casual match. I was never to recall his opponent, but Margot Asquith was there just off the field of play, trying to capture his attention and put him off his game.

His open collar displayed a strong, sunburned neck, and his shirtsleeves were rolled high on his arms, making me think of Joe though they were nothing alike.

He was tall and broad-shouldered with the kind of astounding good looks that owed more to Richard Harding Davis than to my Joe Fletcher. His square jaw was like a line drawing. His teeth flashed white in the sun when he laughed, easily and with a little twist of irony.

To the manner born, I thought, *and almost too good to be true:* just right as a red herring to draw across my mother's path if I could only learn his name and a fact or two to drop in her hearing.

How I meant to carry off being in love with a complete stranger, I don't know. I may have thought unrequited love would serve, that I might languish of it and be sent home. It wasn't the sort of scheme that warrants thinking through.

I drank lemonade on the fringes of a straw-hatted group discussing the University Boat Race. Then I strolled down along a trail like a towpath between the river and the trees. It would have served me right to stumble upon my phantom lover entwined with Margot Asquith under a bush. Instead, like a page from an Ouida novel, he stepped up beside me. He towered over me and fell into step. My plan took flight, and I nearly went with it.

"Miss Nichols?"

I looked up, pretending to see him for the first time. Extraordinary how handsome he was up close. He wore a cream flannel blazer now. His straw boater rode at a carelessly precise angle.

"Mr. . . . ?"

"Drummond. Hugh Drummond."

I made a mental note of the name. "Has our hostess sent you to rescue me?"

"Consuelo isn't known for having the life preservers thrown out, but she may just have mentioned your name in passing."

I decided to stroll on, slowly. There were dips in the path, and Hugh Drummond's hand at my elbow to guide me.

"As we haven't met before," he said, "we must both be outsiders."

"You? I'd have thought you were at the heart of—wherever you are."

"As it happens, I'm just now back in England. I don't suppose you'd care to hear my life history?"

"As it happens, I would, though I'd rather not tell you why."

He gave me his history, or parts of it, with the kind of self-dismissal convincing only in an Englishman. He'd set out to be a soldier, First Battalion of the Scots Guards, but had found it an idle life. Since then, he'd guided hunters over the Serengeti Plain and across the Dakotas, tried his hand at farming in the Cape Colony, and worked as crew on a whaler out of Lahaina in the "Sandwich Islands."

"The Hawaiians, you mean," I said.

"Yes, the Sandwich Islands, as I say." Then betraying slight surprise: "You're American?"

"Intensely. You're not going to say I'm not a bit like the Americans, are you? That's never the compliment it's meant to be."

"I'm not going to say it *now*," Hugh Drummond said, "but you caught me just in time."

"I'm so glad of that," I murmured.

And I was glad again a day or two later when the box of flowers that arrived at Half Moon Street was from Hugh Drummond. I took a time arranging them and left his card among the stems. They were American Beauty roses.

Unwilling to rock the boat, my mother seemed not to take notice. But on that very day Lady Randolph was there with her in the afternoon, their dark heads close and conspiring. When I drew nigh, they waved me away.

I went about my business, for at last I had some. There'd been a note among the roses along with the card, Hugh inviting me to the theater. I wired back my acceptance and wedged his note into my looking-glass frame should prying eyes wish to read it.

"The theater?" my mother said, alarmed. She feared Hugh might be taking me to see *her*.

"A musical at the Royal Strand, I believe. *The Belle of New York*."

"Oh, that's all right then," she said. "And who's the young man?"

I told her, sober as a judge, though Mother would know more about him by now than I did.

"Nice?"

"A gentleman adventurer," I said, more airy than she. "Rugged, but refined. I don't know what his prospects are," I added.

Her mouth opened and closed again. She'd been about to tell me.

Then, between us, we staged a scene I hadn't meant. I might have known that any plan of mine would be shaped by my mother.

On the evening Hugh called for me, he sent me more flowers. I went the distance of wearing them in my hair where I willed them to stay. My gown was of two shades of oleander, lace over satin. It was the year "natural" figures were meant to emerge. The natural figure, though, was seen as slightly swayback, and I was ramrod straight. I've always suffered from this stiffness, as if I were bracing myself against . . . I don't know what. Never sure about such matters, I hoped the dress was the right compromise between demure and seductive.

When I heard Blaine open the front door, I flew to the head of the stairway. Hugh was there below, twice as handsome in black evening clothes as he'd been in tennis whites. Faltering a little, I descended half the stairs, trailing lace.

"Will you have a drink before we go?"

He would, and then it happened as I might have foreseen.

When we entered the drawing room, Mother, who should have been at the theater by now, was there at the far end against the windows. I'd seen the pose before but not the dress. It was another of her absolutely plain ones, in black crepe since this was the season of summer pastels. It clung at her breast and again at her hip and made that sensational turn at the knee. The lamplight, low in the room, drew out all the dusky velvet beneath the smooth flesh of her arms and shoulders. She stood as if on a pedestal, and the color of her eyes was visible across the room.

I was speechless with rage, though I couldn't think why since their meeting promoted my plan.

Hugh was merely speechless. I hadn't thought to see that controlled jaw drop. "Good Lord!" he said. "Eve Waring."

"Have you met my mother, Hugh?"

"Your . . . ? No . . . I haven't had that pleasure, though . . . of course . . . everybody . . . ''

The sight of an Englishman this nonplussed and outflanked was all one could wish for, all that Mother could wish for. She strode across the room in that straightforward, almost masculine way. Hugh stirred himself and moved to meet her, taking her hand.

She could have seduced him on the spot, and I rather wished she would. I'd have thrown any number of human sacrifices to her to win my own freedom, and how much I wanted my freedom at that moment.

But she was as little seductive with him as she could well be. She was playing Mother with stately restraint. The expression in her eyes was direct, not dreamy. She seemed to assess his good intentions toward her daughter without staking him out for herself. She'd never vie for a man with any woman, and certainly not with me.

But still they seemed to merge, these two larger-than-life ebony figures, like silhouettes cut from black paper. In their decorous sparring they stood near to each other, walling me out.

Dear God, I thought, how terrible if I were in love with him.

After the theater we went on to supper at Kettner's in Soho. It was a mildly risqué place with private dining rooms upstairs, like the notorious old Poodle Dog in San Francisco. But we were seated safely on the main floor surrounded by crowds of the overdressed. The show at the Royal Strand had been all swirling skirts and blaring music. My head still buzzed with it.

"Did you enjoy the show?" Hugh asked me.

"I did. I think I did. I've never been to a play before unless you count school productions with girls taking all the parts."

"Never? Surely you've seen your mother's performances."

My gaze fell to a fork I was straightening on the tablecloth. "Never on the stage."

"But why not?"

"She's never allowed it. It's always been strictly forbidden, and seemed to carry over to theater in general. I've felt wicked and corrupt all evening.''

"Astonishing," Hugh said, though somehow an Englishman never looks very astonished. "I was about to suggest we go see her in the Pinero thing one night, *The Second Mrs. Tanqueray*. I've been once already and wanted to see her again.''

I gave him a brave smile, but he didn't heed it.

"She's awfully good, you know. There's no one like her.''

"I know.''

He planted elbows on the table and worked his hands together. "She absolutely dominates the stage—''

"And this table.''

He flinched and pulled back. "I'm sorry. That was thoughtless.''

"Not very," I said. "In time I'll get used to hearing my mother praised, but not just yet. We've lived apart.''

"And now?''

"I'd never thought she had time for me. Now that she does, I'm finding it hard to cope with. She'd like to arrange my life for me, and I'd prefer to arrange it for myself.''

"Will you?''

"I mean to try.''

"I believe you're very fond of her," Hugh said.

"I admire her strengths, but I don't have them. I'm going to have to find my own.''

"I believe you're fonder of her than you'll admit.''

Because he was too wise, I turned the conversation away, and he told me of his adventures. He had the gift of bringing far places near: rain forests and frail ships leaving trails of smoke across empty oceans, and Mandalay that I thought was only a name in a song.

He had a way of standing apart from his own adventures, not above, but beside. I knew that Englishmen were never seen to boast even when they did. But far from boasting, Hugh seemed detached from a world where he'd grown worldly. It was as if he stood at the edge of his own life, and that was something I could understand. He seemed to be without vanity, hard to credit in a man that handsome.

"And were you never in love?" I asked him. It was rather pathetically coquettish for me, but he brought that sort of thing to the surface by merely being there.

"Sixteen times by actual count. Three times on the same night in Yokohama. Or was it Singapore. And you?"

I could parry and thrust too, or try to. "I believe I'm supposed to be in love with you. Here I am a young girl having her first London season, and I find myself quite unchaperoned. My m—a certain person has thrown me at your head."

He rested his chin in his hand. "She may have thought I was too old to pose a threat. Twenty-eight my next birthday."

"Decrepit," I said, "but dangerous still." Then the waiter intervened with the first of many courses in this light supper, and we were spared more sparring for the moment.

"Why have you come back to England?" I asked him later. "If I were as free as a man, I'd—"

"You'd be less impressed with that freedom than you are. Have you never been homesick?"

"Every minute I'm away from San Francisco. Maybe not this very minute, but all the others."

"I missed home too. Scones for tea, good English ale, cubbing in the autumn, and—Nanny up in her attic knitting proper stout school socks."

"Truly?"

"In the attic of every Englishman's mind there's still a Nanny knitting socks. It's an article of faith, like 'Land of Hope and Glory' and chilblains."

"Curious people, you English."

"Mad as hatters, every one of us. But you'll fit in here once you're cured of your youthful seriousness."

"Don't patronize me," I said. "I have a mother for that. Tell me why you came home. Was it to take a wife or a job?"

Hugh glared in mock horror. "Nothing so enterprising. No

. . . I've come home to catch my breath and enjoy myself, before things change.''

"How will they change?''

"Surely you've heard the talk. War's coming. Europe's sickened and surfeited with peace. They're rattling sabers at a great rate now. Even old Joe Chamberlain's reversed himself and gone all imperial. And young Winston, of course.''

"But why?''

"Oh, the reasons are there, but they can't be mentioned. War will fire an economy that seems to be going nowhere. And it will put the lower orders in their place. Have you any idea how much the rich and powerful in this country fear the poor? They're so terrified of revolution they dare not breathe the word. A war looks like an ideal solution, quick and glorious, into the fray against a common foe.''

"How awful,'' I said. "And who will be the foe, Germany?''

"Not while Queen Victoria lives. She's pro-German to the core, and the kaiser's her grandson. No, Germany won't do, this time. If it isn't the Irish, it'll be the Boers in the Transvaal.''

"But isn't there a way—''

"No one wants a way out, Constance. Everyone expects to win.''

"What will you do when it comes?''

"Take back my commission in the Guards, I expect.''

"That's just what I don't understand about men. Why stand and fight in a pointless war when you could—''

"Run from it?''

"Yes, run from it. And *live*, and make your life count instead of squandering it. Women want to do things with their lives, things that matter, and we're told it's not our place. But men throw away—all their advantages.''

He smiled and shook his head. "You're more militant than I am, Constance. I'll make a half-hearted soldier at best. I'm a little cynical, a little old. Far better to be a nineteen-year-old subaltern again who thinks war's heaven and himself invulnerable. But you see if I went to the ends of the earth, there'd still be newspapers there, full of war news and casualty lists with one's friends on them.''

"I still don't understand," I said, fuming. "I don't even want to."

"Let's talk of something else then," Hugh said. "I want to make the most of the time before I have to see my tailor about altering my old uniform to fit this sagging figure.''

And so after all he was vain, a bit. His figure was perfect.

"How do you plan to make the most of the time?''

"Not in riotous living. There'll be enough of that later. I mean to be very country-squirish, as squirish as one can be in town. The Guards are posted back in London now, you see, and I'm already the old war horse beginning to paw the ground. I'll hole up here and view with alarm the war hysteria until it claims me.

"But I mean to hole up in exceedingly comfortable quarters and read ancient, dull books, and acquire an old red dog to lie at my feet, and perhaps even a smoking jacket.''

"Are you ever completely serious?" I asked him.

"I am never really anything else, Constance, but it doesn't do to show it, does it?''

Then the evening was over, too soon it seemed. And when I ascended the stairs at Half Moon Street, I found myself floating.

THIRTY-TWO

The quarters where Hugh Drummond meant to make himself exceedingly comfortable were in a Mayfair mews, tucked away off Hertford Street. It was a curiously rustic old barn lurking at an angle between newer buildings at the back of a cobblestoned yard. He took me there one day to see it.

He'd taken me somewhere every day, and another box of flowers arrived each morning. I floated still and tried to ignore the hat pin jab of conscience. Finally, I had to turn Joe Fletcher's picture to the wall to spare him the sight of me bursting breathless into my room.

My mother was massively discreet. Hugh Drummond must be a better catch than I knew, for she smoothed the way with much accommodating silence. A more practiced mother would have put a roadblock or two in my way, to spur me on.

Hugh and I went everywhere. He knew everyone, and had been born knowing them. While my mother poured from her silver teapot for Lord Curzon and George Wyndham and Lord Esher and the melancholy Lord Rosebery, Hugh took me one afternoon to a livelier tea party at the flat of the beautiful young American actress Ethel Barrymore. She met us at the door wearing a wreath of bronzed leaves in her luxuriant hair. Edna May was there, and Ellen Terry who charmed me nearly to tears by remembering my father. Ethel's schoolboy brother, Jack, was there too, lingering in the doorway agonized by shyness. I hadn't known theater people were such good company, and so kind.

Like young Jack Barrymore, I'd lingered in doorways,

rigid with shyness, but now the doors yawned wide when I entered on Hugh Drummond's arm. I saw too the envy in the faces of girls far prettier than I.

He took me to see his quarters in the mews that he hoped to make livable. The place was as old as time and filthy as a sty. It must have begun as a barn in an open field in the days of the Globe Theatre when London lay well to the east. Later someone had made a misbegotten attempt to turn the place into a sort of bachelor's hall.

Floorboards were laid over stone or the earth itself, and behind curtains of cobweb was paneling, dry now and thirsty for polish. An honest hayloft had been turned into a fake minstrel's gallery with a low balustrade and tapestries now tattered. The only light fell from broken windows set high above this balcony, for the barn was tightly wedged between buildings on either side, and the front was still blank barn doors.

Hugh had warned me to "dress as for the country," and so I was in linen duster and motoring veils and my stoutest boots. He, in green Caledon tweeds and a countrified cap, stood in the center of the main room and surveyed his domain with more hope for the place than was quite reasonable.

"It's worse than Miss Havesham's wedding feast, Hugh. How in the world did you find it?"

He looked a little evasive. "Actually I believe I own it. At least it's one of the family properties, my dear."

My dear, indeed. How quickly a man becomes baronial under his own roof, even this one.

"Hugh, if your family owns half London, don't tell me. I couldn't bear it. I prefer to think of you unfettered and free."

"Nothing like half," he murmured mainly to himself. "Oh, no, nothing like as much." He poked at an awful old load of rubbish and it collapsed, revealing a hearth of sorts, at least a hole with a pothook.

"I suppose," he said in a rare moment of uncertainty, "it might be made habitable." Then we fled the dust we'd raised.

*   *   *

I was falling in love with Hugh Drummond, and writing impassioned letters home to Joe Fletcher. At seventeen I might have expected to fall in love with every other man I met. But like my mother, I could never see any use or excuse in being young. And I took myself much too seriously. I wouldn't dare believe that I could mean very much to Hugh Drummond, and so I drifted on a stronger current than I knew.

A note came from Hugh's mother, inviting me for a weekend party. I hadn't dared think of her existence until now. The letter paper was plain and the handwriting was old-fashioned but firm.

I hoped against hope that Louisa Drummond was a comfortable old body, in a ribboned cap and surrounded by cats. I longed to find her dozing by the fire in a thatched cottage in Kent. And I knew it wasn't to be.

I'd have begged off, to spare myself and confound my mother, but that would mean whole days without Hugh.

"Lady Drummond has written to me," Mother said. She no longer waited up for me, as a pledge of trust, but she'd taken to breakfasting downstairs. We began the days together, I nibbling toast and she tucking into kippers because, I suppose, they were English.

"*Lady* Drummond?" My heart sank. "Does she really have a title?"

Mother glanced at the ceiling in exasperation, reminding me of Aunt Opal. "I wish you'd get over your provincial, American prejudice against titles. It is only a pose."

It was of course. If I believed in equality, I shouldn't notice who was called what. Instead I said, sulkily, "I wonder if Hugh will inherit a title."

"No, of course not," she said, revealing her research. "His late father was knighted by the queen. A diplomat, I believe."

She scanned down the Court Circular column of the *Times*. "Lady Drummond is very old guard, at one time lady of the bedchamber to Queen Victoria."

"What on earth is that?"

"She was lady-in-waiting to the queen." Mother seemed to absorb herself in the newspaper. "I have written back that you'll go for the weekend."

Then, reining herself in, she glanced across at me with that faint, plaintive look in her lovely eyes. "Was that all right? Do you want to go?"

I wouldn't tell her how much.

Because I was off her hands, she was free to go away for the weekend too, to Cowes for the start of Regatta Week. Consuelo Manchester had a seaside villa there. Mother was going provisioned with a mountain of straw hats and white linen suits with brass buttons and Royal Yacht Squadron party gowns. She'd cast Guy Carville into gloom by not arranging an invitation for him as well. Then when she returned, she poured salt into the wound by telling him that Lady Randolph Churchill had spent the entire time in dalliance with a Mr. George Cornwallis-West, a man no older than her own son.

Presumably this report was a warning of how older women could make fools and spectacles of themselves with younger men. But Guy took it quite another way, and railed that if West and Lady Randolph could get away with it, why couldn't . . . certain others.

"Confound it anyway, Eve," he took to saying, pacing the drawing room floor. "I say, it really is too much how you dangle a fellow!" But he dared not make too great a nuisance of himself for fear of being sent away.

Hugh and I started out early in the day for our weekend. His family home had a name, "Wrenfields," I learned with a sinking heart. He'd hired a motorcar, a terrifying De Dion Bouton, which he learned to drive during the trip. Hoskins came along later with the luggage, prudently by rail.

After many hours and breakdowns, we rolled up to an ivy-covered gatehouse. A stout old lady in a patched apron rushed out to open the gate for us, and I wished wanly that this was Hugh's mother.

Perched high on the motorcar, I feared too much for my life to think ahead. But after we'd bucked along for a mile on the crown of the drive, Lady Drummond's country cottage loomed up.

Behind a Tuscan fountain playing in the forecourt stood the main block of the house, severely Palladian, with older, patterned brick wings. Perhaps a hundred rooms, perhaps more. I felt the weight of the ages and much brickwork descending and wondered if our good times were past.

We found his mother in a conservatory. Her tweed skirts were short and leather-bound, and she was bending over a flat of flowers, attacking them in gardening gloves with pruning shears.

She was too intent to notice us at first: a bulky, hardy woman with a delicate eighteenth-century profile and a blue vein at her temple. Her white hair was swept impatiently into a knot.

She turned and let the shears fall among the flowers. "My dear boy!" She held out her arms to take him in. I watched the gardening gloves close behind Hugh's neck and thought that a possessive mother might solve my turmoil. I could simply walk away and leave him to her.

But she was thrusting him aside. "Constance?" Her eyes were merry and wide. "You're not at all what I expected!" She swept me up in just the embrace she'd given her son. "Why you dear creature," she said, holding me tight, "I wouldn't have dreamed you were American."

Behind her, Hugh cast his head down in an attitude of profound shame, but he was grinning wickedly.

THIRTY-THREE

It was a perfect weekend. Hoskins herself as much as agreed. When I asked her how she'd fared in the servants' hall at Wrenfields, she said, "Very nice, miss, I'm sure. Good, plain English cooking."

That was true enough. We dined four times a day in an old guard party with only a scattering of young people as a concession to Hugh and to me. Elderly gentlemen, full of years of service to the queen, spoke of the Crimea. In gowns as fine and faded as themselves, their wives spoke in the ringing tones of the slightly deaf. When I was identified as my mother's daughter, they said, "Who? Who did they say she is? Who is the mother?"

I never felt so safe. We played uncompetitive croquet and undemanding Russian whist. In the corner of the library, always asleep, the old gentleman behind a magnificent white mustache was the duke of Connaught.

Hugh, who was at home anywhere, was most at home here. He slipped away from his guests for long, satisfying conferences with the estate agent. It was all wonderful, and a little dreamlike, and I could seem to do no wrong. On Monday when we left for the harrowing return journey, Lady Drummond embraced me as warmly as before, in her gardening gloves, ready to return to routine. I wanted to flee this too too-perfect place, and I wanted to stay there for the rest of my life.

It was nearly midnight before Hugh and I swerved into Half Moon Street. While the motorcar wheezed and vibrated

in the street, he saw me up the steps, pulling my hand away
when I reached for the knocker to summon Blaine.

Hugh turned me and pushed back my veil. When he bent to
kiss me, I planted a hand on his chest and tried to think of
. . . someone else. I shook my head, but his lips were on
mine. His arms were around me, and then mine around his. It
was only for this moment, and a moment longer. I clung to
him under the lamp where anyone could see us.

I meant to break away, but he would decide when to
release me. When he did, it was only to hold me closer,
against the length of him, with my head tucked tight beneath
his chin.

"I hadn't meant this to happen," he said above me.

Though my heart was in my throat, and throbbing, I said,
"I will survive a kiss. It's not quite my first."

"I didn't mean the kiss," Hugh said. "I meant that to
happen right enough. I mean for it to go on happening, and a
great deal more besides. I didn't mean to fall in love with
you, Constance."

I couldn't hear my heart. It must have stopped.

"This is going to sound stuffy and time-worn," he was
saying, "but I'll speak to your mother."

"What about?" I said, more foolish than I'd ever been in
my whole foolish life.

He held me tighter and may have been smiling. "Constance,
I want you for my wife."

I sat up till dawn, writing a letter to Hugh. I wrote through
many drafts until the floor was deep in paper. I confessed to
him my silly plan to seem to fall in love with a suitable
man—to deceive my mother. I didn't dare tell him how I'd
deceived myself.

Instead, I told him of Joe, how I'd loved Joe Fletcher
before and believed I would again. And I told Hugh what I'd
told no one else in England, not even Guy. I told him how I
meant to become an architect.

It was all very earnest and young. I don't remember how I
phrased it, except for the end:

I must find my own way, Hugh, and though I can
scarcely make myself write the words, I cannot be the
lady of your manor.

                                              Constance

I sent the note around to Hugh's club at first light, and he
was wise enough not to send flowers that day.

My mother noticed. She returned that morning from Cowes,
flushed, I supposed, with social triumphs. It took her no time
at all to see that the daily hothouse of cut flowers had all been
sent to her.

"You haven't quarreled with Hugh, have you?" she said,
as if in passing.

I was stricken and miserable and it was bound to show, but
I meant to keep my guard up. If I couldn't bear to see Hugh
again, I must seem to be seeing him, or she would . . . I
preferred not to think what her next move might be. I preferred not to think of the future at all.

But Hugh was wiser and far more mature than I. He was good
at immediate solutions too, as Joe was good at long plans. A
note came from him before I had to descend into new deceits:

Dear Constance,
    It was presumptuous and high-handed of me to wish
to order your life, even in the name of love. It won't
do, you know—not seeing you again. It's neither feasi-
ble nor civilized, and might have who-knows-what effect upon your mother.
    I put to you a business proposition. You are to become
an architect, and I have a barn wretchedly in need of
radical restorations. I commission you to undertake the
job, a challenge to set you up for your life's work.
                        Consider me your obedient client,
                                              H. Drummond
P. S. I am not done proposing marriage to you, but we
will declare an embargo on all that, at least until you've
made of my hovel exceedingly comfortable quarters. If,
that is, you are up to the job.

I might have been proof against an impassioned letter,
but not that one.

The weeks fled, I never knew where, and all along the
Mayfair byways there were chrysanthemums and gentians in
the windowboxes in place of bright summer blooms. The
social season ebbed with summer, and the cream of society
pulled back to their country places. There were no more
garden parties, and the dinners subsided.

But I was busier than before, and it looked to anyone who
was looking that Hugh Drummond and I had settled to a
courtship too intense to be misunderstood. There may have
been many mothers astounded at the prize I seemed to win in
my first season.

Hugh called for me daily, and I smuggled from the house
my sketchpad of plans and scratchy blueprints. I had no idea
of what I was doing or how to go about it, but I had a barn to
rebuild, and my pride was at stake.

He stood back and steered me away from making gross
mistakes. He could usually summon small armies of competent workmen to do my bidding, cloth-capped cockneys clever
at pulling down and building up. While my mother may have
believed that Hugh and I lunched at the Savoy Grill and spent
easy afternoons over tea at Claridge's, we spent the hours in a
hail of plaster dust, ankle-deep in lumber. I was determined
to regard him as my client and nothing more.

I began to learn things I needed to know, about joists and
joins and bearing walls and space arrangements. By September the old barn was a shell, stripped of dry rot and wood-
worm and any number of rats' nests. The chimney had been
blocked, but it was clear now, and I'd found old Portuguese
tiles for the mantel. Before each new decision, I consulted
my client's wishes. But, provokingly, he would only turn his
palms up and say, "I will live with your decisions, all of
them."

I made appalling blunders. I'd have had the floors scraped
and stained for the pleasure of seeing them done before I'd

thought of replastering the walls. But the workmen, who thought me mad indeed, would intervene and save me if Hugh didn't. Slowly, the place began to take shape. I'd preserved the loft as a bedchamber, and beneath it was space enough for a kitchen and a modern bathroom, though then as now there is nothing very modern about English plumbing.

There was still an overhanging width of balcony left, and under it I planned a dining room on a sort of dais for formality and yet open to the main room. The roof rose now rather majestically to the peaked ceiling.

I set old diamond-paned glass in the high windows and cut a smaller, more welcoming door into the great barn doors at the front. It was going to work, and I began to savor the taste of triumph. There was still the ancient, hand-wrought simplicity of a barn, but refined now and baronial enough to suit the country squire in town. We kept fires going in the hearth to dry new plaster. The chimney drew well, and the fire warmed us.

We found a few pieces of old furniture in the street markets and an old plank board door that could be laid across sawhorses for a refectory table. Surrounded by unmatched, high-backed chairs and candlelit, it would be splendid. There was to be much candlelight. My client had balked at electricity.

Then he rose up in a sudden burst of independence as clients will, and insisted on adding the final touches himself. He left his mark with indifferently cured animal skins from his African safaris, and a profoundly hideous rhinoceros head that might hang on the chimneypiece. And a bed too, rather overcarved, with side curtains. A long bed, and very wide.

Somewhere I'd heard that the architect presents the client with a present at the end. In Shepherd Market I found a brass-bound Georgian box fitted out with square crystal decanters. We drank our first toast from these bottles. These were the happiest days of my life. Nothing before and nothing after quite matched them. It was a happiness not much diminished by my refusal to admit it, even to myself.

Before I returned each time to Half Moon Street, I had to improve my appearance all I could. Then with smuts of dirt on my nose and my duster in a shocking state, I was likely to meet my mother on the stairs to hear her say, "Where *does* that man take you?"

THIRTY-FOUR

Autumn came, colder and sooner than in San Francisco, shortening the days. I was torn now, more than before, but on the strength of a single barn, I felt ready to rebuild the world.

I wrote to Joe to tell him of the work I'd undertaken, if not the client. A courtship quickened between Joe and me through letters filled with bricks and mortar and the crotchets of cabinetmakers and masons.

As far as I knew, I was the only female in history to be in love with two men. At seventeen, there are no precedents. Then just when I'd reduced all human experience to the dimensions of my dilemma, my mother stepped forth with her usual uncanny timing.

We were at breakfast when she said with studied calm, "I hope you are free on Saturday afternoon. There is someone . . . I'm going to the Eshers, and I should like . . . they have asked you too."

I was only mildly annoyed. Since I'd first met Hugh, she'd made no demands upon me. Still, I thought of having him invited too. Even an afternoon apart . . . but she read my mind, saying, "Just the two of us."

I should have wondered at that. She hadn't looked across at me as she spoke, and her cup rattled in its saucer.

I knew that Viscount Esher was an eminent man, a friend of the great. He was a statesman and a director of the opera. I'd seen his handsome, remote profile wreathed in cigarette smoke in my mother's drawing room at teatime, and knew his family were the aristocratic Bretts. They were the sort of powerful people so important to my mother.

Their house was lovely, in magnificent lawns set about with weeping willows. There were wide rose-brick terraces and garden paths that wandered apparently at random to distant gateways and sculpture set in woodland clearings.

The house, called Orchard Lea, was at Winkfield opposite Windsor Great Park. There was a royal shooting party that day in the park and the distant, steady sound of gunfire.

We lunched, a small party, in an echoing dining room like a mead hall, muffled in tapestries and bristling with jeweled rapiers from Lord Esher's collection. I don't recall who was there. There were Brett children, but the boys were away, and the girls, Sylvia and Doll, were younger than I and thus still upstairs.

Lady Esher was frozen in dignity, with a gaze that rarely left her husband. The atmosphere was heavy, along with the food, but these were not people who confused society with amusement. I wondered again at my mother's need for people so much less vivid and alive than herself.

She was beautifully dressed, and soberly, in a midnight-blue frock of heavy silk, deeply braided at the cuffs and high collar. At her throat was a gold brooch set with turquoise stones that someone had given her. She deferred to our hostess in ways I hadn't seen before.

Later Lord Esher showed Mother and me around the grounds. He offered us each an arm and commentaries upon the sculpture. It was a slow-paced day, and my thoughts were probably elsewhere. Lord Esher left us to rejoin his other guests, and my mother and I strolled on. As we approached a little clearing called "Pan's Garden," there were ahead of us two men beside the statue of the grinning little stone god.

The elder man was very stout, gaitered and in tweeds tight across his girth. The younger man was in light blue of a more military cut. Both wore Tyrolean hats, jaunty with high feathers. They stood talking and knocking cigar ash onto the groomed ground. I noticed first the stunted, withered arm of the younger man. They turned, unsurprised to see us there.

I should have known then: the steely blue of the younger man's eyes and the watery gaze of the other. I should have seen at once, but I turned to my mother just as she swept back her skirts, and curtsied, the deep brim of her hat dipping as she bowed.

"Miss Waring, my dear Eve," said the older gentleman with the disciplined gray beard. He was before us, though he'd seemed unmovable, putting out his hand to my mother.

"Sir, my daughter, Constance."

My knee bent, bidden by itself. I curtsied and took the hand of the future king of England.

My ears rang with shock in that moment of complete quiet. There was no sound of distant gunfire. The hunters were here before us in their hunting hats. Among the trees around us, other huntsmen, their attendants, seeming to stroll, stood guard.

"My nephew, Wilhelm," the Prince of Wales was saying. My mother and I curtsied again, now to the German kaiser. He stood rigid before us, not offering his hand, offering nothing but the faint click of his heels.

My mind swerved near hysteria. It was like curtsying to—pictures. There was an unflattering cartoon of Kaiser Wilhelm in every daily newspaper. And the Prince of Wales—on a million cigar boxes. The earth seethed at my feet. I might have fainted, but the ground was too far away.

The kaiser clicked again, signal for another curtsy, and walked away to join his huntsmen in the woods. He wouldn't have loitered, I suppose, in any situation that didn't center on himself. Besides, this chance encounter had been planned, and choreographed.

Crazily, it occurred to me. The future king of England, and, almost incidently the ruler of Germany, had arranged to meet us by chance in that corner of Lord Esher's gardens, to meet *me* because my mother . . .

When the kaiser had withdrawn, Prince Edward fetched up an audible sigh and shook his old head, as if to dismiss all tiresome relatives. He stepped forward, arms akimbo, like a vast teapot with two handles. We were meant to take an arm each side and stroll with him as we'd strolled with the more regal figure of Lord Esher.

"A great pity about the poor boy's arm, you know," the prince said to me, like any uncle. "Withered, as you see. Can't load for himself, of course. Has to have four men standing by, don't you know, to hand him the guns at full cock. But the fellow can shoot with one arm and no mistake. These Germans!"

My feet managed to track as we strolled, and my hand rode naturally enough in the crook of the royal arm against the thick tweedy body.

"Not a bad day, all in all," the prince said, wheezing as we went. "A hundred and seventy-eight pheasants."

"Oh, sir," my mother said (fatuously, I thought), "whatever will you do with them?"

"Send a brace around to you at Half Moon Street I expect, my dear. At Sandringham, of course, we think nothing of—"

It was hopeless. I couldn't follow what he said. It was as if a cigar box were speaking or a tea tin or the signs swinging outside a hundred pubs named "The Prince of Wales." He would turn to me soon, tying my tongue in knots.

"Ride, do you, my dear?"

Ride? ". . . No, sir, I'm afraid not."

"Like your mother in that! Bless me if I didn't think all American women rode—bareback, don't you know, and astride!"

My mother saved me adroitly. "Surely, sir, you cannot picture Lady Lister-Kaye or little Maud Cunard breaking broncos, even on their native soil."

He drew us up to give this exaggerated thought.

"Perhaps not," he said, "but I can see Lady Randolph booted and spurred and riding hell bent for leather, and roping and branding into the bargain!" He threw back his head and roared with laughter, and my mother joined in and so perhaps did I.

"A pity though about your mother," he said aside to me, pressing my arm. "What a fine figure she'd cut in bowler and stock any morning along Rotten Row. With all her swains in full cry behind her. A spectacle that!''

"Fit for a king,'' my mother murmured, and that inclined the royal head in her direction.

We stood at last on the brink of the lawn with the Eshers' house before us. "I think I must turn back now,'' the prince said. "My guests, you know. Make my excuses to Esher, won't you, my dear, and to Lady Esher.'' He freed me from his arm and took my mother's hand in both of his, bending to kiss it.

I was not there for a moment, and then he turned to me with the impartial courtesy of kings. "How pleased I am to know you at last, my dear young lady. Your mother is very proud of you, and justly so.''

"You are kind, sir,'' I said, and because my mother was inclining her head behind him, I knew to curtsy again. He reached out to press Mother's hand again, reluctant to leave her. Then he strolled down the garden path as if he were anyone, and with the ghost of a spring in his step.

THIRTY-FIVE

My mother was the mistress of the Prince of Wales, the man who would be the king of England. The truth of it raged in my brain, not least because I must be the last person in England, and America, too, to know it. I was out of my depth in her world, and always would be.

We didn't speak in the train back to London. I sat far from her, staring out the window until darkness fell, and there was only my blurred reflection in the glass. If I'd looked and listened, if I'd thought beyond myself, I'd have known. Anyone might have told me, and there are always those glad to tell. Maybe they assumed I knew and conspired in this open secret. Maybe they thought I was too young and stupid to understand. Either way there was no solace.

Of course I knew the Prince of Wales had mistresses. It was a mark of his distinction, and theirs. It was what made the Marlborough set dashing and defiant and above ordinary mortals.

It was never to be spoken of around a young girl, but there'd been allusions enough, to Lady Brooke and Mrs. Langtry, speculations about Lady Manchester and Lady Randolph. There were so many speculations about so many hard and high-born women that none of it was real to me. But how real and logical a triumph for my mother. How firmly it fixed her where she'd needed to be, beyond chance and above struggle.

The train was in the station now, sliding past the platform. The first doors banged back, and there was the sulphurous city smell of London. Only when the porters were in the corridors did she rise. She could never do the ordinary, human little things—standing too soon before the train stopped and then sitting down again suddenly, or searching around for gloves gone astray as anyone else did. She left nothing to chance, and staged everything, she who despised the theater.

Why must I meet the prince by that implausible accident when I might have met him at Half Moon Street on those days when I was sent out to shop instead? Or those afternoons when the drawing room doors, and Blaine's mouth, were firmly shut? She wouldn't see her own limitation, that she must create artificial scenes because she couldn't cope with life as it is. My brain boiled, and it got me nowhere.

She'd risen to leave the train compartment, and I was ready to start out into the crowd on the platform behind her. She turned and said, "Are you going to marry Hugh Drummond?"

The audacity of that took my breath away. I'd spent an hour trying and condemning her in my mind, and she'd dismissed all that with a single bald question. She hadn't been on trial at all. *Court* to her had quite a different meaning.

"He has asked me," I said.

"As well he should have, after all this time."

"He asked me some while ago."

"Perhaps he asked too soon," she said.

Or too late, I thought, not daring to say it.

"Do you think he will ask again?"

"He has said he will."

She turned and stepped out of the compartment, and I could only follow in her wake. She'd shaped that moment too and hadn't asked the inevitable final question.

We were silent again in the hansom cab, but when it turned out of Piccadilly, she said, "I have an hour before the theater."

Only then did I realize she'd missed the matinee performance. She heard me realizing that and said, "I gave the matinee to the understudy. To leave the evening to her as well might give her ideas." There was a ripple of lightness in her tone, but she wasn't cajoling.

At home I turned at the landing and would have gone straight up to my room, but she said, briefly, "In here."

I followed her into the drawing room. Guy was there, just turning from the liquor cabinet. Our stern watchdog, Blaine, always admitted him out of habit. I saw in Guy's composed face that he knew precisely what the afternoon had been. At that moment, I didn't see Guy as another betrayed and injured party, my fellow sufferer with reasons of his own to suffer. I only felt a small sense of safety as long as he was there between us.

"A fine day," he said cautiously, "for the time of year."

But a storm was gathering. Mother stood at the mirror drawing the pins from her hat. Her time was limited, or so her gestures said.

"Constance has met the prince this afternoon," she said. "He has been asking to meet her." She turned to look full at me. This was to be a moment of truth, and so we were both on unfamiliar ground. "Sit down, Constance. Yes, Guy, you too."

She'd pulled off her gloves, and I noticed inconsequential things. There were no rings on her hands. Mistresses, in lower life, lived upon diamond rings and pearl necklaces nestled in orchid corsages. I had this on the authority of any amount of cheap fiction. But the mistresses of the prince were not bought with jewelry or money. They couldn't be the sort of women who needed that. My mother had worked herself like a slave, like a machine to place herself . . . where she was. She was not kept. Somehow that made it worse.

The prince gave nothing but tokens, souvenirs—medals for distinguished service. Mother's hand rested on her throat a moment, just touching the almost modest brooch set with turquoise stones.

"She has met the prince," she said, still using Guy, "but I wonder if she is sensible of the honor."

"Oh, come now, Eve," Guy said, "I'm sure she—"

"I'm not sure it was an honor," I said.

She was still standing, speaking down at both of us. "Yes, that's the line I expected you to take." Her eyes, her splendid,

compelling eyes were on me. Her gaze drifted over me, over
the dress I was wearing, taking me in. It was a rather
beautiful one, and it must have cost her a great deal. But she
was above reminding me what I owed her.

"I wanted you here in London with me, Constance. Perhaps that was wrong of me and unwise. I don't often give
way to that sort of personal indulgence. Now I wonder if you
are going to make me pay.

"I wonder," she said while I looked at my hands gripped
in my lap, "I wonder if you expect me to fall on my knees
and beg your forgiveness for what I've achieved."

Achieved, I thought, trying to see what she'd become as an
achievement. Trying to see it that way and failing.

"Perhaps I should have left you in your little life."

"I would have found out," I said, "even there."

"You could have found out anywhere," she said. "Here, I
hoped you'd understand."

"I don't. If you were in love—"

"Ah, I thought that word would come up." She glanced
away, dismissing me. "But I'd hoped not to hear it from you.
You, who've kept one man fully engaged in London and
another on the string in San Francisco. Or are you to be
forgiven everything and I nothing?"

I nearly choked. She'd turned it all back on me again. I
thought of flight. In my mind I was running already.

"I think I should go back to San Francisco. I want to go
home."

She sat down across from me and sighed, not very
dramatically. She'd expected to hear that too, but didn't
bother to say so. "And what will you do when you get
there? Solve everything by marrying the young man in the
photograph?"

Use him to settle my life, she meant, while I accused her
of using . . . another man. How petty and pointless she
could make my life seem. Or perhaps it was. My head
pounded. If I told her what I wanted to do with my life, *mine*,
not anyone else's, she'd wave that contemptuously away. I
was sure of it, sure enough not to tell her.

She looked up at the tall clock at the door, gauging her time. "You must do as you see fit, Constance. No mother can be precisely what a daughter wants and nothing more. In a daughter's eyes, we are all diminished. I have wanted you here, and I want it still. But I won't have you judging me in your ignorance. This is a world beyond your understanding, a world that runs by its own rules for people who were born to it and people who have risen to it. If you cannot bear to see me in it, I think you should go."

If she'd stood then and turned back to her life, I'd have had no choice but to embrace my freedom. But it was Guy who stirred, setting down his untouched drink.

"I say, Eve, I really think I should—"

"I'm not quite finished, Guy," she said, not looking at him. "But if you must go, you must. I'm not able to be to you what you want either. Or what you think you want. Perhaps we should all . . . walk away from each other.

"But you have wanted in your young way to be a part of my life, Guy. You can hear a bit more that I've spared you."

She held the moment lightly in her grip until Guy subsided, and then a little longer.

"I was once younger even than you two. And there was in my life this stranger who was a mother to me. All mothers are strangers. She ran a brothel."

Guy made some movement, but I sat there in a spell.

"I would have thought her incapable of love if it weren't for that other girl, that daughter named Opal."

My eyes must have widened. The door of the past had always been shut tight, and now she threw that door open in a gesture almost casual.

"She loved Opal until it was a sickness they both suffered from. You see, Constance, what that has made of Opal.

"I ran away from the only mother I knew. I pretended to walk, but I was running. Perhaps I'm running still. There's more to the story—a man, of course—but it was that woman I ran from because she would not love me as I thought I should be loved. And because I convinced myself she'd lied to me, though nobody lies to you unless you allow it.

"I ran, and though the world might have swallowed me whole and spat me out, it didn't. I found the force in me I needed, as you can gather your forces, Constance.

"I've tried to make the distance between me and her count for something, but that woman who ran the brothel haunts me still. I won't have you haunted that way by me. That's more burden than any woman needs.

"I believe to this day that woman I once called Mother never loved me. But whether you go or stay, Constance, I cannot have you think the same of me."

She rose then. The curtain fell abruptly on the scene, if this was a scene. I tried to think it was. Yet it differed from all the others. She stood up so quickly that Guy had to struggle out of his chair like an older man than he was.

"Go or stay, the pair of you," she said, straightening her skirts in awkward, jerking gestures. Then so faintly that we might have missed hearing it altogether: "But whatever you do, know that I . . . love you both."

She was gone, out of the room so quickly that she must have run, like an animal fearing us, fearing the word she'd invoked.

A day or two passed, and flowers came again from Hugh. There was no message on his card, or need for one. I must decide now what I would do. It had been too easy to drift and judge. But now even the wrong decision would be better than that. I must choose now among worlds, not schemes.

The flowers came with the post. There was a letter from San Francisco. If it had been from Joe Fletcher, I don't know what that might have meant. But it was a letter from Rose Conklin, whose letters I'd torn open so avidly earlier, when I was newer here and she'd written often. I put it aside for a moment. Until I decided what to do with me.

BOOK 4

The World at Its End

THIRTY-SIX

After all this time, I don't remember how I managed to phrase that letter to Constance in London. I'd been married that day, and so I was no longer Rose Conklin. I sat in a strange house through a long evening, staring down at the gum trees along Van Ness Avenue. The street was dark and slick with the rains of late autumn.

I sat up there the better part of the night, tearing a good handkerchief to shreds, before I could pick up the pen. Because I was frightened, I reached out across the world to my friend.

From our first year at St. Mary's Constance had been my idol. I thought she was always so sure and moved with such purpose.

There was never the hint of jealousy between us. She was far more intelligent than I could hope to be, and there was that loneliness about her that no one could wish for. Certainly I couldn't, for I'd come from a family where warmth and belonging and love were like the staples in the larder.

I hadn't expected to make anything very extraordinary of my life. I wasn't driven as Constance was. I thought happiness was a river, and that I would bob along.

When Constance and I graduated from St. Mary's, dressed in our Maypole dresses and carrying our little diplomas away, I went back home to San Francisco to my mother and father. Constance went off abruptly to London, summoned by her famous mother.

Her going was the kind of exciting, dramatic thing that

happened to other people. But she went grimly, dreading her mother, and she was parted from Joe Fletcher, so I couldn't envy that either.

I couldn't even envy her Joe. It didn't occur to me that any man that funny and sunny and promising would ever notice me. Perhaps in that I was right.

Joe wasn't a man to swerve or be swayed, then or ever. I thought: *This is the man who will marry my dearest friend and be like a brother to me.* It was an innocent view of all our futures.

Even in Constance's absence, Joe continued for a time to come to our Sunday dinners. He was working hard on his first commission, a house out by the Presidio. He meant to use the time until Constance came back to get his career underway.

My mother thought he was overworked and underfed. She fussed and fed him, and we sat long after dinner at the table, reading aloud our letters from London. At first we took comfort in Constance's homesickness. Then I began to look between the lines and wondered if I saw, faintly, another man there—a foreigner. But I refused to believe it. That would have shattered my illusions, and I still had them.

I dreamed of marrying one day and having children and living in the same sort of rambling house I was in no rush to leave. I dreamed of marrying—later, and I didn't know who. I dreamed, but I didn't yearn and sat high in the house, sewing with my mother. We had a pair of Singer machines set to face each other. The treadles clacked with a cozy sound through the afternoons. During the raw days of the San Francisco winter we kept a small fire going in the grate. I should have basked longer in that warmth where I was safe.

My mother was the least pushing of women, but she wanted me to have the advantages of the other girls in the Western Addition and all the better neighborhoods. She'd come from Sacramento where you could conduct a brisk social life and never leave the porch. But I must find my niche in San Francisco, this complicated little Paris that my mother wondered at from the safe side of her parlor windows.

For guidance she read Ned Greenway's column on the society page of the *Chronicle*. She wouldn't countenance William Chambliss's low insinuations in Hearst's *Examiner*. Still, Father subscribed to all the papers, and she gave Chambliss's column quick, horrified glances.

"If this isn't the worst piece of trash that ever I saw printed!" she said to me one day, shaking the *Examiner* in her fist. Then because she didn't really know what she was reading, she read it out to me:

> What exalted actress, the unmatched Eve W— — — –g, who has forgotten what she owes to the San Francisco stage, has become the Golden Friend, the Personal Houri of the Insatiable Prince of a Decadent Empire? It is an acknowledged truth that Our California Destiny is to feed the world . . . but not its Baser Passions!

Mother vibrated with indignation, and not over the dubious grammar. "Why I bet you anything it's Constance's mother that madman is babbling about. They ought to bring back the Vigilance Committee and string the horse thief up."

Horse thief was not a term my mother bandied lightly.

From her more improving reading, she learned of that distinctly San Franciscan institution, cotillions, where every girl who aspired to society made her bow and met men.

To prepare, I must go off to the dancing academy the Lunts ran over on Polk Street for a short course of lessons to lighten my step. I'd learned the rudiments of ballroom dancing at a girls' school, so I had a tendency to lead and had to be broken of that, like a colt.

The cotillions were weekly affairs, held in ordinary hired halls. They were balls organized as clubs, and a girl must be chosen to belong, though young men could drop in on all of them to partner us in the dance, and with any luck for the rest of our lives.

There were three cotillions that counted. Ned Greenway ran the most popular one on Friday nights, "Greenways" it was always called. His enemy, Chambliss, ran another in competition, the Monday Evening Club. There was a third, Inez Shorb's Cotillion Club, to absorb the leavings.

I thought Greenways was well above my sights, and Chambliss was of course out of the question. I'd have settled for Inez Shorb's, out of the full glare of whatever was expected.

I was a broth of a girl, broad in the shoulder and not small in the hip, and I worried that I'd loom large as a wallflower. I was always shy to the point of sickness among strangers. When Constance had taken me along to the artistic parties she and Joe went to at North Beach, I almost swooned with fear. How would I do now, cast out on my own? I hoped the whole cotillion business would pass me by.

But that reckoned without my mother, who developed unsuspected resources. She read that Mrs. Eleanor Martin helped Ned Greenway select his Greenway Girls. There was always speculation about how Greenway Girls were picked, and talk of bribery and mothers who moved heaven and earth. One afternoon I discovered a stranger in our parlor, drinking coffee and eating a slice of Mother's angel cake.

She never entertained anybody but the neighbors, but this was Mrs. Martin. I found I'd been interviewed before I knew it, and accepted. Perhaps no other anxious mother had tried angel cake and simple friendship on Mrs. Martin. I became a Greenway Girl. Provisioned with four new dresses in sweet pea colors and a lump in my throat, I went forth to face my brief season. It was soon over.

The stag line at Greenways was made up of all the eligible young men in San Francisco, but the chief beau was old Mr. Ned Greenway himself. He not only raised the daughters of fond mothers to social visibility, but he catered to their papas too as the local distributor of Mumms Extra Dry champagne. All this and his *Chronicle* column too. The town could scarcely move without him.

He looked like a banty rooster, but he ran his cotillion with military precision and would often pick up the slack by dancing with those of us left along the wall. Of course he was a wonderful dancer and gave me the idea that I followed better than I did. It was almost impossible to tread on his small, quick feet. I thought I did passably well with him until once he remarked, "Miss Conklin, conversation is part of dance, often the better part."

I'd been waltzing with him in the stony silence born of concentration.

"Oh, I don't believe I could do both at the same time," I said without thinking.

But he only answered, "Nonsense, girl, you will learn to fascinate and float, both with an easy grace." Having delivered this optimistic prophecy, he was already peering around my shoulder in search of some damsel in greater distress.

I was often bigger than my partners and had the worst trouble remembering their names, even when their names were Spreckels or Lilienthal or Holladay or Haggin. But all the blades and scorchers from these good families were there, and I had to find my feet and my tongue. I even learned a little feeble trick or two, like carrying a chamois skin in my handkerchief for applying face powder discreetly in public. I managed, but the high point of those Friday nights happened short of the ballroom floor. As I came down the stairs from my room at home, my mother was there waiting to see me in my dancing dress. She stood looking up with her hand on her breast and her eyes shining. I could never be as beautiful in any other eyes.

Then one evening at Greenways I was in the arms of a young man with a face like a pitted moon and very good evening clothes over a very fat figure. He was trying for a mustache, but it was lost in his face as any detail was. He was a college man, Stanford. He told me at once though I hadn't asked.

"You're Rose Conklin," he announced. He announced everything he said and was too pompous for anything. "A friend of Connie Nichols."

I must have wondered how he knew me. Somehow it wasn't as flattering as it might have been.

"Oh, I know everybody," he said, sweeping me around

the floor in a showy way. "You will have heard of me, I expect. I'm Jack Kinsella."

I'd heard of him all right. He was Constance's cousin, one of a pair. The Kinsellas lived not far from us. Constance had always gone there for Christmas Day, dragging her feet.

"Poor Connie," Jack Kinsella said, sweeping and dipping and turning a waltz into a kind of adagio. "Out of her depth in London, I expect."

I wouldn't rise to that, which gave him no pause.

"Her mother is Eve Waring, you know. *The* Eve Waring." Then, leaving nothing to chance, "My Aunt Eve."

I wouldn't rise to that either, but it was of no consequence. Jack Kinsella needed no partnering in conversation or dance. He could float and fascinate himself. To give him credit, he was light on his feet for his weight and didn't turn my hems into lacework as certain partners did. I took what comfort in that I could.

Jack had a disparaging word for everyone. "There's poor Jeannine Fitzhugh," he'd say of a local belle across the room, "in the same dress again."

Or more cryptically, "There's poor Hortense Ferguson." He'd nod toward a girl trying to maintain her dignity in a chair along the wall. "I wonder why she tries."

He declared himself "a complete cynic" and tolerated society, he said, because its presumptuousness amused him. On three successive Friday evenings, this young whale lumbered across the room to claim me.

On the third, he broke his stride in the midst of a waltz. "Oh, Lord," he said in dismay, looking past me to the door. "There's my brother, Terry. A terrible fellow really. You wouldn't dream we were twins."

And I could agree with that pronouncement when I turned to see Terry Kinsella there in the door, imperially slim, giving his chiseled profile to the room.

THIRTY-SEVEN

I married Terry Kinsella late in the November of that year. I had to.

That first night at Greenways he danced with me for the pleasure of cutting in on his brother. In his arms I thought a lightning bolt had struck me, and I thought it was love.

He was as handsome as a—hatchet. There was nothing to see in his narrow face and the shifting emptiness of his eyes. But his sharp profile was the ideal of the time. His nose was deceptively aristocratic. His chin was deceptively strong. I was easily deceived.

In contrast to his brother, he had a shock of blond hair parted perfectly in the middle and smooth as a cap with pale curls feathering his neck above the Arrow collar.

He was lean and lithe as a jockey, not very tall except in my eyes. He moved with the nervous grace of a prizefighter. I could almost put my finger on what Terry Kinsella was or might become, almost but not quite.

Had we grown old together, we'd have looked like those married couples in fiftieth-anniversary photographs: I big-bosomed and full-faced, he whittled narrower by the years. He seated, I standing behind him.

It was his profile that won me, though I needed little winning. I was the duckling that falls in love with the first creature it sees. I saw a good deal of his profile, for even as he courted me, he was looking aside, beyond me. I thought it only natural that his eyes went everywhere. I thought it a

wonder he'd noticed me at all when he could pick and choose
and win any girl, however rich, however lovely.

In that, too, I was deceived, and deceived myself. The
Kinsellas were nowhere near the small magic circle of San
Francisco society. They had money enough to make the
necessary show. There were other families snugly in the
circle with no more taste, and many were less respectable.
But the Kinsellas weren't destined to belong. No more was
my family, but the Kinsellas cared. At least the mother cared.
Opal Kinsella cared, and that was what counted.

Jack protected himself with pomposity. Terry tried to cover
himself with insolence and dash. On the sidelines myself, I
fell for whatever Terry was trying to be. There were other
girls, primed to marry well, who aimed higher, and there
were wiser girls who'd have seen through him. Vain though
he was, I expect Terry knew that.

He wasn't quite twenty, yet he longed to be a man about
town. He longed for that the rest of his life.

His father, Mr. Terrence Kinsella, owned property throughout the city, and so Terry seemed to be in the real estate
business. I believe they made very few repairs on their holdings,
and so there wasn't much to do beyond collecting rents. Terry
had served a brief apprenticeship as a rent collector, but it
required legwork, and he preferred to be seen moving faster
behind a good horse. Out of his allowance that was called a
salary, he hired flunkies to do his work. If his father ever
challenged that, he was overruled by Opal Kinsella.

Jack lingered at Stanford, "reading the classics."

"It is a meager family," Jack once remarked, "that cannot
support one gentleman." But Terry, it was said, had gone
into the business.

He had a great deal of time on his hands. For a short
season he courted me. In all seasons he courted acceptance
harder won than mine. He longed to be a clubman. He had
the leisure for it and the clothes, and he cultivated the right
interests: horses and the track, fighters and the ring, dogs and
the Bench Show at the Mechanics' Pavilion. He worked to

master the vocabularies of yachting and naptha launches and golf.

But no club took him, and his almost-invisible father had no memberships of his own to open the doors. The Bohemian Club was miles out of his reach. So was the Olympic, whose virile members took their famous New Year's Day dip in the Pacific, the club that had produced James J. Corbett. Terry wasn't admitted to these preserves of real men, and it thwarted him more than it should have.

He was almost valiant in the ways he found to fill the day, trying to give it purpose. He stood at the bar at The Mining Exchange or The Tadich Grill. He stood there and drank Pisco punch and ate off the buffet lunch, and, I suppose, tried to strike up conversations with prominent men, sporting men. He tried, too, to hold his liquor, but that was another bitter failure.

It strikes me now that this was the occupation of an elderly man who's outlived his friends. But Terry was young. He was never to be anything but young.

He courted me offhandedly that summer of 1898, sweeping me easily off my feet. If he ever spoke endearments to me, I won't recall them now. I can't believe he did, or that I needed them. What I remember is the way my heart leaped each time he called for me with some sleek little two-wheeler at the curb.

We went where he wished to be seen. On summer afternoons, we drove out to Land's End and Sutro's Gardens. The highway there was an impromptu race course, and Terry must be seen in a smart rig behind a fast horse, with a girl at his side, holding the brim of her hat.

He would never hire anything comfortable. It must be fast and low-slung, no more than a pair of seats swinging between the whirling wheels. I was lucky if there was a splashboard between us and the hooves of the horse. Terry railed at his father for not providing him with horses of his own, or a motorcar. He railed at fate a great deal, and there must have been a time when I thought him misunderstood.

Once a week, and then oftener, he called for me in the

evenings, while I let my hopes build. He'd spend five minutes in the parlor with my innocently pleased mother and father, but never longer. He had no conversation, and my family were not the people he hoped to impress.

We went to the theater, to the Columbia to see Eddie Foy and Josie de Witt and to the Chutes on Haight Street to hear Nora Bayes sing "Shine On, Harvest Moon." We saw Gentleman Jim Corbett in *A Naval Cadet* and Marie Dressler and Eddie Cantor and Sophie Tucker, and always from very good seats, often a box.

Afterwards we went to Zinkard's for supper. Terry's eyes were everywhere in the crowded room, and I tried to be his good companion. I thought I'd be thanked for sharing his solitude. I thought, too, he might turn suddenly from me. Expecting that, I tried to be ready.

Then one day at the end of summer when there's always that little threat of change, he took me to his family's house after a long rambling drive through Golden Gate Park. He'd hardly mentioned his people though he lived with them still. I knew more of them from Constance. Now I wonder what it meant to me that he and Constance were cousins. Perhaps I thought it was another bond between us, another proof.

He didn't ring, but unlocked the front door and pulled me inside. I hardly had time to fear meeting his mother, but she wasn't home. I would learn later that she filled her days with shopping.

There was an afternoon emptiness in the great cluttered house and sounds at the back, of servants. He put his finger to his lips and commanded me with his eyes. He took my hand—I always wanted that—and led me upstairs. It didn't occur to me to resist. He was the one I expected to pull back finally, to resist me and walk forgetful away.

Along the upstairs hall he eased a door open to a small room his mother sewed in. The windows were shuttered, and I barely saw the little fainting-couch against the wall. In the strangeness of being there, I couldn't think. I noticed his mother's sewing basket with the silk tassel and amber beads, and the way the sunlight through the slats at the window sliced him as he looked outside. But there was nobody out there who could see.

He turned and said, "Have you thought of being my wife?"

It seemed I'd never heard his voice before, as if nothing had counted till then.

"Yes," I said, finding the strangeness wonderful now, even the strangeness in his eyes. He wasn't looking aside.

"Then be my wife now."

"What do you mean?" I tried to smile. "Today?"

"Now." He pointed to the couch.

A long time seemed to pass, but it couldn't have. He wouldn't have let it.

"Oh, no," I said, as if he could be reasoned with. "That wouldn't be right." Perhaps I was proud of knowing what he meant.

"If it's ever to be, between you and me," he said, strangely precise, "then it must begin now."

He stepped nearer and was gripping my arms. The fear lurched in me, and he felt it and thrilled to it. He loosened his grip and took me in his arms and kissed me, moving his hands over the buttons down the back of my dress.

I stepped back and felt the low couch pressing against my legs. "Don't make me beg," he whispered. I felt his lips on my ear. "I don't like to beg. I don't have to."

He drew his hands apart across my back, and my dress loosened and gapped forward, trapping my arms.

"No, Terry," I said, whispering because if anyone should—

"It's too late," he said. "It's too late not to." He slipped the sash from my waist, and then he turned from me as if I were free. "Take off your clothes," he said.

He slid out of his coat and hung it on the doorknob, and eased his suspenders off his shoulders. He wouldn't turn back to me until I'd done what he expected. I stepped out of my dress and reached back to my corset strings.

I was frightened of everything, of being discovered, of not being what he wanted. My throat was thick, but I dared not sob, and he was folding his trousers neatly over a chair, the chair at his mother's sewing table.

I saw his legs, white as marble, hazed with golden hair. He was naked now. I saw the narrowness of his waist and the line of his spine. He was turning to me, naked, and I wasn't, quite.

"Leave your stockings on," he said.

"We mustn't," I said, but I knew it was too late. He'd seen me. His hands were already on my naked breasts, and so it was too late.

"Lie down," he said.

"My shoes," I said insanely.

"Leave them on. There isn't time. I'll have to be quick, this time."

He was, I guess. I didn't know. Then there was that awful, breaking pain. My back arched, but he clamped his hand over my mouth. His eyes widened in warning, and so I couldn't cry out.

THIRTY-EIGHT

"Have you told your mother?" Terry said. It was later, after too many afternoons like that one. I forget where we were when he asked. It doesn't matter.

"Yes, I told her." I hadn't. I dreaded it too much, but I wanted him to think she knew.

"Have you told yours?" He looked aside and flared a nostril as if he was above worrying about that, but he wasn't.

"What a mess you've got us into." He lit a gold-banded cigarette, snapping the matchstick.

"Didn't you think it would happen?" I tried to keep the pleading and the panic out of my voice.

"I didn't think anything about it. I suppose you expect me to marry you now."

"You don't have to." But I knew something then without understanding it at all. He wasn't as reluctant as he wished to seem. He'd achieved something through me that meant a great deal to him. He'd be a husband now, and a father. That would prove his manhood to anyone who wondered. A day or so later after he'd made me wait, he brought me an engagement ring, from Shreve. And I thought: *He will learn to love me.*

I told my mother, not choosing my time. If I chose, I'd keep putting it off, and there wasn't time for that. I told her I was engaged to Terry Kinsella.

She turned from whatever she was doing. Her gray hair was escaping from its knot, and her face was flushed, her eyes bright. She clasped her hands before her.

"My stars, child! I wondered if you loved him."

"I do, Mother."

She pulled off her apron and even tossed it on the floor. This was a moment to mark. She put out her arms, and I rushed into them. I clung to her and heard her thoughts, of wedding cakes and bridesmaids in shades of pink, and long white runners down church aisles, of white gladiolus spiky in stands and white paper wedding bells. Of a long white train and points of white lace.

"Won't we be busy?" she said. "So much to do!" But she sensed I was huddled against her, and so she had some warning.

"We will have to make it simple," I said against her soft shoulder, "and soon."

She drew back to see my eyes, but she took my hands in hers. I couldn't meet her look, however long she waited. She waited a while, in hope. Then, breaking my heart, she said, "Oh, my child, how have I failed you?"

Terry sourly took me to meet his mother and father. I'd never been so frightened in my life. It was to be only the four of us. Jack was at Stanford and didn't come home for the event. For many years afterward he would say to anyone who'd listen that Terry had stolen me from him. Jack would say I'd been the love of his life and the reason he never married. Uproariously absurd though that is, I have never been able to laugh at it.

I'd heard enough from Constance about her Aunt Opal to be petrified, but at that first meeting it wasn't as bad as it might have been, and was to be. She didn't suspect then that I was pregnant. It would have undermined her belief in her perfect, golden son.

I wasn't good enough for him, not by a long chalk. She could make that clear with a look, but at first she was only annoyed at me. She expected Terry to do far better. On the other hand, if he'd married into the high circles they both dreamed of, he'd have left her behind. And so she gave me only the grim line of her mouth and saved the rough side of her tongue for later.

The four of us sat at a table for sixteen. Opal Kinsella had silver enough for thirty-six, but I expect we were as large a gathering as ever dined in that room. We sat at great distances from one another.

I hadn't known what to wear. I felt too young for what was happening, and so I wouldn't wear anything girlish. But an evening gown that showed my shoulders seemed brazen. I chose a dark green shot-silk dress with a high collar and buttoned cuffs. For jewelry I wore only the small diamond ring Terry had given me. His mother would not notice it.

Mr. Kinsella, sitting in shadow at the end of the table, took no part, and I was not to be recognized. I don't remember what we ate or how I got it down.

"What plans do her people have for the wedding?" Mrs. Kinsella asked Terry.

He wasn't in the habit of explaining things to his mother. The pale eyebrows in her narrow face were high and inquiring. I dared just a glance at them. Still, she didn't suspect. The reality of sex to her was all but unthinkable, and that was my last scrap of shelter.

At last we worked through the meal, and the coffee was brought in small gold-banded cups, lost in the snowy expanse of the damask tablecloth.

"This is the coffee Terry likes," his mother said, suddenly turning on me. "Folger's grinds it. I will tell you how he likes things."

I had to look at her then. My drooping head might tell too much. I had to look at my future mother-in-law. She was hardly bigger than a child, and her sparse hair was drawn up too tightly, narrowing her face to a knife—not quite a knife. A fish, I thought, or a chicken, sharply beaked. I was nearly hysterical, or sick. I'd been sick in the mornings. I could be sick again, now, over this spotless damask tablecloth.

"He is particular," she was saying. "He is accustomed to having everything done well."

She wore long earrings that seemed to vibrate, and when I

could no longer look at the edge of her face without thinking
of strange animals, I settled for the hollow of her throat, a
deep pit within the frill of her elaborate collar. Her dress was
rich and unfashionable. The sleeves, gray corded silk, were
leg-of-mutton, now out of date and grotesquely big for her
wispy form. If I could have laughed at her then, at this
parody of all mothers-in-law . . . if I could have laughed at
all of them . . .

Terry Kinsella and I were married in the clergyman's study
of Trinity Church on Bush Street. Our parents came. With the
wing of a bird huge and threatening on her hat, Opal Kinsella
was suspicious now and ready for revenge. But she wouldn't
be seen to stay away from the ceremony though the world
could hardly have noticed. I wore a wisp of veiling across my
forehead in place of the long train of lace my mother had
hoped for.

My father-in-law had been instructed to give us a house. A
generous wedding gift, though one of his foreclosures, it
stood on the east side of Van Ness Avenue. It was a vast
frame house within walking distance of the home I'd grown
up in, and nearer still to Opal Kinsella's.

There was no honeymoon trip. Terry was more the sullen
child than before. He left me in the enormous, creaking house
alone on that wedding night and went out. I didn't know
where.

I wrote to Constance in London that first night and many
more like it. I wrote first that I'd married her cousin Terry,
and I could tell her why. There was some comfort in that, a
little. The letter crossed in the mail with one from her.

She, too, had news to share. We were sharing still. Her
news erased the past and left the future blank and empty.
Constance was to be married too. It was a briskly business-
like letter, very like her. She would share, but she didn't spill
her heart across the page.

She was marrying a man I'd never heard of even from her.
He was an Englishman named Hugh Drummond. She needed
love more than she would ever say, and she'd found it again

over across the sea. She didn't say she loved Hugh Drummond, but she did. It was there between the lines.

My eyes swam. The future was shattered now. I was eighteen and longing for happy endings and first hopes fulfilled. Constance was marrying this stranger, a gentleman I supposed, though she was the last person to repeat a pedigree.

I wondered if this meant she'd come to terms with her mother, and what those terms were. I wondered and wept every time I reread the letter when I should have been wishing her well. I looked at maps and despaired at the distance of this kingdom that had claimed Constance.

"I will write to Joe," she said in her letter, "and try to explain."

She wouldn't be coming home now, and she wouldn't be marrying Joe Fletcher. He'd lost her too. I looked around in my world and found no one there.

THIRTY-NINE

Constance and I had always been contrasts, but never more than in our marriages. When I could no longer bear my life, I lived through hers. She sensed that, even after I ceased telling her everything. Her letters grew warmer as she reached across the miles to me.

Marriage was mellowing her. I even came to know Hugh Drummond and saw him in his country tweeds in the midst of London. He seemed a little lordly at times, but affectionate and quite as intelligent as he needed to be to keep pace with Constance. A soldier he had been, and an adventurer. A seasoned man.

I tried to see the place where they lived, a house Constance had rebuilt. "A resurrected cattle barn," she wrote, "masquerading as a honeymoon cottage and startled to find itself hemmed all round by Mayfair."

The house on Van Ness Avenue that Mr. Kinsella gave Terry and me was hemmed in too, by Opal Kinsella. Through the long days I wandered among its rooms, haunted by the relics of the family of strangers who'd lived there before us. As in an old-fashioned melodrama, their every possession had been repossessed. They seemed to have fled in the night, leaving clothes in the closets and, sadly, a child's toy in a room that would be a nursery again. But they were gone, and Terry and I were their inheritors.

It was a substantial house, for grown-ups. But there was no substance in Terry and me, and we were children still. The household only ran because of my mother-in-law. She'd engaged the cook, a Mexican woman who worked cheap, and her own cleaning woman came over from Pacific Avenue two afternoons a week. A handyman did the grates and the lawn. It wasn't much of a staff for a house of twenty rooms, but then there was no life in it.

In those first months I arose early, easing carefully out of my side of the bed. Terry slept long and heavily, his arms thrown back like a child's. He woke late and left the house without a word, dressed impeccably for business in time to have lunch somewhere.

I arose early, but Opal Kinsella was there before me, down in the kitchen giving orders. She planned the daily menu around Terry's favorite dishes, choosing not to know he was rarely there for meals. She telephoned her orders to Paladini's for fish and to Lilienthal & Company for wines and Domingo Ghirardelli for condiments and Goldberg-Bowen for tea and groceries. She returned every afternoon to monitor the deliveries, paying for them herself.

The cook refused to speak to me, shaking her heavily plaited head when I tried a word or two on her. Wisely, she knew she couldn't serve two mistresses. I learned to keep out of the kitchen, but at first my mother-in-law took a cup of morning coffee with me in the dining room. She sat in the glare of the Tiffany lamp that hung over the table and instructed me on the running of a house I wasn't allowed to run. Then one day that was over.

I was beginning to show, disguise it though I would. I dared not appear in my wrapper these mornings, but the bands on my skirts were straining, and a trim shirtwaist would give me away. I draped shawls about me though the fire in the dining room grate burned briskly. I saw in her narrowing eyes that Opal Kinsella knew. Still, she struggled with herself in a state of disbelief until it threatened to make her look foolish.

She rose up from the table one morning and looked me full in the eye, a thing nobody in that family often did.

"Trapped him, didn't you," she said. "How else could you get him?"

She kicked at the swinging door to the kitchen as she left. From then on, I had no need to rise early. When she came to run my kitchen, she entered by the side porch to avoid my contamination.

Terry was in prison too. There were limits to his father's generosity, though he could always get an extra wad of money from his mother. He liked to keep a thick roll of bills bulging in his trouser pocket. I was thought to need no money, and I didn't need much. I rarely left the house, and Terry didn't like me to visit my mother in the afternoons. He wanted me there should he come home, and taught me the wisdom of keeping him from anger outright. He couldn't control his temper. He had no need to.

Terry longed to be free, but I didn't hold him. He longed to be free of his mother though she was the only person in his life. He harped against his father, who was safer, and thought it was money that kept him back. He dreamed of the Yukon.

There'd been a new gold rush up on the Alaska peninsula. Gold fever had swept San Francisco, but the word of rich veins had been exaggerated, and the disappointed were streaming back. Still, Terry could grow almost lyrical about grub-stakes and sled dogs and spring thaws. When he learned there was no point in going, he was free to dream even more extravagant dreams of what might have been. He was looking for himself. He never really looked anywhere else, and for a time the Yukon was his safely unattainable goal.

He looked for companionship too and lowered his sights until he found it. He began to come home later, seeming more drunk perhaps than he was. He stank of whiskey and face powder and spittoons and lay huddled on his side of the bed, whimpering in his sleep.

He came reeling in one night and turned on every light in the bedroom. It was to be an invasion, and I was to understand that.

He was on the bed before I was awake, clawing at the buttons on his trousers. Muttering beneath his breath, he reached for the neck of my nightgown and tore it down the

front. My head leaped from the pillow as he made a shambles
of the bed.

"You'll be fat soon," he said, trying to growl. "Fat as a
hog." He thrust his face into mine and nodded. "Yes, you
will."

He ripped the skirt of my nightgown to the hem. When it
resisted, he sat back on his heels and rent it between his fists,
grinding his teeth until it tore in two.

I could only think he might hurt the baby in me. Then he
fell like a tree on me, and I didn't care if the baby died, or if
I did. His head struck my face, and the hard bone in his
temple chipped one of my teeth. I felt the sharp particle of
tooth loose in my mouth and the taste of blood. He grasped
my legs and fought them apart. I tried not to resist, never
thinking he might want me to. Then he began to thrust into
me, not with the force he wanted, but he tried to make it hurt.

I thought I lay awake all that night, but I didn't. I awoke
just at dawn. He was there on his knees on the bed, naked
now. There was a length of rope over his shoulder, like a
suspender, and he had my wrist in his hands, winding another
rope tight around it.

In this nightmare I began to speak, or cry out, but his eyes
warned me. They were grayer than the day, but they made
themselves clear. The house was empty, and the windows
were shut tight against the neighbors. I might have screamed
without causing any difficulty, but he wouldn't let me.

He tied my wrist to the farthest rail of the bed. Then he
made me give him my other hand, my other wrist. He tied
me, spread-eagle, to the rungs of the brass bed, and stripped
it of the bedclothes and the rags of my nightgown.

He eased backward off the bed, carefully, as if I could
lunge at him. He walked backward to the door. "There
now," he whispered, "that will teach you. You will have to
learn."

He spent a long, leisurely time in his dressing room. Then
he was gone, leaving the house early for once. I heard the
front door bang behind him far away in the house. I lay there
all day, learning not to twist my wrists in the ropes. I lay

there not crying out for fear the Mexican woman downstairs would hear and find me like this, for fear she wouldn't come if I called.

I lay there, hung there all day. There was a fireplace in the bedroom, but it was stone cold. I shuddered with the cold, thinking: *He will come back. He'll set me free. I can hold out till then*.

The clock on my dressing table mocked me all day. In the middle of the afternoon the door opened. It was the cleaning woman, stooped to drag in her basket of polishes. She'd rarely spoken to me. I couldn't think of her name.

She saw me and froze in the door. When she clamped her hands over her mouth, her eyes were big with horror, and disgust. I'd lain there all day. I'd fouled the bed. She was the one who untied the ropes without a word, her head turned away.

My baby was born in June, in the last spring of the old century. A beautiful girl, and I'd hoped for a girl. I told myself I wouldn't know what to do with a boy; I didn't want another Terry.

He was the proud father, and the humidors overflowed with the cigars he gave away to those he wanted to befriend. Through the summer and into the fall, things were better. But I was a little wiser now. I didn't expect a child to heal us. I named her June for her month and Constance for my dearest, only friend.

She was a beautiful baby, and I wanted no other, ever. But from the start, I began to want things for this child I couldn't quite imagine. I knew the danger in wanting to give a child too much, smothering her with secondhand hopes. But I thought my own life was over before it had begun, and so I centered my dreams on a cradle swathed in white tulle and pink bows.

From London Constance sent the baby a very English perambulator: high-wheeled with wickerwork and wine-red lacquered sides. Though I had never met her, Constance's mother sent a heavy silver porringer, very old with ancient hallmarks. My baby would have things, things that belonged to her.

I hadn't known how to be a wife, but now I meant to be a mother. There must have been some fugitive fierceness in me that kept Terry at bay. He was proud of this child in his way and never entered the nursery when he was in drink. He stood there at the foot of the cradle a few times with his thumbs hitched into his waistcoat pockets, gazing down with a hint of wonder in his eyes. I stood guard at the head of the cradle until he went away.

My mother came every day, and we sewed for the baby. I bought a pair of Singer sewing machines at the Emporium and sent the bill to Opal Kinsella, and she paid it. Mother and I sat again with our heads close over our work. There was an echo of old happiness in that.

I lived in that nearly endurable world for the months it lasted. There was new life in this house, and the scent of talcum. The days were measured now with feedings. I sat in a chair that became mine, and my child nursed at my breast.

Then one evening in the fall Terry was home too early. His collar was askew. He'd lost his necktie somewhere, and he'd fallen. There was mud on his trouser knees. He was climbing the hall stairs with absurd care, refusing to grasp the banister, and I stood at the top, watching him. He caught at my arms, but only his grip was strong. His mind was furred by liquor, and we staggered together. I tried not to grapple with him on the shifting carpet. He tried not to pitch backward down the stairs. How easy that would have been.

I fell instead. I believe he pushed me, but perhaps I want to think so. I fell and he didn't, the full length of the flight, turning over and over as I went, thanking God even then that my baby was born. I caught at the rungs in the banister, but I fell to the bottom and lay there on the hall floor. I wasn't badly hurt, and that was fortunate, for when I looked up to the landing, Terry had turned and wandered away.

*   *   *

I lived for my child in her nursery and for the letters from Constance. She'd married at the end of January on her eighteenth birthday, not hurried as I had been.

She wrote of their life together, and so I went with Hugh and her to parties and the balls of the London summer season. I rode out with them through the dappled parks behind a spanking pair and for long weekends to a country house named Wrenfields. I went where I could only go in Constance's letters and sat by their fire in the long English summer twilights, hearing the knock of Hugh's pipe against the hearthstones.

But the autumn came to Constance too, shortening her days. A war was brewing between the British colony at the bottom of Africa and another land, the Transvaal where a grim people called the Boers lived. I could scarcely find these end-of-the-world places on the map, but Constance's letters urged me to know. Her husband was a soldier.

She rejected war and the shrill people calling for it, but the dread of it crept into her letters. Then in October it happened. Soldiers were massed on some godforsaken border and an ultimatum was laid down. The British sent their reinforcements, and war broke over these countries. Hugh Drummond rejoined his regiment, and Constance must raise a flag now, if she couldn't wave it. The tone of her letters changed. They became a little frantic, determined to be hopeful and certain.

The English gentlemen officers outfitted themselves as if they were going to a sporting event. Perhaps that was what it was meant to be. Constance wrote of how Hugh and she must rush around fashionable shops, buying him a dressing case and a picnic hamper and seeing tailors and buying shotguns. He'd take his own horses, and they must be fitted out too by the best saddlers. "So much to do," Constance said, as my mother had once said to me.

Hugh Drummond sailed with his regiment at the end of October on a ship called *The Nubia*. Constance wrote that night. She told of the march before dawn from the Chelsea Barracks to Waterloo Station, and how all the wives and families swelled the crowd, making this a triumphal parade as if the war was already over.

There was a pause between her letters when she found herself alone. She didn't write about that. We didn't tell each other everything. When she wrote again, she'd found something to do. I almost saw the determined set of her chin and the strength of her jaw. An organization of prominent American women in London was mustered by her mother's friend, Lady Randolph Churchill. They formed a committee for war relief and began raising funds to send a hospital ship to South Africa. They seemed to work night and day. Constance's letters shrank to single pages, but her spirits were high.

Once she wrote of their greatest fund-raiser, a lavish theatrical party at Claridge's attended by royalty. There were *tableaux vivants,* and Eve Waring entertained with a scene from her current play.

"It has taken a war," Constance wrote, "to make my mother and me pull together in harness."

The war ground on into another century. Hugh Drummond suffering from enteric fever was invalided to a town called Durban, but then he was back in the line of battle, writing to Constance of the perpetual crackle of the Mauser rifles and the heat and the flies. He was wounded at the Battle of Modder River, and her letters to me spoke in a quieter voice now, hushed by fear.

He was injured finally, grievously, at a place called Spoenkop. Constance wrote the day she heard. He was to be sent home on the *Mondego Castle* sailing from Capetown. Her heart was in her throat. She would see him again, but there would be weeks to wait before she knew what war had done to her husband.

She never told me, precisely. There was gangrene in his wounds. She wrote to me from his bedside in a hospital in the English countryside, in winter.

"His mind is clear," she wrote, "and we relive the summer together." I looked between the lines and saw that he was dying. I loved him too then.

"I lost him today," she wrote on a January evening in

1900. Her hand was firm, but there were spatters of ink on the page. ''I held his hand to the end, and pressed it against me, where the child is.''

She could write no more that night, but my eyes were blind with tears, and I couldn't have read it.

FORTY

Constance wore black for a year. I pictured her now as much older than we were. How could she mourn as she was mourning and remain a girl? In the summer of that year she gave birth to her son, and she named him for her father, Anton.

I sat in my child's nursery and thought of Constance and her fatherless son. I nearly lived in the nursery now with June. I had a metal grate put across the window to keep the child from falling and lived myself within its protection.

June had her first birthday, crawling already and wanting to walk. She'd be ready to leave the nursery before I was. There was a nurse, but I wouldn't have her there at night when Terry came home. Perhaps I wouldn't have had her there in any case. I set up a cot in a corner of the nursery and slept there near my daughter. I locked us in every night.

I wondered at Constance as a mother, yet there was the maternal rising in her too. She resisted her mother's plan to move back to the house in Half Moon Street with her son. Though it wasn't suited for an infant and a nurse, she stayed on in the barn cottage. "I still cling to that," she wrote

She wouldn't live beneath her mother's roof, but she spoke of her more than before, with a new kind of affection and a touch of humor that made her sound very mature:

> . . . My mother is still Eve Waring and always will be. She is as complete and unchanging as you and I used to think all grown women were, that and more.

Old Sir Lawrence Alma-Tadema wants to paint her portrait, and while she shrugs this notion off, I've caught her posing before mirrors in an unmistakably artist's-model attitude.

She is lovely still, lovelier, and if the years begin to tell on her, she'll have a stinging reply. She is as busy on the stage as ever and as impatient with her career. She will do no more Shakespeare.

"Lady Macbeth is not for me," she says, "and I am getting past Juliet." But she closes one drawing room comedy, lavishly costumed, only to open another just like it. And while she sighs with boredom at her career, she keeps a sharp eye on Mrs. Patrick Campbell.

She is secure among the Best People now, though I often wonder why since she is so much more clever than they. She returns from a weekend with Daisy Warwick at Easton Lodge or Alfred Rothschild's, brimming with gossip, her eyes as bright as a girl's. I begin to wonder which of us is the mother and which the daughter.

In Hugh, I married just the sort of man Mother would have chosen for me. Perhaps by now she thinks she did. Fate has cast me as the dutiful daughter, and she proclaims her grandson from the housetops. All London is astonished anew at this glamourous grandmother. I glory in her grandeur, and it worries me less. . . .

Constance wrote another letter I always kept. On the winter day she left off her mourning, old Queen Victoria died after that long reign. Constance's world was plunged into mourning again. She wrote a somber description of the sorrowing city: the long tolling of bells and the black crepe everywhere, even tied in bows on the brooms of the street-sweepers. Then she added,

The shutters are closed today on the house in Half Moon Street. I suppose you know, Rose, the part my mother has played in the life of Prince Edward. It is no secret, or meant to be, and I've long since stopped judging her by my schoolgirl standards.

Mother has always looked beyond the ordinary things that would satisfy an ordinary woman. She's always looked up and reached up. Today the Prince is King, and my mother sits behind her shutters, wondering what changes in her life this rings. . . .

From letters like these, I thought Constance was lost to me forever. She was the English widow of a hero fallen in an English war and the mother of his son. She spoke of royalty as if they actually existed, and she'd made her peace with her mother. On very dark days, I wondered if I'd ever see her again.

I learned to live, I thought, without milestones. I expected nothing from a new day except to live in it with my daughter. She sat on my lap and I read to her fairy stories of princesses in towers, while her cornflower-blue eyes scanned the walls of the narrow nursery.

We read all the old traditional tales, except for those with ogres, and I fashioned even happier endings and pretended to read them on the page. I could give her this and a doting grandmother who came in to hold her against the ample breast I had known. Life was these afternoons.

But I couldn't keep her locked up with my heart forever. We went to Jefferson Square and Lafayette Park where she stood studying from under her hat brim the other children playing there. Though it cost me something, I urged her toward them until she was playing too.

I took her to the park myself, thinking I couldn't trust the nurse for that. I dressed carefully and tried to follow the fashions. For my daughter's sake I must look right in public. And so perhaps I was becoming a Kinsella in fact, comporting myself as if the world noticed.

Though I looked for no milestones, they occurred. Terry's father died suddenly. It was the only surprising thing he ever did. At the door of his offices at Sansome Street and Jackson he slipped on the wet paving stones and fell beneath a team of carter's horses. A hoof struck his temple, and he lay unconscious for a week before he died. Opal Kinsella mourned him extravagantly, throwing herself first into Jack's arms and then Terry's. She was inconsolable.

So was Terry when he learned that all his father's fortune had gone directly to his mother. Her purse strings tightened about it, and Terry was less free than he'd been. For many months he was brought home each night near morning, reeling and reeking, delivered to the door by waiters from the Maison Riche and Delmonico's.

We lived in different rooms of the house like two quarrelsome children who have been told to play apart. Still I could hear the mutterings of his frustration, the oaths and the bottles in his bathroom swept off onto the tiles. June heard too. Her eyes grew enormous, and she clutched at my skirts.

I thought I was grown now, and that being grown was this disillusionment. I was withered inside, but emboldened by my child. I could even present a blank, bold face to my worried mother. Then came more milestones, bringing me down.

On the night in 1903 when Eugene Schmitz was re-elected to his second term as mayor, there were rallies and victory parties. Terry had someplace to go, people to see.

Toward morning, the bell in the front door sounded. It often did. Terry could rarely find his key or fit it into the lock. Often, as I've said, it was a waiter who rang the bell and left Terry like a parcel on the porch.

I slept expecting the sound and dared not ignore it. The child had never seen me in the grip of Terry's anger, and I feared the moment she might.

I came down through the house not bothering to pull on a robe over my nightgown. I went barefoot in the dark, knowing the way. There was nothing to see through the stained-glass front door, so I pulled it open.

A woman stood there. I saw only the glint of jewels in her hair. The collar of a cloak was turned up against her face. She was silent a moment at the sight of me.

"Are you the servant?"

It wasn't the offence it might have been. At least a servant is paid and can leave.

"Forgive me," she said. "Are you Mrs. Kinsella?"

No, I nearly said. *She lives over on Pacific Avenue.* But I just managed to spare us both that. Behind the woman, down in the street a closed cab waited with its sidelamps turned low.

"Yes, I'm Mrs. Kinsella."

"I am Jessie Hayman."

The name meant nothing to me, and I can almost smile now. Any other housewife along Van Ness Avenue would have slammed the door in her face. She was the most notorious woman in San Francisco.

"I have your husband," she said, glancing briefly over her shoulder at the cab. "I wonder if I might come in first for a moment."

I walked before her into the front parlor and fumbled for the light switch. Then I turned to see her and caught my breath. She was strikingly beautiful. Her hair was fiery red, and the jewels in it were diamonds. She was tall and slender within her fine cloak. It was trimmed and banded in sable fur, about her face and down to the hem.

We studied each other for a moment. Under my nightgown I was naked, and the floor was cold beneath my bare feet.

"You don't know who I am, do you, Mrs. Kinsella?"

I shook my head, childish before this perfect creature. "I'm sorry."

"Don't be that," she said with the ghost of a smile. "I meet very few wives, but somehow I think they all know me. I'm in business on Ellis Street. Now do you understand?"

Still I didn't, but she betrayed no impatience.

"It's a parlor house. I'm bringing your husband home from it." She put her head slightly on one side. "Do you know what a parlor house is?"

I nodded, seeing her again for the first time. "Is he drunk? He often is. I won't be—"

"I expect he's drunk," she said, "and if he is, he's drunk

on champagne. I serve nothing else, but I've brought him to you, Mrs. Kinsella, because he has . . . sustained injuries.''

She was studying me still. Now she thought I might clutch my throat or cry out. When I didn't, her look was more direct than before.

''I've had a doctor look at him and stitch up his eyebrow and give him a strong sedative. There was a doctor on the premises. There usually is. I don't believe it's as serious as it looks, but your husband is pretty badly battered. I thought you should be prepared for that.''

I stood dumbly before her, and so she turned. ''I'll have him brought in now.''

I expected to see Terry stumble over the threshold, hanging from the cabby's shoulder. But he was brought in on a stretcher borne by two men in evening clothes, portly, middle-aged gentlemen in silk top hats. There were ruby studs in the shirtfront of one of them. They must have been—what was the word? They must have been this woman's clients. Seeing me in the hall, they'd have taken off their hats if their hands had been free.

One of them said, ''Will you tell us where his bed is, young lady?''

I pointed up the stairs like a sleepwalker. They would have moved off at once, but Jessie Hayman said, ''She had better see him while we're here with her.''

Terry was lying there wrapped in a blanket. If it was Terry. The only light came from the parlor, but it was enough. There was a ghastly mask where his face had been. Beneath the stitched brow one of his eyes was so swollen that it was open and staring. The proud, aristocratic nose was bent and ripped as if an animal had turned on him.

The shadows across his face made it all worse. A handful of his hair was wrenched out, and his swollen lips were drawn back to the gums. One of his teeth was chipped off down low. There was a black space. I went cold with horror, but there was a little thrill of satisfaction at that chipped tooth. I felt Jessie Hayman's eyes on me, reading me.

''A terrible thing,'' one of the gentlemen said. Perhaps he

was somebody's father. "A terrible, terrible thing." They started up the stairs with Terry, and I would have followed, but she led me back to the parlor. Perhaps I was too composed. I'd been horrified by what I'd seen, but perhaps not horrified in a wife's way.

"You will want to know?" she said.

"I suppose I should."

She almost looked away. "I have girls . . . in my employ who will . . . take abuse. They are paid to. Do you see what I mean?"

"I have taken abuse too," I said to this stranger.

"Yes, I thought you might have." Her eyes looked deeper into me, and there was a trace of sympathy in them. "Your husband selected one of the other girls. There was no such arrangement with her. There never is. She's a big woman, big as a man. She'd make two of your husband. When he . . . Well, I don't need to go into that. You've seen."

The men were coming back down the stairs. Jessie Hayman drew herself up to go. It might have been a social call and in a very good class of society.

"You have been very kind," I said to her. "More than kind."

She raised her eyebrows in faint surprise at this gratitude. "When I meet the wives," she said, "I always want to tell them . . . something. I never know what."

She turned up the collar of her cloak. "We won't meet again, Mrs. Kinsella. I won't have your husband back at my place."

"Maybe he's learned his lesson," I said feebly.

"Oh, no." She spoke from behind her furs. "That kind never does."

FORTY-ONE

Until daybreak I could think of nothing to do except dress and listen to Terry's labored breathing loud through the house. When I heard the cook come in the back door, I seemed to know the next step to take.

I was in the kitchen when Opal Kinsella came on her daily round. She was dressed in deepest black for her husband as she would always be. The wings on her hat were from ravens. At the pit of her throat was a mourning brooch the size of a saucer. Behind her veil she started at the sight of me between her and the Mexican woman at the range.

"When you are finished here," I said, "please join me in the dining room."

Her mouth opened and snapped shut. I waited beyond the door until she came. She cut short her interview with the cook. But for the veil, I might have seen caution in her eyes.

"I have a good deal to do and a busy day," she said, looking up over my head. "I am a woman alone now, and everything is on my shoulders."

I stood there, calmer than I was.

"Well, what is it?" Her eyes darted around the room, looking for clues.

"It's Terry. He was brought home badly beaten."

Her hand flew to her mouth, and already there was a black-bordered handkerchief in her clutch. She turned, and her skirts tangled. "I don't suppose you've thought to get a doctor." She was ready to make for the stairs.

"A doctor has seen him."

She was out of the room, hiking her skirts and mounting the stairs in a swirl of black.

He seemed not to have moved in the bed, but his breathing filled the room. In the vague light the pallor of his face had turned greenish, and the bruises and cuts were black. I didn't light the lamp. It might make him look better.

She teetered at the bedside. After one glimpse of him, her head fell back and her hands clamped her face. Except for the terrible noise of his breathing, he seemed a dead man. The thought of that played near my mind.

She reached down at last and smoothed the blanket. He was naked under it, and his chest was furrowed with the rake of sharp fingernails, clotting and crusted. His mother staggered out of the room. Somehow we were down in the dining room again, our place. She lifted back her veil so I could see her eyes.

"Did you do that?"

It shook me, and I hadn't meant to waver. "If I had, if I could have, I wouldn't have shown you."

"Who then? Who else knows about this?"

"I don't know who did it. I don't know her name."

"Her," she said against the handkerchief at her mouth. "Yes, that was a woman's work." Her eyes glowed with hatred for some woman, somewhere.

"It was a whore's work," I said. "They brought him home last night from a whorehouse. The . . . madam brought him herself. He shouldn't have gone to a whorehouse. He doesn't know enough about how to treat a woman even to have a whore."

I never saw her move. Yet I fell back across the table, sending a bowl of wax fruit rolling away. She'd struck me across the face with more than human strength.

I struggled up from the slick tabletop. "He beats me too," I told her.

"He ought to beat you to death," she said. "You're the whore."

She'd have bolted then, but she wouldn't leave her son

behind. I stood up and thought: *If she strikes me again, I'll do her some damage.*

"You'd let him lie up there and suffer, wouldn't you?" She spat out the words. "You'd let him die."

I hadn't thought of it till then. She saw my eyes widen.

"Take him with you," I said.

It was her fondest dream come strangely true, to have him back. Yet like all her dreams, it wasn't enough.

"I could turn you out. This house is as good as mine."

"Take it," I said. "It was always yours."

"I could turn you out and that bastard brat with you. She's nothing but a bastard in my mind, I can tell you that."

I took a step toward her, and she shied, tangling her skirts again.

"I'll take him." She looked aside and fetched up her breath in a sound like panting. "Get him ready to go."

"Get him ready yourself," I said.

Her gardener and her handyman came to carry Terry away. He was conscious, but he had nothing to say about what was happening to him.

That was my moment to return to my own family, to the house on Filbert Street where my child and I might be safe. I ran up the stairs, ready to throw a few things into a valise, a very few things, sweep up my child, and be gone, as if this house had never happened.

Something stopped me on the stairs. The echoing emptiness of the place wasn't ominous now. It was my house, a home suddenly for my child and me. Why should I run? There was nobody here. Why should I shame myself by hurrying home to my mother and father, having failed in the only thing I'd ever done with my life?

I walked up the stairs in command of the place. I looked into June's room. She was still asleep, a little mound beneath the covers. I saw the cot in the corner where I'd slept every night of her life. I hadn't slept in Terry's bed since that long-ago day I'd lain there with the ropes burning my wrists.

I had not gone back in that room, and Terry hadn't lowered himself to notice.

Now the cot looked temporary, uncomfortable. I sent for Opal Kinsella's handyman that very morning and had him set up a permanent bed for me in my child's room. We had the whole house to ourselves now, but there was no reason why we shouldn't be cozy and together. We needed nobody but each other and never had. The thought thrilled me.

My mother-in-law didn't turn me out of her house. She continued to come every day to direct the cook. She couldn't banish me entirely, for that would tell Terry how tightly she held him. I confronted her one morning, in the kitchen as before.

"Why are you here?" I said, and she started again at my daring to be in my own kitchen. "Your son doesn't take his meals in this house and never did."

Her eyes seemed to shift behind her veils, but she thought to order the cook into the pantry with a jerk of her head. "I must see to the running of the house. Somebody has to. You were capable of trapping my son, but you're capable of nothing else. This house is property, and property must be kept up."

"And appearances too," I said, finding the words.

"What would you know about keeping up appearances?" There was a wariness in her tone, and somehow I discovered the next step to take.

"I suppose you are right," I said. "It is your responsibility to see that my child and I are adequately fed."

Her jaw fell open.

"You owe us a great deal, Opal."

Her eyes snapped at this familiarity, and her hand crept to her throat.

"Yes, you do. I've put up with too much from you and yours. You owe me plenty."

She went white with rage and began to sway. I thought she might faint, or spring at me.

"You must see to our needs now. You must provide for us handsomely."

"I'll see you in hell first," she whispered. "I'll find a way to—"

"If we're not well provided for," I said, "you'll find your son in the divorce court."

Her hand closed over a chairback for balance. "You filthy hussy, how dare you mention such a thing in my presence. There'll be no divorce for you. You've brought my family low, but not that low." There was a wildness in her eyes where the wariness had been. Still, she managed to collect herself. "Divorce, indeed," she said, trying to toss her head, but she looked at the pantry door for fear there were ears to hear. "You have no grounds."

I knew nothing about divorce. It was only a word people whispered. Still, I found my way. "I didn't say divorce. I said divorce court. People . . . testify. I'd have to tell how my husband beat me, and how he went to whores. I have . . . witnesses for that."

"Who'd believe them?" she snapped.

"Perhaps no one. But it would all be spoken in a courtroom, Opal. Surely you see that. People would hear and repeat what they heard. I'd mention your name in the courtroom, Opal. Your name would come up. I'd see to that."

She turned from me, horrified. I'd touched her where it hurt, I of all people. She walked out of the house, bent as if in grief, stumbling over the doorsill.

My mother came in the afternoon. I knew I had to tell her. June would begin to notice her father's absence. It would seem nothing to her, for she'd never had him to miss, but she was a little chatterbox. She'd say some innocent thing, and my mother would know.

"Terry has gone back home." Futilely, I tried to sound casual.

She put down her sewing and looked up at me. I worked on, trying not to meet her gaze, until I knew I had to.

"You haven't been happy, Rose. I've known that, and it's grieved me."

"You mustn't, Mother. I've been too weak, but I'm stronger now." Still, I hadn't dispelled the pain in her eyes.

"You should come home to us," she said.

"I couldn't do that. I must be . . . someone's mother, not someone's daughter." But now I'd hurt her, and it was the last thing I'd meant to do.

"You'll always be my daughter, Rose. Don't close me and your father out."

"No," I said, trying to brighten. We'd weep soon, both of us, and that would solve nothing. "You must come here in the afternoons, to call. You must let me find my way and be in charge here."

"What of the future?" she said, wiser than I dared to be.

"Oh, I can't think of that. I must just get through these days."

Terry stayed with his mother the better part of a year. His wounds were the kind slow to heal, and he couldn't face the world with them. His nose was broken, robbing him of his profile. It was put about that he'd been thrown from a horse and dragged. That must have sent peals of laughter ringing up Ellis Street.

Opal Kinsella had no one but Terry now, not even Jack. I read in the society column of the *Call* that Mr. Jacinto Kinsella, Stanford alumnus of this city, had been appointed an apprentice curator for the Metropolitan Museum of Art in New York.

"Many are called, but few are chosen," Jack was quoted as saying when he boarded the eastbound train. Perhaps he could seize this single chance for escape now that Opal possessed his brother.

Then I looked up one day, and it was time for my daughter to go off to her first day at school, another milestone as hard as any of them. The baby chubbiness had melted from her legs, and she'd sit now, quite grown-up and uncomplaining, while I brushed out her corn-silk hair.

"Corn-silk hair and cornflower eyes," I'd say to her, and if it would make her vain, I couldn't help that. She wouldn't let me spoil her very much. She was ready to be gone, dancing out of the house with her new schoolbooks strapped together and the shoes that buttoned high up her legs flashing in the morning of her life.

Terry came home one afternoon.

He rang the bell like any stranger, and I didn't know him through the stained-glass panes. I looked twice before I knew him when I'd opened the door.

He'd grown gross from a mother's feeding. The fine line of him, the knife-edge was gone. His pale blond hair had receded around that patch that had been wrenched out. His nose was someone else's. He looked thick in his clothes, and I wondered if his mother had kept him from his tailor.

I grasped at the door, but his foot jammed it open.

"I'm home again," he said, "to stay."

"No," I said, but he brushed me easily aside and strode in.

"That old bitch was driving me crazy," he said in the hall. He pitched his hat at the hat rack and didn't wait to see it roll into a corner. He turned to me.

"I could do with a drink, and a woman." His hands were on his hips and his feet far apart in some sad show of manly authority.

"This isn't your home anymore if it ever was. I think you'd better go back to your mother. Opal's all the woman you need."

I'd grown too bold in his absence, out of the sight of his mad eyes, and I couldn't have said anything more dangerous. He was on me in that moment, twisting both my arms behind my back.

"Do you want to get upstairs on the bed, the bed in my room, or do you want it here?" he whispered against my ear.

I tried to bring my knee up, but he was ready for that, and I was half blind from the pain twisting in my arms.

Then he demolished everything I had built in his absence: "Where's the kid?"

I longed to tell him she was out of the house, but she wasn't, and he would know. "Upstairs in her room."

"Let's keep her there," he said. "Do just exactly as I say,

or I'll call her downstairs, and I'll show her what I'm going to do to you.''

He eased me almost gently onto the floor of the hall. I fell back and opened my hands to show him I'd do nothing to make him call the child. I lay back, and he loomed over me.

''Not that way,'' he whispered, easing off his coat. ''Turn over on your belly.''

He beat me that night and blackened my eye. It was a halfhearted attack. He was only reasserting his authority in that house. A day passed, or several. They meant nothing to me now. I sent excuses to my mother to keep her away. She mustn't see my bruised face and insist that June and I come away with her. He could always get to me through my child, wherever I went. Hope left me when I saw there was no place to hide.

The bell sounded in the door on this other afternoon, and I came down to answer it.

There was a young woman there, vaguely outlined in the window. I opened to her. I'd have opened to a burglar. I'd already opened to a maniac. I could keep nobody out.

She stood there neatly composed in a trim tailored suit, with a hat that turned back from her face. At her side was a child, a small boy in short pants, holding her hand. We were strangers, and she saw first my eye, swollen shut.

I didn't know her, and she didn't know me, not in that first moment. And then it was Constance.

FORTY-TWO

Constance had come home, becoming again a San Franciscan. She took rooms for herself and her son across the Bay on Piedmont Avenue in Berkeley. Her son, young Anton, was nearly ready for school, and she wanted him educated as an American boy. If his father had lived, things would have been different. She never said that, but then she didn't have to.

I watched Constance fit the pieces of her life together, wondering at the sureness of her touch, as I always had. She meant to enroll at the university. Against all odds, she was determined to study architecture. It wasn't a field that admitted women, but that never stopped her. She was a builder in her bones and saw poetry in bricks and mortar. I didn't know there were such things in a woman.

She returned to her native place and that plan, and Joe Fletcher. Somehow I thought he'd gone away, but he hadn't. A shack he'd once worked in on Telegraph Hill was a substantial house now. He lived in it and worked from his offices there. It may be sentimental to say that the memory of Constance had spoiled the thought of anyone else for Joe. I don't know that. I only know she came home, and he was here for her.

"Your cousin Constance has come home," I said to him, to Terry.

It was evening, and he was dressing to go out. The studs were in his boiled shirtfront, and his suspenders looped down his black trouser legs. He was struggling with a starched collar and a collar button as men must, but his hand was steady enough. He wasn't drunk yet. I stood in the door of his dressing room to give him this news. He seemed not to hear.

"Come fix this damned collar for me," he said. "And help me with my tie. I can't ever get the thing to come out right."

"No. I won't come near you. I'm afraid of you. Isn't that what you want?"

His eyes remained on the mirror as he fought his collar. He was giving me his profile again though it was altered now.

"Rose, I don't have any idea what you're talking about. I wonder if you're in your right mind. They have places for people who talk out of their heads."

He was sober, and these full sentences proclaimed that proud fact. "You ought to get out of the house more," he said.

And so after all he'd heard me say that Constance was back, that now there was someone here for me, someone on my side. It might make a difference, and the thought occurred to him too.

Constance knew. Even when my blackened eye had faded, it wasn't forgotten. She'd already seen through the omissions in my letters. She saw again in that first look at the shabby emptiness of my house and the greater vacancy in my face.

She didn't invade me with her outrage and pity. We talked of other things, talk I was hungry for. We talked of our children and the children we'd been.

My June was a year older than her Anton—Andy—and glad of her advantage. She bossed him, and he bore it with gentlemanly grace. June's astonishment alerted us to his British short pants that must be replaced with American knickerbockers. He needed a checked cap too, and though it looked like a newsboy's, it was all the rage in kindergarten. The children played together very well, all things considered, June the boss, Andy the grave-faced follower. The house on

Van Ness Avenue rang with the unfamiliar sound of womantalk and surprising gusts of laughter.

We talked around some topics and plunged into others. Constance spoke of her mother, who was planning a triumphal return tour of American theaters.

"Mother is feathering her nest now," Constance remarked. "She says she must provide for her old age."

"How old is she?" We'd always wondered.

"She encourages the rumor that she's thirty-five, which means she was twelve at my birth." Constance drew in her cheeks and cocked an eyebrow at me, and we were girls again, at St. Mary's.

We went out together. She saw to that. We took the children to the carousel in the park and to the giant water lilies at the conservatory. The working model of the Panama Canal at the Mechanics' Pavilion drew Andy time and again and us with him. Constance glanced at my hair that I'd ceased to bother about, and we went off to fancy hairdressing salons.

I was so proud to be out with her, waiting with our children for the cable car and strolling the Ladies' Mile along Market Street. I don't suppose she was a pretty woman exactly, but she'd acquired distinction. Her suits were British worsted, and none of her hats fussed. Pince-nez spectacles hung from a button on her tailored jacket and fitted precisely on the bridge of her nose. She spoke now with the slight crispness of an English accent that suited her perfectly.

We gave our children outings on the Saturday afternoons she could get away from her studies. June and I met them off the boat under the new tower of the ferry building. San Francisco was booming as never before, and Constance had to examine and assess all its new architecture. We toured the new Mills building and the Kohl tower and the Merchants' Exchange while she made quick notes and sketches of them in her notebook.

The new James Flood building stood now where the old Baldwin Hotel had been. The Baldwin had burned on the day I was married, and it had been Constance's childhood home.

But she never looked back. She looked up. We threw back our heads to see the dome of the new Claus Spreckels building at Market and Third, the *Call* building that scraped the sky at nineteen stories.

These outings, we said, were for the children, though Constance meant them for me. We haunted circuses and frequented firehouses and parades of paper dragons. Once we took the cars out to the beach when Buffalo Bill's Wild West came to town, performing outdoors in the dunes.

Andy, still a little English boy, so forgot himself during the mock Indian raid that he cheered the redskins on. We saw Buffalo Bill in his flow of white hair and mustaches and the magnificence of his white kid buckskins.

We roared with the crowd for another old veteran of frontier days, the durable equestrian star of the show in his fine black Spanish hat and astride his palomino, Lorenzo Ransom.

We went one day up Telegraph Hill. Constance suggested it casually, but I wasn't fooled. I nearly smiled. She could wax so eloquent about steel girders and speak so matter-of-factly about almost anything else, but on the topic of Joe, she wasn't much short of coy.

We took a motor cab to the foot of the hill and then climbed the sheer, dusty rise of Lombard Street, up among the wheeling seabirds. The hill was still ragtag and rural, but Joe had made much of his old headquarters. The former shack still stood as the main room, encased in stucco behind a walled terrace paved in colorful tiles. He'd added a tower to it with a winding staircase that the children loved. It led to bedrooms above and a flat roof at the top where we sat in garden chairs commanding the town. Alcatraz Island lay below us like a stone ship moored in the Bay.

There was more to the house than that: arches that looked Spanish and hand-hewn beams. I thought even then that Joe hadn't built it for himself alone. It rambled on levels, a part of the hill it hugged. I can't begin to explain it well. Constance could.

That day was the first of many. Joe was older too, nearer

his goals now. He was stockier, but the ginger-colored mustache and the grin were the same. He was as ready as ever to turn back his shirtsleeves to unroll blueprints. His head and Constance's were soon close, poring over some new project of his. He was prospering along with San Francisco.

His gaze rarely left Constance except to study her son. I sat there high in that enchanted tower with them and matched the colors of our old days to this brilliant afternoon.

On another day, Constance said to me, "I've been putting it off, but I suppose I'd better go call on Aunt Opal."

We'd never mentioned Opal Kinsella. We'd hardly mentioned Terry. He'd been there once, come home when she was there. She'd spoken coolly, distantly to him and was astonished at how he'd changed, the look of him, I mean. She'd noticed he was rarely at home. Maybe she took that for a better sign than it was.

She raised a questioning eyebrow at me.

"I don't get along with my mother-in-law," I said.

"Who could?" She poked busily into her handbag. She was trying to ease us into something.

"Still," she said, "I'd better go. I expect she knows I'm back."

"I expect so. Terry would have told her."

"Are you ready yet?" she said.

I couldn't think what she meant, quite.

"Ready to talk about Terry," she said, spelling it out.

"Your being here is enough," I said. "It helps." It was time to tell her more, but still I couldn't. I'd have to speak in the voice of a victim, and I despised the thought of that. I despised myself.

"You come with me to Aunt Opal's."

I flinched, not expecting this.

"As bad as that?"

I nodded.

She thought about that for a moment, and said, "There'd be the two of us, four with the children. We'd have her outnumbered."

She paused then, waiting. We were upstairs in June's

room. The children darted in, playing tag, and darted out
again, echoing along the hall.

"I couldn't take my child there, Constance. Opal Kinsella
has never been a grandmother to her."

"Perhaps that's just as well," Constance said.

"Perhaps it is. She called my daughter a bastard."

Constance watched me giving way. "Words," she said.

"Words and more than that. She struck me once." I
smiled at Constance, though I never could make use of irony.
"I fell across the table. Maybe I need a good beating once in
a while. I often get one."

She might have turned away, but she put out her hand for
me to take. "Do you remember the time on the ferry going
back to school? You said you wouldn't mind if we never
grew up. But we did, Rose."

I told everything then, everything I knew. I had this friend,
and I told her. She heard me to the end and spared me advice.
She heard me out and spoke no more of calling on her Aunt
Opal.

I must have believed that telling Constance was enough,
but it wasn't enough for her. She stayed with me that afternoon until it was dark and Terry came home. "First of all,"
she said to me, "you need a witness." I'd feared a witness,
but now I saw the folly of that.

He came home at last. There'd been small changes in him
lately. He'd been trying to pull himself together, to find some
purpose. Now he wore round black-rimmed glasses that gave
him rather a legal air and drew attention away from his
shapeless nose. He brought papers home from some office,
carrying them in a satchel. He had some scheme that would
see him through a season, something that smelled faintly of
quick money. I don't know what. It doesn't matter.

He saw us there in the stairs. "Well, Connie, here again?"
He planted his satchel on the newel post where she'd notice
that he was a responsible man of affairs, home after a busy
day. He hung his black bowler with care on the halltree.

"Rose has been telling me about you," Constance said,
there on the stairs above him. He had to look up at her. She'd

thought of everything. He looked up too quickly, shattering his show.

"What's she been telling you?" Oddly, he looked back over his shoulder.

"The truth."

"She's a liar," he said. "Believe me. I know women."

She stood there above him.

"Terry, if you ever lay a finger on Rose again, I'll make you wish you'd never been born."

We stood there, statues for a moment.

"I never—"

"You never will again," Constance said.

"I'd like to know what you could do about it."

"No, Terry," she said. "You wouldn't like to know that."

She took a final step down and another toward him. They stood face to face. She wasn't taunting him. I think she was studying him.

FORTY-THREE

The pace of life quickened, even mine. The new century had found its feet, and San Francisco was reaching for the sky. The streets were filling with automobiles powerful enough to crest the hills. The cable cars clanged deep in the granite canyons downtown, and Madame Tetrazzini sang at the Tivoli. It was still San Francisco—the glossy-leafed greenery in the parks and the fog rolling in like a moving mountain—but the city stood taller now, and glittered.

Most of the Nob Hill mansions stood empty, old now as they'd always meant to look. Among them the magnificent Fairmont Hotel, all white marble, was rising at the top of the town like a picture of the Acropolis.

June was in her second year of school, quick and clever in her studies. She gloried in ruled paper and steel-nibbed pens. She brought things home that could hardly have come from school: bullfrogs from rain barrels, a family of ants, fledglings with broken wings. Her room became a menagerie as ranked with specimen bottles as a horse doctor's.

Shyly, she invited her father in to view these treasures. He stood in the doorway looking in on her small universe, another world like mine that existed without him. Terry looked in and went away, but June was busy again, taming a kitten to wear a bandage, waiting with confidence for birds' eggs to hatch.

Terry lingered there on the edge of us for months, nobody's father or husband, only somebody's son. He was friendless too, in the face of my friend.

Constance's mother came to San Francisco in the spring of that year. Constance and Andy traveled as far as Reno to join her and return in her private railroad car. The papers were full of Eve Waring long before the train drew into the Oakland Station. There had not been such hysteria even for Bernhardt. She even eclipsed the great Enrico Caruso and the entire Metropolitan Opera Company arriving for their season.

Every front page was filled with Eve Waring's pictures, encircled in oval frames of American Beauty roses, her symbol. Portraits of her and the king of England were entwined with American flags and Union Jacks. Those who'd forgotten she'd begun in San Francisco remembered now.

People stood in long lines before dawn for tickets to see Eve Waring, quoting to one another from the newspapers and even debating the duties of a royal mistress. They waited to see what the years had done to her legendary beauty and to copy her clothes, even to see if she could act. They waited to claim her as San Francisco dearly loves to do, as one of our own.

I pondered the newspaper pictures, for I'd never seen her in life, but they failed to reveal the astonishing colors of her eyes and hair and skin.

She was to occupy a suite that took up half of the new St. Francis Hotel's sixth floor, with a reception room copied from the Tuilleries. It was noted that her time would be so fully engaged that she begged to be spared social invitations. This provided a challenge to many a hostess though it was not meant to. She traveled with a hundred and sixteen steamer trunks, and Lloyds of London declined to estimate the value of her jewelry. The town was agog at this invasion, just as it was supposed to be.

I meant to withdraw, thinking I had no part, but Constance wouldn't hear of it. So I was in the suite at the St. Francis on the afternoon Eve Waring gave her first interview to the press.

Though I meant to be early, I was late. The crowds in Geary Street and standing on boxes in Union Square were impossible. I fought my way through the lobby and gave my

name to the man in the elevator as Constance had told me to
do. Then I was making my way along a corridor banked with
baskets of flowers, dank with the greenhouse scent of roses.
There were mirrors at intervals, and I straightened my hat in
every one of them. I'd trimmed it myself and thought it was
right, but I wasn't sure.

Her reception room was packed to the door with newspaper-
men. I heard her voice before I could find a gap in the crowd
to see her.

"You haven't played San Francisco for many—several
years, Miss Waring," a rumbling voice said. "Why is that?"

"I have made my home in England for some time now and
have many friends there. My home is there, but a part of my
heart is here." The voice was velvet, giving each simple
word immense meaning. It was strangely intimate, as if she
hadn't raised it.

"San Francisco hasn't seen any of the plays for your run
here, Miss Waring. Is it true you will appear only in work
written for you?"

"Quite true. At my time of life a woman must be either in
complete control or in retirement."

I suppose it must have been audacious for an actress to
mention her time of life and retirement, even when she hadn't
been asked. But she could do no wrong before this regiment
of men, and she could make them see that.

Then I saw her myself, and the next answers were lost to
me. She sat with one hand on the arm of the chair and the
other lying palm up in an attitude of great openness. Every
man in the room must have thought those turquoise eyes were
upon him. She was, of course, the most beautiful woman on
earth, but that was news to nobody.

It is easier to recall details, though there were no details
about her; everything counted. Her hair, blacker perhaps than
it had been, was dressed to recall a coronet. She wore no
jewelry except for a gold brooch set with turquoises that
answered her eyes. She made no gestures. She sat unmoving,
baffling those who expected dramatics.

"And how is the king?" asked a reporter too young.

Her eyes lifted past him. "The audiences all across the country have been more than kind, but I have saved San Francisco until last. There is no theater town to equal San Francisco."

Thus the room learned the topic that could not arise.

I've said she seemed to gaze at everyone directly. But then I felt her gaze on me in fact. "It is time to mention a very important reason for my San Francisco stay," she said, "to be with my family." Constance was sitting next to her in another chair that faced the crowd. Like her mother Constance sat there with a calm imposed. Andy sat on Eve Waring's other side, small in a big chair, keen-eyed and curious, twirling his checkered cap.

She introduced them. "My daughter, Mrs. Drummond, who has returned to California to take up the study of architecture. It is a study well beyond my grasp or understanding. I can take no credit for encouraging her. But it is her life's work, and if I am remembered, I shall be remembered as the mother of this distinguished daughter."

A hush fell on the room, and I wondered if Constance's eyes were misted over. I couldn't tell, for mine were.

Miss Waring introduced Andy, and he slid off the tapestried chair to make his bow. "My grandson, An—Andy Drummond. Need I tell any of you gentlemen that all grandsons are perfect?"

There was a little respectful laughter, and my eyes cleared.

"And another member of my family," Eve Waring was saying, "though I have never met her." It was true. Her eyes had been on me. "My nephew's wife, Rose Kinsella of San Francisco. She should join us here if you gentlemen will make room."

I was handed to the front of the room where a place was made next to Constance. Miss Waring took my hand and pressed it as I made for the empty chair in great confusion. My heart thundered, but the reporters continued their assault, more respectful with each thrust. Time and again she tamed them.

Near the end Eve Waring seemed to scan the room, cutting across a question.

"I see," she said, "there are no lady reporters present. For the benefit of you gentlemen, I had better explain my dress, though none of you has asked."

Again they were thrown back on their defenses and reminded of their job.

She just glanced down at herself. "My clothes are designed now by a brilliant young Parisian designer, Paul Poiret." She spelled the name for them, and waited. "He is the man of the hour in Paris, and means to liberate women from their corsets."

Many a hard-bitten reporter looked up suddenly at this news.

"Poiret draws his inspiration from the colors of contemporary painters and from the simplicity of ballet. The waistline is high now, and the skirts are rising. You may promise your women readers quite simple hats, like turbans, for the next season. Turbans that recall the Directoire period." She spelled *Directoire* for them, and they were routed. She'd turned them from the topic of herself, and they were busy with their spelling.

She rose then, seeming to show them her deceptively simple gown, the color of a ripe plum. It would be several seasons before San Francisco caught up with it. The newsmen stared of course, not at the dress but at the figure within. It was a figure always, inaccurately, called voluptuous—not slim by any means, not as slim as the Poiret dress insisted upon. It was a statue come to a kind of life, the magnificent figure of a woman who must be in her mid-forties, a figure that brought some of the older veterans in the room nearly to their knees.

She was standing now, and this meant the interview was at an end. They filed away, swallowing the last of their questions. She'd told them nothing of her craft or her past or herself, and she'd skewered them with her dressmaker. She'd bested them, and they went away adoring.

The photographers took their place. The room was saffron

yellow with flash powder and loud with their unheeded pleas to strike many poses. She gave them the pose she wanted them to have.

She could talk through all this to Constance and Andy and me. She spoke to me from the first as if she'd always known me. She did know me. Constance had told her a great deal, about me and about Terry Kinsella.

Constance's old friend, Arnold Genthe, was there quietly in the midst of the other photographers, with a small box camera in his hand to put their tripods and elaborate equipment to shame. No newspaper sent him. He was there because beauty never escaped him, and the camera was one of his eyes.

In the midst of this muddle he photographed Eve Waring quickly, just once. That is the picture that's remembered, of the goddess in the timeless gown with the face half in shadow and the faint smile at some mysterious memory.

At last the room emptied, and there lingered a sulphur smell and the man smell of sweat and pursuit. But there was one man left. He sat at the far end on a sofa. His hands were clasped over the head of a walking stick planted between his patent-leathered feet. His chin rested on his clasped hands, the picture of patience.

He was perhaps not quite thirty, with a young-old face and a wonderfully tailored English suit. I'd never heard of him before, but I met him now. He rose and took my hand in a kind of detached warmth, and I was made acquainted with Lord Guy Carville-Paget.

That April afternoon at the St. Francis would have been enough for me to savor, but Constance and her mother came to call at Van Ness Avenue. They came when Eve Waring was still in rehearsal. I think she rehearsed very little, but that was her excuse to decline invitations. She'd give of her best on the stage, but she wouldn't know society people. Perhaps she remembered when they wouldn't know her. Of all people, I was to be her only hostess.

I bustled for days. I even burst in on the Mexican cook and

told her there'd be need of refreshments, and she seemed to comprehend. I told Terry they were coming, to keep him away. He wouldn't face Constance if he could help it, but he told his mother.

I stood in the door, flush-faced, to receive my guests. June stood with me, beribboned as a candy box. The neighbors knew too, though I hadn't told them. They stood on their porches and watched a chauffeur hand Eve Waring down out of a big automobile. Though they only walked together up to the porch, it was a royal progress.

Once inside, they were family. Eve Waring dominated the room, but she couldn't help that. She wore a toque like a turban and another Poiret gown and a long scarf of furs. She deferred to her daughter and made much of mine. The chair she sat in transformed itself into a throne, but she never patronized. Though her voice filled the room, she spoke of comfortable commonplace things and knew how to listen. She became my aunt that afternoon and told me to call her Eve.

The Mexican woman amazed me by appearing unbidden in a starched cap behind a tea cart. It was laden with sandwiches and cakes with a silver tea service I'd never set eyes on in my life. The cook—my cook suddenly—served with mysterious grace and left the cart correctly before Eve, to pour out.

She raised her eyebrows and said, "I see that Opal has given you her tea service. It was always one of her treasures."

I was far more surprised than that. "I've never seen it before. She must have sent it around this afternoon."

Eve smiled without a hint of humor, and we three exchanged glances over June's head. When the child went off to play, Eve sighed. "I shall have to do something about Opal, or she'll pester us all to distraction."

Only a few blocks away my mother-in-law sat, waiting to be recognized by her famous sister. I didn't like to think what she might do at the end of her patience. She'd sent her silver tea service ahead, and she was sure to follow.

"I could send her a ticket for opening night. A box. She'll

like that.'' Eve turned her hand over, to dismiss Opal Kinsella, and said, ''Of course I want you all there opening night.''

The teacup nearly leaped out of Constance's hand. ''Mother!'' she said, ''not me, surely?''

Her mother turned to her, quite startled at this outburst. ''Yes, of course you, Constance. Why ever not?''

''But, Mother,'' she said, all her composure gone, ''you have never let me near a theater where you were playing. Why have you changed now? What's come over you?''

''Nothing has come over me, Constance. Nothing ever does. You're to be an architect, aren't you? You know I don't understand that, but you're quite set on it, aren't you?''

''Yes,'' Constance said, ''of course.''

''Since that's decided,'' Eve said as if this were all perfectly obvious, ''there's no harm in your coming to the theater. I only kept you away before because I was afraid you'd want to go on the stage yourself. I wanted something better for you.''

Constance fell back in her chair. It was one of those rare moments when something is actually made clear between a mother and a daughter, some realization come almost comically late.

''Oh, Mother, how could you think I'd ever want to be an actress? How could you think I'd ever hoped to . . . vie with you? I've always stood in your shadow. I've always had to look elsewhere for myself. Why, I'm not even beautiful.''

Eve's eyes grew large, and her hand worked on the arm of the chair as if she might reach out to Constance.

''Not beautiful?'' she said, deeply baffled. ''How could I know you thought that? You are beautiful to me.''

I am always too ready to weep, and I could have then. Constance had to turn her face away, and there was a wonderful stillness in the room. We sat there so near one another, and then Eve rose to go, drawing back into her famous self.

At the door Constance hesitated. There was one more matter to air, and I thought I saw it coming.

''If we are all to be there opening night,'' she said to her mother, ''there's someone else I should like to invite.''

Eve gave her an eternally maternal look. "A man?"

"Yes, a man. A . . . friend of long standing."

"Not that young man in the photograph all that time ago?"

"Yes, Mother, that man."

"How patient men are," Eve said, shaking her head in wonder. She arranged her furs about her shoulders in gestures that would have played to distant balconies.

"I suppose something can be arranged," she said, speaking in a clear parody of every grande dame in the Western Addition. Then she sailed away to her waiting limousine. Constance followed with a little skip in her stride.

FORTY-FOUR

No one ever forgot that April night in 1906, Eve Waring's opening night. It was a brilliant, hectic evening, frantic with broughams and automobiles making for Mission Street and the Grand Opera House to hear the great Caruso's Don José in *Carmen*. A crossfire of traffic surged to the Majestic Theater on Market Street to see Eve Waring. It was an embarrassment of riches, an overflowing. There was electricity in the air.

I had a parlor maid now, and I persuaded her to stay late with June, though I tucked the child in myself. I hadn't left her before, but there hadn't been a night like this.

I sat in a box with Constance and Joe who was half strangled by unaccustomed evening clothes. Across in the opposite box sat Opal Kinsella and Terry. It had been decided that way. Terry seemed supremely indifferent when he knew I wouldn't sit in the box with my mother-in-law, or with him. Perhaps he was too relieved that she was invited at all. She'd been plaguing him. He was near the end of his rope and growing dangerous again. His mother harped worse than a wife and it wouldn't take very much to push him over another edge.

I don't recall the name of the play. Perhaps it was never performed after Eve Waring's time. She wasn't off the stage except to make her changes. There were eighteen of them, all her own clothes. It was rumored that her jewelry was worth millions, gifts to her. The jewels were all paste, I believe, and purchased for the play. But there was nothing false about

her performance, not a false step though she walked with
such heedless ease through the scenes.

She was the play's only strength. It told the unlikely story
of a worldly woman whose lover was an elderly man of
enormous power, a man who never appeared on the stage.
There was another man, decorative and dedicated to her, who
longed with youthful idealism to redeem her. She hung suspended between these two men through three acts. At the
final curtain she stood somehow lovelier than before at a
stage window, gazing out upon an artificial evening. She was
ready to make her choice, though we were left to wonder
what it was to be. She won her audience with her first
entrance and held them till the end. Then came that rolling
roar of applause like summer thunder, and the stage filled
with flowers. She stood gravely in that garden, just inclining
her head in the least theatrical of bows.

The intermission in the midst of this was very long while
San Francisco society swept up and down the aisles in a
flurry of aigrette feathers and sable. Diamonds glittered like
the sea under the heavy crystal chandelier. I think of it now
as the last moment of some ancient civilization. Perhaps it
was.

Constance was like a young girl at her first party and
couldn't disguise it. She pored over her theater program and
didn't read a word of it. She nearly fidgeted, and I couldn't
look at her when her mother was on the stage. We had new
gowns of course, rather low-necked and woman-of-the-world.
Joe Fletcher was far more amused by us than by the play.

Opposite, Opal Kinsella sat preening in black jet, unfolding a black lace fan. I looked across at Terry and her and saw
how alike they were. I tried to make my eyes skip past these
strangers. They seemed not to notice me, though Opal's eyes
were everywhere, and at the intermission she turned her opera
glasses on the audience. Then she put down her glasses and
took up her fan again, giving her profile to the world. She
played to the house until the curtain rose, and perhaps I was
her only audience.

At the intermission Lord Guy Carville-Paget slipped into

our box. He was a very charming young man, not much to look at but suave beyond the meaning of the word. I had no idea what role he played in Eve Waring's retinue. I thought perhaps he might be her private secretary, though thank heaven I was too shy to ask him.

Before the houselights dimmed again, I looked across and saw Terry leaving. He was reaching for his hat and stick and shrugging off his mother's gloved hand. He left her, and she sat there alone, smaller through the rest of the play.

There was no opening-night party. Constance helped spirit her mother out of the theater ahead of the crowds at the stage door. Constance and Andy were staying with her at the St. Francis. Joe Fletcher found me a cab and put me in. Cabs were hard to come by that night, and so I was late getting home, later than I'd meant to be.

I climbed down out of the cab and hurried up the walk, anxious to relieve the maid and to look in on June. While I was taking off my cloak in the hall, I heard a woman's voice upstairs. I thought it was the maid, but something held me back. I stood there with the theater program still in my hand.

Terry was there weaving at the top of the stairs, looking down at me. He couldn't be drunk that soon, and yet he seemed to be. His shirt was out of his trousers and hanging down. He swayed there on the top step. My heart stopped.

He held my daughter loosely in the crook of his arm. June's bare feet dangled down below her nightgown. She was still asleep, or half asleep, her head drooped against his shoulder. The mop of her hair was bright, brighter than his. He'd snatched her out of her bed, and now he teetered there at the top of the long flight.

Nearly falling, he called out over his shoulder. "Come here," he said to someone behind him. "Come here and see my little girl. I told you I had a little girl, and I do."

His voice was thick, and I thought his knees would buckle. He'd fall and crush June. I dared not move.

He knew I was there, looking up. This was for me to see, but he was still calling out over his shoulder. A woman, a girl, appeared behind him. She'd come out of his room. Her hair hung lank about her head, and she was pinning it up. I could just see her in the dim light on the landing. She was in a tattered petticoat. I saw the livid narrowness of her bare shoulders and the smudge of lipstick across her mouth.

"I don't give a damn," she said. "I'm going. You're no use to me." She spoke through the hairpins in her mouth.

Terry looked down, pretending to see me for the first time. He hitched June closer against him, and I prayed she wouldn't move or twist in his arms.

"Oh, now you're in trouble. Deep trouble." He bawled over his shoulder though the girl was right there behind him. She looked down and saw me too.

"You are in grave trouble now," Terry said to her, "for that is my so-called wife. I told you I had a wife, and I do."

"I'm going," the girl said again.

"Oh, you're not going anywhere," he said. "I'm not through with you." He reached back at her with his free hand, turning and nearly stumbling on the carpet of the top step. June stirred. She couldn't be sleeping through this. She put her hands around his neck.

The girl vanished back into his bedroom and returned at once, a hat jammed on her head and her hands full of her clothes. She eluded him easily and started down the stairs. She stalked down in her unbuttoned boots, wondering perhaps if she'd get by me as easily.

"Wait right there." Terry's voice, quiet—almost gentle—made the girl stop and look back. "Nobody's going anywhere. I'm in charge here. Matters are . . . in my hands."

He shifted June suddenly, too suddenly and surely for a drunk. He held her out at arms' length. Her hands slipped away from his neck. He turned her, and I saw her eyes. They were open and staring in this nightmare.

Never looking away from me, he rested her on the banister, just where it began to curve downward. He took her wrist in his hand, and then he nudged her gently off the narrow banister, into space. Her nightgown billowed, and she swung out over the sheer drop. Then she was awake and screaming, and beginning to turn in the air.

The girl on the stairs whirled toward me. "He's crazy. He's a madman."

My mind went dead, but I was running. Not up the stairs. That would be fatal. I ran along beside the stairway. If he dropped her, I could try to catch her or break her fall. It was a drop of fifteen feet, not much more than that, and I thought—

When he saw me there below, he began to snatch her back. But she was kicking now and shrieking and crying out for me. I didn't know if I dared move from where I was, but I was afraid he'd pulled her back to throw her down the stairs. I heard sounds, but June's shrieks covered them, echoing in the hallway.

I stumbled back and around the newel post. The girl was on her knees at the top. I saw only the dirty lace of her petticoat. I ran up and the girl was there on her knees, with June in her arms. Terry's bedroom door was banging shut behind him.

The child was crying, hysterical, and the girl was rocking her in her arms, beginning to croon. I stood there over them. For some forgotten reason, I was wearing an evening gown. The girl looked up at me, and in a dream I saw her sickly face and the yellowish whites of her eyes. This woman who had saved my child looked up at me as if I might strike her.

We put June to bed. The little night-light lamp was on and a chair was drawn up to the bed, with a magazine lying open on it. I suppose Terry had come back and sent the maid home. I could imagine her being told to get out. I pulled the quilt up to June's neck and she only sobbed once before she was asleep. It might have been a bad dream. I meant for her to think so.

The girl had stepped into her skirt and thrown on the rest of her clothes. There were flowers on her hat and bunches of cherries. "Lady," she said, "you don't want to stay in the same house with him. It ain't safe."

But I only stood there guarding my child, and the woman went away. Perhaps she knew far better than I that there is no safe place.

I locked us in. Terry might not be done with us. He might

never be done with us. I pulled the chiffonier across the door with more strength than I knew I had. Its drawers were full of June's clothes, and the mirror was heavy, but I could shift it. The house was as quiet as if nothing had happened, but I couldn't trust it now. I remembered the time when Terry had gone back to his mother. For that too brief time, the house had been trustworthy, but not now or ever again.

I thought I heard him breathing, just beyond the door perhaps. But my own breath was coming in hard gasps, loud in my ears. There was a design of beadwork on the bodice of my gown. It winked in the dim light as my breast rose and fell. I sank back on my own bed, but leaped up again. I mustn't sleep. I mustn't think of it. He could find a way to my child. If he'd walked through the wall, I wouldn't have wondered. All I could think of was June turning in the air, suspended there from his hand.

I wouldn't sleep. I wouldn't so much as loosen my stays. I'd guard my child, and if I even heard his footfall, I wouldn't wait. I'd go for him.

I settled in the chair beside June's bed, watching her sleep and turn in her sleep. She lay with her face half buried in the pillow. One small hand was drawn loosely into a fist under her chin. Her lashes lay long against her cheek, and she slept soundly as she always did. I thought the sight of her so deeply asleep would calm me, but it didn't. I sat there braced and waiting and listening.

Sometime before daylight I thought I heard the clink of a bottle somewhere in the house, perhaps from Terry's room. I came out of the chair in a crouch, ready to act, but I heard nothing more.

I sat there until the first cool breeze that brings daylight. Pale light turned the room into new shapes. I was stiffened by the chair and the chill air. I hadn't thought to put a blanket over my shoulders. In the gathering day the little lamp on June's bedside table seemed to dim, like a streetlamp. I was watching it and saw it move.

It rocked on its small round pedestal, and then it edged toward me. It slid across the perfectly flat tabletop, and I caught it just as it tipped off the edge. It mustn't fall and wake June.

The room lurched. The floor rose up, and the chair thrust me out. I fell between it and the bed. The mirror on the chiffonier rippled, and I thought it would fall forward and leave the door unguarded.

Into the perfect silence came the roar of an approaching locomotive. It thundered louder and was somehow tunneling through the house. The room writhed in this deafening frenzy, and June sat up suddenly. I saw the circle of her mouth and knew she was screaming though I couldn't hear her.

An enormous, branching hand spread up the wall behind her bed and broke through the wallpaper. The room seemed to divide. The sound of bricks falling outside the window was like madly exaggerated rainfall. Then it was over. My head roared, but there was silence everywhere else. I had struggled up off the floor and lay half across the bed. June merely looked at me curiously in this new nightmare.

The room was thick with plaster dust. It spewed through the rents in the wallpaper and sifted like sugar in silent narrow streams. The chiffonier across the door had held its ground. The mirror looked blankly back as if nothing had happened. In it I saw an old woman wearing an absurd, shimmering gown. A pale, white-haired woman, and it was me covered in the plaster dust. June was white with it too, running her hands across the quilt, looking for the pattern.

I went to the window and looked out, but the house next door still stood, and the leaves on the gum trees were stirring in what might have been breeze.

"It was an earthquake, Mama." I turned back to June. She was sitting up in her bed, pleased with herself for knowing. "Look what it did," she said. "What a mess."

It could come again, I thought. "Get under the bed, June, and stay until I tell you to come out."

She tumbled out, dragging her pillow and quilt with her. It was a game, and she crawled under the bed, burrowing. There was the ghostly sound of laughter beneath her bed as she made her nest.

I don't know who I was in those next moments. With the same strength I'd had the night before, I scraped the chiffonier away from the door. The door itself had jumped off its hinges. When I touched the knob, it keeled outward and exploded onto the hall floor. The air out there was thick with dust, but I could find my way without seeing. I might have taken June and bolted from the house, but it didn't occur to me. Perhaps I thought she was safer where she was. I went to the door of Terry's room and stood there listening.

I turned the knob, but it was loose in my hand and came away. The knob on the far side thumped on the floor. I listened but heard no other sound. I had to know. I put my shoulder to the door and tried to force it open. There was raw wood splintered along the frame, and I leaned harder. The door skidded open perhaps a foot, no more. I edged around it, tearing the skirt of my gown on the splinters.

Then I drew back. The room was a shambles. Daylight poured in from a long wide gash in the ceiling and the roof above it. Much of the ceiling hung down in dangling shapes of broken lath and plaster. The floor was deep in rubble: broken bricks and lengths of rafter and more sections of plaster with the wallpaper still clinging to it.

One of the chimneys had fallen through the dead center of this room. The chimney had fallen across the room, across Terry's bed, just where I used to lie.

I climbed over the debris. I had to see—what there was to see. I slipped once and wedged my foot into bricks and splintered lumber, but freed it again. I reached for the brass rail at the foot of the bed and pulled myself up to see.

He was lying there in his boiled shirt and black trousers in a tangle of bedclothes and bricks. The chimney had missed him by inches. His shoulder rested against rough bricks and gray mortar. He was on his back and breathing heavily. I smelled the liquor where I stood. A broken bottle lay in the bed. He was lying there just lightly dusted by plaster. He had slept through it all.

My hands gripped and turned on the slick brass rail of the bed. He was alive. Why?

I stumbled over the littered floor, working around the bed to his side. I was panting again like an animal.

Standing there beside him at last, I looked down at his face just for a moment, to place him. I smelled the distillery stench of his breath. Then I searched the floor. There was a fragment of the chimney, six or eight bricks still mortared together, all sharp angles. It scraped my hands when I took it up.

It was heavy and cumbersome, but I hefted the burden in my two hands and turned to Terry. He hadn't moved. An earthquake wouldn't wake him. I lifted the clump of bricks high above my head. Then I brought it down with all my might on his face.

His knees jerked, and his feet in the black shoes bounced on the bed. I heard no breathing but my own.

There was blood then—edging the bricks. It ate out in a halo across the pillow slip. I took my hands away from—my weapon. I left the sharp fragment of chimney there where his face had been. I ran my hand down the hard surface of his boiled shirt to where his heart was.

I felt the heartbeat, loud, but just once. It was as if my hand had stilled it. His arm fell off the bed, and his hand, opening, brushed the skirt of my dress. I drew away from him and turned back to go to my child.

FORTY-FIVE

I dressed June. I dressed us both. I had this day and perhaps no other. Though I wanted her out of the house, I wouldn't flee and frighten her. There was no reason to run. The child was safe now, and I didn't believe for a moment that I could escape my fate.

When I took her into the bathroom to wash our faces, there was an aftershock. We heard a distant peal of thunder from the cellar, answered by the rattling pane in the window. The tiles of the floor rippled. June only laughed and capered on the floor that would not lie still. It was covered by water. The reservoir over the water closet had spilled out, but when I turned on the tap, there was only a thin trickle and then nothing.

In dressing June, it didn't occur to me there would be no school today. But it was early yet, hours early. We would have this holiday for as long as it lasted.

"We'll go see Grandma and Grandpa Conklin," I said, perhaps too brightly. I dressed in a wool serge suit. I could do little with my hair though my hands were steady. My murdering hands wouldn't give me away. They were scraped from the bricks, but there was no blood on them. I did my best with my hair, looking into the mirror without meeting my eyes.

The hat I put on was as big as a coal scuttle. I anchored it with a hat pin and saw with satisfaction how its brim shadowed my eyes. I thought about all these things as they happened and not a moment beyond. I would move through the day in just that way.

We walked down through the empty house, down that stairway. I couldn't wait to leave, and so I measured my steps. It was too early for the Mexican woman and the maid if they would come. I pulled the front door shut behind us. It was still on its hinges, but I didn't lock it. Whoever would come through it next, whoever would be the first to know couldn't be kept out.

The landscape was peppered with fallen bricks, and the neighbors were in their nightshirts. I knew then that it had happened, that I hadn't had some vivid and fulfilling dream.

It would be a beautiful day under a cloudless blue sky. We walked up Van Ness Avenue, and I held my child's hand easily in mine. I had served her well with my hands.

It was an oddly everyday kind of morning though the chimneys of every house had toppled. On the lawns children in their nightclothes made building blocks of bricks and shingles. Women stood with folded arms and spoke from porch to porch. Shirtsleeved men in bowler hats propped ladders to survey damage.

We crossed Sacramento Street where the Claus Spreckels mansion stood in a long lawn before its stables. The servants were out among the shrubbery inspecting the foundations, but the houses on Van Ness Avenue all stood enormous and foursquare.

June and I made a leisurely walk of it, both of us savoring the day in our ways. We turned west along Filbert Street to the house where I was born. It was as it had been except for chimneys ragged against the sky. My father and mother stood on the high porch, watching for us. Her hair was still in papers, and he wore a long grocer's apron from his past. My father would lose everything before that day was over, all he'd built in an industrious life. But now they stood with only the broken crockery in the house to concern them.

Here the world began to close in on me. I didn't dare climb the porch stairs, and sent June up instead. These were my own people, and I might falter before them. My hands might run with blood in their presence. I feared them and found excuses. I told them I was worried about Constance and would go to look for her.

Perhaps it was weak of me, but I wanted to be with Constance. I meant to tell her nothing. I was beyond help, but I had to be somewhere. I walked away, not hurrying, and left June where she'd be safe from me and what would happen to me.

The overburdened cable car was just pulling away, but I clung to the back pole. No fares were collected, and that was lucky, for I hadn't thought to bring money. I hadn't thought I'd ever need money again.

The car moved along the rows of houses where here and there a front had fallen off and beds in upstairs rooms hung in space. Just past Leavenworth Street the car shuddered to a halt before a hill of bricks where the street had been. The slot for the cable vanished into debris, and the rails curled back like the runners on a sleigh.

I walked on then, past parties of people making picnics of their breakfasts on front stoops. Union Square was as thronged as the day Eve Waring came to town. There were sightseers there, but nothing much to see except the skittish easterners hurriedly checking out of the St. Francis Hotel and trying to hail cabs.

The St. Francis lobby seethed with people, and for once I took comfort in the company of strangers. There was no real panic though a man stood in the middle of the room, proclaiming over and over, "New York is under water, and Chicago is in flames." And with rather more satisfaction: "Los Angeles lies in ruins." But the bellboys in their bandbox hats flowed around him, bearing silver trays.

I found them in the hotel dining room. In this orderly wilderness of white napery a sort of breakfast was being served. Coffee water had been drawn before the taps gave out, and there was fresh fruit. The electricity would fail, but now breakfast was being served.

Eve Waring presided at their table, flanked by Constance and Andy. Lord Guy Carville-Paget was there too. Constance wore a smart, severe sailor hat. A cravat like a man's tie closed the collar of her crisp shirtwaist. Eve, beautifully made up as if the limelight were still on her, leafed through the early editions of the newspaper, looking for her review. Andy was tucking into his grapefruit. Lord Guy had fitted a monocle into his eye to survey the room, the only time I'd ever seen a monocle in use.

I nearly broke at sight of them. They were as they had been, and I was not. But when they saw me, I had to move forward and join them. We—they talked as if the earthquake was behind us. I thought I looked just disheveled enough to have been through that and nothing else. At a table nearby Caruso himself sat, breakfasting con brio in a fur coat thrown over his pajamas. He'd fled the Palace Hotel in outraged panic and landed here. Arnold Genthe was there too at another table, but he was soon gone, with a box camera in his hand. I passed easily in this crowd.

We spoke as the survivors of a small disturbance, and when we'd accounted for everyone else, Constance said quietly to me, "Where is Terry?"

And I could answer, "I don't know."

Joe Fletcher shouldered his way into the dining room and made straight for Constance. He was in his work clothes and an old plaid jacket and boots that laced to the knee, like a hunter. He wouldn't join us though Eve said, "Sit down, young man" at her imperious best.

His hand was on Constance's shoulder, and his eye was on Andy. "I've got to get going," he said. "They're calling for all available men. We're to report at the Hall of Justice over on Kearney. They're calling out the troops at Fort Mason."

"Whatever for?" Eve asked.

Joe's voice dipped, and he glanced at the next table. "There's fire south of the slot and it's working up toward Market Street."

"But the Fire Department," Constance began.

"Chief Sullivan was hurt in the quake. He's dying. And the engine companies are only getting mud out of the hydrants. The quake broke the water mains. It doesn't look good."

"But what can you do?" Constance asked him.

His shoulders lifted. "Whatever we can," he said, quieter still. "I want you all to go up Telegraph Hill. You'll be all right up there, and I'll know where you are."

"Leave the St. Francis?" Eve said, though she spoke lower than she ever did. "But it's a fireproof structure." Joe and Constance both looked at her then, and she fell silent.

"I wouldn't take much with me, Miss Waring," Joe said, "but if there's anything you—"

"I shall have what I want with me," she said. She rested her hand on Andy's shoulder and looked at the rest of us around her table. Then in an afterthought, she just touched the gold brooch with turquoises at her throat.

Joe turned to go, and Constance's hand slipped down his arm. He'd only taken a step away when Eve said, "Joe!" He turned back. Anyone would have. "I think in future you had better find some way to address me other than 'Miss Waring.' I can't think what it is, but I suggest you find it."

He grinned his crooked grin and was gone.

Lord Guy who had not spoken took up his napkin and touched his lips. Wordless still, he pushed back his chair and rose, bowing to us all. Then he followed Joe Fletcher out of the room.

Eve's mouth dropped open, but she closed it again as if she meant to recover from this aftershock. The chandeliers flickered and went out, but an orchestra, a small one, had been located. In those days an orchestra could be summoned at any hour. It struck up "My Merry Oldsmobile," and Eve Waring poured out again from the coffee pot.

"I propose," she said, "that we finish our breakfast at leisure. It will set an example."

In one of the last cabs available we threaded our way from Union Square to the foot of Telegraph Hill. The first wave of people from south of the slot were already moving above Market Street, and looking back. We spent that day in Joe's house on the crest of the hill. I didn't worry that I was separated from my child. She was in safer hands than mine.

Even the ramshackle houses on Telegraph Hill had stood up well. They were built on solid rock. Everything on Joe's shelves, books and plans and pottery, had pitched off onto the floor, but we three weren't tidying housewives. We climbed at once to the roof of the tower, Andy scampering ahead of us, scenting the difference in this day.

Even at midmorning drifting smoke circled this highest tower. We looked south past Market Street and knew. The tall finger of the *Call* building stood against a blank backdrop of billowing smoke. Constance knew every crevice and cornice in this city and loved it all. She stood there and watched it go, in horror unspeakable.

My horror was of a different order, billowing over me and beading my forehead. But I saw logic in this destruction. When these flames were still flickers I'd known the world was coming to an end. The city might have taken its cue from me. I might even have caused it all. There must be the bodies of the dead throughout the city now, dead in their beds and battered. Constance didn't turn and read my face. We stood at the parapet with our elbows touching, but I was still safe from her.

We heard the clang of the engines and human shouts and the quick thump of dynamite. We brought up Joe's binoculars for closer looks, but finally Constance put them aside.

Before noon Market Street was a long, ragged ribbon of orange fire. The fireproof *Call* building burst suddenly into flame, showing its steel skeleton briefly and burning like a match.

Andy's huge eyes just cleared the parapet. Eve stood behind him like the heroic figure she was, more heroic now, for the Majestic Theater with all her costumes and carloads of sets was clearly gone. Until then I expect she planned to give her evening performance. We would have said nothing, but she did, though mostly to herself: "I have been burned out before."

The fire began to leap Market Street and move nearer. Fire ate across the wholesale district between the towers of town and the Bay. I saw then that the warehouses of the produce neighborhood were gone, and all my father's empire. We didn't speak or point anything out.

We stood there all day, never eating or drinking or sitting down. My mind cleared and dimmed and cleared again. It dawned on me that we were all three widows now. Eve and Constance and I. Their husbands had been taken from them, and I—even in this I was separate.

There was new smoke rising out of the Hayes Valley behind the broken dome of City Hall. These two fires began to gather like a storm, and now the wall of smoke outlined Union Square. "Your Joe was right," Eve said to Constance. A distant fire had reached the elegant St. Ignatius Church at the far end of Van Ness Avenue. Something in me stirred. I didn't know what.

The Bay was alive with boats. Ferries crossing to Oakland and Tiburon rode low in the water, heavy with passengers. The boats maneuvered at cross purposes. A fireboat turned its hoses on its own decks, for the air was full of blowing sparks and burning brands. The weather turned sultry like summer in some other climate.

There'd been dynamiting to stem the tide at Market Street. By midafternoon they were dynamiting much nearer in Portsmouth Square. There was blasting along that low ground where Clay Street begins. As if these charges had set it off, the whole rise of Chinatown blossomed into flame. We felt it on our faces. It unfolded toward us, and yet like so many other people that day, we were too absorbed for flight.

Below us on the slopes of Telegraph Hill the Italian householders rolled casks and barrels out of their doors. They hoisted them up to soak their low roofs with vinegar and red wine. We watched the Palace Hotel go. It had lingered till now somehow, but we saw the flag atop it go out like a single spark.

"I think it's time," Eve said; she was looking down at Andy. Constance's hand clung to the parapet a moment longer. This was the house built for her, as we all knew. But it was time, and she saw that. It was the world at its end.

   She left a note to tell Joe where we'd gone, and I led them
away. It was my time to lead in this day of miracles. I'd take
them to the home of my childhood where at least they would
be safe. We turned from the furnace of the city, Lot's wives
all, but we didn't look back.

FORTY-SIX

We walked across the city to Filbert Street in a long patient line of the Chinese who turned their backs on all they had. It was a parade without paper dragons, of pigtailed, orderly children who shuffled at the pace of the very old beside them. There were bamboo yokes across the men's shoulders with baskets heaped with what they'd saved. A lady with lacquered hair carried a paper fan and a pot lid. People moved toward the parks, hoping for fire breaks and a release from the oven air.

We came abreast of my mother's and father's house, and I began to lead us out of the slow surge of people. Then another very strange thing happened. Eve reached across Constance and took me by the arm.

"Send Andy inside to your mother," she said. "But you—both of you—come with me. There is . . . someplace else."

And so we went on, mystified, Constance no wiser than I. We walked on in the crowds, two or three turns past Fillmore Street. Then Eve, watching the street signs, led us into a street that dipped down toward the Bay. It was lined with small houses seeming to hold one another up. They were battered from the quake, and by time.

She watched for the street numbers on their doors, and Constance looked at me, knitting her brows. We came to a house no different from the others: a single door beside a narrow bay window. The earthquake had separated the stoop from the house. Eve drew up her skirt and climbed the step.

She held back a moment, and then she turned the bell in the door.

A gaunt-faced woman opened, scraping the door across the floor. She was old and slightly bent. Her mouth turned down at the corners, but there was nothing else to notice of her face. She wore a gray dress of corded silk, and might have been anyone.

"Yes, what is it?" She had to look up to Eve. Her hand was on the doorframe, half barring the way. Something came into her expressionless face. "Oh," she said to Eve, "it's you. Well, you're very like your pictures, aren't you."

"May we come in?"

The woman looked down at herself. Then she scraped the door wider and gazed away from us back through the house. Her hair was dressed high on her head with old-fashioned tortoiseshell combs. They were set with brilliants and the sockets where brilliants had been.

There was no front hall. We stood on the sloping floor of her parlor. A lamp had fallen from a marble-topped table, and its cranberry glass shade had shattered on the floor. She'd piled the shards of it in neat patterns among the pendants as if it could be mended. Part of the ceiling had fallen, and the plaster was swept into neat pyramids.

The woman ran her hands down her skirt. "You see how I'm situated. No help now, not like before. Not like back home."

She wouldn't quite meet Eve's eye after that first moment. Her eyes darted, and her movements were quick, or had been. "Not that I'm complaining. I will give the devil his due. You have seen to our needs when . . . others haven't." Her eyes darted again. "Who is these girls with you?"

Eve turned to us awkwardly, nearly missing her footing on the uneven floor. She'd been robbed of something. She wasn't the woman she'd been five minutes before. All her grace had left her.

"This is my daughter, Constance, and this is Rose, Terry Kinsella's wife."

The woman's sharp gaze swept past Constance and rested

on me. I'd never seen her in my life, and yet I half knew who she was.

"We have come to see if you are all right," Eve said.

The woman looked down at the shattered lampshade. "As you see," she said, "nothing serious. I have been through worse. Many a time, God knows." She didn't ask us to sit. If we'd gone away then, it would have suited her.

"And . . . Sarah Ann?" Eve said.

"Oh, she don't know it happened," the woman said, more forthcoming than before. "I told her earthquake, but it didn't signify to her."

"Is she—"

"She has her good days and bad. She don't get up now, of course. I wait on her hand and foot. We have come to that. Oh, she can turn herself in the bed, but that's about the extent of it. I tell her she'll get up again someday, but she won't. I don't complain. What's the use?"

She'd grown nearly animated and could almost meet Eve's gaze. But she turned away, and it was again time for us to go.

"Can we see her, Lena?"

Constance drew nearer me. She was far more lost in this moment than I was, and I was lost enough. The woman shrugged her birdlike shoulders. We followed her down a dark hall to a room at the end of it. It was shuttered and black as night. The woman turned up a coal oil lamp.

We stood there at the foot of a bed. There was a figure in it, propped up but deeply asleep. I was frightened in a childish way. It was a woman, very old. Her face was scarred and wrinkled leather. It was a face carved by some sharp, crude tool. Her hair hung in long gray braids across the blankets. The shawl around her shoulders was held at her neck by a brooch, though I couldn't make it out. Her cheeks were shrunken till they seemed almost to meet.

"She won't wear her teeth," Lena said. "I keep them right here in the drawer, but she won't have them in her head. You know how she can be." And then: "I could wake her. She won't know you. It won't make any difference either way. But I could wake her.''

Eve shook her head and turned away.

We were on the street again, and the door was closing behind us. Eve would have strode away then. She was anxious to be gone, but Constance, who'd been patient, wouldn't move. "Mother," she said, "tell me."

Eve looked at us both. She might have reached out to us, but her hands were clenched in the last of her awkward gestures. "Opal and I are not sisters. We were raised . . . as sisters. But Lena is her mother, and Sarah Ann is mine. The woman in the bed is my mother."

She looked at Constance then, but there was so much old pain in her lovely eyes that Constance couldn't speak. Eve turned to me perhaps because it was easier. "Lena is Terry's grandmother, you see, and so she is your June's great-grandmother."

I suppose I comprehended that at the time. I don't know.

We went in silence to my family's house, and they were there with June beside them. She clung to my waist in excitement at this wondrous day. I remembered that I hadn't meant for her to see me again. I wondered if I was being taunted by some god or God, and made myself take her in my arms.

We were my mother's guests, and she bustled in familiar patterns. Eve Waring, who could move from scene to scene, was herself again. Mother clasped her close, saying, "My stars! The house is a mess. What will you think of us?" Constance and I could only stand aside, reduced to daughters and drugged by other thoughts. I looked at our mothers, though, and couldn't tell which one was the more beautiful.

My father was there, followed about by Andy. Father had been turned back at the barricades the army had set up. He was spared the sight of his lifelong business in ruins, but I saw the despair behind his genial smile. It was in Mother's eyes too every time she looked his way.

But their house was full of guests, and their doors open.

They'd taken down the kitchen range and carried it out into the back yard. There was a ban now on cooking indoors, and no water or electricity, nothing to keep us inside.

All over San Francisco that night people slept in the open air though it was bright with driven sparks and burning debris wheeling like seabirds. Mother had drawn water early. We brought down the pitchers from all the bedrooms and set them full of water around the garden in case there were fires small enough to fight. My mother had a canary, and she brought it out and hung its cage in the branch of a barren apple tree. "A grocer's tree that bears no fruit!" my father had often said, but he didn't say it now. Enraptured by the change, the canary sang all night.

We cooked our meal in this oasis, hearing the dynamite charges and the tramping feet in the street, but these kept their distance. We brought down blankets, and beds we set up in the garden. We sat in our encampment, silent for many reasons, until we faded to shadows and our children were fast asleep together in a big brass bed. The sky wavered with rosy dawn all night.

My mother and Eve slept in the same bed against the board fence that served as bedroom wall. I watched Eve Waring uncoil her hair, darker than the dark, and let it down. There was beauty here, and I must drink it all. My time was growing short.

Constance sat before the range in a rocker from the porch. Her white shirtwaist was luminous in the dark. She sat with her thoughts and wouldn't shut an eye until she saw Joe Fletcher again. My father set up an old camp bed, and lay looking up through the branches.

"Under the stars again," he said, remembering some old time, but they were sparks, not stars.

I hadn't slept the night before and fell into deep sleep then, in the bed I'd slept in as a girl.

The city fell that night. The line the men meant to hold at Powell Street failed. They thought Union Square would break the fire, but they were wrong. The St. Francis was gutted sometime in the early hours. The fire seemed to look about itself for more landmarks, and turned up Nob Hill. It vaulted from street to street. Then in a torch held high over the city it destroyed all the old tycoons' mansions at the crown. It reached for the new Fairmont Hotel and became its first guest. In the morning that white Acropolis was a black shell.

I stirred and half woke in the night. I didn't know where I was except in my familiar bed. It seemed there was someplace I must go, something I must do while there was still time. But I couldn't think what it was and slept again.

In the morning I awoke, like a child, later than the others. My father was feeding the stove. The women were coiling their hair, and the children were playing already. Something must have warned me.

We all heard it. My father straightened and turned toward the house. Someone was walking through it with the insistence of heels ringing down the hallway. There was a shape at the back door, and then she was there on the back porch.

Opal Kinsella stood there. Her eyes darted over the yard, but she saw only me. The black kid gloves were tight on her hands. A black veil hugged her face. An avenging angel. We all stared at her; she'd have been an omen to anybody. Grasping her skirts and stumbling down the stairs, she made straight for me.

She hurried past the others to where I stood, and I tried not to step back. I had this coming.

"Where is Terry?" she said in the voice she had for me and servants. "Tell me where he is."

My brain was too thick for suspicion. I didn't calculate my answer. I thought words couldn't matter, but when I spoke, I couldn't have chosen better: "I thought you'd know."

"He is not with me," she said, blustering now. Not an avenging angel, merely herself. "I am worried sick, and does anybody care?"

I looked for the right words now, safe ones. I looked high and low. "Did you go to the house?" I asked her. "Did you go to Van Ness Avenue?" I spoke carefully, distinctly, but not in my own voice. Constance noticed that.

"I went," Opal Kinsella said. "Of course I went. You left

the door unlocked when they're shooting looters right and
left. I hollered up the stairs and down the cellar and couldn't
raise anybody. You'd all taken to your heels. Off you'd all
gone without a thought, and not a servant in sight. Turn your
back on them for a moment, and they rush out like the tide!''

She caught her breath, and my father said, unexpectedly,
''Where do the servants live?''

Without turning to him she said, ''South of the slot. They're
burned out, I suppose, or burned up. I tell you this is the end
of everything. Half the shingles are off my roof!'' She bristled,
less changed than any of us.

I thought my knees would give under me. I'd been given
one final gift if I could know how to use it. She hadn't found
the dead, disfigured body of her son. She hadn't found me
out. Hope hadn't occurred to me till then, and Opal Kinsella
had brought it.

''I have an idea Terry's gone off to fight the fire,'' my
father said. ''They've called up the young men.''

Pivoting on her heel, she faced him at last. She hadn't
thought of that. Nor had I. I saw my father again as I hadn't
seen him since I was a child, when fathers can work miracles.

''It is like Terry to be the first to volunteer,'' Opal Kinsella
proclaimed. ''I only pray he comes back to me whole!'' She
threw back her head and stared up through the branches,
commanding God. Suddenly, she was through with us. She
stalked toward the porch.

But Eve was there in her path. ''Good morning, Opal,''
she said. They couldn't have met in many years.

Opal froze. ''Effie.'' She reached for her dignity, but her
gloved hand rose to her back hair. Eve stood there in a
wrinkled, slept-in dress while Opal primped and faded.

She rallied. ''Effie, don't tell me you slept out here all
night like . . . an immigrant when you could have had a
good bed at my house!''

Eve made no reply. She seemed to study Opal from a great
distance. It was my innocent mother who spoke. ''Will you
stay and have a cup of coffee with us, Mrs. Kinsella?''

Opal broke from them both. "I couldn't think of it. I am a woman alone, and everything is on my shoulders."

She was gone then. Doors slammed through the house. The garden began to revolve, and I thought of another earthquake. It whirled and blurred, and I'd have fallen, for the bed wasn't where it had been.

But Constance was there with her arm around my waist to hold me steady. "Can you make it to the house?" she said in no more than a whisper. "Can you walk there naturally?"

I nodded though I wasn't sure.

"We'll go inside where we'll be alone. And then, Rose, you can tell me the truth."

FORTY-SEVEN

Constance and I stood in the dining room. Beneath the windows the crowds still moved west, filling Filbert Street. We were alone in the room where so long ago her letters from London were read out around the table.

I'd been stronger when I had no hope. My hands shook now and told some terrible tale. They shook though I wrung them and tried to hide them behind me. Constance watched. "Rose—"

But I was ready to fill up this awful silence that rang in me. "She doesn't know," I said in a rush. My eyes were everywhere in the room. I was cornered now. I was a rat in a trap.

Constance stood there quietly, inflaming me with her patience. "Do you mean Opal? What doesn't she know, Rose?"

I drew away to look down on the milling street. "She doesn't know where Terry is." My fingers played at my lips. My eyes were dry and burning. Perhaps they glowed.

"Do you know where he is, Rose?" Constance hovered nearer.

I was so cold then, shaking with the cold. My teeth danced in my mouth. I nodded yes, yes, I know where Terry is. But the room was turning as the garden had. Constance took my arm and turned me. I didn't see it coming. She slapped me hard across the face. The room went black and returned clearer than before. The morning sunshine played through the window, and every mote of dust was distinct.

"Terry is where I left him, Constance. He's been dead since yesterday morning." I could look at her, and play out my hand. She searched me with her eyes. "I killed him, Constance."

I don't know what she expected, but not that. "If he's dead, surely he was killed in the quake."

"No, the quake didn't kill him. Nothing would kill him so I had to," I said. "I have a child, you know."

I thought she must believe me. She eased me into a chair. I was bone-tired and laid my head on the smooth table. A wave of weariness bore me down; I was afraid I'd sleep. "Who will you tell, Constance?"

"No one."

But her hand tightened on my shoulder, and I raised my head. Her mother was standing in the doorway to the hall. She had just stepped up. If she hadn't, I would have ended differently, somehow differently.

"Is she ill?"

"I don't think so," Constance said.

They spoke from far away, and I had to bring them nearer. "I am well enough." I pushed back the chair and stood, impersonating myself. "Come with me now to the house. If I'm mad, there won't be anything to see. Don't say anything to my mother and father. Give them a little while longer. Leave June with Andy. Just come on with me now." My voice spiraled higher toward the end.

The three of us went out of the house and set ourselves against the crowds. I walked between Eve and Constance in case they thought I might bolt and hide myself in the throngs of people. I'd forgotten why all these people were in the streets, but I'd forgotten nothing else.

Van Ness was ranked now with men in blue uniforms. They stood at parade rest down the center of the street, and two by two in the lawns. Among them people were cooking their breakfasts on kitchen ranges along the curb.

We came at last to the house. The men in blue—they were sailors—were drawing nearer, going from house to house.

I rushed ahead up the steps and across the wide porch. I fumbled at the doorknob, never looking at Eve or Constance. Maybe I'd turned to them once too often. My hand slipped off the slick knob. It resisted me, and I thought that was foolish of it. I began to breathe in sobs. Eve pushed me aside and grasped the knob. "It's locked," she said. "Opal must have locked it behind her."

I laughed then, just one peal.

Constance turned and walked quickly off the porch. I thought she'd left me. I thought she'd had enough of this.

But she was climbing the steps again with something in her hand. It was a clump of bricks mortared together. She moved straight to the door, and Eve and I fell back. She raised the bricks above her head. I knew that gesture. She threw it with all her force at the stained-glass panel in the door. It burst inward. I had never liked it.

We were in the front hall, and there were the stairs. I knew this place. I started up, Constance just behind me. I looked back and saw Eve had remained below. Foolishly, I thought she was afraid. She stood down there with her back to the stairs, like a sentinel.

The door of June's room was down. We walked across it and it teetered. The door to Terry's room was only slightly ajar, perhaps as I had left it. I thought then that maybe nothing had happened, that I'd imagined it all and was insane. I thought there might be some safe place to put me, better than a jail.

But I edged inside, and it was true. The ceiling was gashed wide and the bricks were in the bed. I stumbled over the same debris and reached for the footrail of the bed. Constance was beside me, and Terry was there in the bed. The bricks looked lower where his face had been, more settled.

Constance struggled past me. She was at his side of the bed, looking down. I noticed how her crisp shirtwaist was smokesmudged now and slept-in. Her face, always so composed, was faintly out of focus. There was a smell in the room though it was open to the sky. She looked at Terry's flat shirtfront. There were little mother-of-pearl studs on it. She looked at these and not at me. His dangling hand was not far from her skirt. We stood there so long that the sun shifted and fell in a shaft through the broken roof.

I'd always thought she was so quick to understand. She'd been that way in her schoolwork, while I plodded. But in this I'd been quick, and she was slow. This change in us worried me. She half looked at me. "I don't know, Rose. I don't know what to do."

I wanted to comfort her, and not to burden her. I turned away from Constance and my handiwork, stumbling to the door. I didn't run. Where was there to go? She followed, and in the upstairs hall we heard men's voices below. She gripped my arm. I'd have plunged down to face them. We went to the head of the stairs, and stopped.

Down in the front hall there were four or five of them, sailors in blue uniforms and gaiters. They hadn't looked up to see us. They were looking at Eve Waring who held them in thrall. They couldn't take their eyes off her. Another sailor rolled an oil drum in through the smashed door. He saw Eve Waring too and reached for his cap.

"Dreadful," Eve was saying to them, "but I suppose you must do your duty."

"We have our orders, ma'am. We have others to protect if we can."

"Of course," she said. "Of course."

The sailor with the oil drum rolled it into the parlor.

"We'll have to search the place, ma'am. Are you the lady of the house?"

"No." She turned and looked up the stairs as if she expected us to be there at the top, on cue. We were. "This is Mrs. Kinsella's house."

Constance linked her arm in mine, and we came slowly down the long flight. I faced the sailor. His face was stubbled with beard and blackened with soot. "I am Mrs. Kinsella."

"Ma'am, we have to hold the line at Van Ness Avenue. The fire is moving this way along a tremendous front. We've cleared Polk Street behind you. Ma'am, we've got to dynamite here. Our orders are to level every house on the east side of Van Ness between O'Farrell and Jackson. If the fire jumps this street and catches on the other side, we've lost the whole Western Addition.''

I don't think I understood him. Constance did. I smelled the kerosene they were soaking into the parlor floor and heard the glass go when they broke out the windows.

"Ladies, you're going to have to evacuate right now. Is there anyone else here?''

"No," Constance said. "Mrs. Kinsella and I have looked. There is no one else here.''

They dynamited all the east side of Van Ness Avenue that day. The sailors, the Blue Jackets, went from house to house, soaking them in kerosene so they'd burn hot after the dynamite charges. They worked with gathering speed, for the smoke from the city stood tall behind the houses now. They worked on the run, as efficiently as they could.

We were ordered back across the street and farther west than that. But we didn't go. There were high hedges in the lawns across the street, and we could shelter in them. There weren't enough sailors to flush us out and send us to safety.

We three stood there in our bower while the day lengthened and quickened. The houses to the south thumped and thundered. They fell in upon themselves and flamed up quickly and burned briefly. They dropped like dominoes.

We stood there overlooked. I had to know if some sailor might come at the last moment and enter the house. Some final search. I had to know and so did Constance.

The house with Terry in it went then in its turn. It bulged strangely and rounded a second before the burst of the explosion. The porch fell out on the suddenly scorched lawn, and the house folded in on itself. The cellar took its share, and the smoke screened the rest. It burned as it fell, but we watched until this cloud lifted, and there was nothing above the black foundations. We saw it through.

I'd have run then, for the sheer joy of it, back to my child. But we were three women, and we turned and strolled away. We walked—oh, I don't know how far. Then Eve said to us both, and to neither of us, "Don't tell me. I need never know."

BOOK 5

Stranger by My Side

FORTY-EIGHT

It was a summer evening, almost tranquil. The only screams were the shrieks of the flat-nosed British locomotives steaming in to fill the cavern of the station with more smoke. I'd heard worse screams and on this same platform.

I stood there now, not in my usual nurse's cape, but in civilian clothes that hung oddly on me. It was London on a summer evening, and so the last of the light lingered under the vast shed roof. I was waiting for the train from Hythe and not the usual hospital train bringing the wounded from the Channel ferries.

As I was off duty, the mood might have been different, but I waited behind my usual mask. Trains in wartime often came in at the wrong platform. Often they didn't come at all. The war had taught me how to wait without expectation.

It was the summer of 1918. The younger brothers of boys long dead and half buried were being fed into the hopper now. I'd seen them die on this platform and not seventy miles away in Belgium and France. I'd bent over many a boy with his face peeled by mustard gas and heard his last words and the bubble of his life bursting in his throat. Every time I watched one die, I thanked God I didn't love him, that I didn't love any boy, anywhere.

I thought I was old and would outlive the last one of them. It was my nineteenth birthday that day, though there wasn't anyone within five thousand miles who'd know that.

I expect I liked the idea of nobody knowing. I'd built the stoutest shell possible around that former self of mine, young

June Kinsella from San Francisco. I'd forgotten who she was, just as I'd forgotten parties where young men danced on both their legs and sent flowers in long satin-paper boxes the morning after.

Now it was always the morning after. I went to parties in the day room of the Lancaster Gate Hospital behind a wheelchair with part of a boy in it, a boy who'd done his last dancing. The only flowers stood in jars at bedsides, often very bright flowers by the bedsides of the blinded.

Oh, yes, I was an old veteran now and very likely invulnerable. Still, there was a smoke-blurred mirror fixed to a post on the platform, and I turned to look at myself in it. Even under fire, vanity dies hard.

The mirror was printed across with an advertising slogan for Woodbine cigarettes. I looked to see myself and reached in my handbag. Everybody smoked in wartime, even women and nurses. I groped around in the bag for a loose cigarette before remembering that only whores smoked on station platforms.

The face in the mirror glanced back under a little untrimmed hat that dipped in front, dividing my forehead. They were called tricornes, passing as fashionable in the austere fourth year of the War without End. It was a dark felt hat with a faintly military air you could wear year-round.

My hair was regulation short, a darkening blond softly waved to remind the unblinded of womanhood, but short enough to be dressed in a couple of economical gestures, without mirrors. Once, I'd had my mother's coloring: fresh with a natural blush in the cheeks. Rose, like her name. She had it still, but I'd lost it somewhere. I didn't recognize my mirrored face. It was impassive, meant to reassure. I thought I looked thirty and that I'd earned it.

A hospital train from the coast hissed in behind me. I could smell the wounded and the clinging mustard gas that lived in their uniforms. There'd been a time when that mingled stench had turned my stomach. The train clattered against itself and stopped. There'd be the restaurant carriage for the officers and the dim carriages behind for the other ranks. The stretcher-bearers were moving past me. Off duty, I didn't turn, and heard the first moaning.

Until the platform cleared, I let my mind go out of focus. That was something I learned at the front. It was funny where my mind went when I let it go. It skipped away like a stone over water. But it always sank in the past, the recent past to prove I'd survived it. Never the future. There were only a few taboos left, but the future was one of them.

I'd come to Europe the year before though now I had to reach to remember being anywhere else. We were a group of San Francisco girls who'd been rushed through an abbreviated nursing course. It was that eerie, quickening time when President Wilson was promising to keep the country out of war while easing us into it.

We came in the guise of volunteers to the British WAAC. We couldn't even embark from an American port, sailing instead from Halifax, Nova Scotia. The old *Celtic* brought us over in a convoy, describing long diversionary loops in the north Atlantic to baffle the U-boats if there were any. America entered the war while we were at sea.

We weren't quite sure we were nurses, and when we got here, the British were less sure still. I was quick to take offense. All my life I'd wanted to be a nurse and nothing else, and saw the war as my chance. But few of the girls burned with that zeal. It was still a lark and far more modern than marching for the vote. Nursing had become suddenly a goal for girls from nice backgrounds, pampered girls who'd never seen a naked wound or a naked man. In this I was no different from the others. In our training we were taught mainly from charts. We bathed no naked men. We bathed baby boys with rosebuds between their legs.

That original group of us was dispersed now, and I'd long since unlearned the mistake of making friends. One of the girls was killed by a Mills bomb not far from me. They buried her in France in one of the hasty cemeteries for soldiers under a wooden marker that wouldn't have lasted. One foolish virgin far from home, and I didn't remember her name.

The British considered that American girls were hardy and capable, though perhaps not quite nurses. They sent us to France as ambulance drivers. Once we'd mastered the big Leyland lorries converted to haul the wounded, we shuttled back and forth between the front and the advanced base hospitals.

We began to find out whether we were nurses or not after we'd learned how to scrub out an ambulance without gagging. I learned to carry a man across my shoulders when there was nobody to lift the other end of the stretcher, or no stretcher. More than one of them bled to death down the front of my trench coat.

On the first day, I sat high in the Leyland lorry next to an enormous sergeant of the Royal Welsh Fusiliers who was to teach me how to drive it. He taught me on regular runs with a full load of casualties who screamed at every swerve in the road. In his former life, the sergeant had been a chauffeur—a "shover," as he said.

"I expect, miss," he said to me, "back home in the States you had a shover." He thought that had the beginnings of a joke in it now that I was to be a shover of others.

As it happened, my mother did have a chauffeur now, and a long twelve-cylinder Pierce-Arrow automobile to go with him. It crept in a stately manner through the San Francisco streets and was parked in the St. Francis Hotel garage. But soldierlike, I didn't volunteer this information to my sergeant.

He could gauge the span of the Leyland to an inch for straddling shell holes. We drove on random roads never less than axle-deep in mud through a terrain that had earned its name, no-man's-land. We never knew where we were, and the road signs were long gone. We fought back and forth over the same ground until the earth boiled and the fields sprouted dismembered arms and legs.

There was nothing to breathe but the drifting mist of mustard gas that never lifted and the heady undercurrent of putrifying flesh. The ditches were clogged with upended, scarecrow horses, their stiffened limbs angled like gun barrels at the yellow sky.

The fresh troops were being brought from behind along with more corrugated iron to shore up the trenches. The ambulances moved against them, bearing away the dead and the dying and the fortunately wounded.

The best time of day was dawn when the lines of the Germans, the Boches, were outlined against the morning light. Twilight was the worst when we made better targets in the glow of evening. There was no real night, not with the bright flares of the Very lights blooming above us, turning the world and our hands and faces an acid green.

I was at the front and sometimes ahead of it two and three times a day, in the trenches hip-deep in water. I'd been up there in the mornings so close to the German lines that we could smell their breakfast coffee. The advanced base hospitals were only clusters of Nissen huts connected by duckboards laid over the mud. The big delousing vats stood open to the sky, and so of course did the latrines. I remember coming back once to hear that rats had got in and eaten the tablecloths in the mess. Decaying flesh drew rats, and so the hospitals were infested.

On another day a little Boche aeroplane, a Pfaltz, which means "sparrow," dropped down out of the shellburst and box-kited along above the road. I remember the soldiers pitching themselves into the ditches and the pattern of the bullets splashing in the standing water of the road.

"A very near thing that, miss," said my sergeant, never swerving.

The duty days had no more shape than this, and we all slept through our days off. I learned to tame the Leyland and to dress a wound with rifle-rag when there was no lint. Beside the operating table I found out how to hold my eyes steady above the gauze mask when the surgeon's saw struck bone.

I learned the futility of the crisp, angel-white uniforms we'd been issued and took the boots off a small-footed, dead Tommy. They laced to my knees and lasted. A young lieutenant, dying in the night, handed me his gas mask. It was a superior sort from the Army & Navy Stores in London with special rubber-rimmed goggles that the lieutenant said would be "useful for motoring after the war."

I was never without it and wore an officer's trench coat with the red tabs removed and a service cap, a big one that my hair fit into. We were all like that. We ceased being young girls and became soldiers. There were boys who died in our arms and never knew we were women, if that would have been a solace.

This life required an attitude which like a duty uniform had to be improvised. I learned not to know one broken boy from another. It couldn't much matter whether they lay there comatose or babbled with the nerve-racked compulsions of shell shock. Whether they could be patched and sent back or whether they couldn't.

When there was time, I wrote their letters for them. They had little to say, and some of them couldn't have written it down if they'd had hands. I filled in their disconnections and signed these platitudes with names I didn't notice. The postal service was remarkably good. There were often two deliveries a day, if you were still there at the end of the day. My mother wrote regularly from San Francisco, numbering the letters methodically, and I got most of them. Because I was in France, she inquired about Paris spring collections and asked for news about hemlines and hats.

This makes her sound frivolous, even heartless, but she was merely unknowing. I'd told her nothing of what life had become for me. To become a nurse at all, I'd had to walk away from her with more confidence than I had. Now, I spared her the knowledge that I was a nurse in a charnel house. She pictured me on the starched staff of a rest hospital, a requisitioned château perhaps, set in green lawns quietly in the countryside, and I encouraged her in this view.

She inquired about Paris fashions because it was her business to know. When I was a child, both sides of our family lost everything they had in the great earthquake and fire that killed my father. They'd all been prosperous people once, but after the disaster the responsibility for us all fell to my mother. She and I lived with my grandparents, the Conklins, on Filbert Street. I grew up there, and my mother went into business, beginning as a seamstress. She was skillful with a needle, but never vain of any of her accomplishments. She ascended in life armed with thread and needle and need.

Before San Francisco was rebuilt, she'd opened a little storefront business on Folsom Street where a sort of commercial district had survived the fire. She and Grandma Conklin and two or three employees sewed to restore the wardrobes of women who'd lost their every stitch in the fire. I believe they extended a lot of credit. Now, twelve years later, my mother owned the smartest shop in San Francisco, just off Union Square, where two floors of seamstresses copied the vogues of New York and Paris and did custom tailoring for the wealthiest women in California. There was a ready-to-wear department too, and my mother bought for it in Chicago and New York, her view of the world outside.

She had worked day and night to provide for her family, for me. When she'd succeeded, when her label, simply "Rose Conklin," was carried on the best clothes and the best people, she might have rested a little. But she never looked up. She was driven almost mysteriously, and I sometimes wondered if she was trying to work herself to death.

I'd hurt her of course. Like a man who's built an empire to pass to his son, my mother wanted to pass hers to me. There were, after all, only the two of us now. But I wanted something else. I went off looking for a world of my own and found France and the front. My mother couldn't even indulge me though she was generous to a fault. She sent me tea gowns and stockings sheer as cobweb and moiré slippers with curved heels and jeweled buckles. They arrived in battered parcels at the front.

My wandering mind always returned to the front. That June evening on the station platform I'd been back in England less than a month. The front was still my reality. I smelled it still and could hardly sleep in the calm London nights. They'd sent me back after the big Boche thrust forward in May. We'd been pushed back nearly to Fountainebleau, but it was the last of the enemy's real assaults.

That had been my final bloodbath, and I was sent back to London, nearer exhaustion than I'd admit. Here I was living a very different war, in the lulling routine of Lady Randolph Churchill's Lancaster Gate Hospital. I was a nurse here with my dues paid, more competent with the gassed and the shell-shocked than those who'd never seen the front. Here was a mudless, unmuddled world of carbolic acid and sponge baths, a world of white sheets.

Now I was taunted by the faint siren song of hope. Some of these boys would live, or learn to. Our patients here were more bored than frightened, and this made them talkative. Clean-shaven, they began to have faces and one learned their names.

They called me Sister as all nurses in England are called. I savored the impersonal, nunlike sound of it, and told them no more of my name or of me. When my patients threatened me by becoming real, I remembered the front where they were all stubbled and mud-colored and where trench foot is as great a leveler as artillery.

Taking my cue from the British nurses, I grew brisk and astringent and peremptory with the orderlies. I liked the clean sighing of a fresh apron. The spotless white of my headdress fitted my forehead like a wimple. I could live a long war this way.

But now I stood on the platform in a three-cornered hat and a frock my mother had sent me. I wore cobweb stockings and French-heeled shoes that chafed my feet still swollen from the ice-water trenches. I waited for the train from Hythe which would alter a routine growing sacred. I didn't welcome that. No nurse does.

Worse, I was waiting for a boy, someone I'd known back in some other life. Though he'd be eighteen now, I thought of him still as six years old and knob-kneed. He'd spring from the train, boyish, and find that I was nobody he remembered. Seeing childhood friends again was an obvious error. I might have waited no longer, but his train was pulling in, brashly pretending it wasn't late.

The doors down the carriages banged open, and the porters

were there for the luggage. Then I saw him dodging along the platform among the slower arrivals. There he was, stalking along like a great gazelle. The grin was familiar, but I couldn't quite believe he was six feet tall and handsome as the very devil.

He was grinning and waving something over his head and making straight for me so there was no escape now. He was taking long, American strides in of all things leather puttees and breeches of a ridiculously extreme cut. His tunic, open down the front, was only vaguely military, and a white silk scarf around his throat flapped over his shoulder. A disreputable service cap was on the back of his head, and now the object waving in his hand was an untidy bunch of flowers. He was thrusting them at me.

"Happy birthday," Andy Drummond said.

FORTY-NINE

I hoped that Andy Drummond and I would have nothing to say and could go our separate ways. He'd been in France with the U. S. Air Service of the Signal Corps. Now he was posted to England for a gunnery course on the golf course of Hythe. But he'd go back to the war after this training, back to flying. I didn't know the life expectancy of an airman, but it was measured in weeks.

Better not to have met. Much better only to remember the small, evidently English child in short pants and Eton jacket who'd appeared at Van Ness Avenue beside his mother one day long ago.

We'd been small children together, though I hadn't been as small as he and let him know it. But I was a solitary child, and he'd filled that space even if he was the wrong sex and a year younger. We played tag down long hallways. The houses of childhood seem always to have long hallways and endless flights of stairs that figure in later dreams.

We'd had to be friends because our mothers, Rose and Constance, were as close as sisters—closer. They had bound us then, and they bound us still, or I wouldn't be walking along the platform now with this stranger by my side.

He couldn't walk normally. He had to stride, and I struggled along, hobbled by my skirt. His arm was thrown easily around my shoulders, but this was the wartime way. To take a young man's offered arm was out of date now, fussy and Edwardian, reminiscent of foolish times best forgotten.

He seemed to know nothing of the etiquette of queues.

Dragging me along, he strode directly into the street and flagged down a cab, so startling the cabby that he stopped for us. Andy's knees jutted all over the seat, and he smelled of bay rum.

I kept my defenses strong as a matter of policy. Even before I began to dig trenches and string barbed wire between myself and Andy Drummond, my guard was up. On the platform I'd seen he was bursting with life. I liked him better in the dark.

But he struck a match, and I saw him again. I noticed that he shaved, and chewed gum. He had to park the gum in his cheek to smoke.

"For God's sake, give me one," I said before the cigarette case disappeared back into his tunic. His eyebrows rose. We were two kids still, and now we were smoking behind our mothers' backs.

If he'd come straight off the boat from home, I could have patronized him. But he'd been in France already, and so he'd seen action: those sudden-death duels called "dogfights" fought up in the clouds and the shellburst. I hoped to hear none of his exploits and wondered if he would boast. At least he wore no medals, not on that tunic gapping open. There were only the lieutenant's bars, new and untarnished. He wasn't quite an apple-cheeked boy before battle, but he'd fought cleanly in the air, out of the mud. Not the real war. Only an illusion now that I had none.

I didn't know how to entertain the ambulatory. I thought of pointing out the sights from the cab window, but there was nothing to see but a tart stationed under every dim streetlamp. They were stationed there wanly painted, like sentries standing guard.

"A kiss?" Andy said. His arm was around my shoulders again. He need only draw me closer, and it was nothing more than the familiar pattern: a soldier and a girl in a cab, in wartime.

"Don't be silly. We never kissed—and we're grown up now."

"All the more reason."

I offered him my cheek.

"I'll wait for a real one. Are you still as bossy as you used to be?"

Damn all old acquaintance.

We had only the weekends and the odd days off we could match, and London. But great, gray London's regimented wartime pleasures were running thin: chu chin chow and watered beer, Elsie Janis singing jingoistic songs.

I had no place to entertain him. The only parlor for the nurses' hostel where I lived was the day room of the hospital, ranked with amputees.

Andy stayed, at first, in a club in Piccadilly that offered membership to American officers. We went there that first evening. The war had so shattered the old decencies that female guests were admitted to the club dining room. I'd thought we might go to one of those hectic, low-ceilinged places jammed with soldiers and their girls. Some noisy place where everyone sang "Keep the Home Fires Burning" in a chorus to banish conversation.

But we dined in somber state in the almost-empty dining room of his club, attended by a retainer full of years. We might have been a very old couple living out our days in a very big house.

It was the first quiet place in Europe I had been, an oasis. But it was as dangerous as a minefield. I'd meant to keep us busier than this. I'd meant to be in charge and to look past him.

He had the open face of an American and that disjointed way of sprawling in a chair. Yet he'd had an English father who'd fallen in some former war, an aristocratic father still there in the faintly regular, roughly refined features of the son. His face was not quite finished.

We seemed to strike a silent bargain. We'd speak of the past to keep the present in perspective and the future at bay. Less boyish each time I met his eye, he seemed to know he was as old as he was likely to be.

"Do you remember?" we asked one another. "Do you remember the time . . . ?"

"Do you remember the earthquake and the fire?" Andy said. We were being served now, chill brussels sprouts and gray potatoes under dented silver covers.

"I do and I don't," I said. "Just odd impressions."

"We slept together that night," Andy said, "you and I in a big brass bed out in your grandparents' garden."

"Did we? I suppose I remember. Was there a canary in a cage, up in a tree? Was that the time?"

When our memories wouldn't quite mesh, we wove them tighter. My father and Andy's stepfather, Joe Fletcher, had gone off to fight the fire. I didn't remember their going, and my father never came back.

For a long time afterward I thought he would. There were handbills on lamp posts with the names and descriptions of the missing. I read them all. But the fire storm and the dynamite had leveled and blackened vast stretches of the city. Some unknown number of victims had been overtaken and incinerated. It stood to reason that he was one of them. Since my mother couldn't speak of him at all, I finally relinquished my young father.

Andy and I embroidered our memories, making them last. We remembered Andy's home after his mother married Joe Fletcher. It was at the crest of Telegraph Hill where the fire spared a few acres. We recalled every corner of it and the romantic tower that stood over it where we could command the town. It was a house that might have been designed to please children, a cozy castle. I'd envied him that house and two parents.

After my grandfather and grandmother died, Mother sold the house on Filbert Street and took a suite of rooms at the St. Francis Hotel. It was exorbitant, but she could afford it, and it was close to the shop. The houses of my childhood had a way of disappearing as most things do.

The aged waiter, bent nearly double without bowing, approached, clearing his throat. "Sir, madam, forgive the intrusion, but it's the air raid, you see."

The sirens had gone while we were talking, and we'd only half heard. After where I'd been, I could never take the war over London seriously.

"I can recommend the wine cellar," the waiter was saying, "or under the stairs."

But we decided on the open air in case there was something to see. The old man let us out through the balcony doors, shaking his white head at foolhardy youth.

The searchlights played across low clouds. Beyond Green Park, south where we could see it, the shafts of light crossed each other and caught the long shape of the airship. A zeppelin moved through light and dark as some obscene sea monster moves through water. The beams played wetly on its silver skin. It was too enormous an object to be made by man or to rise in the sky. There was no scale to this scene, or any reason. The guns barked from the ground, but the zeppelin passed on, easily.

We found the rhythm of our days that weekend or the next. There were queues for everything, too many salutes to return on the crowded streets, nothing to see in the shop windows. We took to the parks instead, Green Park and Hyde Park, the orangery of Kensington Palace, the Round Pond, the Serpentine. I knew this was unwise. We should have kept to the jostling queues and the frantic saloon bars, but we tired of them.

It was a San Francisco summer, wet and glossy green. A high haze filtered the sun. We strolled apart down parkland paths among pairs of lovers growing desperate.

We took a cab to Hampstead Heath. Officers, even American ones, didn't take buses, or carry parcels in the streets. This far behind the lines, the war was largely a matter of observing correct forms, the more meaningless, the better.

Hampstead Heath was miles of undulating country hardly shaped by any hand. I'd forgotten countryside could be this peaceful and listened from habit for the whistle of mortars. We had this world to ourselves except for the distant dots of children using the sky for their kites.

On a knoll somewhere up by Whitestone Pond Andy wadded his tunic and made a pillow of it. He rolled his shirtsleeves high on his arms and sprawled. I sat on the ground with the posture of a nurse, as if attending his bedside. Our recollections were moving through the years, growing ominously near. I listened more to my own and less to his.

It seemed that our childhood hadn't lasted long enough, and now we were running through it too quickly again. Andy, the ex-English child, had drifted into baseball and boy exploits that ruled me out: stealing bases and rides on the cable car. Alone again, I began to grow impatient with my bandaged kittens and bottles of candy pills.

We were spared the sight of one another's adolescence. Andy went away to school, to Culver in Indiana, his stepfather's home state. I went away to a despicable boarding school in Maryland that I continued to despise too thoroughly to name. I arrived at that school, feeling at once like the prize in a Cracker Jack box. I was wide-eyed and blond and dressed, thanks to my mother, for all conceivable occasions, most of which never arose. And I failed to fit in.

The hard-eyed, tweedy eastern girls spoke in nasal monotones about horses they didn't have and boys they didn't know. Once, only once, when boys were imported from some neighboring school, my classmates stood in damp clumps and wouldn't cross the room to meet them. Western and breezy, I crossed the dance floor at once and paid for that act with my reputation. But the boys were weirdly like the girls though their clumps were damper. After five excruciating semesters, I refused to go back.

Andy lay, perhaps listening, with his hands locked behind his head and the color of the sky in his eyes. Then he broke the only rule we had.

Seemingly at random he said, "Did you ever see a Rumpler up close? It's a two-seater. The pilot sits ahead of the observer."

I waited, wanting this to go away, smelling the sweet-grass scent of the heath. "I was shot at by a Pfaltz once," I said. "More than once.

"Me too." Andy lay there with his eyes hazing over while the war found our corner of the heath and claimed us.

"The Rumpler's a good plane," he said, "as good a plane as the Boche have, but it hasn't got the maneuverability of a Nieuport Twenty-eight, or I wouldn't be here now."

"What happened?" I said, giving in.

"It was a few weeks ago, up around Saint-Dié. I was in a Nieuport, and this Rumpler came out of nowhere, cutting me out of the pack. It was right there, and I banked away in the couple of seconds I had. They're both armed, you know. The pilot's gun has a stationary setting. He can only fire straight on. But the observer's gun is mounted so he can swing around and cover both sides and the rear.

"They came in after me. I could keep out of the pilot's range, but the observer was writing his name all over my tail. I was dipping and weaving and trying to set him up.

"Then—it's funny how clear you can see up there—the observer ran out of ammunition. I was looking right down his muzzle when it happened. I'd have taken that next round, but I saw him hang his cartridge belt over the side.

"I eased in alongside them, keeping back from the pilot, and I'll be damned if the observer didn't stand up, push his goggles back on his forehead, and stare across at me. It was like he was saying, It's your move now, if you can make it."

A kite drifted over us, throwing its tail like a cat. "What did you do?" I asked Andy finally.

"I didn't have much choice. The Boche were photographing our artillery positions. I dropped back and blasted the Rumpler from behind. It took them out."

"Was it your first . . . kill?"

He shook his head and stared up at the sky. "I wish it had been my last though." He rolled over and pulled at a tuft of grass. "I keep seeing that German guy with his arms folded, watching me, waiting for me to do to him what he'd have done to me. He's still watching me, June."

"It makes a lot of sense, doesn't it?"

"Not much," he said. He didn't have my brittle pose.

"But you'll go back to it."

"Of course."

"Of course."

The pale sun was angling, catching the distant dome of St. Paul's. The ground cooled under us.

"What will you do, June? I'll want to know."

I thought we were saying good-bye then, and so I said, "I hadn't thought until now. But I believe I'll get back to France. Nobody's indispensable, but they can always use another pair of hands. I ve got the experience and know the ropes. I think I'll go back to the front and be blown apart, gladly as a man, and never have to miss—anybody."

I stood up and walked away, wishing he wouldn't follow. I stepped high to keep from stumbling, heading toward the road if there was one and a cab if there was one. I felt him follow, closing with me across the uneven ground as if it were a football field. He was long and lanky. He hadn't had time to fill out his frame.

We'd worked through our memories, and that had led us into the perilous present and the foreshortened future. It had led us to skies of screaming aircraft over graveyard battlefields. I'd condemned us both. I was like that German gunner who'd thrown his empty cartridge belt over the side, refusing to prolong the pretending.

In a few strides he caught up with me.

"You should find yourself a girl, Andy." I looked dry-eyed into the distance to see the way we'd come. "Some empty-headed girl who likes a good time and can give you one. They're easy to find and getting easier."

There was a steep climb ahead of us, the last rise of the heath before the city street. At the top with civilization in sight, Andy took my arm and turned me toward him. From the window of a passing bus we were two lovers, sad after lovemaking.

I could make this clear to him if I explained. "At the hospital there are boys who need me. I don't know their names, but I know their needs. I'm a nurse. Go find a girl."

We stood so near I felt his breath on my forehead, boy breath scented with chewing gum and tobacco. He should be in college now if boys still went to college. He should be kicking footballs through goal posts and clearing the hurdles of track meets with his tireless stride.

"This war's making a little old lady out of you," he said, summing me up unforgivably. "You're fighting it too hard."

"What do you do with a war but fight it? It's too late to run away."

"And yet you were trying to run away just now."

"Don't be wise beyond your years, Andy. I couldn't bear that. We've spoiled everything. We've worn out the past. We've let the present in. We'll be planning the future next when we both know better than that."

I dared to look up at him, and I thought he understood. His eyes were older than eighteen—this is what war does, to baffle and deceive. He was gazing above my head into the sighing summer trees.

"I'll tell you what we need," he said. His hands rested comfortably on my shoulders as if he'd always been taller. "We need some place where we can be by ourselves for the time we have. Some place where we can be kids again."

"You didn't understand a word I said, did you, Andy? There's no such place. There's no place to hide."

But he was nodding with confidence for two. "We'll find it," he said. "It's got to be around here somewhere."

FIFTY

Because there is no rhyme or reason to war, an uncle of mine had been cast up on this foreign shore too. He was my Uncle Jack Kinsella, an eccentric even by English standards.

I seemed hardly a Kinsella at all. My father was dead, and my mother had made only brief mention of this uncle. I had a Grandmother Kinsella too, but I didn't know her. She lived in a large, shuttered house on Pacific Avenue. The neighborhood children thought she was a witch, and my mother appeared to think so too.

Perhaps I met this grandmother once. I seem to remember an ominous little black figure, heavily veiled, walking down porch steps and across a lawn, a garden—somewhere. Or maybe I imagined this.

I knew not to ask about her, and yet of course I did once before I was grown. My mother only said, "She doesn't like children," and that had been warning enough. Later I learned somehow that my mother sent this mysterious grandmother a monthly check to cover her expenses. Whether I thought that natural or strange, I don't know.

She may well have been a witch. Certainly her son Jack seemed to have supernatural powers. How else could he come by all his knowledge of other people's business? Even mine. I wasn't in London a week before he swooped down on me, and no use asking how he so much as knew who I was. His sparse eyebrows only rose in his dinner-plate face, insufferably knowing and outrageously smug.

He swooped down and bore me off to dinner at the Café

Royal, just his sort of place. "It is an absolute must to be seen in the right places, my dear."

"But who would know us here?"

"Who indeed? I often know people who don't know me."

He was a preposterous figure stuffed into black evening clothes going green, a dandy of perhaps the 1890s, and fat and wind-filled as a zeppelin. A watch chain hung from a little gold bar in his buttonhole, and another stretched like the equator across his belly. He was hung with fobs and seals, relics of an earlier century, and seemed to convey the idea that he was a man of sixty-five. He must have been forty.

He could order plausibly in French, and the small fish knife lost in the grip of his bloated white paw was something to see.

"That dress is all wrong for your coloring, my dear June. How badly young women dress these days, and then use the war for an excuse. I saw Lady Diana Manners from the top of an omnibus only yesterday. She was all in mud colors, looking like a sister of charity. Too dismal. And you, my child, are looking positively sallow, but then there is a great deal of jaundice at the front."

Ordinarily I wouldn't have put up with that from a civilian, but Uncle Jack, of all people, had been at the front himself. He'd come over in '16 as a volunteer with the Norton-Harjes ambulance group to drive the wounded between Verdun and Bar-le-Duc. Now he was out of the war and stranded contentedly in London.

I thought they might merely have wearied of him and sent him out of the war. But he may have been wounded and invalided out. Certainly he'd have made a big target, but strange to say, he never crowed about his war exploits and had the tact not to press me about mine. I was never quite sure, but I suspected him of heroism, and that beneath the flatulence lurked a human being.

But he seemed determined to portray himself as an ass out of an Edwardian drawing-room comedy.

"Ah, no, you are not the woman your mother was. Now

there was a splendid-looking girl in her time. Poor Rose. I
suppose she has run to fat by now?''

She was thin as a rail, honed by hard work and polished by
success. But the dessert trolley was being rolled up, heavy
with sherry trifle and dense puddings, distracting Uncle Jack.

"Your mother—in business—in trade! And poor Connie a
house builder or whatever. I picture her with ten-penny nails
in her mouth and a claw hammer in her hand! In England the
better class of women are perfectly content with a bit of
gardening and the odd philanthropy. Look at Lady Dudley.
Much the better way.''

"And what of nursing as a profession, Uncle Jack?''

"Ah, well, of course, look at the splendid work of the
duchess of Sutherland. And Nellie Hozier and of course
Monica Grenfall. There's a war on, you know, and naturally
Florence Nightingale was English.'' He spoke reverentially.

Uncle Jack's new British accent threatened to surpass the
natives. He'd done a lot of eavesdropping to perfect it.

"And Connie's boy, that son she had by poor Drummond.
He is in the war now, I believe. Flying in France.''

"How do you know that, Uncle Jack?''

"My child, I stand in the wings of life, and nothing
escapes me. Besides, I read it in the *Chronicle*. I take in the
San Francisco papers. They arrive weeks late, but their pro-
vinciality is an unfailing source of amusement.''

And so it went. I had a sort of vaudeville uncle, a lonely,
vainglorious blunderbuss of a bachelor who stood in the
wings of life. And now in the wings of mine.

When Andy came to England, Uncle Jack was sure to
know, and did. He sent me a note at once urging me to bring
around Poor Drummond's Boy for "a family evening, a
gathering of the clan.'' It seemed to me that Uncle Jack and I
were something less than a clan, but there was no denying
him. As it happened, our visit was set for the end of that day
on the Heath, just when I needed someone to stand between
Andy and me, another voice as bombastic as possible.

Uncle Jack who dreamed of Mayfair had rooms in a house
off Oakley Street at the far end of Chelsea. A slatternly

landlady let Andy and me in, and the flights up to the top reeked of cabbage cooking. The hallway was unlighted, but the door opened onto pink-shaded grandeur of a sort. My uncle filled the doorframe with his arms wide in welcome.

He wore a winged collar lost in his chins and the only smoking jacket I'd ever seen outside a shop window. It was garnet-colored quilted velvet with taffeta lapels, circled in a silk rope with tassels. There were tassels everywhere, hanging as light pulls from the pink lamps, looping back the damask draperies, depending from sofa pillows. The room was a gimcrack jewel box recalling some earlier, lush time, like a superior secondhand shop. Elaborately framed pictures hung from the ceiling to the baseboard. They were rather academic oils and watercolors: literal still lifes and landscapes with cathedral spires.

There was sculpture too, bronze castings of heroic groups on marble stands. One or two bore price tags. I gathered Uncle Jack dabbled in art dealing to keep himself afloat. I wouldn't have been surprised if his mother sent him money— money my mother had sent her.

My thoughts became circular, and I gave up. Uncle Jack wasn't meant to be explained. He seemed to have plenty of money for luxuries if he stinted on necessities. On one chair lay hanks of bright silk thread, a pair of sewing scissors, and a pillow sham with some sort of unfinished motto on it, being worked in cross-stitch.

"Are they making you comfortable at the club, my boy?" Uncle Jack boomed.

"Sir?" Andy said. Apparently there was nothing very comfortable about a London club.

"There's something to be said for the war if it can get you into a good club!" Uncle Jack pronounced. "I belong to no clubs. I am not a clubbable man." He wagged his huge head fondly at this sorrow. "Nor was my father before me. Nor of course my brother, poor Terry—June's father as I should say."

Poor Andy. He was out of his depth and sinking. He cracked his elbow on a Canova copy—the nude Napoleon—

and sank nearly to the floor in the cushions of a Turkish sofa. He stared in a glazed way through his knees while I found an ottoman that seemed reasonably sittable.

Uncle Jack threw back the doors of a liquor cabinet where a bottle or two stood on long-barren shelves. "Port, the Englishman's drink!" he said, pouring out three ladylike portions into cracked crystal.

"I am not a drinking man," he said, distributing the glasses. "We are not a convivial family, and of course poor Terry drank so. Demon rum! He was not meant for a long life. A terrible fellow really. You wouldn't have dreamed we were twins."

Then in this bravura performance, Uncle Jack set his glass aside and reached into his quilted pocket for an enormous thimble to plant on his finger. He settled into the chair and took up the pillow sham and began to take careful stitches in his fancywork. By reading upside down, I could just make out what the motto would say:

WHEN A MAN IS TIRED OF LONDON,
HE IS TIRED OF LIFE

I expect Uncle Jack thought the saying original with him. Andy's mouth hung open.

"Your mother and I," Uncle Jack said to him, "were children together of course. Poor Connie. I hear she has had to go out to work."

"She's pretty successful in her field, sir," Andy said, trying to rally. "The University of California just accepted her design for the new faculty club. It's a real feather in her cap since she was the first woman granted an architecture degree there."

"Fancy that," said Uncle Jack, bending over his stitchery.

"And she and Joe—my stepfather—have the commission to redesign the Southern Pacific terminal." Andy began to falter.

"Two hearts with but a single thought," Uncle Jack said obscurely. "Ah, yes, Connie married again, did she not? A busy life. She was an intense and withdrawn child, nothing like her mother—Eve Waring. Your grandmother, of course." He gave Andy a nod. "And my Aunt Eve."

Andy rolled his eyes at me, but I could only shrug, and since Uncle Jack missed nothing, I'm sure he caught us at it. It was like him to imagine he was related to Andy's grandmother since she was the famous Eve Waring. And he seemed to believe it, but Andy couldn't let this fantasy pass.

"My grandmother is your aunt . . . sir?"

"Oh, good Lord, yes. Didn't you know? Aunt Eve and my mother—Opal—are sisters. From quite an old pioneering family, I believe. I am astonished at your ignorance. This younger generation never looks back!"

Andy and I, who had done little else, stared into our empty glasses.

"Yes," Uncle Jack was saying, "your grandmother was a great reprobate in her time."

I rose to this. "Eve Waring is the loveliest woman I ever saw."

"Yes, yes, a great beauty," he agreed, "and so thought the old king, bless him. I well remember when he died. When was it? Nineteen ten, and there Aunt Eve was on the mourners' bench with all his other old mistresses in attendance. All big women! Fine figures! Daisy Warwick and Mrs. Keppel and the duchess of Manchester. Lady Randolph Churchill, too, I believe. I will say this for them: They made a virtue out of vice!"

Andy was grinning crazily into his glass.

"Poor Aunt Eve," said Uncle Jack, flowing on, "she was the toast of London. I will tell you where she went wrong."

"Uncle Jack, she never put a foot wrong in her life."

"She did once," he said, "that we know of. It was all that backing and forthing between England and America. She knew all the best people here, and she was never appreciated in the States. Who is? Then just see what happened. She was trapped out there by the war. A great pity, but she should have known better. Has anything been heard of her since?"

This really was going too far. Much had been heard of her since.

Andy cleared his throat. "She's keeping very busy, sir, down in southern California. Still acting."

Uncle Jack's eyebrows flew up. "On the stage in southern California? Los Angeles? That is down and out indeed."

"Not on the stage, sir. She's in moving pictures. Doing very well at it too."

"The cinematograph?" Uncle Jack said. "Well, that has nothing to do with acting, does it?"

"She's rallied the moving picture colony in aid of the war," I said. "Surely you've heard of the funds she's raised for the duchess of Sutherland's hospital at Saint-Omer, Uncle Jack?"

He was threading a needle unerringly. "I may just have read something about that," he remarked. Nothing a duchess did escaped his notice.

"Ah, the fortunes of war," he said. "In the old days Eve Waring was always in the right place at the right time. I have always considered that her greatest talent. Surely people don't live in Los Angeles, do they?"

"I don't know about that, sir. Mother designed a house for Grandmother, a very fine one I believe. It's in a new town called Beverly Hills."

"Beverly Hills? It sounds like an unsuccessful country club. But it is entirely like poor Connie to build a house for her. Connie was always desperate for a mother's love. I saw it as a child, and I suppose we are all the children we were, trapped as we are in these aging bodies. And Aunt Eve was ever the least domesticated of women. What would she want with a house? She was always very much the hotel-suite type. All very sad. I expect she'll be glad to get back to London after the war."

"I expect so, sir."

"She sold the lease of that house she had in Half Moon Street, you know. Houses as I say mean nothing to her. But of course she could always put up at your mother's little place off Hertford Street in Mayfair. I often stroll past there on my constitutionals, and have struck up an acquaintance with the caretaker. It was let out for years, I believe, but the latest tenant bolted when the zeppelin raids began.''

Andy looked at me in bewilderment, but I could only shrug again.

"What house?" he asked.

Uncle Jack looked up at him. "Why the house Connie and poor Drummond lived in. I daresay you were born in it. Don't tell me Connie never mentioned she had a house in London."

"I suppose she probably did." Andy's gaze sharpened for the first time all evening.

"Yes, yes," Uncle Jack said, "the young never listen. I should think it will be your house one day if you want it."

"I'd like it now," Andy said, still looking at me. "I'd like it for these weekends I'm in London."

"But your club—"

"I wasn't born in the club."

Uncle Jack was snipping thread ends with his miniature scissors. His eyes were small slits, concentrating. "Yes, we all need our roots now, as we three poor waifs should know."

Then he looked up, and it was strange to see, even startling. All his pose had drained away: the uplifted eyebrows, the pursed, pontificating lips. It was the face of another man, the real one.

"Why shouldn't you have it now?" he said to Andy. "What better time?" He spoke with a kind of exquisite compassion, perfectly veiled. "I will write a note for the caretaker, and you can walk round there and have a word with him."

FIFTY-ONE

The house stood at an angle of its own off Hertford Street behind Shepherd Market. Piccadilly boomed not far behind it. Hyde Park stretched to the west. The house itself squatted deep in a London tangle of sober eighteenth-century houses that walled it away. It had risen before streets as some kind of outbuilding behind a yard. Now the yard was a shadowed triangle, brick-paved, with only a bottleneck passage half the width of White Horse Street opening to the front. If you didn't walk by it unnoticing, you sensed the magic at once.

Andy dealt with the caretaker whom I'd pictured as a cockney in a cloth cap taking a firm stand against intruders. But he was an elderly man, tall and pale in an alpaca suit, with the unmistakable air of a superior house servant. Where he lived himself, or served, was a mystery.

Andy was welcomed as the rightful tenant and deferred to as if he'd been daily expected. The caretaker handed over the keys and arranged for the housekeeper who turned out to be his wife. She instructed me to call her "Hoskins." Her elderly husband was named Blaine.

It was a dollhouse expanded almost to human scale. There was a little cottage door cut into a bigger barn door. Behind it the house was mainly a single room under a roof steeply peaked and stoutly beamed.

It had been furnished once and never again, though electricity had been added. The wiring for it snaked over doorframes and ran under the old wine-red Persian rugs. The furniture was all old and mostly mahogany, kept dully alive by Hoskins's polishing. Beneath the overhang of the balcony a long dining table stretched like a door on legs, with high-backed chairs at either end, just two. Staring down from all the walls were the trophies of someone's safari: wet-eyed rhinos and the glittering gaze of big cats.

It wasn't a place to be taken entirely seriously, or to be quite grown-ups in. It was unlikely and fantastic in a solid way, a bolt hole for lingering in a little while, for catching your breath.

We played house in it, cautiously until it claimed us. On the first weekend that Andy took up residence, we brought ale and wedges of shepherd's pie from Oscar's public house in the market. I couldn't cook and confessed it, not blaming the primitive kitchen. We picnicked at either end of the table.

"You're a mile away," Andy said, but I liked us at opposite ends. He looked like a small boy there at the foot of those polished planks.

We laid a fire in the hearth. There were little decorative tiles set in around it, and the chimney drew well. A long sofa pulled up so you could plant your feet on the fender, but I liked the old matching wing chairs, one slightly larger than the other, on either side of the fire.

We closed the door against the war and declared a private peace. Occasionally we went out. Andy drifted over to be shaved at Paillard's. We sat sometimes in the sunny patch of pavement before The Bunch of Grapes, drinking lager and lime. It was a village where we lived, but full of Londoners incurious about this young couple so curiously at home. We weren't quite recluses, but we needed nowhere else.

Andy lounged with one breeched leg thrown over the chair arm, reading the newspapers. I sat dozing, letting myself be bone-tired again, dreaming disconnected dreams of other houses. Before, we'd hoped for fine weather. Now we preferred the rain. It drummed far above us on the tight roof. Gusts lashed the leaded windows high up in the balcony beyond the big four-poster bed.

Andy took me back to the nurses' hostel each night. We parted at the door. Inside, the disinfectant hospital smell was a hard reminder. The drab green of the hallways leading to the wards moved in on me, nearer each night. The naked light bulbs hung over my head like a threat, and I saw my future, all of it, in this midnight maze of green walls and movable screens.

I saw the ordered days building into years, the duty days, the regular rounds, the unceasing reassurance offered to strangers. I saw the student nurse weeping over the spilt bedpan, the terminal case coaxed into smiling to please me, the beds never empty of suffering. Here there would always be war and never won.

I had these repeated warnings of my fate until one night I turned on my heel. I darted back into the dark street at last. He'd brought me back that night in a cab, but he was walking home now. He said he would. We were becoming householders now, practicing small economies. Andy would be walking down the Bayswater Road, across a corner of the park, turning at Londonderry House into Hertford Street.

I ran down the black pavement, and if I didn't find him, I'd run all the way. No danger that I'd change my mind and turn back. My coat flapped behind me, and my hat was over my ear. I ran pellmell into the present.

He was there just ahead, the unmistakable shape of him silhouetted in the light of a passing bus. He was striding along, and a puff of cigarette smoke curled up behind him into the damp night. He heard me there. I was running in the ridiculous slippers my mother had sent me. He turned and put out his long arms, and I was in them.

"I haven't come back for you," I said. "I've come back for me." We were inside the house again. The door was barred behind us, and the embers were still red, throwing last light across the wine and mahogany room. Shadows played over the beams above us.

"It can't be on the same terms," Andy said.

"I've forgotten what they were."

He took me in his arms and kissed me, gently to begin with. I willed myself to meet this change, and then I didn't have to. But we wouldn't fall this easily. We stepped apart, creating the last distance between us. I wasn't the hardened woman I'd been. I was a girl now, exactly my age. In another moment I'd be a defenseless child if I wasn't careful.

"I've known you all my life," I told him. "It seems you're the only human being I've ever known."

He waited. I had the floor.

"We can't be sure," I said, "that this isn't just . . . loneliness and being far from home and—"

"The war," Andy said.

"Yes. We mustn't mention—love. Or the future."

"More rules? In a world full of them?"

"Just those two," I said.

He built up the fire, and we sat deep in the sofa together. My hand was lost in his. We heard the sirens go and later the thump of far-off guns. But we'd outdistanced the war. The airships might drift above us, but only as summer lightning that would strike elsewhere.

The fire ebbed, and my hand was damp in his. He stood up, casting a long shadow, and walked to a wooden box set on a stand. Fitted inside were square crystal bottles and glasses.

"Brandy?" he said, not quite impersonating a man of the world.

"Do we need it?"

"I could use it," he said. "I'm scared."

Oh, he shouldn't have said that. In an easy stroke, he demolished the last wall between us. I took the glass.

"I have never—"

"Neither have I," Andy said.

We might have knocked back the brandies and dashed the glasses on the hearthstones, but it was too late for bravado. He stood over me and we sipped.

"Perhaps your mother and father drank this brandy." These two might have been in this room with us, watching from their tolerant distances.

"The last tenants probably left it behind. They were in a hurry."

"I'm glad."

"Maybe my mother and father . . . loved each other here on the rug in front of the fire." He took my glass away and was on his knees before me. I took his face in my hands.

He lay stretched before the fire, his long back and legs smoothed by firelight. I'd seen, touched naked boys before, but never this flawless. I'd rubbed alcohol into their vulnerable backs, and so my hand moved in this pattern across his. We'd made neat, separate piles of our clothes, his beside his chair, mine beside mine. But that was hours ago.

I leaned across his back to be nearer, and my breasts grazed the straight line of his spine. He turned beneath me and took me in his arms. I'd have cradled him in mine, but his shoulders were too broad. I lay there encompassed.

I spoke, to feel my lips against his chest. "Until now I never wanted to be beautiful."

"You were always beautiful," he said. "I just realized it."

He sat up and held me easily in the crook of his arm. He brushed the hair off my forehead with fingers just lightly calloused. His hands moved down me in a memorizing way.

"Did I hurt you?" he said.

"Only a little, and never again."

He eased me beneath him once more, already growing practiced. He covered me and lay there between me and the world.

"Someday," he said, "after the war—"

But I stopped his lips and stilled those forbidden words.

Four more weeks like that, five? I wouldn't ask when they were to be over, and he didn't tell me. We entered the last of our conspiracies together. During the weekdays when he was at Hythe, I rehearsed not having him. At the hospital I grew rigid over minor rules and took extra shifts. I recalled the self I'd been and impressed her into service. But this virgin had deceived herself. I sent her away.

Then one Sunday night was the last. I saw it in his

deliberation. I lay in the big bed up on the balcony and watched him gather up his few possessions. He might have left the little metal box for his soap in the bathroom, but he remembered that too. He laid everything out, as for an inspection, on the bed at my feet.

"This week?"

"Tonight. I won't—want you at the station."

"No."

He laid the keys on the dresser. "Will you look after the house? Keep it until—"

"Yes. I'll want to come here. I'll need to be somewhere."

He made a business of buckling his kit, bending over it in concentration. I watched the top of his head, his hair tousled from the bed. I thought he'd bolt down the stairs and out the door. I thought I wanted him to, but he didn't. Perhaps I'd cost him the last bit of his boyhood.

While I willed him to go, he stepped up and took my hand. This was all wrong. I was the one to stand at the bedside, eternally beside the beds of others.

He looked down at me in the dusk, man's eyes in a man's face. "What can I say to you, June, that isn't about love and the future?"

"I love you," I said. "Come back to me."

Feeding and growing fat on itself, the war ground on into the autumn. Walls were still plastered with recruitment posters. Militant Belgravian matrons still prowled the pavements, distributing white feathers of cowardice to any man not in uniform. The maimed flowed like a river into the wards of the Lancaster Gate Hospital.

I moved among them like a graven image. I worked through the weekends when I could, and came to the house in Hertford Street only for manageable moments. I came to sit an hour or so before the cold hearth. It was nothing to me now, I said, but I needed a quiet place.

Letters came from him, and I read them quickly. I looked again, making sure they were in his handwriting, and then I tore them across. Small bundle though they'd make, I wouldn't bear the burden of them.

In October a final letter came, from Vaubecourt in the Argonne. It was written in the copybook hand of a nurse at a bedside. But it spoke in Andy's voice:

> . . . On the way back, we were attacked by a squadron of Fokkers. They came from behind and killed my observer with their first round. His body jammed against the second cockpit controls, and that knocked out most of my maneuverability. I lost a lot of altitude and couldn't get any of it back. Crash-landed in a field our side of the line. Hands singed. Crick in my back. Nothing serious, but my war's over.
>
> And so is yours.
Andy

I blurred the page to wordlessness while I wept for every woman in the war, for those who could never have a letter like this now, and for those who would. I wept and laughed and held on to the arms of the wing chair to keep from soaring.

The sirens had sounded, and the guns were thundering in the park. A shadow fell across the room, but I'd forgotten the war.

BOOK 6

A Race of Mighty Women

FIFTY-TWO

She greeted me from the middle of her bed as if she'd sent for me from the next room instead of from across Europe. I stood before her in the suit I'd slept in.

Even to kiss her cheek or take her hand, I'd first have to plant a knee on the great bed and stretch, but she only waved me into a chair. She loved chocolates so I'd brought her a box, hand carried from London: Charbonnel & Walker in Bond Street. I put it on the bed where it lay ignored. In her heart she still dieted.

Drawn up close, I was still a distance from her. The bed had been made for her in Paris by Emile Ruhlmann sometime after the market crash. Her great shoulders were propped against a headboard of polished ebony, dark behind her hair. The wall above wavered in mottled green light, reflecting the afternoon sun on the Mediterranean below the window.

It was October of 1939, the second month of the war. I'd tried to hop a flight from Croydon, but they were all full, then canceled, then requisitioned, then full again. The trip from London to Nice had taken the better part of three days and my American passport.

"A tiresome journey?" she asked in a voice fainter than I remembered.

"A far cry from the *Golden Arrow*," I said, "and no chance to climb down and stretch my legs. The platforms from Victoria on were mobbed."

They were all jammed with half-panicked, half-euphoric crowds, the first of the refugees, and everywhere uniforms.

My civilian clothes were beginning to weigh on me. I was more than ready to sign up again. As a kid, I'd been in the last war, a flyer, but those were the box-kite days. Nobody would talk to me in the brave new Spitfire world of the RAF. I was thirty-nine; if I didn't get in on the ground floor somewhere, I'd end up in the Home Guard.

A group was organizing for the Royal Marines, training at Deal, and I harbored some hopes of slipping in there as a somewhat elderly second lieutenant. But my American passport was giving difficulties with that. I'd been born an Englishman though, and so I harbored hopes.

I wondered if she couldn't get me into the war if she tried. Churchill was First Lord of the Admiralty, and she had him in her pocket. He'd often come down here to paint on the rocks below the villa and at Saint-Paul de Vence. And if Churchill wouldn't help, she'd know somebody who would. She knew everybody.

But she wouldn't have sent for me about that, or because the war had rattled her. I didn't know why she wanted me unless she was dying. It was useless to search her face for clues. She'd been an actress; she was an actress still. She offered the world exactly the face she wanted the world to see, and she was calculating. She could have outmaneuvered Hitler from her bed.

She was recalled as the great beauty of her age. I remembered her in her prime, though by then she was already a grandmother—mine. It was a sledgehammer beauty with an overwhelming grand manner to match it. Yet the key to it was mystery: the halftones, the nuances of her sidelong glances, the unnerving secrecy of her amazing turquoise eyes.

Her eyes were as they'd been, still speaking and deceiving for her. Some of her mystery had turned to slyness, but not all, and her beauty hadn't as much faded as gone out of fashion. There was a hint of it left, webbed and widened, but there.

Her hair was snow-white now. I could remember when it was jet black and piled high on her head to balance the astounding figure.

Now its silvery whiteness was cut short and marcelled in the stiff style of five or six years ago. A woman still rode over every morning in the postman's sidecar from Cannes to dress it and to manicure the broad, grooved nails.

When her hair had been black, her skin was tawny. Now the flesh of her face, loose except at the cheekbones, was bronze against the white hair. She looked like an old Indian chief, propped and implacable. She must be eighty now. Nobody knew.

Old men still stopped me on the steps of clubs, even in the street, to tell me about her. Except they never did. They spoke instead of the young men they'd been when they'd stood at the stage door waiting for her, waiting for Eve Waring.

When I was married, my wife and I were invited to Belvedere by the Prince of Wales to meet Mrs. Simpson. Since this was a pretty high social peak for us, we wondered why we were there, but it came clear. At lunch the prince put my wife beside him and regaled her with old stories of Eve Waring.

"She was ever such a favorite with Grandpapa," I heard him say in that high, piercing voice. "If it hadn't been for Mrs. Keppel, I don't know where it might have ended."

I'd enjoyed that, but my wife was less pleased to learn why we'd been invited.

"You're in a daze," Eve said. Her vast hand, heavy with diamonds, lay above the satin counterpane, patient, though she wasn't a patient woman. "Your trip has done you up. When I was touring, I learned to sleep in the train. One had to arrive refreshed, sometimes in most unpromising places."

"I was woolgathering," I said, "thinking of the Prince of Wales."

Something sharpened in her eye. "Which one?"

"The duke of Windsor."

"That whippersnapper. Things were arranged quite differently in my day." Her hand twitched now as she dismissed an entire royal abdication—and closed the case on an old story of her own.

She sighed, and I saw she was more exhausted than I was

and far less willing to admit it. Something had worn her out, and it didn't occur to me that it was something she wanted. Was she bedfast now? Her eyes half closed against the brilliant day. From somewhere out at sea came the throb of a motor launch and voices and laughter from it, already an incongruous, prewar sound.

Summoning herself, she said, "Tell me about the war, Andy."

It was hard to know where to begin. War was declared on the first of September, but that was ancient history now. On the third night the *Athenia* was torpedoed. It was an ocean liner bound for North America packed with civilians, many of them Americans. This was generally thought suicidal on Germany's part, sure to bring America into the war. But it hadn't. The Nazis swept through Poland to divide the spoils with the Russians advancing from the east. On the twenty-seventh day of the war, Warsaw fell.

Still, we—the British—had done nothing but stage practice air-raid drills. There hadn't even been air strikes on the Ruhr for fear of reprisals against France. The Atlantic was a German lake, thick with their U-boats.

"They're turfing up the park around Knightsbridge Barracks for earth to fill sandbags," I told her. "They say if we're not invaded shortly, Hitler will wait till March."

Age had drawn down the corners of her mouth, but her jaw tightened. I told her how the French were putting all their faith in the Ligne Maginot, how they'd carved in the stone of their medieval fortifications: *Ils ne passeront pas,* as if these earthworks could repel Stukas. I meant this for a warning to her. Inevitably, France would fall, but she only flared a nostril in mild contempt.

It was a waste of time to tell her about the war. She was always better informed than anybody. She looked like the least attentive woman in the world, and she was the most. The Paris *Herald Tribune* lay in the folds of her bedclothes, and so did yesterday's London *Times.* I began to wish we'd be interrupted.

People were coming to the villa to say good-bye because of

the war and because, one way or another, they wouldn't see her again. I'd met Cecil Beaton on the stairs and Randolph Churchill and his bride, Pamela, on the landing. Lord Derby, who dominated the British colony on the Riviera, hovered in the background, trying to convince her to get out while she could, but she had no time for him.

She lay there somehow girded for battle, her enormous bosom encased in a bedjacket pinned at the throat with a turquoise brooch set in gold. She bristled with an easy defiance. A loaded revolver in her pillowslip wouldn't have surprised me much.

She'd always had a grim greeting for catastrophe. When she'd brought her theatrical company to San Francisco, the earthquake struck, and the fire destroyed all her costumes and sets. She performed her entire repertory a week later to sell-out crowds in the open-air theater at Berkeley across the Bay. She'd given birth to a new San Francisco in those performances, and her daughter, Constance, the architect, had helped raise the city from ruins. I was Constance's son and had come of this race of mighty women.

But that was all long ago. While minutes passed, I sat beside the bed wondering if time meant nothing to the very old, or too much. In the moments when Eve Waring was silent on a stage, you thought she was reading your mind, even if you were in the last row of the balcony. I'd heard that time and again from old men who remembered. She was famous for her stage silences. We had one now, until she broke it.

"Men," she said. "How you men crave war. War killed your father, you know."

My father, Hugh Drummond, had died in the Boer War. I knew that of course, but I hadn't known him. Joe Fletcher, who married my mother, was the father I knew, and a good one. He was dead now too, in the influenza epidemic at the end of the last war.

"Guy went to the last one," she said. "He must have been then the age you are now. But he went."

She meant Lord Guy Carville-Paget. It was always said he was young enough to be her son. He'd loved her for years, probably without much hope. When he came back from the '14-'18 War having left a leg at Ypres, she married him. She was in fact Lady Carville-Paget, though nobody ever called her anything but Eve Waring. I called her Eve too. Neither of us would have found *Grandmother* quite right. Lord Guy had loved her for years and loved her still. He was somewhere in this vast hotellike house waiting to greet me. She'd send me on to him when she was ready.

"I should have thought you'd suffered enough, from war."

I didn't know where she was leading me so I wondered what age had done to her. She'd never let the past plague her. She'd always cut her losses and invited others to do the same.

Maybe in soldiering I hadn't suffered enough. I'd been crazy about flying and too green and cocksure to be as scared as I should have been. I was eighteen and immortal and maybe too dumb to die.

She meant June. I'd loved June Kinsella, and I'd lost her. She died in the last zeppelin raid on London. She'd died when the last bomb of the war fell on the house in Hertford Street, blasting it apart.

I'd loved June too young and too much, and I was paying for it still and making others pay. I could go months at a time without wondering what damage June's memory had done, but I was wondering now. Eve had invited me to, and all her invitations were commands.

I'd come back to London from the hospital in France to find that June was dead. She'd thought the war would kill me, and it had killed her. In twenty years I'd never mastered the irony of that.

"She was a pretty child, June was," Eve said. "I thought Rose would spoil her, but she didn't."

Like me, June's mother had loved her too much, but she hadn't spoiled her. June was too independent. She went her own way until we met again in the war. There were times when I wished we hadn't. She might have lived. I might have.

When I could get back to San Francisco in 1919, I took
June's ashes home. I'd thought I was going home myself, but
home's never where you left it. Joe Fletcher, my stepfather,
had died in the epidemic. My mother and June's, Constance
and Rose, were the only ones left. Constance closed the
house on Telegraph Hill. She had her work still and his to
carry on. She was grief-stricken and wouldn't show it. When
I came home, she and Rose were living at the St. Francis
Hotel.

I found my mother as controlled as ever, and tighter about
the lips. She'd buried two husbands, and I don't suppose
she'd expected me to get through the war. But she had her
work—and Rose—to look after.

They'd been friends as girls, and now they were bonded
for life. My mother: tightly strung, ambitious. And Rose:
driven too. They lived in two apartments in the Post-Powell
wing of the St. Francis with the door between always ajar.
They were two of the most notable women in San Francisco.
My mother was the most prominent architect in California,
and Rose was one of its most successful merchants. Her
shop, called Rose Conklin, was a cut above I. Magnin. Rose,
who'd been pretty once, was like an aunt to me, but when I
came home I wouldn't have known her.

Reading me like a book, Eve said, "Poor Rose."

An odd thing had happened when I went home twenty
years ago. I remembered it in detail and had never known
what it meant. Maybe Eve would.

"We took June's ashes out to the beach," I said, "and
scattered them in the sea."

Eve turned her head toward me, listening.

"Later, back at the hotel, I came upon Rose and Constance
alone. It was evening, and they didn't see me in the shadows.
"Rose was slumped in a chair and Mother was standing by
her. I still remember what Rose said: 'It's a judgment on me.
There is a God, and He has found a way to make me pay.
And, oh, Constance, He is unforgiving. He took June from
me, and you know why.' "

The memory of that had nagged me all these years. I couldn't match that moment to the women I thought I knew.

"Do you know what she meant, Eve?"

She'd looked away, and her eyes were hooded, but she was alive behind her mask.

"Yes," she said, "well enough."

Somewhere in the room a clock ticked. The sun had dropped lower.

"Are you going to tell me?"

"No."

After a time she stirred herself, blinking her eyes wide as if she'd just awakened, changing the subject neatly.

"Tell me about Constance," she said.

She'd probably heard from my mother since I had, but she waited for an answer.

"She's well, I think. Worried about the war, but busy with her work. She changes very little," I said, hoping it was so.

"Yes, if they blow up the world, Constance will build it back." A rare, small flicker of maternal pride showed in her eye. "You can count on that. You can count on Constance."

I'd never fathomed the relationship between this mother and this daughter. My mother had come to France nearly ten years ago to build this villa for Eve Waring. Then she'd gone home again, homesick for San Francisco and already absorbed in her next project. Constance loved her mother; she'd loved two husbands. She loved me. But something had stilled her tongue. She only spoke through bricks and mortar and long windows giving on to the sea.

"As a child, Constance was warned by life," Eve said unexpectedly. "She had only herself to turn to."

I was willing to hear more. The women of my family rarely reminisced.

"I mothered her too little. I only came to know her when she was grown. I was lucky she would know me."

"You had to provide for her," I said, thinking it was the right thing to say.

"I was providing for myself, and . . . compensating. I'd been deprived of love, and so I deprived Constance. We always withhold what was withheld from us. We cannot even see this cycle, let alone find a way to break it."

"We?" I said.

"You too." Her hands were clasped, holding one another steady. She looked away, changing the scene again, or seeming to. "And Dinah? Is she well?"

Dinah was my wife, had been my wife. We were separated on reasonably civil terms.

"She's trying to get in the war herself. There's talk of requisitioning private cars. They'll probably want her Rover as some general's staff car, and I think Dinah plans to go along with it as chauffeur."

"Good for her! That girl always had more spunk than you did."

She had a point there. After the war I saw nothing for myself in San Francisco and drifted back to London. Disillusioned London in the twenties had just about suited my mood. At twenty-one I was old without the wisdom of the old. I tried a job or two, cushioned by family money. I'd managed my mother's London properties and dabbled in the stock market, losing only a little in '29.

Without much in the way of inner resources, I settled for poses. I took rooms in Albany and had my shirts made in Jermyn Street. Styling myself a writer, I dabbled in journalism. I developed a tolerance for saxophone music. My Yank accent began to fade, and one or two of the less demanding clubs took me. My generation was all gone, so I fell in with a younger crowd where every other girl was trying to look like Gertrude Lawrence. Dinah stood out like a beacon among them. She had the brisk emphasis I'd known from the women of my own family, and June. But she was very much herself.

"A splendid girl," Eve said. "Better than you deserve."

"You'll get no argument from me on that," I said. "I tried to warn Dinah, but she was at the age to think marriage will solve everything."

"What rot you're talking, Andy. You cannot court a girl and warn her at the same time. You were in love with her and might be yet if you let yourself. Did she turn you out?"

"She made it easy for me to go."

"When she knew you'd go anyway. That's not the same thing. Was there another woman?"

". . . Not exactly."

She saw I was thinking of June and looked away. She was only a little impatient with me and hadn't sent for me to deliver a lecture on marriage. It was something else, and she'd come to it when she was good and ready. She seemed to remember what it was suddenly and grew fretful, too like any other old woman. Her hand plucked at the bedclothes.

"You should go and dress for dinner now. The light's fading."

I turned to the window to make sure it was, that she hadn't meant something else. When I looked back, her gaze was fixed on something past my shoulder, behind me in the room.

"Maugham invited himself over from Cap Ferrat for this evening," she was saying, "but I put him off. I think I'll rest a little while now. Just go through there and say hello to Guy if he's awake. He isn't well, you know, and he's so looked forward to seeing you."

When I rose to go, I turned to see what she'd been looking at. There was a table full of photographs, a whole silver-framed forest of them, mostly faded and signed.

In the jumble was one of me, circa 1906, in a Buster Brown collar, and one of Edward VII, inscribed, in coronation robes. The Mountbattens were there, signed "Edwina and Dickie," and the Fairbanks, signed "Mary and Doug." There were several of my mother and Joe Fletcher, and one of Lord Guy long ago. There was one of me in the war, in tunic and white silk scarf. I noticed another, smaller and newer, in a place of unmistakable honor set in front of the rest.

It was a picture of Claire taken on her sixth birthday, a Shirley Temple child, though her curls were dark. It was a picture of my daughter, of Dinah's and mine.

"You're looking haggard," Eve said across the room. "You don't take care of yourself. And your hair's thinning."

When I went to Guy's door, it seemed to me that Eve's gaze never left the picture of my daughter.

FIFTY-THREE

I rapped lightly at the door connecting their rooms. No answer came, so I looked in and saw Guy lying asleep in a chair at the window.

There was a distinct air of military spit-and-polish about the room. Framed photographs of regimental dinners hung on the walls, and his brushes were laid out according to some plan on the dresser top. Among them was a photograph of Eve as Mrs. Cheveley in Wilde's *An Ideal Husband*, like a picture of a soldier's girl proudly displayed in the barracks. The bed had been turned back for his nap, but he'd spurned it. He was in the chair as if he hadn't meant to sleep.

I went across and stood over him, seeing his view of the Mediterranean from the window. He lay there in a very fine dressing gown. His hair was gray, and his face, like a withered boy's, was turned toward the light. For some reason he reminded me of—a broken toy soldier. Then I saw the way his dressing gown lay and realized he wasn't wearing his artificial leg.

I turned to go, quietly, when he opened his eyes. "The damned thing hurts like the very devil. Hello, Andy. You're here at last. Eve will be pleased."

I took his hand, like a bundle of twigs. "How are you, Guy?"

"Oh, not very well, I'm afraid, and I had meant to stay so strong. Curious how happy one is nonetheless. I'm not quite finished, you know. I'd planned to come down to dinner tonight."

"Don't think of it," I said. "I'll come to your room, and we'll have some talks while I'm here."

He smiled an old debonair smile. "That's right," he said. "You must come and say good-bye to me when you go. I don't think you're meant to make a long visit here."

"I see. Then I suppose Eve has plans for me."

He seemed to laugh silently. "Her head is full of plans for other people, and always was. We usually carry them out."

He was tired, and I meant to go, but he said, "I'm not up to much these days. But Eve, don't you find her remarkable? She hasn't altered in all the years I've known her. All that beauty, and just as it was."

It took all my borrowed British phlegm to turn away then, and even at that my eyes were damp. I supposed we were saying good-bye now. So I said over my shoulder, "Guy, what's the secret? You're the happiest married man I know."

Englishmen don't discuss these matters, but he was ready. His voice was thin and precise. "I can speak only for myself. You wait twenty years, go to the war, get your leg blown off, then you hobble across the world and hope she'll have you. I'd have crawled to California, you know."

He gave me a graceful exit, worthy of Eve Waring's husband.

The evening came on, robbing the Mediterranean of color. I made a sketchy business of dressing for dinner, struggling with a collar button in another peacetime ritual growing meaningless.

My usual room was nearly unchanged, with all the impersonal comforts of a good hotel. The only addition was a new electric tea kettle squatting among my shaving things. The paper label was still stuck to its chromium dome, possibly Eve's preparation for war and the scattering of servants.

Their unseen hands had unpacked me. Her servants here were tough peasants of this province who knew the territory and the markets. The French she used on them was uproarious, and their rude replies amused her enormously. That, too, was changing. There were fewer of them in evidence now, and I'd heard sobs coming from their quarters. Whether they wept for their mistress or their country, I didn't know.

It was night when I stepped out for a cigarette on the balcony of my room. Cannes lay glittering across the water. Well out, a motor launch blazed with electricity. The Côte d'Azur was keeping the war at arm's length, and it couldn't last.

This whole overmanicured stretch from Hyères to Ventimiglia had always been something of a joke to Dinah's generation and mine. It was too highly colored, and we had to laugh at the wedding-cake hotels and the palm-court orchestras still playing "The Man Who Broke the Bank at Monte Carlo." The elderly English still dozed over tea on the Carlton Terrace as if Sarajevo had stopped all the clocks.

But I was missing it already. It remembered better times than were coming. There'd be barbed wire on these beaches and mines in the yacht basins, and nothing would be the same.

The villa hung in terraces like Babylon so close to the cliff I could flip my cigarette directly into the sea. My room was muffled by the silence of the house. There were countless bedrooms, and they'd always been filled before. Even when Dinah and I brought the child down for family visits, there was no knowing who'd be here.

Winston Churchill was liable to be running a game of six-pack bezique in the library, and Noel Coward in the music room, playing "Ziguener" on the grand piano in a wreath of smoke. Daisy Fellows was apt to be arriving with six steamer trunks and her aunt, Princesse Edmond de Polignac. I'd once met Coco Chanel coming from the loo. There was just no knowing.

"I've been the Wandering Jew all my life," Eve had said. "Let the world come to me."

It had. Greeks bearing guests had come off their yachts for lunch, and tour buses from American Express slowed at the gate for picture taking. My mother, Constance, had built the place in the style she'd spread from one end of California to the other. It was like an entire village—Monterey in the old days. It stair-stepped down the cliffs in an orderly jumble of roofs and terraces, and all the rooms were ideally proportioned. Constance had made it as a backdrop for Eve. The window walls curved like prosceniums, stages where Eve Waring could take her final calls, make her last bows.

It was just as well my mother hadn't come back from San Francisco to see the place being lived in. Constance always created space without hemming it in. She needed simplicity, austerity. Eve had other needs. She'd emptied warehouses of her belongings and filled the thousand corners of the house to overflowing. It was all good stuff in its way, some of it priceless, but her tolerance for clutter was Edwardian at the latest.

She had a fortune in art. When she was making films in California, she collected paintings while other people were buying on margin. In my dressing room a Corot was casually tacked up beside the shaving mirror, and the long hallway to the stairs was a gallery: Matisse jostled Burne-Jones, and Daumier crayon sketches ranged all the way to the floor.

On the stairs a thought struck me hard. Had she summoned me to say I was to inherit this house? In the best of times I couldn't live in it, and in these times I certainly couldn't sell it. When the Germans came, and they would, this would be occupied territory. I could hear jackboots ringing on the tiles and canvas being ripped out of frames. The thought passed. She hadn't sent for me to hand me a house. She had a firm of solicitors for that.

The picture on the landing always stopped me. It was her portrait, the only artifact in the house from her career. It could almost have been late Sargent. She was painted in her role in *The Second Mrs. Tanqueray*. She'd played it all over the world in her farewell tour before she settled in Hollywood.

She made that part hers. Costumed for Pinero, she's portrayed sitting at a piano, lit with the suggestion of footlights. Her hands, whiter and more delicate than they could have been, rest on the keyboard. She looks aside, not quite at the audience or the painter, eluding them both.

Her Mrs. Tanqueray was still cited in theatrical annals. She played herself, a fascinating older woman trailing intrigue and heading for death in high style. She played a dozen different Mrs. Tanquerays in Hollywood films. She outlasted the vamps and lingered into the Clara Bow era to confound the flappers. They'd have paired her with Valentino, but she didn't share.

"It was tiring and trying, stage and screen alike, and I did it for the money," she said. There was another reason, though, and that involved Lord Guy. I believe it was a long time before he learned to walk with neither cane nor crutches on his new wooden leg. When he could cross the world on it and walk down gangplanks and climb up into trains, he found Eve again in California, or she summoned him.

He was still a young man then, though not as young as he'd been. How he made his transition into films I never knew. I suppose Eve championed him and made demands. Subtly, she and he never appeared in the same picture, but he became a distinguished actor, always playing a polished, world-weary Englishman. At a glance, he looked like Claude Rains. I'd often dropped into a cinema to see my step-grandfather suavely on the screen. He never got the girl, and so his career could have gone on and on. But on the day before the market crash, they abruptly retired, her timing flawless to the end.

She'd left only this enigmatic, unsatisfying portrait to represent her career. All the photographs in her bedroom were of other people, and only they revealed the past. Eve lived in the perpetual present, moving among people who made conversation, not inquiries.

In the drawing room, I went to the liquor cabinet and made myself a drink. After a measured interval, I supposed unseen hands would draw back the dining room doors, and I'd dine in solitary splendor, feeling like a fool.

Halfway through the drink I knew I wasn't alone. I turned to the door to see Eve standing there.

Her back was straight, her eyebrows high. She was cuing her entrance to some line of dialogue I was too surprised to devise. And she was dressed for dinner in a black and silver gown bedizened with beads that seemed to be from the late 1920s. It had no waistline, and that suited her well enough. But it seemed to come from a time when women weren't supposed to have busts, and so it veered a long way from fashion to accommodate her.

Her hair was clenched in tight waves angling across her heavy brow, and her hand was planted on her generous hip in a provocative, dated posture. She was ponderous now, perhaps two hundred pounds. Yet I could see what the old men remembered. I knew we weren't to recall the woman of the afternoon, lying elderly and even a little diminished in her bed upstairs.

Eve Waring walked across the room, a triumph. The beads on her dress made the sound of the sea.

"I could eat a horse," she said.

In the dining room a door stood open to the sea, flickering the candle flame between us. We sat at either end of a very long table.

It was a cold supper, like Sunday evening in an incredibly good club. There were *aubergines à la Turque* to begin; a *loup poché* with *aïoli*, that local, garlic-impregnated mayonnaise; then a *soufflé glacé au citron* like a subtle symphony; and Gruyère after.

Small mats printed with English hunt scenes marked our places. She geared her hospitality to men. She ate like a man herself, savoring every bite and attacking the loup with gusto.

She glanced up at me. All of her glances were different. "How old would you be now, Andy?"

I told her, though I think she knew.

"You're at the age a man looks his best in dinner clothes," she remarked. "It's taken a lot of good tailoring and bad climate to give you the look of an Englishman."

I gave that some thought and then decided to nudge us both forward a step, or try. "Ever since I arrived, you've reminded me that I've left my youth behind me, Eve. My hair's thinning. I don't look after myself. Now I'm being held together chiefly by my clothes. I wonder what you're driving at?"

I might as well have saved my breath. Her hearing had suddenly failed her. She was chasing a morsel around her plate, giving it all her attention.

"Yes," she said, answering herself, "you've adopted an Englishman's ennui, but it's borrowed and doesn't belong to you. Under that boiled shirt and behind those tired eyes you're an American."

"I've never denied it."

"Oh, but you have with every breath. You've thought life was too hard, and so you've been too easy on yourself. You've got grit you haven't used yet."

"Maybe I'll be using it soon."

"Maybe you will."

I meant the war. She didn't. The soufflé came, and she fell upon it.

My guard was up now, quenching my appetite. I gazed around the dining room. Along the far wall that Constance would have left blank hung an enormous panorama by Alma-Tadema. It was as big as a mural, and the wall barely took it. I scanned it, though it was the kind of painting people nowadays said they couldn't look at.

I wouldn't have known the artist at all, but in my desultory journalism career, I'd been called on to write brief, knowing essays of art criticism. This was from Alma-Tadema's early period: Frankish knights in unlikely armor marching immaculately to battle before an unruined landscape.

"I knew him, you know," Eve said.

"Alma-Tadema? Surely not."

"I did. He lived until 1912, something like that. He wanted to paint me, but I wouldn't have it. He made all his women look like monuments, and in my case that would have been redundant."

She gestured over her shoulder with a fork. "It will come into its own again one day if it makes it through the war."

I couldn't think its loss would figure as a major calamity, but kept this to myself.

"I've never been fond of it," she said. "It's not the sort of picture you can get close to. Possessions possess us though. I always remember Evan Charteris telling me about his father— that was Lord Wemyss, you know. The old gentleman had a copy of the 'Mona Lisa,' not an especially good copy, I gather. He insisted to his dying day that his was the original and the Louvre had only a clever fake. And he lived well past ninety." She chuckled silently in Lord Guy's way.

"I know it would break all your rules, Eve," I said, "but you ought to write your memoirs."

She made a lovely gesture in the air, sweeping my notion out to sea. "When a woman is old enough to tell the truth, she can't remember what it was."

After a pause I said, "Maybe you ought to have your pictures stored."

"Stored?" Her fork clattered onto her plate. "Stored where? In England to be bombed? Or torpedoed on the way to America? Or here to be confiscated by the Germans?"

"The Germans may not make it this far."

"You know better than that. What's to stop them? Don't talk to me about Pétain. He'll be no use at all. I knew him in Madrid."

I shifted in my chair, still the schoolboy.

"They'll get this far," she said grimly, "and farther. This war will go on for years. It's meant to. There's money to be made in it, as there always is."

"Then why don't you close up this house and move back to London, to the Dorchester Hotel where they'll make you and Guy comfortable?" To tempt her I added, "The countess of Halifax is at the Dorchester already."

She tossed her head, and the diamonds at her throat caught the candlelight. "I know you think me a snob, but buried alive under rubble even with the countess of Halifax isn't much of a lure. In any case, she'll soon be off to America. The earl's being sent as ambassador to Washington."

Of course she'd know this. I knew only what I heard on the BBC.

She produced a cigarette case from somewhere and lit up a

Balkan-Sobranie. Half hidden behind the smoke screen, her great square face was suddenly younger. Its beauty stirred beyond the candle flame. Upstairs in his bed, Guy was still seeing her clearly.

I looked away and fumbled for a cigarette. "I'd like to see you get through the war, Eve."

Her eyes were on me under the thick black brows. "I don't know that I care to. I lived through the last war. It ruined everything worth having and retained the rest. If war kills me, I'll still have had everything I ever wanted, almost."

"Not everything?"

"Only on the deathbed do people say they have no regrets." She shot me a look. "I'm not on my deathbed yet."

It was no use asking her what she'd lacked in life, and yet she was going to tell me. I saw her readying herself.

"I'd hoped you and June would marry."

I must have reacted somehow.

"I know it's painful for you to remember her. Men keep their old wounds open. I don't know why, but you do. Since you were both children, I'd hoped you and June would marry and have a family. June's grandmother and I were raised as sisters."

I grinned, annoying her. "I see nothing diverting about that," she said. "June's grandmother, Opal, was no laughing matter."

"I was only remembering June's Uncle Jack. He claimed you as his aunt."

"He would." She dismissed him though he was long dead anyway. "He was a fool, and his mother was worse than that. Still, I hoped that you and June would marry and have children. I must have thought of it as a . . . joining that would heal something in me. I suppose we're always looking for ways to heal our childhoods.

"It wasn't to be, and it was foolish of me to want it so much. I don't often give way to sentimentality, and when I do it generally turns out badly."

"You married Lord Guy, and that turned out very well for both of you."

"That wasn't sentimentality," she said. "It was . . . a great deal more than that. Guy had more strength than showed, you know. Like you."

She was coming around to her point now, to the reason she'd sent for me.

"Is there something more you want, Eve, something I can do?"

She drew in her cheeks. I was pushing her again, but in the right direction now.

"Don't make it so easy to ask," she said. "You might not find it easy to grant."

"I'll take my chances."

"You're not thinking of getting into the war, are you—not at your age, surely?" she said, seeming to change the subject.

"As a matter of fact, I am. I even thought you might—"

"What nonsense! You had your war. Surely you're old enough now to know wars aren't for fighting; they're for surviving."

She worked her glittering hands together, suddenly at her wit's end at war's stupidity, and mine.

"And Claire? Your daughter? What of her?"

She had me there. I had an offhand English father's attitude toward my daughter. She was with Dinah, of course, at home in Pont Street. Dinah made no difficulties about my seeing the child, but for weeks at a time, I didn't.

"They'll be evacuating Claire's school," Eve said, "somewhere in the countryside."

"Will they?" I said, wishing I hadn't.

Intent upon Claire, she seemed to pass over my ignorance. ". . . and of course that won't do, as I'm sure you'll agree. She's much too young to be sent away on her own, and besides there won't be a safe corner in England. There may be an invasion."

She was half out of her chair. The beads on her gown swayed and jangled. She was almost beside herself with worry, and something harder for her to show: fear. She'd been thinking of her great-granddaughter all along, and only of her. Claire was the reason I'd been summoned.

She worked to compose herself, reaching for her wine. A bit of it spilled, and she drew her hand back. "There's something I want, Andy, and I want it very much."

I'd never heard the sound of pleading in her voice, but it was there now.

"I won't rest easy, or die happy for that matter, unless she's out of the way of the war. I want you to take Claire to America. Take her to San Francisco. Constance is there. Take her, Andy, and keep her safe. She's . . . all the future we have." Her voice blurred, and her eyes.

I spoke quickly to keep her eyes from filling. "Dinah has custody of Claire, you know." But then I realized that Dinah would want Claire safe. I saw, too, in a quick flash of furtiveness crossing Eve's face, that these two women were in agreement.

Outflanked, I said the only other thing I could think of. "I don't know that an Atlantic crossing would be entirely safe."

"There are Clippers flying from Lisbon," she said. "Safe enough and safer than staying. Heavily booked, of course, but something can be arranged."

And already had been arranged, I thought, if I knew anything about Eve Waring.

"You would have to go with her," she said, the plan already mature. "See her safely there. And stay with her. This is your opportunity, you see."

"My opportunity?"

She almost despaired of me then. She could hardly bear my blindness.

"Your opportunity to be her father. I had no father, Andy, and it made everything harder than it should have been. It makes things harder yet. War would be an easy escape for you. Surely you won't take it."

I shied from that, thinking instead how all the borders might close overnight. Any minute now the Clipper flights from Lisbon could become one more memory of peacetime. But even then I knew I'd do it. I'd do it to please her, to keep her from weeping. I'd never seen her weep; maybe nobody had.

A servant entered the dining room, a beefy-armed woman with her hair in a kerchief. She may have been listening against the door. Eve leaned heavily on her to be helped out of her chair, but she wouldn't take my arm into the drawing room where the coffee was. She tottered a little, but her spine was a poker.

The drawing room was full of ghosts. It was a room meant for a multitude, and the pink-shaded lamps lit more corners than we could fill. We sat across a little table under a haunting Gustave Courbet elaborately framed on the wall. She poured out from a silver pot, disciplining her hands to deal with the sugar tongs.

"I wonder," she said mildly, "who will have this silver next." Her smile was wry, and she wasn't referring to her heirs. She handed me a cup.

"We can't be bothered about that," she went on. "It will either go or stay." She looked about the room, assuming an air of great ease. "The Nazis may rather like some of this stuff," she remarked. "A good deal of the art is representational, and I believe the Germans understand nothing else. It's entirely possible that some field marshal may requisition this place for himself and keep it quite intact."

While she was relinquishing her entire house to the invading horde, she was taking a ring off her finger. It left her hands heavily laden with stones, but it was mammoth, a massive square-cut diamond set among many more. She handed it across the table to me.

"Take this to Dinah," she said. "It has no sentimental connotations. I had it made up for myself." The ring fell heavily into my hand.

"I don't imagine you'll have much difficulty getting it back to England undiscovered. Dinah won't want to wear it of course, but it might come in very handy for her. You never know how meaningless money might become, whereas jewelry . . ." Her voice trailed off, but her meaning was clear.

This was to seal our agreement. Dinah was already party to the plan, and I'd been persuaded. Still, there must be no hitch, no last-minute shirking. I was to take the ring to

Dinah, and we were to pull together in getting Claire away.
As a device, it was a bit obvious, and probably from some
old play.

"She'll be very touched, Eve," I said. "But I would have
seen her anyway, you know."

But she was deaf to me again, staring away in space, with
her great-granddaughter firmly in her eye. I'd have surren-
dered to her plan at that moment, but there was something that
would never have occurred to her. I wanted something too.
I'd have to begin by catching her off guard.

"If I'm to take Claire to America, I don't see why I
shouldn't take you and Guy too."

Her eyes flashed green fire. She looked at me, horrified.
"What rubbish! I wouldn't consider it."

"And yet you'd like nothing better. You could live in
comfort with your daughter and your great-granddaughter. It
was always a family of women, wasn't it? The men never
really counted for much. I don't count for much except as a
link, between you and my child, between now and the future.
If you went to California, you could be a family. Your
audiences have always loved happy endings. Are you so
different after all?"

"It's out of the question." Her jaw clamped down hard.

I knew it was. She wouldn't go back to die in Constance's
arms. She wouldn't impose herself. She and my mother
would stand separate and adoring, and Eve would die just
exactly as she'd lived. Though I was only a man, I understood that much.

"Very well then." I stirred as if I would rise. "I'll come
to the bargain I'm willing to make."

Her jaw fell open, and I heard the beads again. She made
no bargains.

"I'll take Claire to California," I said, "and I'll sit out the
war with her there. It's just possible that Hitler can be
defeated without my help. After all, Dinah will be defending
England. If they fight to the last woman, I have no doubt it
will be Dinah."

Eve began to allow herself a cautious smile.

"I'll do what you want," I said, "if you and Guy will get away from here and go to England. You have no family there, and so you won't think yourself a burden to anyone. You have friends there. And if you must die, you'd rather be killed in an air raid than be held captive here, and so would Guy. He's an old soldier. Don't let him be taken. The Nazis may like your art, but they're damned bad company."

Her hands were working on the chair arms. "Guy isn't at all well," she said uncertainly. "We are too old to be uprooted."

"Tell that to the Germans and see where it gets you."

"There is no need to take that bullying tone with me, Andy," she said, but of course there was every need.

"Is that your final word?" she said after a moment.

"It is. And time's short."

"When I suggested you show a little grit, I didn't mean at my expense," she said, richly ironic. But I knew I'd won.

"Then you'll go to England?"

"Yes, of course. What choice do you leave me? I'm old and helpless." But she was laying on the irony with a trowel, and suddenly she was all business. She drew herself up, and the poker returned to her back. "The Clipper tickets—"

"Are already at Cook's, aren't they?"

She smiled.

"And Dinah, I trust, is in complete agreement."

"You're not to think," Eve said, "that she and I have gone behind your back."

"Preposterous thought."

"Don't mock and spoil things." She sat back in her chair, exhausted by relief. I rose to ring for the servant to take her upstairs, knowing she wouldn't let me help her.

I stood over her, thinking she had slept, instantly. But she stirred. "You are wrong, you know," she said very low. "You are not merely my link to your child. I love you, boy."

FIFTY-FOUR

I was up at first light because I had a long trip ahead of me and no talent for good-byes. At dawn the house was more stage set than it had been. There was bustle backstage; unseen hands were packing for their mistress who would be going away.

I found breakfast on the sideboard and the solitary, brawny womanservant. I'd have swilled coffee standing up and slipped a slice of toast into my pocket for later. But she gestured me to the table with all the command of her employer.

I'd never heard this woman speak English, but then the French are secret linguists. In a gravel voice she said, "Madame is taking only the jewelry. She leaves the pictures."

"As Madame sees fit," I said, not chancing my French on her.

The woman stood over me, superintending my breakfast. "We," she said, striking her breast, "will take the pictures and hide them." She shrugged. "In the hills perhaps. The Boches will never find them." She tapped my arm significantly with a long finger. "Have no fear there."

I looked up at this unknown woman. She was a country-woman with a Romany look about her. There were crosses in her ears, and her upper lip was faintly brushed with black down. She wouldn't be leaving. She was already home.

"There will be risk enough for you," I said. "Madame would worry more for your safety than for her pictures."

The woman looked deeply at me, black eyes alive, and then she looked away. "Was there ever such a one as she?"

"No, never." And then I had to go, quickly.

A car had been sent for to take me to the train. The driver was waiting at the top of the stone steps. He was lounging against the bonnet of an ancient Peugeot.

We were drawing away when I looked back for a last glimpse of the villa. The sun was catching the tiles of the towers and roofs, azure and orange against the blue Mediterranean. It stood like a merry fortress, and all its striped awnings were bright flags. Now I'd never see its colors struck.

The postman from Cannes shot along the road past us, and in his sidecar, the hairdresser. Following a curve along the coast, the car gave me a glimpse of a high balcony. The shutters were thrown back, and Eve was standing there, one hand gripping the balustrade.

In her other she waved a long scarf, silver-white in the morning air, like her hair. She stood in a billowing nightdress and waved and waved until the car negotiated another curve, and the villa dropped from sight, suddenly into the sea.

Not so many days later I walked down the pier to the Clipper bobbing in the river. Behind us the domes of Lisbon stood pink and green against the cloudless sky. At the end of my hand a little girl walked, one small hand in mine, the other holding the brim of her hat, a hat with streamers whipping in the breeze. She was my daughter, and I was being born now as her father. Her blue coat might have been copied from one of Princess Margaret Rose's, and her eyes were wide with wonder.

She had fewer reservations than I did about crossing the Atlantic in this eggshell-thin airplane. She skipped a little on the planking, and I saw the plane in her eyes. It was a toy for a bathtub made magically big as things become in a child's imagination.

"Will we sleep in it?" she asked.

"Yes."

"And when we wake up, will we be there?"

"No. Then we take the train, and we sleep in it too."

"And then will we be there, and will I like it?"

I nodded, but I hadn't thought that far. There were other people queuing along the pier with children in their hands. We thought we were leading them away from the war, but our children were already looking ahead, finding the end of the journey.

On the gangplank, Claire hurried ahead of me, eager to be gone and to begin. She peered inside the plane, her head darting, her profile sharpened by curiosity. She was an English child, Dinah's, in her dress and the kind of antic dignity English children acquire early.

But I saw my mother in her too, Constance in the brisk economy of her movements and the assurance to carry her into uncharted territory.

I was saddled by the two small bags we could carry aboard, and Claire looked back at me, impatient. I saw Eve in her then, in her un-English coloring and the beginnings of command. And in her beauty. Claire would be a beauty of course. A father is permitted such thoughts.

I wondered about all the women in her, even women I'd never known, and I wondered where she was leading me. The engines throbbed, and the propellers began their first revolutions, slow before they whirred, as I followed my daughter into the future.